WATCHMEN

ALAN MOORE
writer

DAVE GIBBONS
illustrator/letterer

JOHN HIGGINS
colorist

WATCHMEN

Published by DC Comics Inc., 666 Fifth
Avenue, New York, N.Y. 10103. Copyright
© 1986, 1987 by DC Comics Inc. All Rights
Reserved. The stories and incidents mentioned
in this book are entirely fictional. WATCHMEN
and all characters featured in this publication,
the distinctive likenesses thereof and all
related indicia are trademarks of DC Comics
Inc. Originally published in twelve issues in
magazine form, 1986–1987.

DC Comics Inc.
A Warner Communications Company Ⓦ
Printed in Canada
Third Printing
10 9 8 7 6 5 4 3

Book design by Julia Sabbagh

JENETTE KAHN
president and publisher

DICK GIORDANO
v.p.–executive editor

LEN WEIN & BARBARA RANDALL
editors–original series

BARRY MARX
editor–collected edition

RICHARD BRUNING
art director

TERRI CUNNINGHAM
mgr. editorial admin.

PAT BASTIENNE
mgr. editorial coord.

ANGELINA GENDUSO
managing ed.–collected edition

BOB ROZAKIS
production director

PAUL LEVITZ
executive v.p.

JOE ORLANDO
v.p.–creative director

BRUCE BRISTOW
marketing director

MATTHEW RAGONE
circulation director

PATRICK CALDON
controller

With special thanks to
Neil Gaiman, Mike Lake,
Pat Mills, and Joe Orlando.

CHAPTER 1

"HEY, SO IT IS! WELL, LISTEN, BETWEEN YOU AND ME, I THINK WE CAN RULE HIM OUT AS A SUSPECT.

"A JOB LIKE THIS JUST ISN'T HIS STYLE."

THAT'D BE REAL FUNNY IF WE HAD ANY BETTER LEADS TO GO ON.

I MEAN, WHAT IS THIS? A LITTLE MONEY GOT STOLEN, BUT NO WAY IS THIS A STRAIGHT BURGLARY...

"SOMEBODY REALLY HAD IT IN FOR THIS GUY."

I MEAN, HOW DID HE GO OUTTA THE WINDOW?

MAYBE HE TRIPPED AGAINST IT.

FORGET IT. THAT'S STRONG GLASS, MAN. YOU TRIP AGAINST IT, EVEN A BIG GUY LIKE THAT, IT DON'T BREAK.

"I THINK YOU'D HAVE TO BE THROWN."

WELL, IF THIS EDWARD BLAKE WAS AS BIG AS YOU SAY HE WAS, THEN ONE GUY WOULD NEVER LIFT HIM, SO WE'RE TALKING TWO ASSAILANTS HERE.

WHICH FLOOR YA WANT?

OH, UH, GROUND FLOOR, PLEASE.

"GROUND FLOOR COMIN' UP."

3

SO LOOK, YOU HAVEN'T ANSWERED MY *QUESTION*... IS THIS A *BURGLARY*, OR DO WE LOOK FOR SOME *OTHER* MOTIVE?

LISTEN, IT *COULD* JUST HAVE BEEN A BURGLARY... MAYBE A BUNCH'A *KNOT-TOPS* ON *KT-28*s OR 'LUUDES...

"YOU KNOW HOW IT IS...A LOT OF CRAZY THINGS HAPPEN IN A CITY THIS SIZE.

"THEY DON'T *ALL* NEED MOTIVES."

SO, WHAT YOU'RE *SAYING* IS...

I'M *SAYING* LET'S NOT RAISE TOO MUCH *DUST* OVER THIS ONE. WE DON'T NEED ANY *MASKED AVENGERS* GETTING INTERESTED AND *CUTTING IN*.

FOLLOW IT UP *DISCREETLY*, SURE. BUT IN *PUBLIC*...

"...WELL, WHAT SAY WE LET THIS ONE DROP OUT OF *SIGHT?*"

I DUNNO. I THINK YOU TAKE THIS *VIGILANTE* STUFF TOO *SERIOUSLY*. SINCE THE *KEENE ACT* WAS PASSED IN '77, ONLY THE *GOVERNMENT-SPONSORED WEIRDOS* ARE ACTIVE.

THEY DON'T INTERFERE.

SCREW THEM. WHAT ABOUT *RORSCHACH?*

"*RORSCHACH* NEVER RETIRED, EVEN AFTER HIM AND HIS BUDDIES FELL OUTTA GRACE.

"RORSCHACH'S STILL *OUT* THERE SOMEWHERE."

HE'S CRAZIER THAN A SNAKE'S ARMPIT AND WANTED ON TWO COUNTS *MURDER ONE.*

WE GOT A COZY LITTLE *HOMICIDE* HERE. IF *HE* GETS INVOLVED, WE'LL BE UP TO OUR *BUTTS* IN *CORPSES*...

WHAT'S THE *MATTER?*

UH, NOTHING ...JUST A *SHIVER.*

MUST BE GETTIN' A *COLD.*

4

AT MIDNIGHT, ALL THE AGENTS...

6

HURM.

SO, THERE I WAS IN THE SUPERMARKET BUYIN' *DOGFOOD* FOR OL' *PHANTOM* HERE, I TURN THE CORNER OF THE AISLE AND *WHAM!* I BUMP INTO THE *SCREAMING SKULL!* YOU *REMEMBER* HIM?

I THINK I HEARD YOU *MENTION* HIM...

OH, I PUT HIM AWAY A DOZEN TIMES IN THE *FORTIES*, BUT HE *REFORMED* AN' TURNED TO *JESUS* SINCE THEN. MARRIED, GOT TWO KIDS...

WE TRADED ADDRESSES, NICE GUY.

UH, HOLLIS, LISTEN ... IT'S ALMOST MIDNIGHT. I OUGHTTA *GO.*

OH, SURE. LOST TRACK O' THE TIME THERE, TALKIN' 'BOUT ALL THAT OLD STUFF.

YOU MUSTA BEEN BORED AS HELL.

YOU KNOW BETTER THAN *THAT.* THESE SATURDAY NIGHT *BEER* SESSIONS ARE WHAT KEEPS ME *GOING.*

YEAH, WELL, US OLD RETIRED GUYS GOTTA STICK TOGETHER.

LEMME PUT THIS OUT AND I'LL BE RIGHT WITH YA.

Y'KNOW, IT WAS A CRYIN' SHAME THEY PUT YOU YOUNGSTERS OUT TO GRASS IN '77. YOU WERE A BETTER *NITE OWL* THAN I *EVER* WAS.

HOLLIS, WE *BOTH* KNOW THAT'S BULLSHIT, BUT THANKS *ANYWAY.*

HEY, WATCH WITH THE *LANGUAGE!* THIS IS THE LEFT HOOK THAT FLOORED *CAPTAIN AXIS,* REMEMBER?

HOW COULD I *FORGET* THANKS FOR ANOTHER GREAT NIGHT, HOLLIS. TAKE *CARE* OF YOUR-SELF.

YOU *TOO,* DANNY.

GOD BLESS.

9

...LOOK DOWN YOUR BACK STAIRS, BUDDY, SOMEBODY'S LIVING THERE AN' THEY DON'T REALLY FEEL THE WEATHER...

CHLOP.

THLUP.

SHORP.

LEP.

HELLO, DANIEL.

GOT HUNGRY WAITING. HELPED MYSELF TO SOME BEANS.

HOPE YOU DON'T MIND.

RORSCHACH..?

10

UH ... THAT IS, *NO*! NO, OF *COURSE* I DON'T MIND ...

UH ... YOU WANT ME TO HEAT THOSE *UP* FOR YOU OR ANYTHING ..?

NO NEED. FINE LIKE THIS.

SO, UH ... LONG TIME NO *SEE*!

HOW HAVE YOU *BEEN* KEEPING?

OUT OF PRISON. SO FAR.

TAKE A LOOK AT THIS.

UHH ... WHAT *IS* IT?

THIS LITTLE *STAIN*, IS THAT *BEAN JUICE*, OR ..?

THAT'S RIGHT. HUMAN BEAN JUICE. HA HA.

BADGE BELONGED TO THE *COMEDIAN*. BLOOD TOO.

HE'S DEAD.

DEAD? WHAT, YOU'RE TALKING ABOUT *THE* COMEDIAN?

INVESTIGATED A ROUTINE HOMICIDE. VICTIM NAMED EDWARD BLAKE. FOUND THE COSTUME IN BLAKE'S WARDROBE. SEEMS HE WAS THE COMEDIAN.

SOMEBODY THREW HIM OUT OF A WINDOW.

SOMEBODY ...?

UH, LISTEN, MAYBE WE COULD TALK ABOUT THIS DOWN IN MY *WORKSHOP*. I FEEL KINDA *EXPOSED* UP HERE.

ALSO, THAT WAY YOU CAN USE THE HIDDEN REAR EXIT. UH, WHEN YOU *LEAVE*, THAT IS ...

RIGHT DOWN THIS WAY.

UH, YOU HAVEN'T BEEN *DOWN* HERE FOR A WHILE ...

11

NEITHER HAVE YOU. LOT OF DUST.

YEAH, WELL, Y'KNOW. SOMETIMES I COME AND SIT DOWN HERE FOR A WHILE, BUT THERE DOESN'T SEEM MUCH POINT SINCE I RETIRED.

LISTEN, ABOUT THE COMEDIAN...

MIGHT IT JUST HAVE BEEN AN ORDINARY BURGLARY OR SOMETHING? MAYBE THE KILLER DIDN'T KNOW WHO BLAKE WAS...

AN ORDINARY BURGLAR? KILL THE COMEDIAN?

RIDICULOUS.

HMM. I GUESS IT DOESN'T SEEM VERY LIKELY.

I HEARD HE'D BEEN WORKING FOR THE GOVERNMENT SINCE '77, KNOCKING OVER MARXIST REPUBLICS IN SOUTH AMERICA...

MAYBE THIS WAS A POLITICAL KILLING?

MAYBE.

OR MAYBE SOMEONE'S PICKING OFF COSTUMED HEROES.

UM. DON'T YOU THINK THAT'S MAYBE A LITTLE PARANOID?

THAT'S WHAT THEY'RE SAYING ABOUT ME NOW? THAT I'M PARANOID?

THE COMEDIAN WAS ACTIVE FOR FORTY YEARS. MEN MAKE A LOT OF ENEMIES IN THAT TIME.

HOW'S YOUR FRIEND HOLLIS MASON THESE DAYS?

HOLLIS? WHAT DOES HE...?

THEY WERE BOTH MINUTEMEN, WHEN BLAKE WAS SIXTEEN AND MASON WAS THE FIRST NITE OWL.

THAT BOOK MASON WROTE. HE SAID SOME BAD THINGS ABOUT THE COMEDIAN IN IT.

RORSCHACH, I DON'T LIKE WHAT YOU'RE IMPLYING HERE. HOLLIS IS AN OLD MAN. IF YOU'RE THINKING ABOUT GOING OVER THERE AND SCARING HIM...

IMPLYING NOTHING.

JUST AN OBSERVATION.

12

ANYWAY, THOUGHT I'D LET YOU KNOW. IN CASE SOMEBODY'S GUNNING FOR MASKS.

BETTER GO NOW. THINGS TO DO.

YEAH, WELL, THE TUNNEL BRINGS YOU OUT IN A **WAREHOUSE** TWO BLOCKS **NORTH...**

YES. I REMEMBER. USED TO COME HERE OFTEN. BACK WHEN WE WERE PARTNERS.

OH, UH, YEAH... YEAH, THOSE WERE GREAT TIMES, RORSCHACH! **GREAT** TIMES. WHATEVER **HAPPENED** TO THEM?

YOU QUIT.

13

RORSCHACH'S JOURNAL. OCTOBER 13TH, 1985.

SLEPT ALL DAY. AWOKEN AT 4:37. LANDLADY COMPLAINING ABOUT SMELL. SHE HAS FIVE CHILDREN BY FIVE DIFFERENT FATHERS. I AM SURE SHE CHEATS ON WELFARE.

SOON IT WILL BE DARK.

BENEATH ME, THIS AWFUL CITY, IT SCREAMS LIKE AN ABATTOIR FULL OF RETARDED CHILDREN. NEW YORK.

ON FRIDAY NIGHT, A COMEDIAN DIED IN NEW YORK.

SOMEBODY KNOWS WHY.

DOWN THERE...

SOMEBODY KNOWS.

THE DUSK REEKS OF FORNICATION AND BAD CONSCIENCES.

HAPPY HARRY'S

BAR GRILL

I BELIEVE I SHALL TAKE MY EXERCISE.

14

RUH.

ROR. ROR.

RORSCHACH! HAR HAR HOW YA *DOIN'*, FELLA?

I'M FINE, HAPPY HARRY.

YOURSELF?

FINE! I'M FUH, I'M *FINE!*

AND I'M, AND I'M, AND I'M GLAD *YOU'RE* FINE, TOO!

AND UH, AND UH...

OH, GOD.

PLEASE DON'T KILL ANYBODY.

GUY WENT SIDEWALK DIVING, FRIDAY NIGHT. I DON'T THINK HE WAS ALONE WHEN IT HAPPENED.

NAME WAS EDWARD BLAKE.

FRIEND OF MINE.

HEY, YOU HEAR *THAT?* HE'S GOT *FRIENDS!* MUSTA CHANGED HIS *DEODORANT!*

STEVE, FOR GOD'S SAKE, MAN, SHUT *UP*...

I--I GOTTA TAKE A *LEAK*...

15

H-HEY! HEY, I DIDN'T **MEAN** ANYTHING...

I, UH, I HAVEN'T **BEEN** IN THE APPLE TOO LONG, AND I...

...I, UH...

HEY, WHAT...?

AAAAAA

I'VE JUST BROKEN THIS GENTLEMAN'S LITTLE FINGER.

WHO KILLED EDWARD BLAKE?

OH. OUHH...

EEYIIAA

...AND HIS INDEX FINGER.

WHO KILLED EDWARD BLAKE?

PLEASE...

PLEASE, WE DON'T **KNOW**...

AW, **GOD**, MAN, LEAVE HIM **ALONE**...

FIRST VISIT OF EVENING FRUITLESS. NOBODY KNEW ANYTHING. FEEL SLIGHTLY DEPRESSED.

THIS CITY IS DYING OF RABIES. IS THE BEST I CAN DO TO WIPE RANDOM FLECKS OF FOAM FROM ITS LIPS?

HURM.

never despair. never surrender.

I LEAVE THE HUMAN COCKROACHES TO DISCUSS THEIR HEROIN AND CHILD PORNOGRAPHY. I HAVE BUSINESS ELSEWHERE, WITH A BETTER CLASS OF PERSON.

16

THE COMEDIAN DEAD? BUT *WHY*?

YOU WERE ALWAYS SUPPOSED TO BE WORLD'S SMARTEST MAN, VEIDT.

YOU TELL ME.

I NEVER CLAIMED TO BE ANYBODY *SPECIAL*, RORSCHACH. I JUST HAVE SOME OVER-ENTHUSIASTIC *P.R. MEN*.

LISTEN... COULD IT HAVE BEEN A *POLITICAL* KILLING? MAYBE THE *SOVIETS*...

DREIBERG SAID SAME THING. DON'T BELIEVE IT.

AMERICA HAS DR. MANHATTAN. REDS HAVE BEEN RUNNING SCARED SINCE '65. THEY'D NEVER DARE ANTAGONIZE US.

I THINK WE'VE GOT A MASK-KILLER.

NOT *NECESSARILY*.

THE COMEDIAN HAD PLENTY OF *OTHER* POLITICAL ENEMIES TO CHOOSE FROM, EVEN *DIS-COUNTING* THE RUSSIANS...

THE MAN WAS PRACTICALLY A *NAZI*.

HE STOOD UP FOR HIS COUNTRY, VEIDT. HE NEVER LET ANYBODY *RETIRE* HIM.

NEVER *CASHED* IN ON HIS REPUTATION.

NEVER SET UP A COMPANY SELLING POSTERS AND DIET BOOKS AND TOY SOLDIERS BASED ON HIMSELF.

NEVER BECAME A PROSTITUTE.

IF THAT MAKES HIM A NAZI, YOU MIGHT AS WELL CALL ME A NAZI, TOO.

HM.

17

RORSCHACH...

I *KNOW* WE WERE NEVER *FRIENDS*, BUT EVEN SO, YOU'RE BEING *UNFAIR*.

NOBODY RETIRED ME. I *CHOSE* TO QUIT ADVENTURING AND GO *PUBLIC* TWO YEARS *BEFORE* THE POLICE STRIKE MADE THE *KEENE ACT* NECESSARY.

YES. GOOD TIMING.

I CAME HERE TO WARN YOU ABOUT THE MASK-KILLER. SO YOU DIDN'T END UP SMARTEST MAN IN THE MORGUE.

BUT I GUESS THERE'S WORSE THINGS TO END UP AS.

BE SEEING YOU.

SURE.

HAVE A NICE DAY.

ADRIAN VEIDT : PRE

18

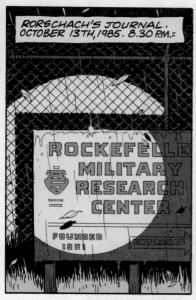

ROCKEFELLE MILITARY RESEARCH CENTER

FOUNDED 1981

ENTRANCE

MEETING WITH VEIDT LEFT BAD TASTE IN MOUTH. HE IS PAMPERED AND DECADENT, BETRAYING EVEN HIS OWN SHALLOW, LIBERAL AFFECTATIONS.

POSSIBLY HOMOSEXUAL? MUST REMEMBER TO INVESTIGATE FURTHER.

DREIBERG AS BAD. A FLABBY FAILURE WHO SITS WHIMPERING IN HIS BASEMENT.

WHY ARE SO FEW OF US LEFT ACTIVE, HEALTHY AND WITHOUT PERSONALITY DISORDERS?

THE FIRST NITE OWL RUNS AN AUTO-REPAIR SHOP.

THE FIRST SILK SPECTRE IS A BLOATED, AGING WHORE, DYING IN A CALIFORNIAN REST RESORT.

CAPTAIN METROPOLIS WAS DECAPITATED IN A CAR CRASH BACK IN '74.

MOTHMAN'S IN AN ASYLUM UP IN MAINE.

THE SILHOUETTE RETIRED IN DISGRACE, MURDERED SIX WEEKS LATER BY A MINOR ADVERSARY SEEKING REVENGE.

DOLLAR BILL GOT SHOT. HOODED JUSTICE WENT MISSING IN '55.

SPECIAL TALENT QUARTERS

PRIVATE

THE COMEDIAN IS DEAD.

SPECIAL TALENT QUARTERS

PRIV

ONLY TWO NAMES REMAINING ON MY LIST.

BOTH SHARE PRIVATE QUARTERS AT ROCKEFELLER MILITARY RESEARCH CENTER.

I SHALL GO TO THEM.

I SHALL GO AND TELL THE INDESTRUCTIBLE MAN THAT SOMEONE PLANS TO MURDER HIM.

CLEAR 2 ONL

KEEP

GOOD EVENING, RORSCHACH.

19

GOOD EVENING, DR. MANHATTAN.

WHAT ARE *YOU* DOING HERE, RORSCHACH? THIS IS A *GOVERNMENT* BASE AND I HEAR YOU'RE WANTED BY THE *POLICE.*

EHH.

GOOD EVENING, MISS JUPITER.

THAT'S *JUSPECZYK.* "JUPITER" WAS JUST A NAME MY *MOTHER* ASSUMED BECAUSE SHE DIDN'T WANT ANYONE TO KNOW SHE WAS *POLISH.*

YOU HAVEN'T ANSWERED MY *QUESTION.*

APOLOGIES.

CAME TO WARN YOU BOTH AND BRING BAD NEWS.

THE COMEDIAN IS DEAD.

20

YES. SINCE HE AND I ARE THE ONLY TWO **EXTRANORMAL OPERATIVES** CURRENTLY EMPLOYED BY THE GOVERNMENT, I WAS INFORMED ON SATURDAY MORNING.

I UNDERSTAND THE C.I.A. SUSPECTS THE **LIBYANS** WERE RESPONSIBLE.

HAVE MY OWN THEORIES ON THAT.

TAKE IT YOU'RE NOT TOO CONCERNED ABOUT BLAKE'S DEATH.

A LIVE BODY AND A DEAD BODY CONTAIN THE SAME NUMBER OF **PARTICLES**.

STRUCTURALLY, THERE'S NO DISCERNIBLE **DIFFERENCE**.

LIFE AND DEATH ARE UNQUANTIFIABLE **ABSTRACTS**. WHY **SHOULD** I BE CONCERNED?

ENNK.

ANYWAY, IT COULDN'T HAVE HAPPENED TO A NICER **PERSON**.

BLAKE WAS A BASTARD. HE WAS A **MONSTER**. Y'KNOW HE TRIED TO **RAPE** MY **MOTHER** BACK WHEN THEY WERE BOTH **MINUTEMEN**?

UHM.

SO YOU SUPPORT THE ALLEGATIONS MADE IN HOLLIS MASON'S BOOK CONCERNING BLAKE?

WHAT MASON SAID IN "**UNDER THE HOOD**" IS WHAT **HAPPENED**. GOD KNOWS I'M NOT MY MOTHER'S **BIGGEST** ADMIRER, BUT SOME THINGS SHOULDN'T HAPPEN TO **ANYBODY**.

WHY DO YOU THINK BLAKE NEVER **SUED** MASON?

≥CRONCH. CRONCH≥

MORAL LAPSES?

I'M NOT HERE TO SPECULATE ON THE MORAL LAPSES OF MEN WHO DIED IN THEIR COUNTRY'S SERVICE. I CAME TO WARN...

RAPE IS A **MORAL LAPSE**? YOU KNOW HE BROKE HER **RIBS**? YOU KNOW HE ALMOST **CHOKED** HER?

JON, GET THIS CREEP **OUT** OF HERE.

21

YOU SEEM TO BE UPSETTING *LAURIE*.

I THINK YOU OUGHT TO GO.

WITH RESPECT, DR. MANHATTAN, I WARNED VEIDT AND DREIBERG AND I INTEND TO WARN YOU AND YOUR LADY FRIEND.

I BELIEVE SOMEONE IS ELIMINATING MASKED ADVENTURERS, POSSIBLY SOME OLD FOE WITH A GRUDGE. I BELIEVE...

I SAID I THINK YOU OUGHT TO GO.

SPENT A LOT OF TIME GETTING IN TO SEE YOU.

NOT LEAVING BEFORE I'VE...

...HAD MY SAY.

HURM.

22

HE'S GONE.

ARE YOU STILL *UPSET?*

YEAH. I JUST DON'T *LIKE* RORSCHACH. HE'S *SICK.* SICK INSIDE HIS *MIND.*

I DON'T LIKE THE WAY HE *SMELLS* OR THAT HORRIBLE MONO-TONE *VOICE* OR ANYTHING.

THE SOONER THE POLICE PUT HIM *AWAY,* THE *BETTER.*

JON?

YES, LAURIE?

I WAS JUST THINKING THAT I MUST BE REALLY *EDGY* TO LET A *MAGGOT* LIKE *RORSCHACH* GET TO ME LIKE THAT.

I JUST FEEL *COOPED UP* SOME-TIMES. MAYBE I COULD USE A *NIGHT OUT.*

YOU KNOW, RORSCHACH MENTIONED *DAN DREIBERG.* WE HAVEN'T SEEN DAN IN *YEARS.*

MAYBE I'LL CALL HIM UP, ASK HIM OUT TO *DINNER.*

IF YOU DON'T *MIND,* THAT IS.

OF COURSE NOT.

THAT'S *FASCIN-ATING.*

I'D *JOIN* YOU, BUT I THINK I'M CLOSE TO LOCATING A *GLUINO,* WHICH WOULD COMPLETELY VALIDATE *SUPERSYMMETRICAL THEORY* IF WE COULD INCLUDE IT IN THE *BESTIARY.*

I'LL CALL *DAN.*

HELLO, *DAN?* *LAURIE.* LAURIE *JUSPECZYK.* I'M *FINE.* HOW ARE *YOU?*

GREAT. LISTEN, I JUST REMEMBERED I HADN'T *SEEN* YOU IN AGES AND WONDERED IF WE COULD HAVE *DINNER* SOMETIME.

WELL, HOW ABOUT *TONIGHT?* RAFAEL'S AT 9:30?

THAT'S *TERRIFIC.*

JON? OH, YEAH. YEAH, JON'S IN PRETTY GOOD SHAPE.

SEE YOU LATER, DAN.

'BYE.

23

On friday night, a comedian died in new york.

Someone threw him out of a window and when he hit the sidewalk his head was driven up into his stomach.

Nobody cares.

Nobody cares but me.

Are they right? Is it futile?

Soon there will be war. Millions will burn. Millions will perish in sickness and misery.

Why does one death matter against so many?

Because there is good and there is evil, and evil must be punished. Even in the face of armageddon I shall not compromise in this.

But there are so many deserving of retribution...

...and there is so little time.

24

WELL, I GUESS IT'S GETTING PRETTY LATE.

IT'S BEEN A GREAT EVENING, LAURIE. YOU'RE SURE YOU WON'T LET ME PICK UP THE TAB?

NAH. IF I'M GONNA BE A KEPT WOMAN FOR THE MILITARY'S SECRET WEAPON, THEN THE MILITARY CAN STAND ME A BOWL OF SPAGHETTI AFRICAINE EVERY ONCE IN A WHILE.

HEY, YOU SOUND BITTER.

NO. NOT REALLY. IT'S JUST THAT THE ONLY REASON I'M KEPT AROUND IS TO KEEP JON RELAXED AND HAPPY.

UH... IS EVERYTHING OKAY WITH YOU AND JON?

ME AND JON?

OH, YEAH. YEAH, EVERYTHING'S FINE.

COULDN'T BE BETTER.

IT'S JUST I KEEP THINKING "I'M THIRTY-FIVE. WHAT HAVE I DONE?"

I'VE SPENT EIGHT YEARS IN SEMI-RETIREMENT, PRECEDED BY TEN YEARS RUNNING ROUND IN A STUPID COSTUME BECAUSE MY STUPID MOTHER WANTED ME TO!

YOU REMEMBER THAT COSTUME?

WITH THAT STUPID LITTLE SHORT SKIRT AND THE NECKLINE GOING DOWN TO MY NAVEL? GOD, THAT WAS SO DREADFUL.

GOD, YES. DREADFUL.

Y'KNOW, WHEN I THINK BACK... WHY DID WE DO IT? WHY DID WE DRESS UP LIKE THAT?

THE KEENE ACT WAS THE BEST THING THAT EVER HAPPENED TO US.

YEAH. YOU'RE PROBABLY RIGHT.

25

At midnight, all the agents and superhuman crew, go out and round up everyone who knows more than they do.

—Bob Dylan

UNDER THE HOOD

We present here excerpts from Hollis Mason's autobiography, UNDER THE HOOD, leading up to the time when he became the masked adventurer, Nite Owl. Reprinted with permission of the author.

I.

The lady who works in the grocery store at the corner of my block is called Denise, and she's one of America's great unpublished novelists. Over the years she's written *forty-two* romantic novels, none of which have ever reached the bookstores. I, however, have been fortunate enough to hear the plots of the last twenty-seven of these recounted in installments by the authoress herself every time I drop by the store for a jar of coffee or can of beans, and my respect for Denise's literary prowess knows no bounds. So, naturally enough, when I found myself faced with the daunting task of actually starting the book you now hold in your hands, it was Denise I turned to for advice.

"Listen," I said. "I don't know from writing a book. I have all this stuff in my head that I want to get down, but what do I write about first? Where do I begin?"

Without looking up from the boxes of detergent to which she was fixing price tags, Denise graciously delivered up a pearl of her accumulated wisdom in a voice of bored but benign condescension.

"Start off with the saddest thing you can think of and get the audience's sympathies on your side. After that, believe me, it's a walk."

Thank you, Denise. This book is dedicated to you, because I don't know how to choose between all the other people I should be dedicating it to.

The saddest thing I can think of is "The Ride of the Valkyries." Every time I hear it I get depressed and start wondering about the lot of humanity and the unfairness of life and all those other things that you think about at three in the morning when your digestion won't let you sleep. Now, I realize that nobody else on the planet has to brush away a tear when they hear that particular stirring refrain, but that's because they don't know about Moe Vernon.

When my father upped and left my Granddad's farm in Montana to bring his family to New York, Moe Vernon was the man he worked for. Vernon's Auto Repairs was just off Seventh Avenue, and although it was only 1928 when Dad started working there, there was just about enough trade for his wages to keep me and Mom and my sister Liantha in food and clothing. Dad was always really keen and enthusiastic about his work, and I used to think it was just because he had a thing about cars. Looking back, I can see it was more than that. It must have meant so much to him, just to have a job and be able to support his family. He'd had a lot of arguments with his father about coming east rather than taking over the farm, like the old man had planned for him, and most of the rows had ended with my grandfather predicting poverty and moral ruination for my dad and mom if they so much as set foot in New York. To be living the life that he himself had chosen and keeping his family above the poverty line in spite of his father's warnings must have meant more to my dad than anything in the world, but that's something I only understand now, with hindsight. Back then, I just thought he was crazy for crankshafts.

Anyway, I was twelve years old when we left Montana, so during those next few years in the big city I was just the age to appreciate the occasional trips to the auto shop with my dad, which is where I first set eyes on Moe Vernon, his employer.

Moe Vernon was a man around fifty-five or so, and he had one of those old New York faces that you don't see anymore. It's funny, but certain faces seem to go in and out of style. You look at old photographs and everybody has a certain look to them, almost as if they're related. Look at pictures from ten years later and you can see that there's a new kind of face starting to predominate, and that the old faces are fading away and vanishing, never to be seen again. Moe Vernon's face was like that: three chins, a wiseacre cynical curl to his lower lip, a certain hollowness around the eyes, hair retreating back across his head, attempting a rendezvous with the label on his shirt collar.

Vernon's Auto Repair c. 1928. (left to right) *My father; myself, age 12; Moe Vernon; Fred Motz.*

I'd go into the shop with my dad and Moe would be sitting there in his office, which had glass sides so he could watch the men working. Sometimes, if my father wanted to check something out with Moe before going ahead with his work, he'd send me over to the office to do it for him, which meant that I got to see the insides of Moe's inner sanctum. Or rather, I got to hear them.

You see, Moe was an opera buff. He had one of the new gramophones over in the corner of his office and all day he used to play scratchy old seventy-eight recordings of his favorites just as loud as he could manage. By today's standard, "as loud as he could manage" didn't amount to a whole lot of noise, but it sounded pretty cacophonous back in 1930, when things were generally quieter.

The other thing that was peculiar about Moe was his sense of humor, as represented by all the stuff he used to keep in the top right side drawer of his desk.

In that drawer, amongst a mess of rubber bands and paper clips and receipts and stuff, Moe had one of the largest collections of tasteless novelty items that I had seen up until that point or have seen at any time since. They were all risqué little toys and gadgets that Moe had picked up from gag shops or on visits to Coney Island, but it was the sheer range of them that was overwhelming: every cheap blue gimmick that you can remember your dad bringing home when he'd been out drinking with the boys and embarrassing your mom with; every ballpoint pen with a girl on the side whose swimsuit vanished when you turned it upside down; every salt and pepper crewet set shaped like a woman's breasts; every plastic dog mess. Moe had the works. Every time anybody went into his office he'd try to startle them by displaying his latest plaything. Actually, it used to shock my dad more than it did me. I don't think he liked the idea of his son being exposed to that kind of stuff, probably because of all the moral warnings my grandfather had impressed upon him. For my part, I wasn't offended and I even found it kind of funny. Not the things themselves...even by then I was too old to get much amusement out of stuff like that. What I found funny was that for no apparent reason, a grown man should have a desk drawer full of such ludicrous devices.

Anyway, one day in 1933, a little after my seventeenth birthday, I was over at Vernon's Auto Repairs with Dad, helping him poke around in the oily innards of a busted-up Ford. Moe was in his office, and although we didn't find out till later, he was sitting wearing an artificial foam rubber set of realistically painted lady's bosoms, with which he hoped to get a few laughs from the guy who brought him the morning mail through from the front office when it arrived. While he waited, he was listening to Wagner.

The mail arrived in due course, and the guy handing it over managed to raise a dutiful chuckle at Moe's generous cleavage before leaving him to open and peruse the morning's missives. Amongst these (again, as we found out later) there was a letter from Moe's wife Beatrice, informing him that for the past two years she'd been sleeping with Fred Motz, the senior and most trusted mechanic employed at Vernon's Auto Repairs, who, unusually, hadn't shown up for work on that particular morning. This, according to the concluding paragraphs of the letter, was because Beatrice had taken all the money out of the joint account she shared with her husband and had departed with Fred for Tijuana.

The first anyone in the workshop knew about this was when the door of Moe's office slammed open and the startlingly loud and crackling rendition of "Ride of the Valkyries" blasted out from within. Framed in the doorway with tears in his eyes and the crumpled letter in his hand, Moe stood dramatically with all eyes turned towards him. He was still wearing the set of artificial breasts. Almost inaudible above the rising strains of Wagner swelling behind him, he spoke, with so much hurt and outrage and offended dignity fighting for possession of his voice that the end result was almost toneless.

"Fred Motz has had carnal knowledge of my wife Beatrice for the past two years."

He stood there in the wake of his announcement, the tears rolling down over his multiple chins to soak into the pink foam rubber of his bosom, making tiny sounds in his chest and throat that were trampled under the hooves of the Valkyries and lost forever.

And everybody started laughing.

I don't know what it was. We could see he was crying, but it was just something in the toneless way he'd said it, standing there wearing a pair of false breasts with all that crashing, triumphant music soaring all around him. None of us could help it, laughing at him like that. My dad and I were both doubled up and the other guys slaving over the nearby cars were wiping tears from their eyes and smearing their faces with oil in the process. Moe just looked at us all for a minute and then went back into his office and closed the door. A moment or two later the Wagner stopped with an ugly scraping noise as Moe snatched the needle from the groove of the gramophone record, and after that there was silence.

About half an hour passed before someone went in to apologize on behalf of everybody and to see if Moe was all right. Moe accepted the apology and said that he was fine. Apparently he was sitting there at his desk, breasts now discarded, getting on with

I graduate from Police Academy (1938)

normal routine paperwork as if nothing had happened.

That night, he sent everybody home early. Then, running a tube from the exhaust of one of the shop's more operational vehicles in through the car's window, he started up the engine and drifted off into a final, bitter sleep amongst the carbon monoxide fumes. His brother took over the business and even eventually reemployed Fred Motz as chief mechanic.

And that's why "The Ride of the Valkyries" is the saddest thing I can think of, even though it's somebody else's tragedy rather than my own. I was there and I laughed along with all the rest and I guess that makes it part of my story too.

Now, if Denise's theory is correct, I should have your full sympathy and the rest will be a walk. So maybe it's safe to tell you about all the stuff you probably bought this book to read about. Maybe it's safe to tell you why I'm crazier than Moe Vernon ever was. I didn't have a drawer full of erotic novelties, but I guess I had my own individual quirks. And although I've never worn a set of false bosoms in my life, I've stood there dressed in something just as strange, with tears in my eyes while people died laughing.

II.

By 1939 I was twenty-three years old and had taken a job on the New York City police force. I've never really examined until now just why I should have chosen that particular career, but I guess it came as a result of a number of things. Foremost amongst these was probably my grandfather.

Even though I resented the old man for the amount of guilt and pressure and recrimination he'd subjected my dad to, I suppose that the simple fact of spending the first twelve years of my life living in my grandfather's proximity had indelibly stamped a certain set of moral values and conditions upon me. I was never so extreme in my beliefs concerning God, the family, and the flag as my father's father was, but if I look at myself today I can see basic notions of decency that were passed down direct from him to me. His name was Hollis Wordsworth Mason, and perhaps because my parents had flattered the old man by naming me after him, he always took a special concern over my upbringing and moral instruction. One of the things that he took great pains to impress upon me was that country folk were morally healthier than city folk and that cities were just cesspools into which all the world's dishonesty and greed and lust and godlessness drained and was left to fester unhindered. Obviously, as I got older and came to realize just how much drunkenness and domestic violence and child abuse was hidden behind the neighborly facade of some of these lonely Montana farmhouses, I understood that my grandfather's appraisal had been a little one-sided. Nevertheless, some of the things that I saw in the city during my first few years here filled me with a sort of ethical revulsion that I couldn't shake off. To some degree, I still can't.

The pimps, the pornographers, the protection artists. The landlords who set dogs on their elderly tenants when they wanted them out to make way for more lucrative custom. The old men who touched little children and the callous young rapists who were barely old enough to shave. I saw these people all around me and I'd feel sick in my gut at the world and what it was becoming. Worse, there were times when I'd upset my dad and mom by loudly wishing I was back in Montana. Despite everything, I wished no such thing, but sometimes I'd be mad at them and it seemed like the best way to hurt them, to reawaken all those old doubts and worries and sleeping dogs of guilt. I'm sorry I did it now, and I wish I could have told them that while they were alive. I wish I could have told them that they were right in bringing me to the city, that they did the right thing by me. I wish I could have let them know that. Their lives would have been so much easier.

Masked adventurers make the front page. (New York Gazette, October 14th, 1938) Note artist's impression of "The Hooded Vigilante."

When the gap between the world of the city and the world my grandfather had presented to me as right and good became too wide and depressing to tolerate, I'd turn to my other great love, which was pulp adventure fiction. Despite the fact that Hollis Mason Senior would have had nothing but scorn and loathing for all of those violent and garish magazines, there was a sort of prevailing morality in them that I'm sure he would have responded to. The world of Doc Savage and The Shadow was one of absolute values, where what was good was never in the slightest doubt and where what was evil inevitably suffered some fitting punishment. The notion of good and justice espoused by Lamont Cranston with his slouch hat and blazing automatics seemed a long way from that of the fierce and taciturn old man I remembered sitting up alone into the Montana night with no company save his bible, but I can't help feeling that if the two had ever met they'd have found something to talk about. For my part, all those brilliant and resourceful sleuths and heroes offered a glimpse of a perfect world where morality worked the way it was *meant* to. Nobody in Doc Savage's world ever killed themselves except thwarted kamikaze assassins or enemy spies with cyanide capsules. Which world would you rather live in, if you had the choice?

Answering that question, I suppose, was what led me to become a cop. It was also what led me to later become something more than a cop. Bear that in mind and I think the rest of this narrative will be easier to swallow. I know people always have trouble understanding just what brings a person to behave the way that I and people like me behave, what makes us do the sort of things we do. I can't answer for anybody else, and I suspect that all our answers would be different anyway, but in my case it's fairly straightforward: I like the idea of adventure, and I feel bad unless I'm doing good. I've heard all the psychologists' theories, and I've heard all the jokes and the rumors and the innuendo, but what it comes down to for me is that I dressed up like an owl and fought crime because it was fun and because it needed doing and because I goddam felt like it.

Okay. There it is. I've said it. I dressed up. As an owl. And fought crime. Perhaps you begin to see why I half expect this summary of my career to raise more laughs than poor cuckolded Moe Vernon with his foam teats and his Wagner could ever hope to have done.

For me, it all started in 1938, the year when they invented the super-hero. I was too old for comic books when the first issue of ACTION COMICS came out, or at least too old to read them in public without souring my promotion chances, but I noticed a lot of the little kids on my beat reading it and couldn't resist asking one of them if I could glance through it. I figured if anybody saw me I could put it all down to keeping a good relationship with the youth of the community.

There was a lot of stuff in that first issue. There were detective yarns and stories about magicians whose names I can't remember, but from the moment I set eyes on it I only had eyes for the Superman story. Here was something that presented the basic morality of the pulps without all their darkness and ambiguity. The atmosphere of the horrific and faintly sinister that hung around the Shadow was nowhere to be seen in the bright primary colors of Superman's world, and there was no hint of the repressed sex-urge which had sometimes been apparent in the pulps, to my discomfort and embarrassment. I'd never been entirely sure what Lamont Cranston was up to with Margo Lane, but I'd bet it was nowhere near as innocent and wholesome as Clark Kent's relationship with her namesake Lois. Of course, all of these old characters are gone and forgotten now, but I'm willing to bet that there are at least a few older readers out there who will remember enough to know what I'm talking about. Anyway, suffice it to say that I read that story through about eight times before giving it back to the complaining kid that I'd snitched it from.

It set off a lot of things I'd forgotten about, deep inside me, and kicked all those old fantasies that I'd had when I was thirteen or fourteen back into gear: The prettiest girl in the class would be attacked by bullies, and I'd be there to beat them off, but when she offered to kiss me as a reward, I'd refuse. Gangsters would kidnap my math teacher, Miss Albertine, and I'd track them down and kill them one by one until she was free, and then she'd break off her engagement with my sarcastic English teacher, Mr. Richardson, because she'd fallen hopelessly in love with her grim-faced and silent fourteen-year-old savior. All of this stuff came flooding back as I stood there gawking at the hijacked comic book, and even though I laughed at myself for having entertained such transparent juvenile fantasies, I didn't laugh as hard as I might have done. Not half as hard as I'd laughed at Moe Vernon, for example.

Anyway, although I'd occasionally manage to trick some unsuspecting tyke into lending me his most recent issue of the funnybook in question and then spend the rest of the day leaping tall buildings inside my head, my fantasies were to remain as fantasies until I opened a newspaper in the autumn of that same year and found that the super-heroes had escaped from their four-color world and invaded the plain, factual black and white of the headlines.

The first news story was simple and unpresupposing enough, but it shared enough elements with those fictions that were closest to my heart to make me notice it and file it in my memory for future reference. It concerned an attempted assault and robbery that had taken place in Queens, New York. A man and his girlfriend, walking home after a night at the theater, had been set upon by a gang of three men armed with guns. After relieving the couple of their valuables, the gang has started to beat and physically abuse the young man while threatening to indecently assault his girlfriend. At this point, the crime had been interrupted by a figure "Who dropped into the alleyway from above with something over his face" and proceeded to disarm the three attackers before beating them with such severity that all three required hospital treatment and that one subsequently lost the use of both legs as a result of a spinal injury. The witnesses' recounting of the event was confused and contradictory, but there was still something in the story that gave me a tingle of recognition. And then, a week later, it happened again.

Reportage on this second instance was more detailed. A supermarket stick-up had been prevented thanks to the intervention of "A tall man, built like a wrestler, who wore a black hood and cape and also wore a noose around his neck." This extraordinary being had crashed in through the window of the supermarket while the robbery was in progress and attacked the man responsible with such intensity and savagery that those not disabled immediately were only too willing to drop their guns and surrender. Connecting this incidence of masked intervention with its predecessor, the papers ran the story under a headline that read simply "Hooded Justice." The first masked adventurer outside comic books had been given his name.

Reading and rereading that news item, I knew that I had to be the second. I'd found my vocation.

"AW, WILLYA *LOOK* AT HER? PRETTY AS A PICTURE AN' *STILL* KEEPIN' HER *FIGURE!*"

"SO, HONEY, WHAT BRINGS *YOU* TO THE CITY OF THE DEAD?"

MOM, BEING *LAZY* ISN'T A TERMINAL CONDITION, SO SPARE ME THE *"CITY OF THE DEAD"* CRAP. BROUGHT YOU SOME *FLOWERS.*

OHHH! BIG *SPENDER!*

WHERE'S *JON?*

"JON'S AT SOME *FUNERAL.* I DIDN'T FEEL LIKE *ATTENDING,* SO HE TRANSPORTED ME *HERE,* TO CALIFORNIA."

"I JUST GOT THROUGH THROW-ING UP IN THE *LADIES' ROOM.*"

ALWAYS GETS ME THE SAME. ONE SECOND *NEW YORK,* THE NEXT, *WHAM,* CALIFORNIA! SO LONG *BREAKFAST.*

POOR BABY.

SO, THIS *FUNERAL:* ANYONE I *KNOW?*

"THE *FUNERAL?* OH, NO, THAT'S JUST, Y'KNOW, SOME LITTLE *OFFICIAL* THING."

"JON *HAD* TO GO. PROTOCOL. THEY MADE HIM PUT *CLOTHES* ON AND EVERY-THING..."

IT'S EDDIE BLAKE'S FUNERAL, RIGHT?

MOM...

LAURIE, DON'T TREAT ME LIKE A *KID!* I CAN STILL *READ.* I SAW IN THE *PAPER* HE GOT MURDERED.

"I GUESS HE FINALLY REACHED THE *PUNCH-LINE,* HUH?"

"POOR *EDDIE.*"

POOR EDDIE? MOM, HOW CAN YOU *SAY* THAT? AFTER HE ALMOST...

LAURIE, YOU'RE *YOUNG,* YOU DON'T *KNOW.* THINGS *CHANGE.*

WHAT *HAPPENED,* HAPPENED FORTY *YEARS* AGO...

"IT'S HISTORY."

1

YEAH, WELL, SO'S *DACHAU.* I'D *NEVER* FORGIVE SOMEBODY WHO DID THAT...

LISTEN, GETTIN' *OLD,* YOU GET A *DIFFERENT PERSPECTIVE.* THE *BIG* STUFF LOOKS *SMALLER* SOMEHOW.

"IN THE END, YOU JUST WASH YOUR HANDS OF IT AND SHUT IT AWAY."

OH, *RIGHT.* JUST LIKE *THAT.*

SO, WHAT, YOU WANT I SHOULD CURL UP AND *WHIMPER* FOR FORTY YEARS? YOU WANT I SHOULD GO BE A *NUN?*

"LIFE GOES ON, HONEY."

"LIFE GOES ON."

PLUS, IT'S A *BEAUTIFUL DAY!* Y'KNOW... ≥AHUH-HEMM≥ ...

Y'KNOW, YOU AND *JON* OUGHTTA MOVE OUT HERE, FOR THE *WEATHER.* WAS IT THIS SUNNY IN *NEW YORK* TODAY?

"UH, YEAH. YEAH, PRETTY MUCH..."

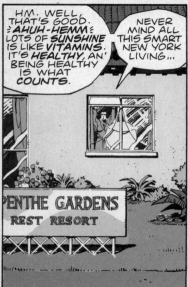

HM. WELL, THAT'S GOOD. ≥AHUH-HEMM≥ LOTS OF *SUNSHINE* IS LIKE *VITAMINS.* IT'S *HEALTHY,* AN' BEING HEALTHY IS WHAT *COUNTS.*

NEVER MIND ALL THIS SMART NEW YORK LIVING...

PENTHE GARDENS
REST RESORT

"I MEAN, WITHOUT YOUR *HEALTH* WHERE *ARE* YOU?"

AT *MY* AGE ≥AHHUM≥ YOU WANNA TAKE *CARE* OF YOUR-SELF. ALL YOUR OLD *BUDDIES* HAVE PASSED *ON,* AND...

MOM, IT'S *OKAY.* YOU DON'T NEED ANY MORE *DOORS* OR *WINDOWS.* LOOK, I'M PUTTING IT, *OUT,* OKAY? IT'S *DEAD.*

EXTINGUISHED.

2

ABSENT FRIENDS

Y'KNOW, THAT MAKES JUST *THREE* OF US MINUTEMEN LEFT NOW. ME, *HOLLIS MASON,* AND POOR *BYRON LEWIS,* IN THE *BUGHOUSE* IN MAINE.

FUNNY... *EDDIE* WAS THE *YOUNGEST.* ALWAYS JOKIN' ABOUT HOW *OLD* WE ALL WERE.

"HE SAID HE'D *BURY* US.

"Y'SEE, THAT WAS *EDDIE,* ALWAYS TALKIN' LIKE HE WAS ON *TOP* OF IT, LIKE IT WAS NEVER GOING TO *HAPPEN* TO HIM..."

EDWARD MORGAN BLAKE 1924-1985

HE WAS *THE COMEDIAN.*

HE ALWAYS THOUGHT HE'D GET THE LAST LAUGH.

3

YEAH? WELL, JON TOLD ME ABOUT SOME OF THE STUFF BLAKE DID IN 'NAM. SOUNDS LIKE HE HAD A STRANGE SENSE OF HUMOR.

OH! SPEAKING OF WHICH, THAT REMINDS ME...

YOU REMEMBER THAT GUY WHO WRITES ME LETTERS? WELL, HE SENT ME AN ITEM OF MEMORABILIA...

THE ONE WHO ASKED FOR YOUR OLD COSTUME? HONESTLY, MOM, YOU ENCOURAGE THESE GUYS...

WHAT IS IT?

IT'S A TIJUANA BIBLE... A LITTLE EIGHT-PAGE PORNO COMIC THEY DID IN THE '30S AND '40S...

THEY DID 'EM ABOUT NEWSPAPER FUNNIES CHARACTERS LIKE BLONDIE, EVEN REAL PEOPLE LIKE MAE WEST.

THIS ONE'S ABOUT ME.

ABOUT...?

OH, GOD! MOTHER, THIS IS JUST GROSS! SOMEBODY SENT YOU THIS?

SURE. LISTEN, THOSE THINGS ARE VALUABLE, LIKE ANTIQUES. EIGHTY BUCKS AN' UP. I THINK IT'S KINDA FLATTERING.

FLATTERING...?

BEING REMINDED THAT PEOPLE USED TO SLOBBER OVER ME? SURE. FLATTERING. WHY NOT?

LAURIE, I'M 65. EVERY DAY THE FUTURE LOOKS A LITTLE BIT DARKER. BUT THE PAST, EVEN THE GRIMY PARTS OF IT...

...WELL, IT JUST KEEPS ON GETTING BRIGHTER ALL THE TIME.

OKAY, THAT'S IT! NICE PICTURE, FOLKS!

WE CAN MOVE? I CAN FINALLY SCRATCH MY ARMPIT?

OOOH! I GOT SPOTS IN MY EYES...

4

REALLY? LEMME TAKE A *LOOK* AN' SEE IF I CAN FISH 'EM OUT FOR YA...

OH, EDDIE! GIVE ME A *BREAK*!

OKAY, MR. OWL, THAT'S *EIGHT PRINTS*. THEY'LL BE READY IN A *WEEK*.

BOY! REAL *PHOTO SESSIONS*! DO YOU THINK MY *HAIR* WILL COME OUT LOOKING *OKAY*, H.J.?

FRANKLY, SALLY, I DON'T GO IN FOR ALL THIS *RAZZLE DAZZLE*. I'D RATHER BE ON THE *STREETS*, DOING MY *JOB*.

STREETS *NOTHING*! WHY DON'T *UNCLE SAMMY* GET US INTO *EUROPE*, WHERE THE *ACTION* IS?

WELL, *FIRSTLY*, WE AREN'T AT *WAR*. SECONDLY, WE SHOULD *AVOID* POLITICAL SITUATIONS...

PERHAPS THE *POLES* THOUGHT SO TOO, EH? YOU *AGREE*, SALLY?

WELL, I'M SURE *I* WOULDN'T KNOW ANYTHING ABOUT WHAT THE *POLISH PEOPLE* THINK!

ME, I HOPE WE KEEP OUT OF IT. JUST *THINKING* ABOUT *WAR*, IT SCARES ME...

HEY! WATCH WITH THE *WINGS*!

C'MON... WHAT'S ALL THIS *DISCORD* I HEAR? MEETING'S *OVER*!

LISTEN, EVERYONE MEET IN THE *LOBBY* IN FIVE MINUTES. WE'LL GO BACK TO THE *OWL'S NEST* FOR A *BEER*.

FINE. YOU GUYS GO AHEAD. I GOTTA *CHANGE*.

HI.

5

EDDIE? WHAT THE HELL ARE YOU DOING HERE? YOU KNEW I WAS CHANGING...

SURE I DID. YOU ANNOUNCED IT LOUD ENOUGH.

C'MON, BABY. I KNOW WHAT YOU NEED. YOU GOTTA HAVE SOME REASON FOR WEARIN' AN OUTFIT LIKE THIS, HUH?

E-EDDIE, NO...

SURE. NO. SPELLED Y, E...

SPELLED ENN OH!

AAK

EDDIE?

AHHHUUGHH

GUHH

MOLOCH'S SOLAR MIRROR WEAPON

OH, NO.

OH, NO, EDDIE, DON'T...

OH, GODDD...

SALLY? WHAT'S KEEPING YOU?

GHUUCHH

6

7

GET UP...

AND, FOR GOD'S SAKE, *COVER YOUR-SELF.*

MOTHER, THIS IS *VILE!*

OH! TREAT ME ROUGH, SUGAR.

OH SAY, BABY, THIS IS *TOPS!*

ACME BRUSH CO.

I JUST, JEEZ, I JUST DON'T KNOW HOW YOU CAN STAND BEING *DEGRADED* LIKE THIS. I MEAN, DON'T YOU *CARE* HOW PEOPLE *SEE* YOU?

MOTHER?

HM?

I *SAID,* DOESN'T THIS SLEAZEBALL IMAGE BOTHER YOU? *HONESTLY,* MOTHER, YOU...

WHY DO YOU ONLY CALL ME "*MOTHER*" WHEN YOU'RE *MAD?*

ANYWAY, WHAT ABOUT *YOUR* IMAGE? AT LEAST *I* DON'T SLEEP WITH AN *H-BOMB...*

JON IS *NOT* AN *H-BOMB!*

HONEY, THE ONLY *DIFFERENCE* IS THAT THEY DIDN'T HAVE TO GET THE *H-BOMB LAID* EVERY ONCE IN A WHILE.

TO SALLY JUPITER BEST WISHES *Varga.*

UH-*HUH.* RIGHT. I *SEE.*

OF COURSE, YOU *REALIZE* YOU'RE BEING TOTALLY *UNFAIR?*

YEAH? WELL, THINGS ARE TOUGH ALL *OVER,* CUPCAKE, AN' IT RAINS ON THE *JUST* AN' THE *UNJUST* ALIKE...

...EXCEPT IN *CALIFORNIA.*

8

MAN THAT IS BORN OF WOMAN HATH BUT A SHORT TIME TO LIVE, AND IS FULL OF MISERIES.

HE COMETH UP, AND IS CUT DOWN, LIKE A FLOWER. HE FLEETH AS IT WERE A SHADOW, AND NEVER CONTINUETH IN ONE STAY.

IN THE MIDST OF LIFE, WE ARE IN DEATH.

OF WHOM MAY WE SEEK SUCCOR BUT OF THEE, O LORD, WHO FOR OUR SINS ART JUSTLY DISPLEASED.

WELL, FIRSTLY, LET ME SAY I'M PLEASED TO SEE SO MANY OF YOU HERE.

VERY PLEASED.

SECONDLY, FOR THOSE WHO ONLY KNOW ME AS CAPTAIN METROPOLIS, THE NAME'S NELSON GARDNER. CALL ME NELSON.

THIRD, UH, I GUESS I SHOULD WELCOME EVERYBODY TO THE FIRST EVER MEETING OF THE CRIMEBUSTERS!

≀BURRUP≀

FRENCH WITHDRAW MILITARY COMMITMENT FROM NATO

HEART TRANSPLANT PATIENT STABLE

9

WHY *"THE CRIME-BUSTERS"?*

WELL, AS YOU KNOW, THIS COUNTRY HASN'T HAD AN ORGAN-IZATION OF *MASKED ADVENTURERS* SINCE THE *MINUTEMEN* DISBANDED IN '49.

SPECIALIZED LAW ENFORCEMENT IS STANDING *STILL.* CRIME *ISN'T.*

NEW SOCIAL EVILS EMERGE EVERY DAY: *PROMISCUITY, DRUGS, CAMPUS SUBVERSION,* YOU *NAME* IT! NOW, BY BANDING TOGETHER AS THE *CRIME-BUSTERS,* WE...

BULLSHIT.

WHAT?

I SAID *BULLSHIT.* THIS WHOLE IDEA, THIS *CRIMEBUSTERS* SHTICK, IT *STINKS.*

WHAT IT *IS,* NELLY, IS THAT *YOU'RE* GETTIN' *OLD* AND YOU WANNA GO ON PLAYIN' *COWBOYS* AND *INDIANS!*

TH-THAT ISN'T *TRUE...*

UH, LISTEN, LET'S NOT THROW THE IDEA OUT RIGHT AWAY. ME AND *RORSCHACH* HAVE MADE HEADWAY INTO THE *GANG* PROBLEM BY POOLING OUR EFFORTS...

OBVIOUSLY, I AGREE -- BUT A GROUP *THIS* SIZE SEEMS MORE LIKE A *PUBLICITY EXERCISE* SOMEHOW. IT'S TOO *BIG* AND *UNWIELDY...*

SURELY, THAT'S JUST AN *ORGANIZATIONAL* PROBLEM? WITH THE RIGHT PERSON *COORDINATING* THE GROUP, I THINK...

OH, AN' I *WONDER* WHO *THAT* WOULD BE?

GOT ANY *IDEAS,* OZZY? I MEAN, YOU *ARE* THE SMARTEST GUY IN THE *WORLD,* RIGHT?

IT DOESN'T REQUIRE *GENIUS* TO SEE THAT AMERICA HAS *PROBLEMS* THAT NEED *TACKLING...*

DAMN *STRAIGHT.* AN' IT TAKES A *MORON* TO THINK THEY'RE *SMALL* ENOUGH FOR CLOWNS LIKE *YOU* GUYS TO HANDLE.

WHAT'S *GOING DOWN* IN THIS WORLD, YOU GOT *NO IDEA.*

BELIEVE ME.

I THINK I'M AS WELL-INFORMED AS *ANYONE*. GIVEN CORRECT HANDLING, *NONE* OF THE WORLD'S PROBLEMS ARE *INSURMOUNTABLE*.

WHICH YOU GOT IN *SPADES*, RIGHT?

ALL IT TAKES IS A LITTLE *INTELLIGENCE*.

YOU PEOPLE ARE A *JOKE*. YOU HEAR MOLOCH'S BACK IN TOWN, YOU THINK "OH, *BOY!* LET'S *GANG UP* AND *BUST* HIM!"

YOU THINK THAT *MATTERS?* YOU THINK THAT *SOLVES* ANYTHING?

WELL, OF *COURSE* IT MATTERS. IF...

IT DON'T MATTER *SQUAT*. HERE --LEMME SHOW YA *WHY* IT DON'T MATTER...

HEY! WH-WHAT ARE YOU DOING?

IT DON'T MATTER SQUAT BECAUSE INSIDE *THIRTY YEARS* THE *NUKES* ARE GONNA BE FLYIN' LIKE MAYBUGS...

PROMISCUITY

ANTI-WAR DEMOS

DRUGS

BLACK UNREST

MY DISPLAY...

...AND THEN *OZZY* HERE IS GONNA BE THE SMARTEST MAN ON THE *CINDER*. NOW, PARDON *ME*, BUT I GOT AN *APPOINTMENT*.

SEE YOU IN THE *FUNNY PAPERS*.

JON, I THINK I'D LIKE TO GO *HOME* NOW, PLEASE.

LISTEN, UH, NELSON...THIS ISN'T WORKING OUT. MAYBE...

PLEASE! DON'T ALL *LEAVE*...

SOMEBODY HAS TO DO IT, DON'T YOU *SEE?*

SOMEBODY HAS TO SAVE THE *WORLD*...

... O LORD MOST MIGHTY, O HOLY AND MOST MERCIFUL SAVIOR, DELIVER US NOT INTO THE BITTER PAINS OF ETERNAL DEATH.

11

I SUPPOSE V.V.N. NIGHT MUST MEAN SOMETHING TO THEM.

NAH. AVERAGE VIETNAMESE DON'T GIVE A DAMN WHO WON. IT MEANS SOMETHING TO THE DINKS AN' IT MEANS PLENTY TO US...

I MEAN, IF WE'D LOST THIS WAR... I DUNNO. I THINK IT MIGHT HAVE DRIVEN US A LITTLE CRAZY, Y'KNOW? AS A COUNTRY.

BUT THANKS TO YOU WE DIDN'T, RIGHT?

DOWNA HATCH.

YOU SOUND BITTER. YOU'RE A STRANGE MAN, BLAKE. YOU HAVE STRANGE ATTITUDES TO LIFE AND WAR.

STRANGE?

LISTEN... ONCE YOU FIGURE OUT WHAT A JOKE EVERYTHING IS, BEING THE COMEDIAN'S THE ONLY THING MAKES SENSE.

THE CHARRED VILLAGES, THE BOYS WITH NECK LACES OF HUMAN EARS... THESE ARE PART OF THE JOKE?

HEY... I NEVER SAID IT WAS A GOOD JOKE! I'M JUST PLAYIN' ALONG WITH THE GAG...

HA! LOOKITHAT!

THERE HE IS. FIRST PRESS HELICOPTER INTO SAIGON SINCE THE CEASEFIRE. HE'S GOT THE NEXT ELECTION IN THE BAG FOR SURE.

ME, I'M TAKIN' THE FIRST CHOPPER OUT!

YOU'RE ANXIOUS TO LEAVE?

DOC, ARE YOU KIDDING? I HATE THIS PLACE. I HATE THE TEMPERATURE. I HATE THE SMELL, I HATE THIS ROTTEN CHEAP BOURBON.

FIRST CHOPPER OUT, MAN, I'M GONE.

MR. EDDIE?

13

OH, GREAT. OH, THANK YOU, GOD. THAT'S JUST WHAT I NEEDED...

NOW WAR IS OVER, MR. EDDIE.

NOW I MUST TALK WITH YOU.

LISTEN, WE GOT NOTHIN' TO TALK ABOUT. I'M LEAVIN'. SAIGON NUMBER TEN, NEW YORK NUMBER ONE, OKAY?

YOU... WALK AWAY... FROM THIS?

SURE.

BUT ME, I CANNOT WALK AWAY FROM WHAT GROWS IN MY BELLY. I CANNOT FORGET!

WELL, THAT'S UNFORTUNATE, BECAUSE THAT'S JUST WHAT I'M GONNA DO...

FORGET YOU, FORGET YOUR CRUDDY LITTLE COUNTRY, ALL OF IT.

I DO NOT THINK SO.

I THINK YOU REMEMBER ME AND MY COUNTRY.

I THINK YOU REMEMBER US AS LONG AS YOU LIVE.

HUH? WHAT'S...

GORDON GIN

MY FACE...

GHUUHUHH

WHAT DID YOU DO, YOU BITCH, YOU HURT MY FACE, YOU WHORE, YOU...

...FILTHY, STINKING, WORTH- LESS...

BLAKE?

...LOUSY PIECE OF...

BLAKE, DON'T...

14

...DO IT.

MEDIC.

GOTTA FIND THE GODDAMN MEDIC.

OWWW. THAT BITCH...

BLAKE, SHE WAS PREGNANT. YOU GUNNED HER DOWN.

YEAH. YEAH, THAT'S RIGHT. PREGNANT WOMAN. GUNNED HER DOWN. BANG. AND Y'KNOW WHAT?

YOU WATCHED ME.

YOU COULDA CHANGED THE GUN INTO STEAM OR THE BULLETS INTO MERCURY OR THE BOTTLE INTO SNOWFLAKES! YOU COULDA TELEPORTED EITHER OF US TO GODDAMN AUSTRALIA...

...BUT YOU DIDN'T LIFT A FINGER!

YOU DON'T REALLY GIVE A DAMN ABOUT HUMAN BEINGS. I'VE WATCHED YOU.

YOU NEVER CARED ABOUT WHATSERNAME, JANEY SLATER, EVEN BEFORE YOU DITCHED HER.

SOON YOU WON'T BE INTERESTED IN SALLY JUPITER'S LITTLE GAL, EITHER.

YOU'RE DRIFTIN' OUTTA TOUCH, DOC.

YOU'RE TURNIN' INTO A FLAKE.

GOD HELP US ALL.

...FOR AS MUCH AS IT HATH PLEASED ALMIGHTY GOD OF HIS GREAT MERCY TO TAKE UNTO HIMSELF THE SOUL OF OUR DEAR BROTHER HERE DEPARTED, WE THEREFORE COMMIT HIS BODY TO THE GROUND,...

15

EARTH TO
EARTH...

ASHES
TO
ASHES...

...DUST
TO DUST.

PLEASE...
IF EVERYBODY
WILL JUST
CLEAR THE
STREETS...

LISSEN, YOU LITTLE
PUNKS, YOU BETTER
GET BACK IN YA RAT
HOLES! I GOT RIOT
GAS, I GOT RUBBER
BULLETS...

16

17

"I HEARD A VOICE FROM HEAVEN, SAYING UNTO ME, WRITE..."

"FROM HENCEFORTH, BLESSED ARE THE DEAD WHICH DIE IN THE LORD, EVEN SO SAITH THE SPIRIT, FOR THEY REST FROM THEIR LABORS."

"LORD HAVE MERCY UPON US."

"CHRIST HAVE MERCY UPON US."

"LORD HAVE MERCY UPON US."

"OUR FATHER, WHICH ART IN HEAVEN, HALLOWED BE THY NAME..."

"THY KINGDOM COME, THY WILL BE DONE, ON EARTH AS IT IS IN HEAVEN. GIVE US THIS DAY OUR DAILY BREAD, AND FORGIVE US OUR TRESPASSES..."

"AS WE FORGIVE THOSE THAT TRESPASS AGAINST US..."

"AND LEAD US NOT INTO TEMPTATION..."

"BUT DELIVER US FROM EVIL."

"AMEN."

19

AAAAAAAA

20

OH, GOD, PLEASE...

PLEASE, THIS MUST BE A MISTAKE! YOU HAVE THE WRONG PERSON...

NO.

EDGAR WILLIAM JACOBI, ALSO KNOWN AS EDGAR WILLIAM VAUGHN, ALSO KNOWN AS WILLIAM EDGAR BRIGHT...

...ALSO KNOWN AS MOLOCH.

I... I DON'T KNOW WHAT YOU'RE TALKING ABOUT. I'M A BUSINESSMAN, A RETIRED BUSINESSM--

AAAA!

LYING. DO IT AGAIN, BROKEN ARM. NOT JOKING.

OH, GOD, PLEASE...I SPENT THE SEVENTIES IN JAIL. I'M NOT MOLOCH ANYMORE. I JUST WANT TO BE LEFT ALONE. WHAT DO YOU WANT WITH ME?

HEARD YOU ATTENDED FUNERAL TODAY.

WHY?

THE FUNERAL? I...I DON'T KNOW. I DON'T KNOW WHY I WENT.

I JUST FELT I SHOULD. I'D BEEN THINKING ABOUT THE COMEDIAN SINCE HE VISITED ME, AND...

AUHH! OH, GOD! WHAT DID I SAY?

HOW?

HOW DO YOU KNOW EDWARD BLAKE WAS THE COMEDIAN?

WH-WHEN HE BROKE IN, TO SEE ME! HE WAS DRUNK. HAD HIS MASK OFF. THE GUY WAS SCARED OF SOMETHING, CRYING...

ENEMIES FOR FORTY YEARS. WHY SHOULD HE VISIT YOU?

I DON'T KNOW. I WOKE UP, HE WAS THERE, IN MY ROOM, DRUNK, BABBLING, NOT MAKING SENSE...

I SAT IN BED, SCARED STIFF. HE SOUNDED CRAZY. I THOUGHT HE WAS GONNA KILL ME.

"THIS WAS, LIKE, A WEEK BEFORE I HEARD HE'D DIED.

"I GUESS IT WAS HIS LAST PERFORMANCE."

21

IT'S A JOKE. S'ALL A JOKE.

I MEAN, LEMME *TELLYA*, WHEN I STARTED *OUT*, WHEN I WAS A *KID*, CLEANIN' UP THE *WATER-FRONTS*, IT WAS, LIKE, REAL *EASY*.

THE WORLD WAS *TOUGH*, YOU JUST HADDA BE *TOUGHER*, RIGHT?

NOT ANYMORE.

I MEAN, I THOUGHT I KNEW HOW IT *WAS*, HOW THE *WORLD* WAS. BUT THEN I FOUND OUT ABOUT THIS *GAG*, THIS *JOKE*...

YOU'RE PART OF IT, MOLOCH OL' PAL. Y'KNOW THAT?

IF I THOUGHT YOU *DID* KNOW... I SAW YOUR NAME ON THE *LIST*, YOU AND *JANEY SLATER*, BUT IF I *THOUGHT* YOU WERE *IN* ON THIS...

...I'D KILL YOU. YOU UNDER-STAND?

KILL YOU.

I MEAN, YOU *FOUGHT* THAT BIG BLUE *GEEK!* YOU KNOW WHAT HIS *HEAD'S* LIKE!

I TELLYA, WHO *KNOWS* WHICH WAY HE'LL JUMP IF ANYBODY *MESSES* WITH HIM...

HE MIGHT... HE MIGHT JUST...

NAH. I DON'WANNA THINK. I DON'WANNA *THINK* ABOUT IT.

DON'TCHA GOT ANY *BOOZE* IN THIS PLACE?

I MEAN, WHAT GETS *ME*, RIGHT? WHAT GETS *ME*, I NEED NEVER HAVE *LOOKED* OUTTA THE AIRSHIP WINDOW AT THAT MOMENT, NEVER SEEN THE GODDAMN *ISLAND*, NEVER GOT *INVOLVED*...

HAH! THERE Y'ARE, YA SUMBITCH...

NK — NK — NK

PAHH

IT STINKS.

IT ALL *STINKS*.

22

I MEAN, THIS JOKE, I MEAN, I THOUGHT I WAS THE COMEDIAN, Y'KNOW?

OH, GOD, I CAN'T BELIEVE IT. I CAN'T BELIEVE ANYBODY WOULD DO THAT...

I CAN'T...

I CAN'T BELIEVE...

AHUHH.

AHUH AHUH AHHUHHH.

OH, JESUS, LOOK AT ME. I'M CRYIN'! YOU DON'T KNOW. YOU DON'T KNOW WHAT'S HAPPENING.

ON THAT ISLAND THEY GOT WRITERS, SCIENTISTS, ARTISTS, AND WHAT THEY'RE DOING...

I MEAN, I DONE SOME BAD THINGS. I DID BAD THINGS TO WOMEN.

I SHOT KIDS! IN 'NAM I SHOT KIDS...

BUT I NEVER DID ANY-THING LIKE, LIKE...

OH, MOTHER. OH, FORGIVE ME.

FORGIVE ME, FORGIVE ME, FORGIVE ME...

I MEAN, WHAT'S FUNNY? WHAT'S SO GODDAMNED FUNNY?

I DON'T GET IT. SOMEBODY EXPLAIN...

SOMEBODY EXPLAIN IT TO ME.

...AND THEN HE LEFT.

I DON'T KNOW.

I DON'T KNOW WHAT THE HELL IT WAS ABOUT...

23

HURM.

FUNNY STORY.

SOUNDS UNBELIEVABLE.

PROBABLY TRUE.

S-SO, WHAT, YOU MEAN THAT'S IT? I'M CLEAN?

CLEAN?

YOU?

SEARCHED YOUR HOUSE, BEFORE YOU GOT BACK. KNEW YOU WOULDN'T MIND. FOUND ILLEGAL DRUGS.

ILLEGAL...? BUT I DON'T USE DRUGS! LISTEN, IF YOU'RE PLANTING EVIDENCE...

LAETRIL. PHONY MEDICATION. MADE FROM APRICOT PITS. OUTLAWED THREE YEARS AGO.

ILLEGAL.

OH, COME ON ... YOU'RE NOT SERIOUS? LOOK, I HEARD MAYBE IT DIDN'T WORK, BUT WHEN YOU'RE DESPERATE YOU'LL TRY ANYTHING. PLEASE DON'T CONFISCATE IT.

I HAVE CANCER.

CANCER? WHAT KIND CANCER?

HEH.

WELL, NOW, Y'KNOW THAT KIND OF CANCER THAT YOU EVENTUALLY GET BETTER FROM?

YES.

WELL, THAT AIN'T THE KIND OF CANCER I GOT.

HUHNH.

VERY WELL. COPIED DOWN NAME OF COMPANY. REPORT THEM LATER.

YOU'RE OFF HOOK. FOR NOW.

BE SEEING YOU.

KEEP OUT OF TROUBLE.

24

42ND STREET: WOMEN'S BREASTS DRAPED ACROSS EVERY BILLBOARD, EVERY DISPLAY, LITTERING THE SIDEWALK.

WAS OFFERED SWEDISH LOVE AND FRENCH LOVE....

...BUT NOT AMERICAN LOVE.

AMERICAN LOVE; LIKE COKE IN GREEN GLASS BOTTLES...

THEY DON'T MAKE IT ANYMORE.

THOUGHT ABOUT MOLOCH'S STORY, ON WAY TO CEMETERY.

COULD ALL BE LIES. COULD ALL BE PART OF REVENGE SCHEME, PLANNED DURING HIS DECADE BEHIND BARS.

BUT IF TRUE, THEN WHAT? PUZZLING REFERENCE TO AN ISLAND. ALSO TO DR. MANHATTAN. MIGHT HE BE AT RISK IN SOME WAY? SO MANY QUESTIONS.

NEVER MIND. ANSWERS SOON. NOTHING IS INSOLUBLE.

NOTHING IS HOPELESS.

NOT WHILE THERE'S LIFE.

25

In the cemetery, all the white crosses stood in rows, neat chalk marks on a giant scorecard.

Paid last respects quietly, without fuss.

EDWARD MORGAN BLAKE 1924-1985

Edward Morgan Blake. Born 1924. Forty-five years a comedian, died 1985, buried in the rain.

Is that what happens to us? A life of conflict with no time for friends...

...so that when it's done, only our enemies leave roses.

EDWARD MORGAN BLAKE 1924-1985

Violent lives, ending violently. Dollar Bill the Silhouette, Captain Metropolis... we never die in bed.

Not allowed.

Something in our personalities, perhaps? Some animal urge to fight and struggle, making us what we are?

Unimportant. We do what we have to do.

Others bury their heads between the swollen teats of indulgence and gratification, piglets squirming beneath a sow for shelter...

...but there is no shelter...

...and the future is bearing down like an express train.

PROMISCUITY

ANTI-WAR DEMOS

DRUGS

BLACK UNREST

26

BLAKE UNDERSTOOD. TREATED IT LIKE A JOKE, BUT HE UNDERSTOOD. HE SAW THE CRACKS IN SOCIETY, SAW THE LITTLE MEN IN MASKS TRYING TO HOLD IT TOGETHER...

HE SAW THE TRUE FACE OF THE TWENTIETH CENTURY AND CHOSE TO BECOME A REFLECTION, A PARODY OF IT.

NO ONE ELSE SAW THE JOKE. THAT'S WHY HE WAS LONELY.

HEARD JOKE ONCE:

MAN GOES TO DOCTOR. SAYS HE'S DEPRESSED. SAYS LIFE SEEMS HARSH AND CRUEL.

SAYS HE FEELS ALL ALONE IN A THREATENING WORLD WHERE WHAT LIES AHEAD IS VAGUE AND UNCERTAIN.

DOCTOR SAYS "TREATMENT IS SIMPLE. GREAT CLOWN PAGLIACCI IS IN TOWN TONIGHT. GO AND SEE HIM. THAT SHOULD PICK YOU UP."

MAN BURSTS INTO TEARS.

SAYS "BUT, DOCTOR...

"...I AM PAGLIACCI."

27

GOOD JOKE. EVERYBODY LAUGH.

ROLL ON SNARE DRUM.

CURTAINS.

And I'm up while the dawn is breaking, even though my heart is aching.
I should be drinking a toast to absent friends instead of these comedians.

—Elvis Costello

28

UNDER THE HOOD

III.

Presented here are the excerpts from UNDER THE HOOD. In these next chapters Hollis Mason discusses the formation of the Minutemen. Reprinted with permission of the author.

From the moment that I decided somewhere deep inside myself that I wanted to try my hand at being a costumed adventurer, to the moment I first stepped out into the night with a mask on my face and the wind on my bare legs, took about three months. Three months of self-doubt and self-ridicule. Three months of self-conscious training down at the Police Gymnasium. Three months figuring out how the hell I was going to make myself a costume.

The costume was difficult, because I couldn't start designing it until I'd thought of a name. This stumped me for a couple of weeks, because every name I came up with sounded stupid, and what I really wanted was something with the same sense of drama and excitement as "Hooded Justice."

Eventually, a suitable handle was provided inadvertently by one of the other cops that I worked with down at the station house. He'd invited me out for a beer after work two or three times only to be turned down because I wanted to spend as much of my evenings working out in the Police Gymnasiums as possible, after which I'd usually go to bed around nine o'clock and sleep through until five the next morning, when I'd get up and put in a couple of hours workout before donning my badge and uniform in readiness for my day job. After having his offer of beer and relaxation turned down yet again by reason of me wanting to be in bed early, he finally gave up asking and took to calling me "Nite Owl" out of sarcasm until he finally found somebody else to drink with.

"Nite Owl." I liked it. Now all I had to come up with was the costume.

A masked adventurer's costume is one of those things that nobody really thinks about. Should it have a cape, or no cape? Should it be thick and armored to protect you from harm, or flexible and lightweight to allow maneuverability? What sort of mask should it have? Do bright colors make you more of a target than dark ones? All of these were things that I had to consider.

Eventually, I opted for a design that left the arms and legs as free as possible, while protecting my body and head with a tough leather tunic, light chainmail briefs, and a layer of leather-over-chainmail protecting my head. I experimented with a cloak, remembering how the Shadow would use his cloak to misguide enemy bullets, leading them to shoot at parts of the swirling black mass where his body didn't happen to be. In practice, however, I found it too unwieldy. I was always tripping over it or getting it caught in things, and so I abandoned it for an outfit that was as streamlined as I could make it.

With the mail and leather headpiece hiding my hair, I found I only really needed a small domino mask to conceal my identity, but even this presented problems that weren't obvious at first glance. My first mask was attached to my face by the simple expediency of a string, but this nearly got me killed during my first ever outing in full costume, when a drunk with a knife hooked his fingers into the eyeholes of the domino and pulled it down so that I could only see out of one eye. If I'd been less fit and alert or he'd been less drunk my career might well have ended then. As it was I was able to tear off the mask completely and then disarm him, trusting that the alcohol would fog any clear recollection of my face. After that, I dispensed with the string and stuck the mask to my face using spirit gum, such as actors use to attach false beards or mustaches.

I first became Nite Owl during the early months of 1939, and although my first few exploits were largely unspectacular, they aroused a lot of media interest simply because by 1939, dressing up in a costume and protecting your neighborhood had become something of a fad, with the whole of America at least briefly interested in its development. A month after I made my debut, a young woman who called herself The Silhouette broke into the headlines by exposing the activities of a crooked publisher trafficking in child pornography, delivering a punitive beating to the entrepreneur and his two chief cameramen in the process. A little after that, the first reports of a man dressed like a moth who could glide through the air started to come in from Connecticut, and a particularly vicious and brutal young man in a gaudy yellow boiler suit started cleaning up the city's waterfronts under the name of The Comedian. Within twelve months of Hooded Justice's dramatic entrance into the public consciousness, there were at least seven other costumed vigilantes operating on or around America's West Coast.

There was Captain Metropolis, who brought a knowledge of military technique and strategy to his attempt at eradicating organized crime in the inner urban areas, and who is still active to this day.

There was The Silk Spectre, now retired and living with her daughter after an unsuccessful early marriage, who in retrospect was probably the first of us ever to realize that there could be commercial benefits in being a masked adventurer. The Silk Spectre used her reputation as a crimefighter primarily to make the front pages and receive exposure for her lucrative modeling career, but I think all of us who knew her loved her a little bit and we certainly didn't begrudge her a living. I think we were all too unsure of our own motives to cast aspersions upon anybody else.

There was Dollar Bill, originally a star college athlete from Kansas who was actually employed as an in-house super-hero by one of the major national banks, when they realized that the masked man fad made being able to brag about having a hero of your own to protect your customer's money a very interesting publicity prospect. Dollar Bill was one of the nicest and most straightforward men I have ever met, and the fact that he died so tragically young is something that still upsets me whenever I think about it. While attempting to stop a raid upon one of his employer's banks, his cloak became entangled in the bank's revolving door and he was shot dead at point-blank range before he could free it. Designers employed by the bank had designed his costume for maximum publicity appeal. If he'd designed it himself he might have left out that damned stupid cloak and still be alive today.

There was Mothman and The Silhouette and The Comedian and there was me, all of us choosing to dress up in gaudy opera costumes and express the notion of good and evil in simple, childish terms, while over in Europe they were turning human beings into soap and lampshades. We were sometimes respected, sometimes analyzed, and most often laughed at, and in spite of all the musings above, I don't think that those of us still surviving today are any closer to understanding just why we *really* did it all. Some of us did it because we were hired to and some of us did it to gain publicity. Some of us did it out of a sense of childish excitement and some of us, I think, did it for a kind of excitement that was altogether more adult if perhaps less healthy. They've called us fascists and they've called us perverts and while there's an element of truth in both those accusations, neither of them are big enough to take in the whole picture.

Yes, some of us were politically extreme. Before Pearl Harbor, I heard Hooded Justice openly expressing approval for the activities of Hitler's Third Reich, and Captain Metropolis has gone on record as making statements about black and Hispanic Americans that have been viewed as both racially prejudiced and inflammatory, charges that it is difficult to argue or deny.

Yes, I daresay some of us did have our sexual hang-ups. Everybody knows what eventually became of the Silhouette and although it would be tasteless to rehash the events surrounding her death in this current volume, it provides proof for those who need it that for some people, dressing up in a costume did have its more libidinous elements.

Yes, some of us were unstable and neurotic. Only a week ago as of this writing, I received word that the man behind the mask and wings of Mothman, whose true identity I am not at liberty to divulge, has been committed to a mental institution after a long bout of alcoholism and a complete mental breakdown.

Yes, we were crazy, we were kinky, we were Nazis, all those things that people say. We were also doing something because we believed in it. We were attempting, through our personal efforts, to make our country a safer and better place to live in. Individually, working on our separate patches of turf, we did too much good in our respective communities to be written off as a mere aberration, whether social or sexual or psychological.

It was only when we got together that the problems really started. I sometimes think without the Minutemen we might all have given up and called it quits pretty soon. The costumed adventurer might have become quietly and simply extinct.

And the world might not be in the mess that it's in today.

IV.

There's no mystery behind how the Minutemen first got together. Captain Metropolis had written to Sally Jupiter care of her agent, suggesting that they might meet with a view to forming a group of masked adventurers who could pool their resources and experience to combat crime. The Captain has always had a strategic approach to crimefighting, so I can see why the idea would appeal to him, although back then I was surprised that he'd made an effort to get in touch with Sally. He was so polite and reserved that Sally's drinking, swearing and mode of dress were guaranteed to shock him speechless. Later, I realized that Sally was simply the only costumed vigilante forethoughtful enough to have an agent whose address was in the phone book.

Sally's agent (and, much later, her husband) was an extremely shrewd individual named Laurence Schexnayder. He realized that without the occasional gimmick to revitalize flagging public interest, the fad for long underwear heroes would eventually fade, reducing his girl Sally's chances of media exposure as The Silk Spectre to zero. Thus it was Schexnayder, in mid-1939, who suggested placing a large ad in the Gazette asking other mystery men to come forward.

One by one we came, over the next few weeks. We were introduced to Sally, to Captain Metropolis, to each other and to Laurence Schexnayder. He was very organized and professional, and although only in his mid-thirties he seemed very mature and respectable to us back then. Maybe that was just because he'd be the only person in the room not wearing their boxer shorts over their pants. By the fall of '39 he'd arranged all the publicity and the Minutemen were finally born.

The *real* mystery is how the hell we managed to *stay* together.

Dressing up in a costume takes a very extreme personality, and the chances of eight such personalities getting along together were about seventy-eleven million to one against. This isn't to say that some of us didn't get along, of course. Sally attached herself pretty swiftly to Hooded Justice, who was one of the biggest men I've ever seen. I never found out his real name, but I'd be willing to bet that those early news reports weren't far off in comparing him to a wrestler. Strangely enough, even though Sally would always be hanging onto his arm, he never seemed very interested in *her*. I don't think I ever saw him kiss her, although maybe that was just because of his mask. Anyway, they started going out together, sort of, after the first Minutemen Christmas Party in 1939, which is the last time I can remember us all having a real good time together. After that, things went bad. We had worms in the apple, eating it from inside.

The first Minutemen Christmas party, 1939 (from left to right; The Silhouette, Silk Spectre, Comedian, Hooded Justice, Captain Metropolis (in mirror), Nite Owl, Mothman, Dollar Bill)

The worst of these was the Comedian. I'm aware that he's still active today and even respected in some quarters, but I know what I know, and that man is a disgrace to our profession. In 1940 he attempted to sexually assault Sally Jupiter in the Minutemen trophy room after a meeting. He left the group shortly thereafter by mutual consent and with a minimum of publicity. Schexnayder had persuaded Sally not to press charges against the Comedian for the good of the group's image, and she complied. The Comedian went his way unscathed...even though he was badly wounded in an unconnected stabbing incident about a year later. This is what made him decide to change his flimsy yellow costume for the leather armor he wears at present. He went on to make a name for himself as a war hero in the Pacific, but all I can

Newsreel footage of the Comedian in the South Pacific, 1942

think of is the bruises along Sally Jupiter's ribcage and hope to God that America can find itself a better class of hero than *that*.

After that, things deteriorated. In 1946, the papers revealed that the Silhouette was living with another woman in a lesbian relationship. Schexnayder persuaded us to expel her from the group, and six weeks later she was murdered, along with her lover, by one of her former enemies. Dollar Bill was shot dead, and in 1947 the group was dealt its most serious blow when Sally quit crimefighting to marry her agent. We always thought she might come back, but in 1949 she had a daughter, so that clinched that. Eventually, those of us who were left didn't even fight crime anymore. It wasn't interesting. The villains we'd fought with were either in prison or had moved on to less glamorous activities. Moloch, for example, who had started out aged seventeen as a stage magician, evolving into an ingenious and flamboyant criminal mastermind through underworld contacts made in his world of nightclubs, had moved into impersonal crime like drugs, financial fraud and vice clubs by the late '40's. Eventually, there was just me, Mothman, Hooded Justice and Captain Metropolis sitting around in a meeting hall that smelled like a locker room now that there weren't any women in the group. There was nobody interesting left to fight, nothing notable to talk about. In 1949, we called it a day. By then, however, we'd been around long enough to somehow inspire younger people, God help them, to follow in our footsteps.

The Minutemen were finished, but it didn't matter. The damage had already been done.

Early publicity poster of Moloch, 1937

DELIRIOUS, I SAW THAT HELL-BOUND SHIP'S BLACK SAILS AGAINST THE YELLOW INDIES SKY, AND KNEW AGAIN THE STENCH OF POWDER, AND MEN'S BRAINS, AND WAR.

WE OUGHTTA *NUKE RUSSIA*, AND LET *GOD* SORT IT OUT.

FALLOUT SHELTER

I *MEAN*, I *SEE* THE *SIGNS*, READ THE *HEADLINES*, LOOK THINGS INNA *FACE*, Y'KNOW?

THE HEADS NAILED TO ITS PROW LOOKED DOWN, THOSE WITH EYES; GULL-EATEN; SALT-CAKED; LIPLESSLY MOUTHING, "NO USE! ALL'S LOST!"

THE WAVES ABOUT ME WERE SCARLET, FOAMING, HORRIBLY WARM, YET STILL THE FREIGHTER'S HIDEOUS CREW CALLED OUT, "MORE BLOOD! MORE BLOOD!"

FALLOUT SHELTER

MISSING WRITER:

I'M A *NEWSVENDOR*, GODDAMNIT! I'M *INFORMED* ON THE SITUATION! WE OUGHTTA NUKE 'EM TILL THEY *GLOW*!

ITS TAR-STREAKED HULL ROLLED OVER ME. IN DESPAIR I SANK BENEATH THOSE FOUL, PINK BILLOWS, OFFERING UP MY WRETCHED SOUL TO ALMIGHTY GOD, HIS MERCY AND HIS JUDGMENT.

'COURSE, THAT'S JUST *MY* OPINION.

1

THE JUDGE OF ALL THE EARTH

FOR WHAT THAT'S **WORTH**, Y'KNOW?

INNA FINAL **ANALYSIS**.

WAKING FROM NIGHTMARE, I FOUND MYSELF UPON A DISMAL BEACH-HEAD, AMONGST DEAD MEN AND THE PIECES OF DEAD MEN.

INSTITUTE FOR EXTRASPATIAL STUDIES

LISSEN, I SEE EVERY GODDAMN FRONT PAGE INNA **WORLD**. I ABSORB INFORMATION! I MISS **NOTHING**.

BOSUN RIDLEY LAY NEARBY. BIRDS WERE EATING HIS THOUGHTS AND MEMORIES.

F'R'INSTANCE ...THE MORE **DISASTERS** HAPPEN, THE MORE **PAPERS** I SELL! EXPLAIN **THAT**!

READER, TAKE COMFORT FROM THIS: IN HELL, AT LEAST THE GULLS ARE CONTENTED.

SEE, EVERYTHING'S **CONNECTED**. A NEWSVENDOR **UNNERSTANDS** THAT. HE DON'T RETREAT FROM **REALITY**.

FOR MY PART, I BEGGED THAT THEY SHOULD TAKE MY EYES, THUS SPARING ME FURTHER HORRORS.

UNHEEDED, I STOOD IN THE SURF AND WEPT, UNABLE TO BEAR MY CIRCUMSTANCES.

THE WEIGHT O' THE **WORLD'S** ON HIM, BUT DOES HE **QUIT**? NAH! HE'S LIKE **ATLAS**! HE CAN **TAKE** IT!

HE'S A **SURVIVOR**.

IT'S LIKE THIS AFTERNOON: NOVA **EXPRESS** IS HOLDIN' ITS **FRONT PAGE**, SO NO **DELIVERY** 'TIL TONIGHT! A **CATASTROPHE**!

...BUT I **COPED**!

EVENTUALLY, TEARS CEASED. MY MISFORTUNES WERE SMALL: I WAS ALIVE...

NEWSVENDORS **ALWAYS COPE**! THEY'RE **INDESTRUCTIBLE**! THEY **THRIVE** ON DISASTER! THEY...

...AND I KNEW THAT LIFE HAD NO WORSE NEWS TO OFFER ME.

OH. GOOD AFTERNOON, SIR.

THE END IS NIGH

GOOD AFTERNOON.

IS IT HERE YET?

2

HUH?

OH! YOUR COPY O' THE *NEW FRONTIERS-MAN!* *SURE* IT'S HERE. I KEEP IT FOR YA EVERY DAY, DON'T I?

HOW'S THE ENNA THE WORLD COMIN' ALONG?

IT'LL HAPPEN TODAY. I'VE SEEN SIGNS. NATIONAL EXAMINER REPORTED A TWO-HEADED CAT BORN IN QUEENS.

TODAY FOR CERTAIN.

YOU'LL KEEP MY PAPER FOR ME TOMORROW?

UHH... SURE. SURE I WILL. NO *SWEAT.*

HAVE A NICE *DAY.*

YOU WON'T FORGET?

FPFFF

I HAD A SUDDEN MEMORY OF CLINGING FAST TO SOMEONE THROUGH THE TEMPEST. THE FIGUREHEAD LAY AT MY FEET, BLINDFOLDED BY SEAWEED. ALONE UPON THAT DREADFUL SHORE, SHE SMILED.

I MADE TO TAKE THE RIBBON OF KELP FROM OFF HER PAINTED EYES, THEN THOUGHT BETTER OF IT, NOT WISHING HER TO SUFFER THE TERRIBLE DISTRACTIONS OF THAT GRIM TIDELINE.

*I*T WAS ALL I COULD DO FOR HER, THOUGH SHE HAD BORNE ME THROUGH SEAS OF BLOOD, THOUGH HER COLD, WOODEN BREAST HAD NOURISHED ME IN THE HEART OF THE STORM.

*H*ER DAMP EMBRACE HAD PREVENTED ME FROM DRIFTING BEYOND REACH, YET THIS SMALL COMFORT WAS ALL I COULD OFFER...

3

I COULD NOT LOVE HER AS SHE HAD LOVED ME.

MURRMM. JON? WHEN DO YOU HAVE TO DO THAT T.V. INTERVIEW THIS EVENING? IS IT SOON?

NO. WE HAVE PLENTY OF TIME.

PHPP

GOOD. HEY, YOUR FINGER, IT'S LIKE LICKING A FLASH-LIGHT BATTERY. IT'S ALL SORT OF...

UHH...

AAAAAA

OH, GOD! OH, GOD, THAT'S HORRIBLE! STOP IT!

LAURIE? DON'T BE UPSET.

I THOUGHT YOU'D ENJOY IT. I DO TRY TO PLEASE YOU...

JON, BE ONE PERSON AGAIN!

I--I KNOW. I'M SORRY. I OVER-REACTED.

YOU, YOU JUST STARTLED ME, IS ALL.

LOOK, I GOTTA GO FIND A CIGARETTE. I'LL BE ALL RIGHT.

I'M SORRY. I DON'T KNOW WHAT STIMULATES YOU ANY-MORE.

JON, PLEASE, IT'S OKAY. JUST FORGET IT. I'M FINE REALLY. IT DOESN'T...

4

...MATTER.

WELL, IF YOU'RE SURE...

PERHAPS I'LL GET READY FOR MY INTERVIEW.

LAURIE?

LAURIE? ARE YOU OKAY?

AM I OKAY?

LAURIE, TRY TO UNDERSTAND...

JON, HOW THE HELL LONG HAVE YOU BEEN WORKING OUT HERE?

UNDERSTAND NOTHING! WERE YOU WORKING IN HERE AT THE SAME TIME AS WE WERE IN BED?

LAURIE, MY WORK'S AT AN IMPORTANT STAGE! IT SEEMED UNNECESSARY TO...

SHUT UP! I HATE YOU!

OH, GOD, JON, HOW COULD YOU?

LAURIE, CAN'T WE TALK?

I'M LEAVING. I'M GETTING DRESSED AND I'M LEAVING.

IF YOU THINK THERE'S A PROBLEM WITH MY ATTITUDE, I'M PREPARED TO DISCUSS IT.

LAURIE?

"I REMEMBER SOON AFTER HE FAILED TO PREVENT J.F.K.'S ASSASSINATION, WE ARGUED. I SAID, "JON, YOU KNOW HOW EVERY DAMN THING IN THIS WORLD FITS TOGETHER EXCEPT PEOPLE!""

5

HE COULDN'T *RELATE* TO ME. NOT *EMOTIONALLY.* *CERTAINLY* NOT *SEXUALLY.*

WITHIN *THREE YEARS* HE'D *DUMPED* ME FOR SOME *SIXTEEN-YEAR-OLD* WHO RAN AROUND IN HER UNDERWEAR.

"ONE DAY, *HE'LL FIND OUT.* HE'LL FIND OUT WHAT IT *FEELS* LIKE."

SPECIAL TALENT QUARTERS

VISITORS ENTRANCE

"I SEE. SO, MS. *SLATER,* HOW DO *YOU* FEEL, NOW THAT YOU'VE LEARNED ABOUT YOUR *CONDITION?*"

BITTER. BITTER AS *HELL.* I STARTED *SMOKING...* THREE PACKS A *DAY!* I FIGURE, "WHY NOT?"

I MEAN, I HAVE NO *ILLUSIONS...*

"I MEAN, NOBODY'S GONNA *MISS* ME! AFTER I'M *GONE,* NOBODY'S GONNA MISS ME. *I* KNOW *THAT.*"

"ESPECIALLY NOT *HIM.*"

ROCKEFELLER MILITARY RESEARCH CENTER

OFF TAXI

Y'SEE, HE DOESN'T *CARE! HE* DOESN'T HAVE TO GET *OLD!* THAT'S... ≥AHH-HUH≤ EXCUSE ME...

THAT'S WHY I'M TALKING TO *YOU* PEOPLE. I WANT THE WORLD TO KNOW ABOUT HIM, WHAT HE *DID* TO ME...

"I KEPT *QUIET* ALL THESE *YEARS,* BUT THEN THIS *LATEST* THING HAPPENED AND I HAD TO LET IT ALL *OUT...*"

"≥AHHUK≤"

"EXCUSE ME."

6

≈AHEK≈ ≈AHEK≈ AFTER ALL HE MEANT TO ME... AFTER ALL THE TIMES HE SAID HE *LOVED* ME...

IT'S OKAY, MS. SLATER...

≈AHEK-HECH-HECH-HECH≈ OH, I'M SORRY...

Where is the essence that was so divine?

"...IF YOU WANT, WE CAN STOP HERE."

Nostalgia *by* VEIDT

TREASURE ISLAND

≈EHUK≈ ≈EHUK-HEH-EHUK-EHUK≈

UH, MS. SLATER, I'D LIKE TO *THANK* YOU FOR HELPING *NOVA EXPRESS* SO MUCH WITH THESE INVESTIGATIONS. I'M SURE AFTER THE PAPER FINALLY GOES *OUT* TONIGHT YOU'LL FEEL SO MUCH *BETTER*...

≈AHEHH≈

"NO, I *WON'T*. ≈AHEHHM≈ NOT AFTER WHAT HE DID TO *ME*. SOME THINGS, ONCE THEY'RE *BUSTED*, THEY CAN'T *EVER* BE FIXED..."

...BUT I'M GLAD YOUR PAPER *CONTACTED* ME, AND I'M GLAD THAT AFTER THAT *SHOW* TONIGHT, *EVERY-BODY'S* GONNA KNOW WHAT HE DID.

OH, GOD, IT'S SUCH A *RELIEF*...

"IT'S SUCH A RELIEF JUST TO *TALK* TO SOMEBODY."

LAURIE?

7

UH, WELL, COME ON *IN!* IT'S GOOD TO *SEE* YOU. SORRY ABOUT ALL THIS *MESS...* I'M HAVING A NEW *LOCK* FITTED.

UH, FINE. THANK YOU.

S'OKAY, FRIEND. ALMOST THROUGH HERE.

GORDIAN KNOT LOCK CO.

IF YOU WANT TO COME ON INTO THE *KITCHEN,* I'LL MAKE COFFEE.

IT'S *FUNNY...* I WAS HOPING I'D RUN INTO YOU SO I COULD THANK YOU FOR THAT *DINNER* LAST WEEK...

I THOUGHT MAYBE YOU'D BE AT THE *FUNERAL,* BUT *JON* SAID YOU'D HAD TO VISIT YOUR *MOTHER.*

HERE... TAKE A *CHAIR...*

YOU TAKE *SUGAR* WITH YOUR COFFEE?

UH, YES YES, TWO SUGARS.

NO PROBLEM.

SO, ANYWAY, HOW IS YOUR MOM? *HOLLIS MASON* WAS ASKING AFTER HER JUST THE OTHER *WEEK...*

OH, SHE'S *GREAT.* JUST *GREAT.*

HELL, I THOUGHT I HAD MORE SUGAR THAN *THAT.* IS *ONE* LUMP OKAY OR SHOULD I *GO OUT...?*

NO. ONE LUMP'S FINE. JUST *FIII...*

UHUHUH

UHUHUHUH

HHHUCH

UH...LAURIE? HEY... HEY, WHAT'S THE *PROBLEM?*

AHUHU

FNFF OH, GOD OH, GOD, I'M SO *SORRY...*

HEY, LOOK, IT'S *OKAY.* HERE'S SOME *KLEENEX...*

I MEAN, UH, LISTEN... WHATEVER'S *BOTHERING* YOU, IT'S NOT THE END OF THE *WORLD,* RIGHT?

I LEFT JON.

OH, I SEE. THAT IS, I, UH...

I'M SORRY. I DON'T KNOW *WHY* I'M DUMPING IT ON *YOU.* I JUST...

I JUST DON'T NUH-*KNOW* ANYBODY ELSE! I DON'T KNOW *ANY-BODY* EXCEPT GODDAMNED SUH-SUPER-HEROES!

8

WELL, LOOK, I DON'T KNOW... MAYBE YOU'RE MAKING TOO **MUCH** OUT OF ONE **ARGUMENT** OR SOMETHING...

YOU THINK THIS IS OUR **FIRST** ARGUMENT?

DAN, **LIVING** WITH HIM, YOU DON'T KNOW WHAT IT'S **LIKE**...

"THE WAY HE **LOOKS** AT THINGS, LIKE HE CAN'T REMEMBER WHAT THEY **ARE** AND DOESN'T PARTICULARLY **CARE**...

"THIS WORLD, THE **REAL** WORLD, TO **HIM** IT'S LIKE WALKING THROUGH **MIST**, AND ALL THE **PEOPLE** ARE LIKE **SHADOWS**..."

JUST SHADOWS IN THE **FOG.**

"I MEAN, **TONIGHT**, RIGHT? I WALKED **OUT**, AFTER **TWENTY YEARS**, AND Y'KNOW WHAT I BET HE'S **DOING**? HIS BIG, EMOTIONAL **REACTION**?

"HE'S EITHER **SMARTENING** UP FOR HIS T.V. INTERVIEW, OR WATCHING **QUARKS** GET STUCK TO **GLUINOS**. MAYBE **BOTH.** "

SO, UH, WHERE WILL YOU **GO**? DO YOU HAVE ANY-PLACE TO **STAY** TONIGHT?

YEAH, WELL, I GUESS I'LL SPLASH OUT ON SOME **OVERNIGHT ACCOMMODATION** AND THINK THINGS **THROUGH.** JUST A **HOTEL** OR SOME-PLACE...

"SOMEWHERE **NORMAL.** "

≧HAHHH≧

DAN, I'M **SORRY.** I'VE TURNED UP IN **HYSTERICS** WHEN YOU WERE PROBABLY ABOUT TO **DRESS** FOR GOING **OUT.**

LISTEN, I JUST WISH YOU'D DROP IN MORE **OFTEN.** AS FOR TONIGHT, I'M ONLY CALLING ON **HOLLIS**...

"... AND HE DOESN'T CARE **HOW** PEOPLE DRESS."

NOW, YOU DRINK THIS WHILE IT'S **HOT.**

HERE'S LOOKING AT YOU, KID.

9

YEAH. HERE'S LOOKING AT *ME*.

Y'KNOW, *SOMETIMES* I LOOK AT MYSELF AND I DON'T *UNDERSTAND*...

"SOMETIMES I LOOK AT MYSELF AND THINK, 'HOW DID EVERYTHING GET SO *TANGLED UP*?'"

ANYWAY, YOU DON'T WANT TO GET INTO ALL *THAT* STUFF.

C'MON... I'M HOLDING YOU UP FROM VISITING *HOLLIS*. GRAB YOUR *COAT* AND I'LL WALK OVER THERE *WITH* YOU.

DON'T YOU WANT YOUR *COFFEE*?

"*NAH*. I'M SORRY....IT'S TOO *BITTER*.

"ANYWAY, I'D RATHER BE SOME-WHERE ELSE THAN SITTING HERE FEELING *SORRY* FOR MYSELF."

WELL, LOOK, IF YOU'RE *SURE* YOU WOULDN'T RATHER SIT AND *TALK*. *HOLLIS* WOULD UNDERSTAND IF I WAS *LATE*...

DAN, LISTEN, IT'S ALMOST *SIX FIFTEEN* ALREADY, AND YOU *KNOW* NEW YORK ON A SATURDAY NIGHT...

"SOMETIMES THE CABS JUST DIS-APPEAR AND GETTING FROM *A* TO *B* TAKES *FOREVER*."

WELL, I'M ALL *THROUGH* HERE. YOU'RE *SAFE AS HOUSES*. WHAT *HAPPENED* ANYWAY? Y'GET *ROBBED*?

UH, NO. NO ... A *FRIEND*. HE CALLED WHEN I WASN'T *EXPECTING* HIM...

HAH! I GOT *BUDDIES* LIKE THAT, ALWAYS TURNIN' UP *DRUNK*...

"COMPLETELY *OUTTA THE BLUE*!"

INCIDENTALLY, LADY, I HEARD WHAT YOU *SAID*, ABOUT *CABS*. WHY DON'T YOU CALL MY *BROTHER'S* COMPANY, THE *PROMETHEAN*? IT BEATS *WALKIN'*! THESE ARE *BAAAD* NEIGHBOR-HOODS.

THAT'S OKAY.

I'M IN A *BAAAD* MOOD.

10

OH! SO, DR. OSTERMAN FINALLY *ARRIVES* AND NOBODY THINKS TO *TELL ME!* MARVELOUS!

DUH--DON'T BLAME ME! I ONLY JUST TOOK OVER *RECEPTION* AN' HE JUST *APPEARED!*

I FEEL *SICK.* THEY'RE NOT PAYING ME *ENOUGH* FOR THIS...

"THEY'RE NOT PAYING ME ENOUGH TO HANDLE *MONSTERS* FROM *OUTTA SPACE!*"

YOU HAVEN'T LEFT US TIME FOR MAKEUP! THAT *BLUE* IS FAR TOO *LIGHT* FOR *TELEVISION...*

DR. OSTERMAN? I'M *FORBES,* ARMY *INTELLIGENCE.* HERE'S A LIST OF *NO-GO* AREAS. OBVIOUSLY, *AFGHANISTAN* WILL ARISE, BUT PLAY IT *COOL...*

"...AND TRY NOT TO GET INTO ANY *TIGHT CORNERS.*"

IS *THIS* DARK ENOUGH?

MY GOD.

UHH, WELL, YES. YES, THAT'S JUST *PERFECT* ...

"THAT'S *CERTAINLY* DARK ENOUGH FOR MY PURPOSES."

11

IF THE **GENEVA TALKS** COME UP, THE **OFFICIAL** POSITION IS THAT THEY CAN'T RESUME UNTIL THE SOVIETS AGREE TO EXCLUDE **YOU** FROM THE AGENDA.

SHHH! WE'RE ON!

LADIES AND GENTLEMEN, I THINK WE'RE READY TO **START...**

"... AND BELIEVE ME, WE HAVE SOMETHING REALLY **SPECIAL** FOR YOU TONIGHT."

IN HIS **FIRST EVER** LIVE QUESTION-AND-ANSWER SESSION, LET'S HAVE A **BIG HAND** PLEASE FOR **DOC MANHATTAN** HIMSELF, **DR. JONATHAN OSTERMAN!**

JON, I HOPE YOU'LL FORGIVE ME FOR **ASKING** YOU THIS...

"... BUT WHAT'S **UP**, DOC?"

"HAHAHAHAHAHAHAHA!"

"UP" IS A **RELATIVE** CONCEPT. IT HAS NO **INTRINSIC** VALUE.

UHH... **RIGHT!** OKAY! SO LET'S GET ONTO THE **QUESTIONS.** YOU ... OVER THERE ...

DOC, IF THE **REDS** ACT UP IN **AFGHANISTAN...**

"... WILL **YOU** BE PREPARED TO ENTER **HOSTILITIES?**"

KLAPKLAPKLAPKLAPKLAPKLAPKLAP

12

AS FAR AS I KNOW, THERE *IS* NO SITUATION IN AFGHANISTAN CURRENTLY REQUIRING MY *ATTENTIONS.*

OKAY, FINE. NOW HOW ABOUT YOU OVER *THERE.* YES, YOU, SIR. AND *PLEASE...*

"LET'S TRY AND KEEP IT *SNAPPY.*"

DR. OSTERMAN, I'M *DOUG ROTH,* I WRITE FOR *NOVA EXPRESS.*

I WONDER IF YOU REMEMBER *WALLY WEAVER.* BACK IN THE EARLY *SIXTIES,* THE NEWSPAPERS CALLED HIM "*DR. MANHATTAN'S BUDDY.*"

HE DIED OF *CANCER* IN 1971.

"I BELIEVE IT WAS QUITE *SUDDEN* AND QUITE *PAINFUL.*"

I REMEMBER *WALLY* AS A GOOD FRIEND. I ATTENDED HIS *FUNERAL.*

REALLY?

HOW ABOUT *EDGAR W. JACOBI,* ALSO KNOWN AS *MOLOCH?* YOU ENCOUNTERED *HIM SEVERAL* TIMES DURING THE *SIXTIES* IN BATTLES, CONFLICTS...

"...WHATEVER IT IS YOU SUPER-PEOPLE DO."

13

DID YOU KNOW THAT JACOBI *ALSO* HAS TERMINAL CANCER?

MOLOCH...? NO...NO, I DIDN'T KNOW THAT. I'D RATHER NOT...

WHAT'S THE *MATTER*, DOCTOR? DON'T YOU LIKE THE LINE OF *QUESTIONING*?

"AM I STARTING TO MAKE YOU FEEL *UNCOMFORTABLE*?"

THEN HOW ABOUT *THIS* ONE: DID YOU KNOW THAT MS. *JANEY SLATER*, LINKED ROMANTICALLY WITH YOU IN THE SIXTIES, IS CURRENTLY SUFFERING FROM LUNG CANCER?

DOCTORS HAVE GIVEN HER SIX MONTHS TO LIVE.

NOTICE ANY CONNECTION?

"...BECAUSE FROM WHERE *I'M* STANDING, IT'S STARTING TO LOOK PRETTY *CONCLUSIVE*."

JANEY...? BUT...I WASN'T *TOLD*...

ARE...ARE YOU SUGGESTING...?

OKAY, THAT'S *IT*! NO MORE *QUESTIONS*! THE DOCTOR'S *TIRED*. ABOUT THIS, FOLKS...

"...BUT THE SHOW'S *OVER*."

14

DANNY! HOW *ARE* YA?

YOU'RE *LATE*. I THOUGHT YOU'D HAD AN *ACCIDENT!*

NO... NO, I JUST HAD A LITTLE *SKIRMISH*...

YOU'RE NOT THE *ONLY* ONE. I JUST BEEN WATCHIN' *DOC MANHATTAN* ON T.V.! THEY JUST ABOUT *CRUCIFIED* THE POOR GUY...

JON? UH...

WHAT DO YOU *MEAN*?

SOME GUY STOOD UP AN' ACCUSED HIM OF GIVING A LOT OF PEOPLE *CANCER*, INCLUDING *JANEY SLATER.*

DOC LOOKED REAL *SHAKEN*, STARTED SHOUTING TO BE LEFT *ALONE*. ONE MOMENT, THE CAMERAS WERE IN *CLOSE* ON HIM...

...THE *NEXT*, THE SCREEN WENT *BLOOEY* AND THEN WE WERE GETTIN' PICTURES OF A *PARKING LOT.*

HE'D TELEPORTED EVERYBODY OUTTA THE T.V. BUILDING, CAMERAS AN' ALL.

BUT... BUT I WAS JUST WITH *LAURIE*. SHE DOESN'T KNOW...

EDITED REPLA

WELL, SHE'LL KNOW SOON *ENOUGH*. THAT SHOW WENT OUT ON *PRIME TIME.*

THE WHOLE *WORLD* WILL KNOW SOON ENOUGH.

EDITED REPLA

17

HA! I KNEW IT! WILLYA LOOKIT THAT!

SORRY THEY'RE *LATE.* THEY WANTED TO *WAIT* 'TIL THE *T.V. SHOW* WAS ON THE *AIR* BEFORE THEY PLAYED THE *GRAND SLAM.*

NOVA EXPRESS

DR MANHATTAN CANCER LINK: NEW EVIDENCE

INSIDE: JANEY SLATER SPEAKS

THE FREIGHTER'S MURDEROUS ONSLAUGHT HAD SURPRISED US.

WE'D BEEN BLASTED TO FRAGMENTS BEFORE WE COULD WARN DAVIDSTOWN OF THE HELL-SHIP'S APPROACH. I ALONE SURVIVED UPON MY REMOTE ATOLL.

CANCER! I MIGHTA *KNOWN!* THEY OUGHTTA *DEPORT* THE RADIO-ACTIVE *GOON!* PUT HIM IN *EXILE!*

HA! INSIDE, HIS *EX* SAYS THEY COULDN'T RELATE *SEXUALLY! THAT* MEANS HE'S QUEER AS A THREE-DOLLAR *BILL!*

MY *WIFE,* SHE'D *FANTASIZE* ABOUT THIS *CREEP!* I SUSPECTED ALL ALONG...

I THOUGHT OF MY FAMILY: VULNERABLE, UNSUS-PECTING...

...NEVER DREAMING THAT DAMNATION BORE DOWN UPON THEM, SAILS PREGNANT WITH A PIRATE WIND, A NECKLACE OF HEADS ABOUT ITS PROW.

CRAZED WITH HELPLESS-NESS, I CURSED GOD AND WEPT, WONDERING IF HE WEPT ALSO.

BUT THEN, WHAT USE HIS TEARS, IF HIS HELP WAS DENIED ME?

HEY. IT'S *RAININ'.* LEND ME YOUR *CAP,* MAN, I'M GETTIN' *WET.*

NO CHANCE. I DON'T *LEND* THINGS. IT'S MY *PHILOSOPHY.*

SUIT Y'SELF, JIVE-ASS.

IN *THIS* WORLD, YOU SHOULDN'T RELY ON HELP FROM *ANYBODY.* IN THE *END,* A MAN STANDS *ALONE.*

FALLOUT SHELTER

MY OWN SOBBING HAD FRIGHTENED THE GULLS. THEY DEPARTED...

...AND IN THE TERRIBLE SILENCE I UNDERSTOOD THE TRUE BREADTH OF THE WORD "ISOLATION."

SHELTER

ALL ALONE.

INNA FINAL ANALYSIS.

18

WALKIN' ON...

WALKIN' ON THE MOOOO-OOOON...

DANGER QUARANTINE AREA

WHAT ARE YOU DOING?

WAAGH!

I--I'M *SORRY,* DR. *OSTERMAN,* YOU, YOU JUST *STARTLED* ME. HAHAHA. I, I WAS PAINTING UP THIS WUH-*WARNING* NOTICE, AS, AS *ORDERED...*

A-AFTER THAT *T.V.* SHOW, WE THOUGHT IT *BEST* TO COMPLY WITH *SAFETY REGULATIONS...*

SAFETY REGULATIONS. I SEE.

IT SEEMS I'M *INCAPABLE* OF COHABITING *SAFELY* EITHER *EMOTIONALLY* OR *PHYSICALLY.* PERHAPS YOU'D BEST TELL MS. *JUSPECZYK* AND YOUR *SUPERIORS* THAT I'M *LEAVING.*

LEAVING?

YES. FOR *ARIZONA* FIRST, I THINK, AND THEN *MARS.*

M...? AAWWW... HAH HA HA HAH! DOC, YOU HAD ME *GOIN'* THERE! HA HA HA! HEY, Y'KNOW, YOU'RE A *REG'LAR* KINDA...

...GUY...

HOLY CHRIST.

SERGEANT?

SERGEANT, I GOT A *MESSAGE* FOR YA...

19

THAT NIGHT, I SLEPT BADLY BENEATH COLD, DISTANT STARS, PONDERING UPON THE COLD, DISTANT GOD IN WHOSE HANDS THE FATE OF DAVIDSTOWN RESTED.

WAS HE REALLY THERE?

HAD HE BEEN THERE ONCE, BUT NOW DEPARTED?

21

THE MORNING SUN FOUND ME NO MORE WISE, N'O LESS TROUBLED. FURTHER DOWN THE SHORE, SEVERAL OF THE BEACHED CORPSES HAD BECOME INFLATED BY GAS.

YOU SEEN *THIS*? HE'S *GONE*! NEW FRONTIERSMAN SAYS IT'S THE *RUSSIANS*!

I SET ABOUT BURYING THE SODDEN CARCASSES, MATCHING ODD LIMBS AS BEST I COULD. WITH THEM, I BURIED ALL HOPE FOR MY FAMILY'S SURVIVAL.

I *MEAN*, WHAT'S *NEXT*, Y'KNOW?

GIVE ME A GAZETTE, AS WELL.

SURE. THERE Y'ARE. Y'KNOW, I HAD IT TAGGED FOR A *RED SMEAR* FROM THE *START*. I'M A *NEWS-VENDOR*.

HOW ABOUT *YOU*? I SEE THE *WORLD* DIDN'T END *YESTER-DAY*.

ARE YOU SURE?

*U*SING DRIFT-WOOD, I BEGAN A PIT, DEEP AND WIDE. I HAD NEVER SEEN NOR IMAGINED SO MANY DEAD PEOPLE.

*N*OON CAME AND WENT. BY DUSK, THE CRATER WAS DEEP ENOUGH AND I COMMENCED HAULING THOSE COLD, MAIMED, WRETCHED THINGS INTO THE BED I HAD PREPARED.

*D*RAGGING AND CURSING, I HOPED MY WIFE AND DAUGHTERS MIGHT BE TUCKED IN BY GENTLER HANDS WHEN THEIR TURN CAME.

I BEGAN TO WEEP AGAIN. DEAR GOD, WHO WOULD *PROTECT* THEM?

HEY! ARE YOU BACK *AGAIN*? LISTEN, WHEN ARE YA THINKIN' O' *PAYIN'* FOR THAT *FUNNY BOOK*?

*T*HE FREIGHTER WAS ALMOST UPON THEM. WHO WOULD CARE FOR THEM, NOW I WAS *GONE*?

22

GONE?

WHAT DO YOU MEAN, HE'S GONE?

I DON'T KNOW WHERE YOU SPENT LAST *NIGHT*, MS. JUSPECZYK, BUT HAVEN'T YOU READ THE *PAPERS?* *DR. MANHATTAN* LEFT EARTH.

NOW, PLEASE... WE HAVE TO GIVE YOU A *CANCER SCAN* AND ASK SOME *QUESTIONS*...

CANCER SCAN? WHAT *IS* THIS? WHO'RE ALL THESE PEOPLE?

LEAVE THAT *ALONE!* THAT'S MY *MOTHER'S!*

MS. JUSPECZYK, WE *HAVE* TO ASK... DID YOU PLACE DR. OSTERMAN UNDER ANY *EMOTIONAL STRESS* LAST NIGHT?

WHAT? ARE... ARE YOU *BLAMING* ME FOR SOMETHING?

WH-WHO DO YOU THINK YOU *ARE?* LISTEN, WHEN JON GETS BACK, YOU'RE IN *BIG* TROUBLE...

JESUS CHRIST, I HAVE TAKEN ENOUGH OF THIS.

LISTEN, LADY, IF OUR *PSYCHOLOGISTS* ARE RIGHT, "JON" IS QUITE POSSIBLY *NEVER* COMING BACK! YOUR *MEAL TICKET* HAS FLOWN THE *COOP!*

THE *LINCHPIN* OF AMERICA'S STRATEGIC SUPERIORITY HAS APPARENTLY GONE TO MARS!

BUT YOU'RE *RIGHT...*

I AM IN *BIG* TROUBLE...

...AND *YOU'RE* IN *BIG* TROUBLE...

23

"...AND WE'RE ALL IN BIG TROUBLE!"

WMUH?

≶FNFF≶

≶FNFF-FNFF≶

GOOD MORNING, DANIEL.

BROUGHT YOU YOUR SUNDAY PAPER.

THE COMEDIAN MURDERED, DR. MANHATTAN EXILED...

TWO OF US GONE. ALL WITHIN A WEEK.

WHO NEXT? VEIDT? JUSPECZYK? ME?

YOU?

BY THE WAY, YOU NEED A STRONGER LOCK. THAT NEW ONE BROKE AFTER ONE SHOVE.

MY NEW LOCK?

POOR CHOICE. GET MORE EXPENSIVE ONE. CAN'T BE TOO SECURITY CONSCIOUS.

ESPECIALLY NOT THESE DAYS.

THESE DAYS, NOBODY'S SAFE.

BE SEEING YOU. THANKS FOR THE COFFEE AND CEREAL.

SUNDAY SECTIONS   New York Gazette

DR. MANHATTA LEAVES EARTH

BENNY ANGER

24

Y'KNOW, SUPER-HEROES ARE FINISHED. THESE DAYS, IT'S ALL PIRATES.

EXHAUSTED, I SLEPT ATOP THE GRAVE, DREAMS RINGING WITH THE HORRIBLY FAMILIAR SCREAMS OF CHILDREN. I SAW THE BLACK FREIGHTER BEARING DOWN ON ALL I LOVED...

...BUT I WAS POWERLESS TO STOP IT.

CONTINUED NEXT MONTH.

BACK IN '39, BEFORE THE REAL MASKED MEN SHOWED UP, SUPER-HERO COMICS WERE ENORMOUS. GUESS THEIR APPEAL WORE OFF...

I REMEMBER THERE WAS SUPER-MAN, FLASH-MAN...

UH-OH! HERE'S THE EVENIN' EDITION DELIVERY...

HEY, MAN, I AIN'T BUYIN' THIS! RIPOFF STORY AIN'T GOT NO ENDIN'!

GIMME A BREAK, WILLYA? I'M ACCEPTIN' A CONSIGNMENT!

THANKS, CHUCK.

JUST LEFT HANGIN' WITH THAT SHIP COMIN' IN GONNA KILL EVERYBODY. SHEE-IT. I'M GOIN' HOME.

LET'S SEE WHAT'S HAPPENIN' IN THE WORLD THIS FINE SUNDAY NI...

OH, JESUS.

JIVE PIRATES, MAN. YOU CAN KEEP IT.

WHAT?

NO... NO, YOU... YOU CAN HAVE IT...

AN' Y'CAN HAVE MY CAP, TOO. LISTEN, YOU GET HOME TO YOUR MOM, OKAY? YOU BE GOOD TO HER...

I MEAN... I MEAN WE ALL GOTTA LOOK OUT FOR EACH OTHER, DON'T WE?

I MEAN, THAT'S MY PHILOSOPHY...

UHH... SURE! HEY, THANKS FOR THE STUFF, MAN. LISTEN, I GOTTA GO. YOU TAKE CARE, MAN.

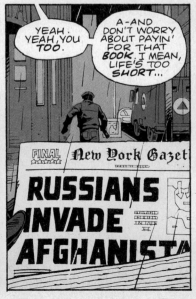

YEAH. YEAH, YOU TOO.

A-AND DON'T WORRY ABOUT PAYIN' FOR THAT BOOK. I MEAN, LIFE'S TOO SHORT...

FINAL / New York Gazet
RUSSIANS INVADE AFGHANISTA

INNA FINAL ANALYSIS.

25

"MR. *PRESIDENT*? THE LATEST ANALYSIS IS THROUGH. IF THE SOVIETS *CONTINUE* INTO *PAKISTAN*, IT'S 60% CERTAIN THEY'LL TRY TAKING *WESTERN EUROPE* ALSO."

"HUH. IF HE *WANTED* TO LIVE ON A *RED PLANET*, HE SHOULD HAVE STAYED *HOME*."

WELL, GENERAL? WHAT DO *YOU* THINK?

WE CAN BE READY FOR A *FIRST STRIKE* WITHIN SEVEN DAYS. I'D ADVISE AGAINST LEAVING IT *LONGER*.

WE HAVE A 54% CHANCE OF WIPING THEM *OUT* BEFORE *HALF* THEIR BIRDS ARE *AIRBORNE*.

"I'M TALKING *TOTAL* DEVASTATION."

HMM. AND WOULD *OUR* LOSSES BE *ACCEPTABLE*?

I'M RUNNING A PROGRAM *NOW*, WHICH ASSUMES THAT WE'VE KNOCKED OUT THE *EASTERN BLOC* BUT THAT A PERCENTAGE OF THEIR *WARHEADS* WERE ALREADY *EN ROUTE* ...

"...ANY MOMENT *NOW* WE'LL BE ABLE TO GIVE YOU AN *OVERVIEW*."

AHH... *THERE* WE ARE. BRITAIN DOWN, GERMANY DOWN ...

HMM. WELL, I'VE SEEN *WORSE* SCENARIOS.

IS THAT SOME HEADING FOR OUR *EAST COAST* THERE? AT THIS POINT IN OUR *CONTINGENCY* PLANS, WHERE SHOULD WE *BE*?

26

"SOMEWHERE ELSE, HENRY."

"UH-OH. THERE GOES BOSTON... AND NEW YORK... BALTIMORE ..."

"...WASHINGTON..."

WOW. THAT'S, UH ...

"...THAT'S PRETTY BREATH-TAKING."

"I'LL SAY. DO YOU HAVE A PROJECTION OF THE FALL-OUT DRIFT FROM THAT?"

COMING UP NOW. WITH ANTICIPATED WIND PATTERNS, LOOKS LIKE MEXICO WOULD CATCH THE WORST. WE COULD PROBABLY SALVAGE A LOT OF THE FARM-BELT...

LOSING THE EAST COAST, WE'D NEED TO. I DON'T KNOW...

"I'D ALWAYS KIND OF HOPED THAT THE BIG DECISION WOULD REST WITH SOMEBODY ELSE.

"THIS IS GOING TO TAKE SOME THINKING ABOUT."

IT'S LIKE OLD NAVAL BATTLES. SO MUCH DEPENDS UPON A QUIRK OF THE WIND.

THE WIND'S A FORCE OF NATURE. IT'S TOTALLY IMPARTIAL ...

27

Shall not the Judge of all the earth do right? —GENESIS chapter 18, verse 25

UNDER THE HOOD

Presented here are the excerpts from UNDER THE HOOD. In this next chapter Hollis Mason discusses the traumas of the 1950s and the emergence of the new super-heroes. Reprinted with permission of the author.

V.

The Minutemen didn't get to usher in the 1950s with a Christmas celebration the way we'd ushered in the '40s, and perhaps that's appropriate. The decade following the disbanding of the group was cold and bleak, both for me in particular and for masked adventurers in general. Plus, it seemed to go on forever.

I think the worst thing was the belated realization of just how much a fad we'd always been, something to fill the dead columns of the newspapers right alongside the Hula Hoop and the Jitterbug. Ever since Sally Jupiter married her manager, his tireless, shrewd efforts as a publicist had been noticeably absent. He'd recognized that the day of the costumed hero was over — even though we hadn't — and he'd gotten out while the getting was good. Consequently, we found our exploits being reported less and less frequently. When they were reported, the tone

1947: Sally Jupiter marries Laurence Schexnayder. Can you spot the famous faces in the crowd?

was often derisive. I can remember a lot of hooded vigilante jokes coming into circulation during the early fifties. The mildest was one that suggested we were called The Minutemen due to our performance in the bedroom. There were an awful lot of bright blue gags about Sally Jupiter. I know, because she told me most of them herself the last time I saw her.

Sally had a baby girl named Laurel Jane in 1949, and it seemed to be right about then that her marital problems started. These were widely discussed, so I don't think I need repeat them here. Suffice it to say that the marriage ended in 1956, and since then Sally has done a first rate job of bringing her daughter up into a bright, spunky youngster that any mother could be proud of.

The thing about that particular decade is that things first started getting *serious* then. I remember thinking at the time that it was funny how the more serious things got, the better the Comedian seemed to do. Out of the whole bunch of us, he was the only one who was still right up there on the front pages, still making the occasional headline. On the strength of his military work he had good government connections, and it often seemed as if he was being groomed into some sort of patriotic symbol. At the height of the McCarthy era, nobody had any doubts about where the Comedian's feet were planted politically.

That was more than could be said for the rest of us. We all had to testify before the House UnAmerican Activities Committee, and were all forced to reveal our true identities to one of its representatives. Galling though this was, it didn't present any immediate problems for most of us. With Captain Metropolis having such an outstanding military record and with my own service in the police force, we both were more or less cleared of suspicion right away. Mothman met with more difficulty, mostly because of some left-wing friends he'd cultivated during his student days. He was eventually cleared, but the investigations were both lengthy and ruthless, and I think that the pressure he was under at that time prompted the beginnings of the drinking problem that has contributed so much to his later mental ill-health.

Only Hooded Justice refused to testify, on the grounds that he was not prepared to reveal his true identity to anyone. When pressed, he simply vanished...or at least that's how it seemed. Vanishing is no big problem when you're a costumed hero — you just take your costume off. It seemed quite likely that Hooded Justice had simply chosen to retire rather than reveal his identity, which the authorities seemed perfectly happy with.

The only detail concerning the disappearance of America's first masked adventurer that still nags at me was trivial, and maybe not even connected at all; it was brought up in an article that appeared in *The New Frontiersman*, almost a year after Hooded Justice vanished. The author mentioned the disappearance of a well known circus strongman of the day named Rolf Müller, who had quit his job at the height of the Senate Subcommittee hearings. Three months later, a badly decomposed body that was tentatively identified as Müller's was pulled from the sea after being washed up on the coast of Boston. Müller, assuming the

(left) Hooded Justice (right) Rolf Müller.
Were they the same man?

body actually was that of the renowned weightlifter, had been shot through the head. The inference of the article was that Müller, whose family was East German, had gone on the run for fear of being uncovered while the Communist witch hunts were at their most feverish. The piece also implied that Müller had probably been executed by his own Red superiors.

I always wondered about that. Müller disappeared at almost exactly the same time as Hooded Justice was last seen, and the two men had corresponding builds. Whether the body washed up on that Boston shoreline belonged to Müller or not, neither he nor Hooded Justice were ever seen or heard from again. Were they the same man? If they were, were they really dead? If they were dead, who killed them? Was Hooded Justice really working for the Reds? I don't know. Real life is messy, inconsistent, and it's seldom when anything ever really gets resolved. It's taken me a long time to realize that.

One of the big problems that faced costumed heroes at the time was the absence of costumed criminals of any real note. I don't think any of us realized how much we needed those goons until they started to thin out. You see, if you're the only one who'd bothered to turn up for a free-for-all in costume, you tended to look kind of stupid. If the bad guys joined in as well, it wasn't so bad, but without them it was always sort of embarrassing. There had never been as many costumed criminals as heroes, but with the end of the 1940s the trend grew much more pronounced.

Most of the crooks turned in their costumes along with their criminal careers, but some just opted for a less extroverted and more profitable approach. The new breed of villains, despite their often colorful names, were mostly ordinary men in business suits who ran drug and prostitution rackets. That's not to say they didn't cause as much trouble...far from it; I just mean that they weren't as much fun to fight. All the cases I ended up investigating during the '50s seemed sordid and depressing and quite often blood-chillingly horrible. I don't know what it was...there just seemed to be a sort of bleak, uneasy feeling in the air. It was as if some essential element of our lives, of all our lives, was vanishing before we knew entirely what it was. I don't think I could really describe it completely except maybe to somebody who remembered the terrific elation we all felt after the war: we felt that we'd taken the worst that the 20th century could throw at us and stood our ground. We felt as if we'd really won a hard-earned age of peace and prosperity that would see us well into the year 2000. This optimism lasted all through the '40s and the early '50s, but by the middle of that latter decade it was starting to wear thin, and there was a sort of ominous feeling in the air.

Partly it was the beatniks, the jazz musicians and the poets openly condemning American values whenever they opened their mouths. Partly it was Elvis Presley and the whole Rock 'n' Roll boom. Had we fought a war for our country so that our daughters could scream and swoon over young men who looked like *this*, who sounded like *that?* With all these sudden social upheavals just when we thought we'd gotten everything straight, it was impossible to live through the 1950s without a sense of impending catastrophe bearing implacably down upon the whole country, the whole world. Some people thought it was war and others thought it was flying saucers, but those things weren't really what was bearing down upon us. What was bearing down upon us was the 1960s.

The '60s, along with the mini-skirt and the Beatles, brought one thing to the world that was significant above all others — its name was Dr. Manhattan. The arrival of Dr. Manhattan would make the terms "masked hero" and "costumed adventurer" as obsolete as the persons they described. A new phrase had entered the American language, just as a new and almost terrifying concept had entered its consciousness. It was the dawn of the Super-Hero.

Manhattan's existence was announced to the world in the March of 1960, and I don't think there can have been anybody on the planet who didn't feel that same strange jumble of emotions when they heard the news. Foremost amongst this assortment of sensations was disbelief. The idea of a being who could walk through walls, move from one place to another without covering the intervening distance and re-arrange things completely with a single thought was flat-out impossible. On the other hand, the people presenting this news to us were our own government. The notion that they might simply have made it up was equally improbable, and in the face of this contradiction, it became gradually easier to accept the dream-like unreality of those first newsreel images: a blue man melting a tank with a wave of his hand; the fragments of a disassembled rifle floating there eerily in the air with nobody touching them. Once accepted as reality, however, such things became no easier to digest. If you accept that floating rifle parts are real you also have to somehow accept that everything you've ever known to be a fact is probably untrue. That peculiar unease is something that most of us have learned to live with over the years, but it's still there.

The other emotions that accompanied the announcement were perhaps harder to identify and pin down. There was a certain elation...it felt as if Santa Claus had suddenly turned out to be real after all. Coupled with and complementary to this was a terrible and uneven sense of fear and uncertainty. While this was hard to define precisely, if I had to boil it down into three words, those words would be, "We've been replaced." I'm not just talking about the non-powered costumed hero fraternity here, you understand, although Dr. Manhattan's appearance was certainly one of the factors that led to my own increased feelings of obsolescence and my eventual decision to quit the hero business altogether. You see, while masked vigilantes had certainly been made obsolete, so in a sense had every other living organism upon the planet. I don't think that society has fully realized yet just exactly what Dr. Manhattan's arrival means; how much it's likely to change every detail of our lives.

Although Dr. Manhattan was the most prominent by far of the 'New Breed' of costumed heroes, he wasn't quite the first nor by any means the last. In the closing months of 1958, the papers mentioned that a major opium and heroin smuggling racket had been busted by a young adventurer named Ozymandias, who seemed to have quickly gained a reputation amongst the criminal fraternity for his boundless and implacable intelligence, not to mention a large degree of athletic prowess.

I met both Dr. Manhattan and Ozymandias for the first time at a charity event in the June of 1960. Ozymandias seemed to be a nice young fellow, although I personally found Dr. Manhattan to be a little distant. Maybe that was more my fault than his, though, since I found it very difficult to feel easy around the guy, even once I'd got used to the shock of his physical presence. It's a strange feeling...the first time you meet him your brain wants to scream, blow a fuse and shut itself down immediately, refusing to accept that he exists. This lasts for a couple of minutes, at which time he's still there and hasn't gone away, and in the end you just accept him because he's standing there and talking to you and after a while it almost seems normal.

Almost.

Anyway, at that charity event...I think it was Red Cross relief for the ongoing famine in India...a lot of things became apparent to me. Looking around at the other adventurers there, I wasn't happy with what I saw: The Comedian was there, imposing his overbearing personality and his obnoxious cigar smoke upon anyone within reach. Mothman was there, a glass in one hand, slurring his words and letting his sentences trail off into incoherence. Captain Metropolis was there, his paunch starting to show despite a strict regimen of Canadian Air Force Exercises. Finally, leaving the two younger heroes aside for a moment, there was me: Forty-six years old and starting to feel it, still trying to cut it in the company of guys who could level a mountain by snapping their fingers. I think it was when that moment of self insight hit me that I first decided to finally hang up my mask and get myself a proper job. I'd been about due to retire from the police force for some time, and I started wondering about what I wanted to do now that the thrill of adventure had finally started to pale. Looking back over my life, I tried to work out what I'd been doing during my existence's happier stretches, in order to form a basis for my future contentment.

After much deliberation, I concluded that I'd never been happier than when helping my dad beat some sense into an obstinate engine down at Moe Vernon's yard. After a life of crime-fighting, no notion seemed sweeter to me than that of spending my autumn years contentedly making dead vehicles run again in the confines of my own auto repair shop.

In the May of this year, 1962, that's exactly what I opted to do.

I retired. To mend cars. Probably for the rest of my life. As I see it, part of the art of being a hero is knowing when you don't need to be one anymore, realizing that the game has changed and that the stakes are different and that there isn't necessarily a place for you in this strange new pantheon of extraordinary people. The world has moved on, and I'm content to watch it from my armchair with a beer by my side and the smell of fresh oil still on my fingers.

Part of my contentment comes from knowing that there have maybe been some overall consequence of my twenty-three years behind the mask. This knowledge came to me in the shape of a letter from a young man whose name I'm not at liberty to reveal. He told me of his great admiration for my efforts as Nite Owl and proposed that since I'd retired and would no longer be using the name, perhaps he could borrow it since he intended to follow my example and become a crime-fighter. I've visited his home since then and seen some of the fabulous technology he intends to bring to bear on the war against crime. I was certainly far too impressed to refuse him the use of what I'd always thought was a dumb name to begin with, so by the time this sees print there may well be a new Nite Owl patrolling the streets of New York. Also, Sally Jupiter tells me that as soon as little Laurie's old enough she wants to be a super-heroine just like her mom, so who knows? It seems as if from being a novelty nine-day wonder, the super-hero has become a part of American life. It's here to stay.

For better, or for worse.

THE PHOTOGRAPH IS IN MY HAND.

IT IS THE PHOTOGRAPH OF A MAN AND A WOMAN. THEY ARE AT AN AMUSEMENT PARK, IN 1959.

IN TWELVE SECONDS TIME, I DROP THE PHOTOGRAPH TO THE SAND AT MY FEET, WALKING AWAY. IT'S ALREADY LYING THERE, TWELVE SECONDS INTO THE FUTURE.

TEN SECONDS NOW.

THE PHOTOGRAPH IS IN MY HAND.

I FOUND IT IN A DERELICT BAR AT THE GILA FLATS TEST BASE, TWENTY-SEVEN HOURS AGO.

IT'S STILL THERE, TWENTY-SEVEN HOURS INTO THE PAST, IN ITS FRAME, IN THE DARKENED BAR.

I'M STILL THERE, LOOKING AT IT.

THE PHOTOGRAPH IS IN MY HAND. THE WOMAN TAKES A PIECE OF POPCORN BETWEEN THUMB AND FOREFINGER. THE FERRIS WHEEL PAUSES.

SEVEN SECONDS NOW.

IT'S OCTOBER, 1985. I'M ON MARS. IT'S JULY, 1959. I'M IN NEW JERSEY, AT THE PALISADES AMUSEMENT PARK.

FOUR SECONDS. THREE.

I'M TIRED OF LOOKING AT THE PHOTOGRAPH NOW.

I OPEN MY FINGERS. IT FALLS TO THE SAND AT MY FEET.

I AM GOING TO LOOK AT THE STARS.

THEY ARE SO FAR AWAY, AND THEIR LIGHT TAKES SO LONG TO REACH US...

ALL WE EVER SEE OF STARS ARE THEIR OLD PHOTOGRAPHS.

I AM TWO HUNDRED AND TWENTY-SEVEN MILLION KILOMETERS FROM THE SUN.

ITS LIGHT IS ALREADY TEN MINUTES OLD. IT WILL NOT REACH PLUTO FOR ANOTHER TWO HOURS.

TWO HOURS INTO MY FUTURE, I OBSERVE METEORITES FROM A GLASS BALCONY, THINKING ABOUT MY FATHER.

TWELVE SECONDS INTO MY PAST, I OPEN MY FINGERS. THE PHOTOGRAPH IS FALLING.

I AM WATCHING THE STARS. HALLEY'S COMET TUMBLES THROUGH THE SOLAR SYSTEM ON ITS GREAT SEVENTY-SIX-YEAR ELLIPSE.

MY FATHER ADMIRED THE SKY FOR ITS PRECISION. HE REPAIRED WATCHES.

IT'S 1945. I SIT IN A BROOKLYN KITCHEN, FASCINATED BY AN ARRANGEMENT OF COGS ON BLACK VELVET. I AM SIXTEEN YEARS OLD.

IT IS 1985. I AM ON MARS. I AM FIFTY-SIX YEARS OLD.

THE PHOTOGRAPH LIES AT MY FEET, FALLS FROM MY FINGERS, IS IN MY HAND.

I AM WATCHING THE STARS, ADMIRING THEIR COMPLEX TRAJECTORIES, THROUGH SPACE, THROUGH TIME.

I AM TRYING TO GIVE A NAME TO THE FORCE THAT SET THEM IN MOTION.

2

WATCHMAKER

IT IS AUGUST 7TH, 1945. THE BROOKLYN MORNING IS HUMID AND THE FIRE ESCAPE DOOR HAS BEEN LEFT OPEN.

JON? WHERE ARE YOU?

IN HERE. I'M PRACTICING ON YOUR OLD POCKETWATCH, BEFORE IT'S TIME FOR SCHOOL.

FORGET POCKET-WATCHES! HAVE YOU SEEN THE NEWS?

NEWS?

THEY DROPPED THE ATOMIC BOMB ON JAPAN! A WHOLE CITY, GONE!

ACH! THESE ARE NO TIMES FOR A REPAIRER OF WATCHES...

New York Times
ATOMIC BOMB DROPPED ON HIROSHIMA

THIS CHANGES EVERYTHING! THERE WILL BE MORE BOMBS. THEY ARE THE FUTURE.

SHALL MY SON FOLLOW ME INTO AN OBSOLETE TRADE?

FATHER? WHAT ARE YOU DOING?

I'M DOING WHAT IS BEST FOR YOU. THIS ATOMIC SCIENCE... THIS IS WHAT THE WORLD WILL NEED! NOT POCKET-WATCHES!

HEY! GIVE ME THAT BACK!

PROFESSOR EINSTEIN SAYS THAT TIME DIFFERS FROM PLACE TO PLACE. CAN YOU IMAGINE?

IF TIME IS NOT TRUE, WHAT PURPOSE HAVE WATCHMAKERS, HEIN?

WAIT! DON'T...

MY PROFESSION IS A THING OF THE PAST. INSTEAD, MY SON MUST HAVE A FUTURE.

FATHER, NO!

FORTY YEARS AGO, COGS RAIN ON BROOKLYN...

ONE HUNDRED AND FIFTEEN MINUTES INTO THE FUTURE, THE METEORITES HAIL DOWN THROUGH THE RAREFIED ATMOSPHERE OF MARS...

IT IS 1948, AND I AM ARRIVING AT PRINCETON UNIVERSITY.

IT IS 1958, AND I AM GRADUATING WITH A PH.D. IN ATOMIC PHYSICS.

THE COGS ARE FALLING...

3

IT'S MAY 12TH, 1959: MY FIRST DAY AT GILA FLATS. PROFESSOR GLASS IS SHAKING MY HAND, ASKING WALLY WEAVER TO SHOW ME AROUND.

THE SCENT OF HIS TURKISH CIGARETTE IS THICK IN THE CRAMPED OFFICE.

I'M THIRTY YEARS OLD...

SO YOU'RE THIS NEW GUY FROM PRINCETON WE HEARD ABOUT, HUH? SAY, WASN'T EINSTEIN AT PRINCETON?

NOT WHILE I WAS. HEARD HIM LECTURE ONCE, THOUGH.

GEE, THAT MUSTA BEEN SOMETHIN'. Y'KNOW, I HEARD HE ARGUED WITH HIS WIFE. CRAZY, HUH? A GUY LIKE THAT, A GENIUS, EVEN HE COULDN'T FIGURE WOMEN!

WELL, I GUESS HE'S JUST HUMAN, LIKE EVERYBODY ELSE.

WHAT'S THIS PLACE?

AHH, THIS IS JUST WHERE THEY'RE DOIN' THE INTRINSIC FIELD EXPERIMENTS. IT'S LIKE, WHAT IF THERE'S SOME FIELD HOLDIN' STUFF TOGETHER, APART FROM GRAVITY?

BEATS HELL OUTTA ME, BUT I'M ONLY AN ASSISTANT...

AND THIS?

THIS IS OUR TIME-LOCK TEST VAULT, SO THAT WHEN THEY'RE TRYIN' TO SEPARATE OBJECTS FROM THEIR INTRINSIC FIELDS, NO RADIATION GETS OUT.

WE GOTTA LOT O' NEW SAFETY FEATURES LIKE THAT HERE.

BUT HEY, LISTEN...NOBODY AT GILA GIVES A DAMN ABOUT ALL THIS JUNK.

C'MON...I'LL SHOW YOU WHERE THE REAL HEAVY-DUTY THINKIN' GETS DONE AROUND HERE.

WE CALL IT THE BESTIARY...

4

IT'S RIGHT THROUGH HERE...

WALLY STEERS ME FROM THE ARIZONA SUNLIGHT INTO THE CROWDED BAR. THERE'S A SUDDEN SENSATION OF *DÉJÀ VU*: I'VE SEEN THIS PLACE *BEFORE*...

...EXCEPT THAT IT WAS *DESERTED* THEN, DERELICT, WITH STARLIGHT SHINING DOWN UPON ITS ROTTED FLOORBOARDS, THROUGH THE COLLAPSED CEILING...

THE ILLUSION VANISHES, ALMOST BEFORE IT HAS REGISTERED. IT'S MAY 12TH, 1959. WALLY IS INTRODUCING ME TO SOMEONE...

JANEY SLATER, MEET JON OSTERMAN. JON'S FROM *PRINCETON*.

OHHH... THE *NEW GUY*! YOU'RE REPLACING *HANK MEADOWS*, RIGHT?

I AM?

I *GUESS* SO. HANK DIED LAST *FALL*, SOME KINDA *TUMOR*. THERE'S HIS *PICTURE* BEHIND THE *BAR* THERE. THE GUY WITH *GLASSES*.

Y'KNOW, YOU'RE PRETTY *YOUNG* FOR A *RESEARCH SCIENTIST*.

WELL, YOU KNOW... MY *DAD* SORT OF *PUSHED* ME INTO IT. THAT HAPPENS TO ME A *LOT*. OTHER PEOPLE SEEM TO MAKE ALL MY MOVES *FOR* ME.

MM. I'LL BET.

CAN I GET YOU A *DRINK*?

SHE BUYS ME A BEER, THE FIRST TIME A WOMAN HAS EVER DONE THIS FOR ME. AS SHE PASSES ME THE COLD, PERSPIRING GLASS, OUR FINGERS TOUCH...

IT'S 1963. WE'RE MAKING LOVE AFTER AN *ARGUMENT*, OUR *TENDERNESS* IN DIRECT PROPORTION TO ITS *VIOLENCE*...

IT'S 1966, AND SHE'S *PACKING*: TEARFUL, CARELESS WITH ANGER...

THE PHOTOGRAPH LIES IN THE SAND AT MY FEET.

5

IT'S JULY, 1959. I'M RETURNING TO NEW JERSEY ON VACATION, VISITING OLD UNIVERSITY FRIENDS.

JANEY SHARES THE TRIP FROM ARIZONA. HER MOTHER LIVES IN JERSEY.

SHE CALLS HOME FROM THE STATION, BUT NOBODY ANSWERS. WE VISIT THE AMUSEMENT PARK, KILLING *TIME* UNTIL HER MOTHER RETURNS.

HEY, YOUNG LOVERS! HOLD IT!

BUT WE'RE NOT...

THERE! THAT'S JUST *BEAUTIFUL*. A BEAUTIFUL *PICTURE*, PARTICULARLY OF THE *LADY*...

HE GIVES US AN ADDRESS WHERE WE CAN PICK UP 75-CENT PRINTS, AND WE WALK OFF TOWARDS THE TILT-A-WHIRL, LAUGHING AT HIS MISTAKE.

BY THE SHOOTING GALLERY, JANEY'S WATCHBAND SNAPS. BEFORE I CAN PICK IT UP, A FAT MAN STEPS UPON IT. I TELL HER I CAN FIX IT.

HER MOTHER STILL ISN'T ANSWERING. WE DECIDE TO CALL AGAIN FROM MY HOTEL. WE BOTH KNOW WHAT'S GOING TO HAPPEN. EVENTS MESH TOGETHER WITH SOFT PRECISION...

WE REACH THE HOTEL. SHE CALLS AGAIN. HER MOTHER STILL ISN'T HOME.

SHE ASKS IF I CAN REALLY FIX HER WATCH. WE SIT TOGETHER ON THE EDGE OF THE BED, EXAMINING THE DAMAGE.

IT'S 1959. A PULSE FLUTTERS IN HER BELLY, BENEATH MY CHEEK.

IT'S 1966. THE SUITCASE WON'T SHUT AND SHE'S CRYING.

IT'S 1985. IN ONE HUNDRED MINUTES, THE METEORITE SHOWER BEGINS.

6

IT'S AUGUST, 1959. WE'VE BEEN BACK FROM JERSEY A MONTH. IN MY FUTURE, THE **ACCIDENT** IS WAITING FOR ME.

JON? DID YOU FIX MY **WATCH** YET?

YES! MATTER OF FACT, I **DID!** IT'S RIGHT...

OH.

WHAT'S THE **MATTER?**

NOTHING. I LEFT IT IN MY **LAB COAT** WHEN WE WERE RESETTING THE **I.F. CHAMBER** THIS MORNING. YOU WAIT RIGHT **THERE.**

I CROSS THE SQUARE TO THE INTRINSIC FIELD CENTER. MY COAT'S INSIDE THE **TEST CHAMBER.** I CAN SEE IT THROUGH THE FOOT-THICK **WINDOW...**

THE ACCIDENT IS ALMOST **UPON** ME NOW.

OPERATI

THE OTHERS RETURN FROM LUNCH AND I ASK THEM TO LET ME OUT, LAUGHING AT MY OWN **STUPIDITY.**

NOBODY ELSE LAUGHS. DR. GLASS IS TURNING WHITE.

HE EXPLAINS THAT THE DOOR HAS LOCKED AUTOMATICALLY WHILE THE GENERATORS WARM UP FOR THIS AFTERNOON'S **EXPERIMENT:** REMOVING THE **INTRINSIC FIELD** FROM CONCRETE BLOCK **FIFTEEN.**

I ASK HIM WHAT HAPPENED TO THE OTHER **FOURTEEN...**

...AND HE **TELLS** ME.

NO! NO, NO, **NO!**

I--I'M **SORRY,** OSTERMAN. THE PROGRAM'S **LOCKED IN,** AND WE CAN'T OVERRIDE THE **TIME-LOCK.** IT...

...IT'S A SAFETY FEATURE.

OH, **GOD,** LET ME **OUT.** LET ME **OUT** OF HERE...

JANEY? DON'T **GO!** I NEED...

NO! DON'T **ASK** ME! OH, **GOD,** I **CAN'T** STAY AND WATCH. PLEASE, I...

I JUST **CAN'T,** OKAY?

7

THE DOOR SLAMS BEHIND HER. I LOOK AT DR. GLASS BUT HE LOOKS AWAY. I CAN HEAR THE SHIELDS SLIDING BACK FROM THE *PARTICLE CANNONS.*

THERE'S SOMETHING IN MY POCKET. I TAKE IT OUT TO EXAMINE...

GOOD AS NEW.

THE AIR GROWS TOO WARM, TOO QUICKLY. I WANT VERY MUCH FOR A BEAUTIFUL WOMAN TO HAND ME A GLASS OF VERY COLD BEER...

ALL THE ATOMS IN THE TEST CHAMBER ARE SCREAMING AT ONCE.

THE *LIGHT*...

THE LIGHT IS TAKING ME TO *PIECES.*

IT'S SEPTEMBER. A TOKEN FUNERAL SERVICE IS BEING HELD. THERE'S NOTHING TO BURY.

IT'S OCTOBER. JANEY PLACES OUR JERSEY SNAPSHOT BEHIND GLASS IN THE BESTIARY. IT'S THE ONLY PHOTOGRAPH OF ME ANYONE HAS.

IT'S NOVEMBER...

DID YOU READ ABOUT THIS COMMUNIST GUY WHO'S RUNNING CUBA? THIS CASTRO?

I SAW A PICTURE! JESUS H. CHRIST, WHAT'S WRONG WITH GUYS THESE DAYS? THAT BEARD!

I MEAN, I REMEMBER WHEN OUR CAROL-ANNE STARTED STICKIN' UP PICTURES OF THAT PIMPY-EYED SINGER, THAT PUNK PRESLEY...

I THOUGHT I'D JUST ABOUT SEEN IT ALL.

EEEEIIIIGHH!

IT'S NOVEMBER 10TH NOW. THERE IS A CIRCULATORY SYSTEM WALKING THROUGH THE KITCHEN...

NOVEMBER 14TH: A PARTIALLY MUSCLED SKELETON STANDS BY THE PERIMETER FENCE AND SCREAMS FOR THIRTY SECONDS BEFORE VANISHING...

A FLATS T BASE

REALLY, IT'S JUST A QUESTION OF REASSEMBLING THE COMPONENTS IN THE CORRECT SEQUENCE...

9

Y'KNOW, I'M THINKING OF QUITTING THIS PLACE. SOME-THING'S HAUNTING US...

WALLY, PLEASE. I DON'T WANT TO HEAR ABOUT IT.

GEE, I'M SORRY, BUT...

HEY, CAN YOU HEAR THAT? THAT WHISTLING? IS IT IN MY EARS, OR WHAT...?

NO. NO, I CAN HEAR IT. IT'S ... HEY! MY ARM! ALL THE HAIRS ARE STANDING UP...

DON'T PANIC! NOBODY PANIC!

AAAA! WHAT'S HAPPENING? THE CUTLERY, IT'S SPARKING ...

OH, HOLY GOD. WILLYA LOOK AT THAT...

JON ?

THEIR BLEACHED FACES STARE UP AT ME, PALE AND INSUBSTANTIAL IN THE SUDDEN FLARE OF ULTRAVIOLET.

SUNBURN IN NOVEMBER.

10

IT'S OCTOBER, 1985. I'M BASKING IN THE TWO-MILLION-YEAR-OLD LIGHT OF **ANDROMEDA**. I CAN SEE THE **SUPERNOVA** THAT **ERNST HARTWIG** DISCOVERED IN 1885, A CENTURY AGO.

IT SCINTILLATES, A WINK INTENDED FOR THE **TRILOBITES**, ALL LONG DEAD.

SUPERNOVAS ARE WHERE **GOLD** FORMS; THE ONLY PLACE. **ALL** GOLD COMES FROM **SUPERNOVAS**.

IT'S CHRISTMAS, 1959...

DO...DO YOU **LIKE** IT? I MEAN, IS THAT THE SORT OF THING THAT YOU LIKE, NOW THAT YOU'RE, UH...

YOU KNOW.

I LIKE IT VERY **MUCH**. ITS **ATOMIC** STRUCTURE IS A PERFECT **GRID**, LIKE A **CHECKERBOARD**. IT'S...

JANEY? WHAT'S UP? ARE YOU **COLD**? I CAN RAISE THE **TEMPERATURE**...

NO...I'M NOT COLD.

I'M **SCARED**.

OF **ME**?

NO. YES OH, **GOD**, LOOK, I...

I'M JUST SCARED BECAUSE EVERYTHING FEELS **WEIRD**. IT'S AS IF **EVERYTHING'S** CHANGED. NOT JUST **YOU**: EVERYTHING!

I MEAN, **I** DON'T KNOW WHAT YOU ARE. **NOBODY** DOES. YOU WERE **DISINTEGRATED**, YOU PUT YOURSELF BACK **TOGETHER**...

THEY SAY YOU CAN DO **ANYTHING**, JON. THEY SAY YOU'RE LIKE **GOD** NOW.

I DON'T THINK THERE **IS** A GOD, JANEY. IF THERE **IS**, I'M NOT HIM.

I'M STILL THE SAME PERSON. NOTHING'S CHANGED. I STILL **WANT** YOU...

I'LL **ALWAYS** WANT YOU.

AS I LIE I HEAR HER SHOUTING AT ME IN 1963; SOBBING IN 1966. MY FINGERS OPEN. THE PHOTOGRAPH IS FALLING...

11

IT'S FEBRUARY, 1960, AND EVERYTHING IS FROZEN. I ACCEPT THAT I SHALL NEVER FEEL COLD OR WARM AGAIN.

PERFECT.

WHEN WE GO PUBLIC NEXT MONTH, EVERY MAGAZINE IN THE WORLD'S GONNA WANT THESE PICTURES!

HOW DO YOU LIKE YOUR COSTUME? PRETTY SLICK, HUH?

I DON'T LIKE IT...ESPECIALLY THIS HELMET. WHAT'S THIS SYMBOL STAND FOR?

UH, WELL, IT MEANS, LIKE, ATOMS, ATOMIC POWER, LIKE THAT...

IT'S MEANINGLESS. A HYDROGEN ATOM WOULD BE MORE APPROPRIATE. I DON'T THINK I SHALL BE WEARING THIS.

B-BUT THAT'S THE ONLY PLACE WHERE YOUR SYMBOL SHOWS! THE MARKETING BOYS SAY YOU NEED A SYMBOL...

THEY DON'T KNOW WHAT I NEED.

YOU DON'T KNOW WHAT I NEED.

IF I'M TO HAVE A SYMBOL, IT SHALL BE ONE I RESPECT.

THERE.

I...I LIKE IT! IT'S GOT SOMETHING, YOU KNOW? IT'S SIMPLE, BUT IT'S...

YEAH! YEAH, THAT'S GOOD. PEOPLE WILL REMEMBER IT. WHEN THEY SEE IT THEY'LL THINK OF DR. MANHATTAN.

DOCTOR WHAT?

THEY EXPLAIN THAT THE NAME HAS BEEN CHOSEN FOR THE OMINOUS ASSOCIATIONS IT WILL RAISE IN AMERICA'S ENEMIES. THEY'RE SHAPING ME INTO SOMETHING GAUDY AND LETHAL...

York Times

ATOMIC BOMB DROPPED ON HIROSHIMA

IT'S ALL GETTING OUT OF MY HANDS...

12

MARCH, 1960...

...STILL *REELING* FROM THIS MORNING'S ANNOUNCEMENT, POSSIBLY THE MOST *SIGNIFICANT* EVENT IN RECENT WORLD HISTORY.

WE *REPEAT:* THE *SUPERMAN EXISTS*, AND HE'S *AMERICAN.*

ACCORDING TO PENTAGON SOURCES, THIS ASTONISHING INDIVIDUAL CAN CONTROL *ATOMIC STRUCTURE* ITSELF. WE SEE HIM HERE DISMANTLING A *RIFLE* WITHOUT *TOUCHING* IT...

...AND *HERE*, DEMONSTRATING THAT A *PATTON TANK* POSES HIM NO GREATER DIFFICULTY.

THERE HAS BEEN NO RESPONSE FROM THE KREMLIN AS OF THIS TIME...

...AND INDEED, HOW THIS ALMOST UNBELIEVABLE DEVELOPMENT WILL AFFECT THE RACE IN *WEAPONRY* AND *SPACE TECHNOLOGY* HAS YET TO BE ASSIMILATED.

ALTHOUGH PHOTOGRAPHED LATE THIS AFTERNOON AT THE *GILA FLATS TEST BASE*, THE *SUPERHUMAN...* CODE-NAMED *DR. MANHATTAN...* HAS NOT SPOKEN TO THE *PRESS.*

GILA FL... TEST B... PER DOLOREM A... ...RNMENT PROP...

INSTEAD, WE ASKED THOSE *COSTUMED VIGILANTES* REMAINING FROM THE 1940'S *MASKED HERO* FAD HOW *THEY* FELT.

WELL, UHH, WE'RE *PLEASED*, OBVIOUSLY.

CAPTAIN METROPOLIS

VERY, *VERY* PLEASED.

WELL, YOU KNOW ...THEY SAY HE WALKS THROUGH *WALLS* AND STUFF.

I'LL *BELIEVE* IT WHEN I *SEE* IT.

HA! YOU KNOCKED 'EM ALL DEAD!

"THE SILK SPECTRE" (SALLY JUPITER)

I MEAN, YOU WEAR AN OLD DOUBLE-BREASTED *SUIT* FOR THAT *PHOTO SESSION*, AND NEXT THING, EVERY-BODY'S TALKING ABOUT ITS *FASHION SIGNIFICANCE!* CAN YOU *IMAGINE?*

YOU'VE *ARRIVED.*

HAVE I?

SOMETIMES I FEEL AS IF I'VE BEEN HERE ALL THE *TIME.*

I'M THERE *NOW*, IN 1960, SAYING THOSE WORDS, WATCHING THAT T.V. SET...

13

NOW IT'S *JUNE*, A CHARITY EVENT WITH SEVERAL COSTUMED ADVENTURERS ATTENDING ... FRIENDLY MIDDLE-AGED MEN WHO LIKE TO DRESS UP. I HAVE NOTHING IN COMMON WITH THEM.

ONLY THE YOUNGEST, CALLED *OZYMANDIAS*, SEEMS INTERESTING...

IT'S NOVEMBER. THE NEWSPAPERS CALL ME A CRIMEFIGHTER, SO THE PENTAGON SAYS I MUST FIGHT CRIME. IN MOLOCH'S UNDER-GROUND VICE-DEN, THE SIGHS TURN TO SCREAMS OF TERROR.

THE MORALITY OF MY ACTIVITIES ESCAPES ME.

IT'S SEPTEMBER, 1961. JOHN KENNEDY IS SHAKING MY HAND, ASKING WHAT IT'S LIKE TO BE A SUPER-HERO. I TELL HIM HE SHOULD KNOW AND HE NODS, LAUGHING...

TWO YEARS LATER, IN DALLAS, HIS HEAD SNAPS FORWARD AND THEN BACK. TWO SHOTS...

14

IN MAY, 1962, A MASKED MAN RETIRES TO OPEN AN AUTO BUSINESS. HIS REAL NAME IS **HOLLIS MASON.** WE ARE TALKING AFTER A CIVIC BANQUET IN HIS HONOR.

DALLAS IS STILL EIGHTEEN MONTHS AWAY...

SEE **THIS?** ALMOST MAKES ME SORRY I'M **QUITTING** THIS RIDICULOUS BUSINESS.

THEN WHY HAVE YOU CHOSEN TO RETIRE NOW? IS IT YOUR **AGE?**

PARTLY. PARTLY, I GUESS IT'S **YOU** ...

WITH SOMEONE LIKE **YOU** AROUND, THE WHOLE **SITUATION** CHANGES. YOU CAN DO **ANYTHING.** ALL **I** GOT TO OFFER IS A GOOD **LEFT HOOK.**

NAH, I'M BETTER OFF **RE-TIRING,** WRITING MY **AUTOBIOGRAPHY,** REPAIRIN' FOLKS' CARS FOR 'EM... CARS ARE SOMETHING I'M **HAPPY** WITH...

... AND IT'LL BE AWHILE BEFORE EVEN **YOU** AFFECT **GENERAL MOTORS.**

SEE, I **UNDERSTAND** CARS, HOW THEY **WORK.** THAT'S MORE'N I CAN SAY FOR THE **REST** O' THIS WORLD.

WELL, THE NEW **ELECTRIC CARS** SHOULD BE EVEN **SIMPLER.**

ELECTRIC?

THAT'S RIGHT. THEY'D HAVE APPEARED BEFORE, BUT THERE WASN'T ENOUGH **LITHIUM** TO MASS-PRODUCE **POLYACETYLENE BATTERIES.** OF COURSE, **I** CAN SYNTHESIZE IT EASILY.

ANYWAY, IT'S BEEN INTERESTING MEETING YOU AGAIN. I HOPE YOU ENJOY YOUR **RETIREMENT.**

Y-YEAH.

YEAH, I HOPE SO TOO.

EIGHTEEN MONTHS AWAY, AN ELECTRIC LIMOUSINE IS PULLING ONTO DEALEY PLAZA...

15

SO WHAT YOU'RE SAYING IS YOU KNEW HE'D GET SHOT?

JON, I... I MEAN, IF YOU'RE SERIOUS, I MEAN, WHY DIDN'T YOU DO SOMETHING?

PRESIDEN SHOT-FEAR CRITICAL

I CAN'T PREVENT THE FUTURE. TO ME, IT'S ALREADY HAPPENING.

JON, WHAT ARE YOU SAYING? THAT YOU KNOW THE FUTURE? ABOUT EVERYTHING? ABOUT US?

IN 1959, I COULD HEAR YOU SHOUTING, HERE, NOW, IN 1963. SOON WE MAKE LOVE...

JUST LIKE THAT? LIKE I'M A PUPPET? JON, YOU KNOW HOW EVERYTHING IN THIS WORLD FITS TOGETHER EXCEPT PEOPLE. YOUR PREDICTION'S WAY OFF, MISTER.

NO. WE MAKE LOVE RIGHT AFTER WALLY ARRIVES WITH THE EARRINGS I ORDERED FOR YOU...

SHUT UP! YOU'RE MESSING UP MY MIND, JON! SOMETIMES I THINK YOU'RE MESSING EVERYTHING UP!

I MEAN, ALL THIS NEW TECHNOLOGY, ALL BECAUSE OF YOU! THINGS ARE HAPPENING TOO FAST. THINGS SHOULDN'T...

WAS THAT THE DOORBELL?

JANEY? THE MAILMAN DELIVERED THIS TO ME BY MISTAKE. SORRY I DIDN'T DROP IT BY EARLIER. SAY HI TO JON FOR ME.

UH....

UH, SURE. THANKS, WALLY.

JON?

I...I'M SCARED. I FEEL LIKE THERE'S BIG INVISIBLE THINGS ALL AROUND ME.

WILL YOU HOLD ME, PLEASE?

IT'S 1963. AN HOUR INTO THE FUTURE HER SWEAT COOLS AND DRIES IN THE NOVEMBER BEDROOM.

16

IT'S 1964. I'M INFORMING THE PENTAGON THAT I'LL NO LONGER BE WEARING THE WHOLE OF MY COSTUME.

IT'S 1966. I'M IN A ROOM OF PEOPLE WEARING DISGUISES.

...THIRD, UH, I GUESS I SHOULD **WELCOME** EVERYBODY TO THE **FIRST EVER** MEETING OF THE **CRIMEBUSTERS!**

A VERY YOUNG GIRL SITS TO MY RIGHT. SHE LOOKS AT ME AND SMILES...

IN 1985, MY HANDS ARE ENCIRCLING HER FACE.

IN 1966, THE COSTUMED PEOPLE ARE ARGUING. JANEY IS TUGGING AT MY ARM...

WHAT'S THE MATTER?

YOU WERE STARING AT THAT **GIRL** IS THE MATTER! NOW PAY **ATTENTION.**

OBVIOUSLY, I AGREE ... BUT A GROUP **THIS** SIZE SEEMS MORE LIKE A **PUBLICITY EXERCISE...**

SHE'S BEAUTIFUL. AFTER EACH LONG KISS, SHE PLANTS A SMALLER, GENTLER ONE UPON MY LIPS, LIKE A SIGNATURE.

IN 1966, THE MASKS ARE STILL SQUABBLING...

SOON, THE MEETING BREAKS UP. JANEY'S VOICE IS COLD, FURIOUS...

JON, I THINK I'D LIKE TO GO **HOME** NOW, PLEASE.

PLEASE! DON'T ALL **LEAVE** ...

OUTSIDE, JANEY ACCUSES ME OF "CHASING JAILBAIT." SHE BURSTS INTO ANGRY TEARS, ASKING IF IT'S BECAUSE SHE'S GETTING OLDER.

IT'S TRUE. SHE'S AGING MORE NOTICEABLY EVERY DAY...

...WHILE I'M STANDING STILL.

17

MAY, 1966...

IT'S NICE OF YOU TO COME OUT ON *PATROL* WITH ME. MY MOM TAUGHT ME EVERYTHING SHE *KNEW*, BUT I'M STILL PRETTY *NEW* TO ALL THIS.

UH... YOUR *GIRL-FRIEND* WON'T *MIND*, WILL SHE?

YOU *PIG!* I *KNEW* YOU WERE SEEING HER! I *KNEW* IT!

YOU'RE *SICK!* HOW *OLD* IS SHE? FOURTEEN? FIFTEEN?

PIG!

I...I DON'T KNOW WHAT I SHOULD *CALL* YOU. MY NAME'S *LAURIE*. DO *YOU* HAVE ANOTHER NAME, APART FROM *DR. MANHATTAN?*

YES.

MY NAME'S JON.

YOU *TELL* HER! YOU TELL HER WHAT IT'S GONNA BE *LIKE* WHEN HER *FACE* WRINKLES UP AND HER *BOOBS* START SAGGING AND YOU'RE STILL GODDAMNED *THIRTY!*

YOU *TELL* HER, AND SEE WHAT SHE SAYS TO *THAT!*

IT'S 1959. JANEY IS HANDING ME THE GLASS.

IT'S 1966, AND SHE'S PACKING; TEARFUL; CARE-LESS WITH ANGER...

THE PHOTOGRAPH LIES IN THE SAND AT MY FEET.

18

IN 1969, I'M RECEIVING NEWS OF MY FATHER'S DEATH.

IN 1959, HE'S OPENING A TELEGRAM FROM THE MILITARY INFORMING HIM OF HIS SON'S ACCIDENTAL DISINTEGRATION. I NEVER CORRECT THEIR MISTAKE.

GILA FLATS CLOSES DOWN IN 1970. ON LAURIE'S TWENTIETH BIRTHDAY, WE MOVE INTO OUR NEW WASHINGTON APARTMENT.

I'VE REVEALED MY TRUE NAME TO THE PUBLIC. AFTER FATHER'S DEATH, THERE SEEMS LITTLE POINT IN CONCEALING IT.

IN JANUARY, 1971, PRESIDENT NIXON IS ASKING ME TO INTERVENE IN VIETNAM, WHILE TEN YEARS EARLIER, KENNEDY IS AVOIDING ANY MENTION OF CUBA.

LATER IN NOVEMBER, I'M TOLD THAT WALLY WEAVER HAS DIED OF CANCER, AGED 34.

IT'S MARCH. I'M IN SAIGON, BEING REINTRODUCED TO EDWARD BLAKE, THE COMEDIAN. HE WORKS MOSTLY FOR THE GOVERNMENT NOW. I SUPPOSE I DO, TOO.

BLAKE IS INTERESTING. I HAVE NEVER MET ANYONE SO DELIBERATELY AMORAL.

HE SUITS THE CLIMATE HERE: THE MADNESS, THE POINTLESS BUTCHERY...

AS I COME TO UNDERSTAND VIETNAM AND WHAT IT IMPLIES ABOUT THE HUMAN CONDITION, I ALSO REALIZE THAT FEW HUMANS WILL PERMIT THEMSELVES SUCH AN UNDERSTANDING.

BLAKE'S DIFFERENT.

HE UNDERSTANDS PERFECTLY...

...AND HE DOESN'T CARE.

19

IT'S MAY. I HAVE BEEN HERE TWO MONTHS.

THE VIETCONG ARE EXPECTED TO SURRENDER WITHIN THE WEEK. MANY HAVE GIVEN THEMSELVES UP ALREADY...

OFTEN, THEY ASK TO SURRENDER TO ME PERSONALLY, THEIR TERROR OF ME BALANCED BY AN ALMOST RELIGIOUS AWE.

I AM REMINDED OF HOW THE JAPANESE WERE REPORTED TO HAVE VIEWED THE ATOMIC BOMB, AFTER HIROSHIMA.

IT'S JUNE, V.V.N. NIGHT, AND THE COMEDIAN IS SLIDING A GUN FROM ITS HOLSTER, BLOOD STREAMING FROM HIS LACERATED FACE...

IT'S OCTOBER, 1985. DECIDING TO CREATE SOMETHING, I TURN AWAY FROM STARS THAT MAY HAVE BURNED OUT AEONS AGO. I NO LONGER WISH TO LOOK AT THEM.

I NO LONGER WISH TO LOOK AT DEAD THINGS.

20

IT'S 1975. THE PAPERS ARE FULL OF THE PRESIDENT'S PROPOSED **CONSTITUTIONAL AMENDMENT**, ALLOWING HIM TO RUN NEXT YEAR FOR A THIRD TERM.

AMIDST ALL THIS, THE UNMASKING AND RETIRE-MENT OF **OZYMANDIAS** GOES ALMOST UNNOTICED.

OZYMAN QUITS

ADRIAN VEIDT ALIAS OZYMANDIAS

HIS REAL NAME IS **ADRIAN VEIDT**, A SELF-MADE MILLIONAIRE. AFTER RETIRING FROM ADVENTURING HE INVITES LAURIE AND ME TO VISIT HIM AT HIS ANTARCTIC RETREAT.

OOH! WHAT **IS** IT? IT'S **BEAUTIFUL**!

THAT'S **BUBASTIS**. SHE'S A GENETICALLY ALTERED **LYNX**. THEY COST RATHER A LOT TO **FEED**, I'M AFRAID.

I HADN'T REALIZED THAT **EUGENICS** WAS SO **ADVANCED** NOW...

IT'S LEAPT **FORWARD** IN THE LAST FIFTEEN YEARS. **EVERYTHING** HAS, FROM QUANTUM PHYSICS TO **TRANSPORT**.

FOR **EXAMPLE**, I UNDERSTAND THAT FAST AND SAFE **AIRSHIPS** MAY SOON BE ECONOMICALLY **VIABLE**...

...AND WE OWE IT ALL TO **YOU**. WITH YOUR HELP, OUR SCIENTISTS ARE LIMITED ONLY BY THEIR **IMAGINATIONS**.

AND BY THEIR **CONSCIENCES**, SURELY?

LET'S HOPE SO.

HIS EYES ARE SAD AND KNOWING. HIS SERVANTS BRING US INDONESIAN FOOD AND HE TALKS ABOUT HIS BUSINESS PLANS, ALL THE TIME FEEDING SCRAPS TO HIS BEAUTIFUL MONSTROUS CAT...

21

IT'S 1985. CHOOSING A SPOT TO BEGIN MY CREATION, I SIT DOWN. PINK SAND LIES POOLED IN MY BLUE PALM.

THIS DESERTED PLANET = IT IS SO WONDERFULLY, COMPLETELY SILENT.

IN 1977, A CITY IS SHOUTING.

CLAIMING THAT COSTUMED ADVENTURERS ARE MAKING THEIR JOB IMPOSSIBLE, THE POLICE ARE ON STRIKE. EVERYONE IS FRIGHTENED, SCENTING ANARCHY.

BELOW ME, LAURIE HAULS THE RINGLEADERS FROM THE CROWD; BUT THE PROCESS IS TOO SLOW...

LOOK AT HIM! LOOK AT THAT FREAK! IT'S AGAINST GOD!

I'D BEST DO SOMETHING...

PAY ATTENTION. YOU WILL ALL RETURN TO YOUR HOMES.

GIVE US OUR POLICE BACK!

BADGES NOT MASKS

OH, YEAH? AND WHAT IF WE DON'T, YA BIG BLUE FRUIT?

YOU MISUNDERSTAND ME.

IT WAS NOT A REQUEST.

JESUS.

THE NEXT DAY, I AM READING IN THE PAPER OF TWO PEOPLE WHO SUFFERED HEART ATTACKS UPON SUDDENLY FINDING THEMSELVES INDOORS. MORE WOULD HAVE SUFFERED DURING A RIOT, I'M CERTAIN.

AUGUST 3RD, 1977: THE EMERGENCY BILL PROPOSED BY **SENATOR KEENE** HAS BEEN PASSED.

VIGILANTISM IS NOW **ILLEGAL** AGAIN, AS IT WAS BEFORE THEY ALTERED THE LAWS TO ACCOMMODATE STRATEGICALLY USEFUL TALENTS SUCH AS MYSELF.

AS LONG AS I CONTINUE TO ACT UNDER U.S. GOVERNMENT SUPERVISION, I AM EXEMPT FROM THE LAW. THEY CAN HARDLY OUTLAW ME WHEN THEIR COUNTRY'S DEFENSE RESTS IN MY HANDS.

BLAKE IS ALSO EXEMPT, SINCE HE TOO WORKS ENTIRELY FOR THE GOVERN-MENT.

LATER, AFTER HIS HANDLING OF THE IRANIAN HOSTAGE SITUATION, EVEN HIS HARSHEST CRITICS FALL SILENT. LAURIE STILL HATES HIM, HOWEVER.

SHE HERSELF HAS BEEN FORCED TO RETIRE BY THE KEENE ACT, BUT HAVING NEVER REALLY ENJOYED THE LIFE, SHE DOESN'T MIND.

HER MOTHER IS MORE DISAPPOINTED THAN SHE IS.

THE NEW **NITE OWL** HAS STATED THAT HE WILL BE RETIRING, ALTHOUGH HE WILL NOT BE MAKING HIS IDENTITY PUBLIC.

LAURIE'S MET HIM SEVERAL TIMES. SHE SAYS HIS NAME IS DREIBERG.

THE ONLY OTHER ACTIVE VIGILANTE IS CALLED **RORSCHACH**, REAL NAME UNKNOWN.

HE EXPRESSES HIS FEELINGS TOWARD COMPULSORY RETIREMENT IN A NOTE LEFT OUTSIDE POLICE HEAD-QUARTERS ALONG WITH A DEAD MULTIPLE RAPIST.

23

IT'S 1981 NOW. LAURIE AND I ARE SETTLING INTO OUR NEW QUARTERS AT THE ROCKEFELLER MILITARY RESEARCH CENTER IN NEW YORK.

IT'S WELL-EQUIPPED FOR MY WORK, BUT LAURIE FEELS WE'VE LOST OUR *PRIVACY*.

SHE'D LIKE IT HERE.

THROUGH MY BLUE FINGERS, PINK GRAINS ARE FALLING, HAPHAZARD, RANDOM, A DISORGANIZED STREAM OF SILICONE THAT SEEMS PREGNANT WITH THE POSSIBILITY OF EVERY CONCEIVABLE SHAPE...

...BUT THIS IS ILLUSION. THINGS HAVE THEIR SHAPE IN TIME, NOT SPACE ALONE. SOME MARBLE BLOCKS HAVE STATUES WITHIN THEM, EMBEDDED IN THEIR FUTURE.

IN NEW YORK, WE GO WALKING.

THE STREETS SMELL OF OZONE RATHER THAN GASOLINE. FLAT INTANGIBLE BLOTS OF GRAY SLIDE ACROSS THE SUMMER SIDEWALKS, THE SHADOWS OF OVERHEAD AIRSHIPS.

IN 1959, A CHILD IS WEEPING FOR ITS LOST BALLOONS.

ANY MOMENT NOW, JANEY'S WATCHBAND WILL BREAK. SOMEWHERE, THE FAT MAN IS ALREADY LUMBERING TOWARD THE SHOOTING GALLERY, STEPS HEAVY WITH UNWITTING DESTINY.

IT'S AUGUST, 1985. I'M WALKING THROUGH GRAND CENTRAL STATION WITH LAURIE. WE STOP AT THE NEWSSTAND AND BUY A COPY OF TIME MAGAZINE, COMMEMORATING *HIROSHIMA WEEK*.

ON THE COVER THERE IS A DAMAGED POCKET-WATCH, STOPPED AT THE INSTANT OF THE BLAST, FACE CRACKED...

...HANDS FROZEN.

24

IT'S SATURDAY, OCTOBER 12TH, 1985, AND WE ARE BEING INFORMED OF EDWARD BLAKE'S MURDER.

LAURIE'S MOOD SEEMS RESTLESS FOR THE REMAINDER OF THE WEEKEND.

WEDNESDAY THE 16TH. LAURIE IS VISITING HER MOTHER WHILE I ATTEND BLAKE'S FUNERAL.

A THIN MAN IN A BLACK COAT LEAVES ROSES, THEN WALKS AWAY. DO I KNOW HIM?

SATURDAY THE 19TH NOW. MY HANDS ENCIRCLE LAURIE'S FACE...

IN 1966, THE COSTUMED PEOPLE ARE ARGUING.

IN 1959, I AM TELLING JANEY I SHALL ALWAYS WANT HER.

IT'S LATER. LAURIE IS WALKING OUT ON ME.

ON A ROOFTOP IN THE PAST, I PULL HER SIXTEEN-YEAR-OLD BODY TO ME, BREATHING HER PERFUME, NEVER WANTING TO LOSE HER, KNOWING THAT I SHALL.

SPECIAL TALENT QUARTERS

VISITORS ENTRANCE

LATER STILL, AND IN THE CROWDED T.V. STUDIO, I AM BEING ACCUSED OF KILLING THOSE CLOSEST TO ME.

THE WORD "CANCER" RUNS THROUGH THE AUDIENCE ON A FIRECRACKER STRING OF ANXIOUS WHISPERS.

I AM TIRED OF THIS WORLD; THESE PEOPLE. I AM TIRED OF BEING CAUGHT IN THE TANGLE OF THEIR LIVES.

IN ARIZONA, I'M ENTERING THE RUINED BAR WITH A SENSATION OF DÉJÀ VU...

...AND I'M TAKING THE SNAPSHOT FROM ITS BROKEN FRAME...

...AND I'M GONE.

25

Soviet heartland that assured his eventual defeat, and though it was paid for mostly by Soviet lives, the entire world reaped the benefits. In time, the Russian contribution to the war effort has been downplayed and dismissed—most noticeably as our political differences became wider—as we glorified our own contribution while forgetting that of our estranged former allies. The Russians, however, have not forgotten. There are still those who remember the horror of a war fought on their soil, and almost certainly there are members of the Politburo in that category. From my reading of various pronouncements made by the Russian high command over the years, I am convinced that they will never again permit their nation to be threatened in a similar manner, *no matter what the cost.*

The presence of a deterrent such as Dr. Manhattan has doubtless curbed Soviet adventurism, as there have been numerous occasions when the U.S.S.R. has had to step down over some issue rather than risk escalation into a war it certainly could not win. Often, these reversals have been humiliating, and this has perhaps fostered the illusion that the Soviets will suffer such indignities endlessly. This is a misconception, for there is indeed another option available.

That option is Mutually Assured Destruction. Stated simply, Dr. Manhattan cannot stop all the Soviet warheads from reaching American soil, even a greatly reduced percentage would still be more than enough to effectively end the organic life in the northern hemisphere. The suggestion that the presence of a superhuman has inclined the world more towards peace is refudiated by the sharp increase in both Russian and American nuclear stockpiles since the advent of Dr. Manhattan. Infinite destruction divided by two or ten or twenty is still infinite destruction. If threatened with eventual domination, would the Soviets pursue this unquestionably suicidal course? Yes. Given their history and their view of the world, I believe that they would.

Our current administration believes otherwise. They continually push their unearned advantage until American influence comes uncomfortably close to key areas of Soviet interest. It is as if—with a real live Deity on their side—our leaders have become intoxicated with a heady draught of Omnipotence-by-Association, without realizing just how his very existence has deformed the lives of every living creature on the face of this planet.

This is true in a domestic sense as well as a broader, international one. The technology that Dr. Manhattan has made possible has changed the way we think about our clothes, our food, our travel. We drive in electric cars and travel in leisure and comfort in clean, economical airships. Our entire culture has had to contort itself to accommodate the presence of something more than human, and we have all felt the results of this. The evidence surrounds us, in our everyday lives and on the front pages of the newspapers we read. One single being has been allowed to change the entire world, pushing it closer to its eventual destruction in the process. The Gods now walk amongst us, affecting the lives of every man, woman and child on the planet in a direct way rather than through mythology and the reassurances of faith. The safety of a whole world rests in the hands of a being far beyond what we understand to be human.

We are all of us living in the shadow of Manhattan.

DR. MANHATTAN:

2

FEARFUL SYMMETRY

I I I WASN'T ...

I WASN'T GOING TO POINT IT AT YOU.

HHUHHH!

NO, PLEASE, WHAT ...?

GUN.

NO LICENSE.

I CHECKED.

VERY BAD.

4

ALSO, YOU'RE SWEATING. LOOKS UNPLEASANT.

SHOULD COOL DOWN.

AAK!

OH, GOD ...LOOK, PLEASE, WHAT DO YOU WANT WITH ME?

NOTHING. JUST PASSING.

OLD AND ALONE. THOUGHT YOU MIGHT APPRECIATE COMPANY.

THEN, UH, C-CAN I GET OUT OF THE FRIDGE?

NO.

THOUGHT WE MIGHT DISCUSS COMEDIAN. HE VISITED HERE. MENTIONED A LIST= YOU AND JANEY SLATER ON IT. TALKED ABOUT SOMEONE MESSING WITH DR. MANHATTAN.

DAYS LATER, MANHATTAN PUBLICLY DISGRACED. ALLEGATIONS HE'D GIVEN PEOPLE CANCER= YOU, JANEY SLATER.

FORCED INTO EXILE.

TOUGH BREAK.

BUT ...I DON'T UNDERSTAND. WHY ARE YOU LAYING ALL THIS HEAT ON ME?

BECAUSE I THINK BLAKE'S LIST WAS CANCER LIST. SOMEBODY WROTE IT. SOMEBODY PUT YOUR NAME ON IT. SOMEBODY GAVE IT TO THE MEDIA.

WONDER WHO?

FUNNY ...DR. MANHATTAN AND COMEDIAN WERE ALWAYS YOUR BIGGEST ENEMIES. NOW THEY'RE BOTH GONE. VERY CONVENIENT.

WHO IS IT, MOLOCH?

WHO'S BEHIND THIS?

I...I DON'T KNOW. I ALREADY TOLD YOU. I DON'T KNOW ANYTHING.

NO GOOD. WRONG TONE OF VOICE.

NOT CONVINCING ENOUGH.

OH NO. OH NO, GOD, DON'T...

RORSCHACH, PLEASE, IT WASN'T ME. I DON'T KNOW!

I DON'T KNOW WHO IT WAS!

5

HURRM.

BETTER.

OUHH.

OH GOD.
OH GOD
...

GOING NOW. IF ANYTHING SHOULD REFRESH MEMORY, CONTACT ME BY LEAVING NOTE, TRASH CAN OPPOSITE GUNGA DINER, AT FORTIETH AND SEVENTH.

PLUS GET GUN LICENSE. SOON.

YES. AHHUHH. OH, GOD, YES, ANYTHING...

SORRY ABOUT MESS.

CAN'T MAKE OMELETTE WITHOUT BREAKING FEW EGGS.

RORSCHACH'S JOURNAL. OCTOBER 21ST, 1985:

LEFT JACOBI'S HOUSE 2:35 A.M. HE KNOWS NOTHING ABOUT ANY ATTEMPT TO DISCREDIT DR. MANHATTAN. HE HAS SIMPLY BEEN USED.

BY WHOM? RUSSIANS SEEM OBVIOUS CHOICE: MANHATTAN AND COMEDIAN BOTH KEY MILITARY FIGURES.

BUT COMEDIAN REFERRED TO AN ISLAND, ARTISTS AND WRITERS LIVING ON IT. DOESN'T FIT.

CAN'T CONCENTRATE. TOO TIRED. NO SLEEP SINCE SATURDAY.

WALKED HOME PAST TRASHCANS STUFFED WITH RUMORS OF WAR, WEIGHING FACTORS; BODIES; MOTIVES...

WAITING FOR A FLASH OF ENLIGHTENMENT IN ALL THIS BLOOD AND THUNDER.

6

WE NEED TO KNOW *EVERYTHING*, MRS. HIRSCH...

WAR.

HE SAID THERE WAS GONNA BE WAR WITH THE *RUSSIANS*. SAID HE WANTED TO *SPARE* THE *LITTLE ONES*.

DOMINIQUE, SHE KEPT SAYING "*WAH*", WHICH IS, LIKE, "*WAR*". SHE'S JUST *THREE*, SHE *REPEATS* THINGS. AND THEN... OH.

OOOHHHHHH.

OKAY, MRS. HIRSCH. NO MORE *QUESTIONS*. OFFICER CAPALDI WILL DRIVE YOU TO THE *HOSPITAL*.

JESUS. WHAT *HAPPENED*?

GUY WORRIED ABOUT *NUCLEAR WAR*. KILLED BOTH KIDS IN FRONT OF THEIR MOM, THEN OPENED HIS *JUGULAR*.

THERE'S GONNA BE *MORE* LIKE THIS.

YEAH. WELL, ME, I THINK IT'S *ASTROLOGICAL*. HALLEY'S COMET IS COMING BACK AROUND NOW. THAT'S AN OMEN OF *DOOM*.

YEAH. SO'S *RUSSIA* INVADING *AFGHANISTAN*.

AHH, THAT'LL BLOW OVER. WORLD WAR THREE, IT'LL NEVER HAPPEN. NOBODY'S *CRAZY* ENOUGH.

BOY. WHAT DID HE USE ON *THESE*?

KITCHEN KNIFE. THEIR NAMES WERE *CLARE* AND *DOMINIQUE*.

NICE *NAMES*. SORTA FILM *STAR* NAMES.

YEAH.

SO, YA WANNA GO GET SOME *BREAKFAST*?

YEAH.

GOOD. LISTEN, DON'T LET THIS RUIN YOUR DAY. THESE *PSYCH-OUTS* ARE MOSTLY MEDIA INSPIRED.

THE MEDIA INSPIRES *BOREDOM* NOT WAKING UP ONE MONDAY MORNING AND BUTCHERING YOUR KIDS.

THAT TAKES SOMETHING *ELSE*, MAN.

THAT TAKES A WHOLE DIFFERENT *KIND* OF INSPIRATION.

7

MY HOME AND FAMILY WERE DOOMED, MY WORLD REDUCED TO RUIN. FATE HAD DEALT ITS HAND CASUALLY, DESPITE MY BITTER PROTESTATIONS.

HEY, TURKEY! QUIT SPLASHING!

WHERE SHOULD I RECHARGE? NOW QUIT OBSTRUCTIN' THE CURRENT...

THE SAME WAVES GNAWED MY ISLAND AND DAVIDSTOWN ALIKE, YET SWIMMING WOULD SURELY BE MADNESS.

S'BETTER. GOT TODAY'S GAZETTE?

SURE. THIS WAR'S LOOKIN' SERIOUS. MAKES A GUY START FIGURING ESCAPE ROUTES, Y'KNOW?

IT WAS THEN I CONCEIVED OF BUILDING A RAFT...

I MEAN, MY FATHER, WHEN THINGS DETERIORATED IN 'THIRTIES GERMANY, HE SPLIT.

SURE. IN WORLD WAR TWO. IN WORLD WAR THREE WHERE'S TO SPLIT TO?

... ALTHOUGH INWARDLY I DOUBTED IT WOULD FLOAT.

ANYWAYS, THAT'S ENOUGH JUICE TO MAKE CONNECTICUT. SEE YOU NEXT DELIVERY DAY.

YEAH. SURE...

THE ISLAND'S TREES DID NOT LOOK BUOYANT ENOUGH TO REACH DAVIDSTOWN. NOT UNAIDED...

SUDDENLY, I RECALLED THE GAS-BLOATED STOMACHS OF THE BURIED MEN, THEN SHUDDERED AT THE IDEA I FOUND MYSELF CONSIDERING.

"WHERE'S TO SPLIT TO?"

HUMM.

I ATTEMPTED TO BANISH THIS REPULSIVE NOTION...

AHH, IT'LL NEVER HAPPEN. WONDER WHAT'S DELAYIN' THE NEW FRONTIERSMAN?

... BUT IT WOULD NOT LET ME BE.

NEXT MONTH'S COMIC BOOKS ARRIVE EARLY, TODAY'S FRONTIERSMAN ARRIVES LATE.

GODDAMN WAR'S SCREWIN' EVERYTHING UP.

FINALLY APPROACHING THE SHALLOW GRAVE, I BEGAN DIGGING. MY SCHEME WAS LOATHSOME, BUT I HAD NO CHOICE.

NOT WHEN I CONSIDERED THE NATURE OF MY SITUATION.

SHEE-IT!

ABSOLUTELY EVERYTHING.

8

EVERYTHING I LOVED, EVERYTHING I LIVED FOR DEPENDED UPON MY REACHING DAVIDSTOWN IN ADVANCE OF THAT TERRIBLE FREIGHTER.

CLINGING TO THE MEMORY OF MY WIFE'S EYES, I DRAGGED MEN UP FROM UNDERGROUND, SAND TRICKLING FROM THEIR SOCKETS.

REMOVING THEIR CLOTHING, I TORE IT TO RIBBONS, BINDING THEM TOGETHER.

OCCASIONALLY, I WOULD PAUSE IN MY WORK, ENTRANCED BY THE STARTLING BEAUTY OF A TATTOO OR THE ENIGMA OF AN OLD SCAR.

BY AFTERNOON, I'D FELLED ENOUGH YOUNG PALMS TO BUILD THE DECK OF MY CONVEYANCE, AFFIXING IT TO THE HUMAN FLOAT BENEATH.

SATISFIED, I WAITED FOR DUSK AND EBB TIDE, THEN EMBARKED, HEADING EAST.

EAST, ACROSS THE NIGHT SEAS.

EAST, BORNE ON THE NAKED BACKS OF MURDERED MEN.

WITH DAWN CAME THE GULLS, DRAWN TO THE CARRION UPON WHICH MY TRANSPORT RESTED.

LENT SPEED BY MY HUNGER, I WAS ABLE TO RIP ONE FROM THE AIR. I HAD NOT EATEN SINCE THE SHIPWRECK.

STOMACH FILLED WITH RAW MEAT; GULL BLOOD CAKED UPON MY CHIN, I DRIFTED ON TOWARDS DAVIDSTOWN. MY **HOME** WAS THERE.

NOTHING WOULD TAKE IT FROM ME.

9

THEY SAID I CAN'T *LIVE* THERE ANY-MORE, NOW THAT *JON'S* GONE.

PLUS, THEY SUSPENDED MY *EXPENSE ACCOUNT*, SO ALL I HAVE IS MY *SAVINGS*. IT WAS JUST "OKAY, WE'RE TAKING YOUR HOME AND MONEY. CHEW ON THAT."

SO, WHERE WILL YOU *STAY*? DID YOU CALL YOUR *MOTHER*?

OH, SHE'D *LOVE* THAT. I'D SOONER SLEEP ON A *GRATING*.

NAH, I'LL GET BY. IT JUST BURNS MY ASS TO BE SO DAMN *DISPOSABLE*.

ANYWAY, THANKS FOR BUYING ME *LUNCH*. I BETTER GO FIND A *CHEAP ROOM* SOME-WHERE.

SAY, ARE YOU *OKAY*? YOU LOOK KINDA *UNCOMFORTABLE*...

NO, NO, I'M FINE. I GUESS I'LL SEE YOU *AROUND* SOME TIME.

SURE. 'BYE, DAN.

LAURIE, *WAIT*.

YOU *KNOW* THERE'S, UH, THERE'S ALWAYS *MY PLACE*.

OH, I COULDN'T IMPOSE...

OH, IT'D BE NO *IMPOSITION*. I HAVE A LOT OF *ROOM* THERE.

I MEAN, WE'RE BOTH *FRIENDS*; WE'RE BOTH IN THE SAME LINE OF *WORK*; WE'RE BOTH, UHH... WE'RE BOTH,...

WE'RE BOTH *LEFTOVERS*.

10

RORSCHACH'S JOURNAL. OCTOBER 21ST, 1985 :

WOKEN AT ELEVEN BY SHOUTING OUTSIDE. DISTURBED TO FIND I HAD FALLEN ASLEEP WITHOUT REMOVING THE SKIN FROM MY HEAD. TIREDER THAN I THOUGHT. SHOULD BE MORE CAREFUL.

ACROSS STREET, BOYS WITH SPRAY CANS WERE DEFACING ABANDONED BUILDING. MEMORIZED THEIR DESCRIPTIONS, THEN PREPARED FOR WORK.

FIRST, PEELED OFF FACE, FOLDED IT, HID INSIDE JACKET. WITHOUT MY FACE, NOBODY KNOWS.

NOBODY KNOWS WHO I AM.

ON WAY OUT OF ROOM, MET LANDLADY. USUAL COMPLAINTS RE HYGIENE AND RENT. THERE WERE PURPLE BITE MARKS ON HER FAT WHITE NECK. FRESH ONES.

SHE REMINDS ME OF MY MOTHER.

OUT IN STREET, INSPECTED DEFACED BUILDING = SILHOUETTE PICTURE IN DOORWAY, MAN AND WOMAN, POSSIBLY INDULGING IN SEXUAL FOREPLAY.

DIDN'T LIKE IT. MAKES DOORWAY LOOK HAUNTED.

ON FORTIETH AND SEVENTH, SAW DREIBERG AND JUSPECZYK LEAVING DINER. THEY DIDN'T KNOW ME.

AN AFFAIR, PERHAPS? DID JUSPECZYK ENGINEER DR. MANHATTAN'S EXILE TO MAKE ROOM FOR DREIBERG? ALSO, SHE HATED COMEDIAN. MUST INVESTIGATE FURTHER.

ENTERING DINER, BOUGHT COFFEE, THEN SAT WATCHING MY MAILDROP, IMMEDIATELY ACROSS STREET.

PASSERS-BY MADE VARIOUS DEPOSITS: CANDY WRAPPERS, NEWSPAPERS, A PAIR OF KEDS STRANGLED BY OWN LACES, TONGUES LOLLING OUT HORRIBLY.

THIS CITY IS AN ANIMAL, FIERCE AND COMPLICATED. TO UNDERSTAND IT I READ ITS DROPPINGS, ITS SCENTS, THE MOVEMENT OF ITS PARASITES...

I SAT WATCHING THE TRASHCAN, AND NEW YORK OPENED ITS HEART TO ME.

11

TELLYA THE TRUTH, THIS WHOLE BLOODY MESS, IT GIVES ME A FUNNY FEELIN' *INSIDE* Y'KNOW?

THERE WAS A GULL IN MY STOMACH.

AFGHANISTAN: IS PAKISTAN NEXT?

IT'S LIKE, I DUNNO HOW LONG WE CAN HOLD *ON.*

AS THE SUN CLAMBERED PRECARIOUSLY OVER THE WORLD'S SLIPPERY RIM, THE ENORMITY OF MY SAVAGE BREAKFAST STRUCK ME AND I GREW FAINT.

I'D SWALLOWED TOO MUCH BIRDFLESH. I'D SWALLOWED TOO MUCH HORROR.

I MEAN, WORLD WAR THREE, IT'S A *NIGHTMARE.* THE ONLY PEOPLE WHO CAN EVEN *THINK* ABOUT IT ARE THE *ARMS COMPANIES.*

YOU *WATCH.* YOU WATCH THE FINANCIAL PAGES. THOSE GUYS, THEY'RE GONNA MAKE A *KILLING.*

EVERYTHING TILTED. ABOVE, SCAVENGERS WHEELED HUNGRILY, JUST SCREAMS DRESSED IN FEATHERS.

THEY'RE *GREEDY.* GREEDY FOR CASH THEY WON'T HAVE THE TIME TO *SPEND.*

I MEAN, DON'T PEOPLE SEE THE *SIGNS?* DON'T THEY KNOW WHERE THIS IS *HEADED?*

HEY MAN, I'M READING.

AFGHAN PAKISTA

SEE? APATHY! EVERYBODY ESCAPIN' INTO COMIC BOOKS AN' T.V.! MAKES ME *SICK.*

THE GULLS' SLAUGHTERHOUSE CHORUS AFFORDED NO DISTRACTION FROM MY NAUSEA, AND I FELL, RETCHING, TO MY KNEES. BETWEEN MY RAFT'S TIMBERS, BOSUN RIDLEY STARED UP AT ME.

THIS SUDDEN CONFRONTATION WITH MORTALITY INDUCED AN ODD CLARITY WITHIN ME.

I MEAN, ALL THIS, IT COULD ALL BE *GONE:* PEOPLE, CARS, T.V. SHOWS, MAGAZINES...

EVEN THE WORD 'GONE' WOULD BE GONE.

SEE, NEWS-VENDORS *UNDERSTAND.* THEY GET TO SEE THE *WHOLE PICTURE.*

LIGHT-HEADED, I GAZED INTO THE INVERTED WORLD BENEATH, WHERE DROWNED GULLS CIRCLED. A MADMAN WITH BLOOD-CAKED LIPS GAZED BACK AT ME.

HIS EYES, HIS NOSE, HIS CHEEKS SEEMED INDIVIDUALLY FAMILIAR, BUT MERCIFULLY I COULD NOT PIECE THEM TOGETHER. NOT INTO A FACE I KNEW.

IT'S OUR *CURSE.* WE SEE EVERY *CONNECTION.*

EVERY DAMNED *LINK.*

AFGHANISTAN: IS PAKISTAN NEXT?

12

TIME'S RUNNING **OUT**, MR. VEIDT. YOU BETTER **HURRY**.

YES. YES, I KNOW.

IT'S THE **TOY** PEOPLE I HAVE TO SEE THIS MORNING, ISN'T IT?

THAT'S RIGHT. THEY WANT SOME NEW **CHARACTERS** IN THEIR **OZYMANDIAS** LINE. MAYBE SOME OF YOUR **MAJOR VILLAINS** OR SOMETHING.

THE **MAJOR VILLAINS** ARE ALL **DEAD**.

OH **WOW**, WHAT **IS** IT WITH EVERYBODY TODAY? EVERYBODY'S ON THIS TOTAL **DEATH TRIP**.

LIKE ON THE **NEWS** THIS MORNING, SOME GUY WENT NUTS, KILLED HIS **KIDS**. YOU' SEE THAT?

NO. NO, I DIDN'T.

APPARENTLY, HE WAS SCARED THERE WAS GONNA BE A **WAR**! ISN'T THAT **DUMB**?

NOBODY WOULD BE **CRAZY** ENOUGH TO **START** ONE, SO WHY'S EVERYBODY ON SUCH A **DOWNER** ABOUT IT?

PERHAPS THEY DON'T HAVE YOUR **YOUTH** AND **OPTIMISM**.

WELL, I DUNNO. I THINK MAYBE IT'S THE **DECOR** ROUND HERE. ALL THIS **EGYPTIAN** STUFF. IT'S VERY MORBID. VERY OBSESSED WITH **DEATH**.

DEATH WASN'T MORBID TO THE ANCIENT EGYPTIANS. THEY SAW IT AS LAUNCHING ON A VOYAGE OF SPIRITUAL DISCOVERY.

DON'T YOU FIND THAT A COMFORTING THOUGHT?

ARE YOU **KIDDING**?

I MEAN, LOSING TEN **POUNDS**, **THAT'S** A COMFORTING THOUGHT. MY NEXT **RAISE** IS A COMFORTING THOUGHT.

GLORIA VANDERBILT, M.T.V., **THESE** ARE COMFORTING THOUGHTS...

SPIRITUAL DISCOVERY, ON THE OTHER HAND, I CAN TAKE IT OR...

OH, GOD.

OH, **GOD**, LOOK OUT, HE'S...

13

16

DURING THE AFTERNOON, I DOZED FITFULLY, MY ENEMIES' HIDEOUS BANNER FLAPPING DISMALLY IN MY DREAMS.

WAR, CHILD MURDER, ATTEMPTED ASSASSINATION...THIS FRONT PAGE IS A NIGHTMARE!

SOMEBODY CHOPS UP THEIR KIDS, SOMEBODY ELSE SHOOTS AT ADRIAN VEIDT...

THAT DEATHS-HEAD BANNER; IT FLIES ABOVE US ALL...

I MEAN, WHO'D WANNA KILL A GUY LIKE THAT?

TALES OF THE BLACK FREIGHTER

...AND THE HEADS NAILED TO THE SHIP'S BLACK PROW, THOSE HEADS ARE OUR HEADS.

IT'S LIKE, IF SOMEBODY WANTS TO OFF A SAINT LIKE VEIDT, WHAT CHANCE DO ANY OF US GOT?

VEIDT'S A REAL HERO. DID CHARITY WORK. REVEALED HIS NAME LIKE HE HAD NOTHING TO HIDE.

TRULY, WHO-EVER WE ARE, WHEREVER WE RESIDE, WE EXIST UPON THE WHIM OF MURDERERS.

JEEZ. WHERE'S IT GONNA END?

INDUSTRIALIST MURDER

I AWOKE AT DUSK AND DRANK A LITTLE SALT WATER. I HAVE HEARD THAT ON LESS THAN A PINT DAILY, A MAN MIGHT SURVIVE.

HELL, NO WONDER PEOPLE GO CRAZY.

LIKE THIS GUY KILLED HIS KIDS. A WEEK AGO, THAT WAS A NORMAL FAMILY.

YOU NEVER KNOW. YOU NEVER KNOW WHAT'S BEARING DOWN ON YOU.

INSTITUTE OF EXTRASPATIAL STUDIES

BENEATH MY RAFT, SOMETHING MOVED.

IRRATIONALLY, MY FIRST THOUGHT WAS OF THE CORPSES, BURSTING THEIR BONDS, ATTEMPTING TO CLAMBER UP INTO THE AIR AND DRYNESS, BUT NO. SOMETHING HAD BRUSHED BENEATH ME.

I MEAN, ALL WE SEE IS WHAT'S ON THE SURFACE.

I BET THERE'S ALL KINDA STUFF WE NEVER NOTICE...

MY PLATFORM LURCHED AGAIN. AHEAD, IN THE DARKENING WATER, I HEARD A SPLASH. SHADOWY FORMS APPROACHED. WERE THEY BOATS COME TO RESCUE ME?

THE END IS NIG

New York
OCTOBER 21

...UNTIL IT'S TOO LATE.

NO. NOT BOATS.

FINS.

17

RORSCHACH'S JOURNAL. OCTOBER 21ST, 1985 :

SOMEONE TRIED TO KILL VEIDT. PROVES 'MASK KILLER' THEORY. MURDERER IS CLOSING IN.

CHECKED MAILDROP. MESSAGE FROM MOLOCH. CONNECTED PERHAPS?

R-
Call tonight, 11.30 p.m. Have information. URGENT.
Jacobi

NEXT, WENT TO RETRIEVE FACE FROM ALLEY. OUTSIDE UTOPIA, POLICE RESTRAINED A YOUTH ON KT-28S.

HE WAS SCREAMING SOMETHING ABOUT PRESIDENT NIXON. SOMETHING ABOUT BOMBS.

UTOPIA C

THINGS
TO COM

IS EVERYONE BUT ME GOING MAD? OVER 40TH STREET, AN ELEPHANT WAS DRIFTING.

Gunga Diner

BEYOND THAT, UNSEEN, SPY SATELLITES. IF THEY SO MUCH AS NARROW THEIR GLASS EYES, WE SHALL ALL BE DEAD.

THIS RELENTLESS WORLD : THERE IS ONLY ONE SANE RESPONSE TO IT.

THE ALLEYWAY WAS COLD AND DESERTED.

MY THINGS WERE WHERE I'D LEFT THEM.

WAITING FOR ME.

PUTTING THEM ON, I ABANDONED MY DISGUISE AND BECAME MYSELF, FREE FROM FEAR OR WEAKNESS OR LUST.

Oh, how the ghost of you clings...

MY COAT, MY SHOES, MY SPOTLESS GLOVES.

MY FACE.

HAD THREE HOURS BEFORE CALLING ON MOLOCH.

AWAY DOWN ALLEY, HEARD WOMAN SCREAM, FIRST BUBBLING NOTE OF CITY'S EVENING CHORUS.

APPROACHED DISTURBANCE. AN ATTEMPTED RAPE / MUGGING / BOTH.

CLEARED THROAT. THE MAN TURNED AND THERE WAS SOMETHING REWARDING IN HIS EYES.

SOMETIMES, THE NIGHT IS GENEROUS TO ME.

18

DAN, REALLY YOU DON'T KNOW HOW *GRATEFUL* I AM FOR THIS.

AFTER WHERE I *THOUGHT* I WAS GONNA BE SLEEPING TONIGHT, THIS IS LIKE *HEAVEN*.

WELL, YOU KNOW, IT ISN'T MUCH BUT IT SHOULD BE *COMFORTABLE* AND I'M SLEEPING RIGHT DOWN THE HALL IF YOU WAKE UP IN THE NIGHT AND *NEED* ANYTHING.

UH, LIKE *COFFEE*. OR *ASPIRIN*. STUFF LIKE *THAT*.

OH, I'LL BE *FINE*. I'M SO *TIRED* I'M GONNA SLEEP TILL *THURSDAY*. THANKS FOR LOOKING *OUT* FOR ME, DAN. YOU'RE LIKE A BIG *BROTHER*, YOU *KNOW* THAT?

SURE. WELL, GLAD I COULD *HELP*.

GOODNIGHT, LAURIE.

G'NIGHT, DAN.

SWEET DREAMS.

HELL AND DAMNATION.

19

GOOD READERS, KNOW THIS: HADES IS WET. HADES IS LONELY.

TEETH THAT SEEMED TO MOVE INDEPENDENTLY OF THE LIPS TORE AT MY RAFT'S SUPPORTS. TINY PREHISTORIC EYES GLISTENED, SEEMING MAD WITH RAGE EVEN IN REPOSE.

WHATEVER WAS BENEATH MY BOAT COMMENCED A VIOLENT THRASHING, ALMOST SPILLING ME AMONGST THE GNAWING HORRORS.

I CLUNG TO MY MAST AS THE PLATFORM TILTED FURTHER. THE WATER BEGAN TO BOIL WHITE. SOMETHING WAS SURFACING.

HOW SHALL I DESCRIBE IT? IT WAS MASSIVE, LIKE NO SHARK I'D EVER HEARD TELL OF, WITH SKIN NEITHER BLACK NOR WHOLLY WHITE, BUT A PALE AND MOTTLED YELLOW.

FURTHER, IT WAS ENTANGLED IN MY ROPES.

TERRIFIED LEST IT SHOULD RE-SUBMERGE AND DRAG ME WITH IT, I FELL TO MY KNEES CLUTCHING A SPLINTER OF MAST THAT HAD SNAPPED OFF IN MY HAND.

THE SHARK'S STAINED MARBLE EYE LOOKED UP AT ME....

...AND, IN THAT INSTANT, WE KNEW EACH OTHER.

HALF BLIND; HALF DEAD; WHOLLY DERANGED BY AGONY; THE YELLOW LEVIATHAN ATTEMPTED TO SWIM AWAY, DRAGGING MY RAFT IN ITS BLOODY WAKE.

I HUNG ON DESPERATELY, CURSING IN THE BITTER, STINGING SPRAY.

20

THIS GODDAMN PAIN IN THE BUTT RAIN! DON'T IT EVER LET UP?

EVENTUALLY, THE SHARK DIED...

... AND SHORTLY THEREAFTER STOPPED SWIMMING.

WHO NEEDS IT? THIS WHOLE JOB'S LIKE PADDLING AGAINST THE TIDE!

WORKING THE STREETS THESE DAYS TAKES A REAL MENSCH.

MAN, CAB DRIVING'S BUSTING MY NUTS! GIMME A COPY HUSTLER.

HI, JOEY. HOW'S THE PROMETHEAN? STILL BRINGING LIGHT TO THE WORLD?

RELIEF WAS FLEETING, MY PROSPECTS STILL DARK.

WE SURE NEED LIGHT WITH THIS AFGHANISTAN CRAPOLA.

WHO'S THIS MONTH'S CENTERFOLD?

AHH, AFGHANISTAN'S A LONG WAY AWAY.

THE OTHER SHARKS CIRCLED CLOSER THAN WAS COMFORTABLE.

IT'S PAKISTAN OUGHTTA WORRY. THEY'RE WIDE OPEN.

MMM.

WELL, WE'RE ALL PRETTY VULNERABLE.

THEY WORRIED THE MORSELS FROM MY RAFT, WHICH I PRAYED WOULD SATISFY THEM.

THAT REMINDS ME. I GOTTA POSTER MAYBE YOU COULD DISPLAY, SO IT WON'T GET TORN UP.

AFTER EATING, THEY DEPARTED, REPLETE. FOR THE MOMENT, I WAS SAFE.

THAT NIGHT, EATING SHARK, I WOULD HAVE CHUCKLED AT THE INVERSION OF NATURAL ROLES HAD NOT MY PARCHED LAUGHTER SEEMED SO HATEFUL.

GAY WOMEN AGAINST RAPE?

IS THIS A JOKE?

IT'S A BENEFIT GIG. NOW YOU GONNA NAIL IT UP OR AM I GONNA ALTER YOUR LOOKS?

MY RAFT GREW INCREASINGLY GROTESQUE, REFLECTING MY OWN GRADUAL TRANSFORMATION.

PINK TRIANGLE LIVE AT THE

GAY WOMEN AGAINST RAPE BENEFIT CONCERT

WITH SUCH THOUGHTS TO COMFORT ME, I DRIFTED ON, MASTLESS INTO THE DAWN.

"BRINGING LIGHT TO THE WORLD."

MY ASS.

21

Y'KNOW, THE WAY THE WORLD IS TODAY, I GUESS NONE O' THESE *MESSIAHS* AND *ILLUMINATED* TYPES REALLY AMOUNTED TO A WHOLE HILL OF *BEANS*.

THAT'S THE *PHONE*.

WELL, THERE'S *NEVER* BEEN ANY MARKET FOR PEACE AND ENLIGHTENMENT.

HEH. I USED TO *OWN* THE RECORD HAD THIS *SLEEVE* DESIGN.

HANDS OFF. IT'S *EVIDENCE*. INCIDENTALLY, THE *PHONE'S* RINGING.

SURE. Y'KNOW, ALL TODAY I'VE HAD THIS FUNNY FEELING. IT'S LIKE THERE'S SOMETHING IN THE *AIR*...

Gunga Diner

THAT'S *SOUND WAVES*, MAN. THEY'RE COMING FROM THE *PHONE*.

NO, I MEAN, FIRST THAT *KIDDIE MURDER*, THEN SOMEBODY TRIES TO WHACK ADRIAN *VEIDT*. IT'S LIKE THERE'S A *PATTERN, LEADING* SOMEWHERE. IT'S...

STEVE, WILLYA JUST ANSWER THE GODDAMN *PHONE*?

I *MEAN*, I'D DO IT *MYSELF* IF I DIDN'T HAVE ALL THIS *BLAKE CASE* PAPERWORK THAT YOU *FORGOT* ABOUT...

OKAY, OKAY, I'M *ANSWERING* IT.

HELLO? YEAH DETECTIVE FINE *SPEAKING*.

A *TIP*? SURE. WHAT'S YOUR *NAME*..?

NO NAME, HUH? OKAY, THAT'S *ACCEPTABLE*. SO WHAT DO YOU *HAVE*?

RAW *WHAT*? DID YOU SAY *SHARK*? *RAW SHARK*? WHY SHOULD I WANT TO KNOW WHERE TO *FIND*...

BLAKE E. 801108

...RAW SHARK.

OKAY. YEAH, I KNOW WHO WE'RE TALKING ABOUT. NOW WHERE..? OKAY. GOT THAT. WHEN WILL HE *BE* THERE? IS HE..?

YEAH. UNDERSTOOD. WE'RE ON OUR WAY. 'BYE.

STEVE, YOU'RE *KIDDING*! THAT WASN'T ABOUT..?

DAMN *RIGHT* IT WAS. AFTER ALL THESE YEARS, SOMEBODY JUST HANDED US THAT BASTARD'S *HEAD* ON A *PLATE*.

C'MON, MAN. WE GOT A *DATE*. LET'S GO IGNORE SOME *RED LIGHTS*.

22

ELEVEN THIRTY.

GOOD EVENING, JACOBI.

GOT YOUR NOTE. BEEN WONDERING WHY YOU WANTED TO SEE ME.

HEAR ABOUT THAT?

THE COMEDIAN, DR. MANHATTAN, OZYMANDIAS... SOMEBODY'S KILLING MASKS, JACOBI. SOMEBODY WANTS US DEAD.

MAYBE SOME OLD ENEMY. MAYBE SOMEONE YOU MET IN PRISON.

BEEN RUNNING THROUGH NAMES.

WAS IT UNDERBOSS? WAS IT JIMMY THE GIMMICK OR THE KING OF SKIN? LOT OF QUESTIONS. NO ANSWERS...

MAYBE YOU CAN ENLIGHTEN ME.

RORSCHACH?

24

THIS IS THE POLICE, RORSCHACH.

WE KNOW YOU'RE IN THERE.

IT'S ALL OVER.

NOW, IF THERE'S ANYBODY IN THERE WITH YOU, I WANT YOU TO SEND THEM OUT FIRST UNHARMED...

NO.

NO, NO, NO.

...THEN YOU FOLLOW THEM WITH BOTH HANDS CLEARLY VISIBLE. I'M GOING TO GIVE YOU THIRTY SECONDS...

FRAMED. SET UP. WALKED RIGHT INTO IT.

STUPID STUPID STUPID.

...AFTER THAT I CAN'T MAKE ANY PROMISES FOR YOUR SAFETY.

C'MON, RORSCHACH. LET'S MAKE THIS A NICE CLEAN SURRENDER.

HEHN. NEVER. NEVER SURRENDER.

TIME'S TICKING AWAY, RORSCHACH. LISTEN, WE'VE GOT MEN OUT FRONT AND BACK, WE'VE GOT GUNS AND TEARGAS, WE GOT A WHOLE LOT OF HARDWARE HERE.

WEAPONS. YES...

FIFTEEN SECONDS.

TEN SECONDS. RORSCHACH, YOU'RE MAKING THIS TOUGH ON YOURSELF. FIVE. FOUR...

OKAY. THAT'S IT. TIME'S UP AND WE'RE COMING IN. I HOPE YOU'RE READY.

WHEN YOU ARE.

25

HELLO IN THERE?

JEEZ, HE BETTER *BE* HERE. IF THAT WAS A *BUM* TIP...

YOU SEE THAT *LOCK*, MAN? HE'S *BEEN* HERE ALRIGHT.

WE'LL TAKE THE GROUND FLOOR FIRST AND WORK *UP*.

AND *REMEMBER*, HERE BE *TYGERS*. WATCH OUT HE DOESN'T ...

YAAAAAAGH!

OH, SHIT...

I'M ON *FIRE*! OH, *GOD*, I'M *BURNING*!

WATCH OUT! WATCH OUT, HE'S TORCHING THE *STAIRS* ...

OH, CHRIST, WHAT *HAPPENED*? GET SOME WATER FROM THE *KITCHEN* AND PUT THIS *OUT*!

GET *AFTER* HIM. THERE'S NO WAY *OUT*!

OH, JEEZ.

HEY! WE NEED MORE *WATER* UP HERE! AND WHERE'S OUR GODDAMNED *BACKUP*?

WHERE *IS* HE? ALL THIS *SMOKE*...

HE'S ⌐HUFF⌐ HE'S JUST AHEAD ON THE ⌐HURRF⌐ ON THE THIRD FLOOR.

DAMMIT, ARE THEY FOLLOWING US, OR *WHAT*?

THEY'RE RIGHT BEHIND US. OKAY... OKAY, HE'S UP HERE SOME- WHERE...

MAN, I DON'T *LIKE* THIS. THE GUY'S AN *ANIMAL*...

26

...BUT AT LEAST ACCORDING TO THE **FACT SHEETS** HE DON'T USUALLY GO ARMED. HE...

AAAA! JESUS GOD, MY EYES!

HELP ME, MAN. I CAN'T SEE...

GET OUT OF THE WAY! GET OUT OF THE WAY, I DON'T HAVE ROOM TO...

...SHOOT...

CHARLIE, WHAT'S **HAPPENING**? MY **EYES**, MAN. MY EYES...

WILLIS AND GREAVES ARE **HURT**. FORGET THE **FIRE** AND FOR GODSAKES GET **UP** HERE!

AAHUH.

AAAHH-HUHG.

HE'S IN THE **BEDROOM**! WE'VE GOT HIM!

CHARLIE? IS CHARLIE HURT? I CAN'T **SEE**. WHAT'S GOING **ON**?

WHAT'S GOING ON UP THERE, STEVE? THAT WAS SOMEONE **SCREAMING**...

IT'S OKAY. IT'S OKAY, WE'VE GOT HIM TRAPPED. WE **MUST** HAVE.

IT'S A **DEAD** END.

HE CAN'T GET **OUT**.

RRAAAARRL

27

Tyger, Tyger
burning bright,
In the forests
of the night,
What immortal hand or eye
Could frame thy fearful symmetry?
—William Blake

A

s discussed in our last chapter, the close of the 1950s saw E.C.'s line of Pirate titles dominating the marketplace from a near unassailable position. The brief surge of anti-comic book sentiment in the mid-fifties, while it could conceivably have damaged E.C. as a company, had instead come to nothing and left them stronger as a result. With the government of the day coming down squarely on the side of comic books in an effort to protect the image of certain comic book-inspired agents in their employ, it was as if the comic industry had suddenly been given the blessing of Uncle Sam himself—or at least J. Edgar Hoover. Unsurprisingly, as one of the few companies to anticipate the coming massive boom in pirate-related material, E.C. flourished and their hold upon the field remained unchallenged.

Until May, 1960. That date saw the first publication of an extraordinary new title from National Comics, now DC. The book was called 'Tales of the Black Freighter', and while its sales never

The following is reprinted from chapter five of the Treasure Island Treasury Of Comics (Flint Editions, New York, 1984) with permission of the author and publishers.

science fiction and horror to the different atmospheric demands of pirate stories than many of his E.C. contemporaries, he was perhaps the best respected artist in a rapidly burgeoning field, and fans awaited the first issue of TALES OF THE BLACK FREIGHTER with relish.

Nor were they disappointed. The first issue is classic Orlando. The script—by then-newcomer Max Shea—while sturdy enough, is cliched and predictable in comparison with the work that Shea did later, and in that first issue was easily outshone by the darkly compelling majesty of Orlando's textures, shadows and faces.

The story served as an introduction to the vessel that lent the book its title, and which was itself apparently borrowed from a ship referred to in Brecht and Weill's 'THREEPENNY OPERA'. In that first story, three men with different paths through life have all been led to the same dockside tavern in search of work. The place is deserted save for a shadowy innkeeper who serves them ale in silence and the large, dark figure of a sea captain who sits at the next table and listens to them recount their stories to each other.

The stories are recounted as small, self-contained tales within the larger narrative that frames them, and are all effective if predictable twist-ending yarns that reveal the various tellers to be utterly unprincipled and worthless creatures capable of almost any act of treachery. Overhearing their stories, the sea captain says he is impressed and offers them passage upon his ship. By the time the men are aboard the ship and have noticed the dreadful, deathly smell that seems to exude from the ship's timbers, it is too late. The three hapless sailors learn that the ship is a vessel from Hell itself to take on board the souls of evil men so that they may walk its blood-stained decks for all eternity.

The identity of the captain is never made clear—is he meant to be Satan, or is he himself a victim of the ship? But this scarcely matters when confronted with Orlando's breathtaking rendition. From the marvelous scene in the first man's story where two ghouls fight to the death with shovels in

A MAN ON FIFTEEN DEAD MEN'S CHESTS

quite topped those of the E.C. giants such as PIRACY and BUCCANEERS, in terms of critical acclaim and influence upon later books of the same type, TALES OF THE BLACK FREIGHTER made an impression upon the comic book landscape that remains to this day. Indeed, with DC comics currently reprinting the first classic thirty issues of the title and apparently meeting with considerable success, it would seem that its impact remains undiluted despite the quarter century that has elapsed since the original publication.

What exactly was it that made TALES OF THE BLACK FREIGHTER so special? Despite the fact that nowadays most people are attracted by the controversy surrounding the later issues of the book, it should be remembered that this title was very popular from the outset. So: What was it that fascinated all those thousands of readers in the first place?

Well, to begin with, it was almost certainly the artwork of Joe Orlando, who drew the entire book from its first issue through issue nine, with the exception of GALAPAGOS JONES, a rather insipid back-up feature that lasted until issue six. Orlando, having been successfully tempted away from his well-received run of 'SARGASSO SEA STORIES' in E.C.'s PIRACY by National editor Julius Schwartz, was regarded as a star amongst pirate artists, and a prize catch. Having adapted more smoothly from

the worm-infested tunnels beneath a churchyard, right through the haunting and evocative final shots of the horrible black ship drifting away into the white mist, the art is breathtaking, conveying a tangible sense of doom and evil even in those places where the writing fails to do so.

With the issues that followed, Orlando's art continued to shine while the scripts supplied by Shea

JOE ORLANDO, CIRCA 1953

also began to gradually improve in quality as the writer became used to the medium. With rapidly increasing confidence, Shea began attempting ideas for stories which at the time seemed wildly radical and innovative. The third issue's story, "Between Breaths", is told from the viewpoint of a man who is drowning, alternating between memories of his past life as they flash before his bulging eyes and horrific descriptions of what it is like to drown. Even read today, the story induces an almost tangible sense of suffocation, so that finishing the story and putting the book down is actually a relief. The closing images, with a multitude of dead and drowned men walking across the ocean bed towards the anchor rope of the Black

Freighter which they climb to take their rightful positions on board the ship, remain some of Orlando's most haunting work on the series.

By issue five, reader reaction was obviously in favor of the title, and the praise seemed to be divided equally between Orlando and Shea. According to insiders, receiving fan mail for the first time in his life had an adverse effect upon the writer, who began to see himself as the driving force of the book, becoming increasingly resentful of Orlando's clearly important role and harassing the artist with impossibly detailed panel descriptions and endless carping requests for revisions of artwork already drawn.

Despite growing friction within the creative team, both lasted on TALES OF THE BLACK FREIGHTER until the ninth issue, when Orlando asked Schwartz to take him off the book, citing the ego of the writer as being the major factor in his decision. During those nine issues they crafted many memorable stories together, including the most famous of all, "The Shanty of Edward Teach", in issue seven. In this story, narrated in rhyme by the dead pirate Edward Teach (otherwise known as Blackbeard), we first begin to see the dark and pessimistic moral sensibilities showing that were later to form most of Shea's work on the series. These are more than adequately matched by Orlando's artwork, and there can be few readers of that period who will forget the heart-stopping close-up shot of Blackbeard, portrayed as violent and leering evil incarnate, in which he seems to look out at the reader and remind them that their own position is perhaps no more noble than Teach's own: "I tread a lurching timber world, a reeking salt-caked hell; and yet, perhaps, no worse a world than yours, where bishops stroll through charnel yards with pomanders to smell; where vile men thrive and love crawls on all fours."

After Orlando's departure, the art for the series was taken over by a relatively unknown but supremely capable artist named Walt Feinberg, previously best known for his work upon numerous western titles where he would often provide excellent fill-in issues that nevertheless seemed

EAST, ACROSS THE NIGHT SEAS.

EAST, BORNE ON THE NAKED BACKS OF MURDERED MEN.

to go unnoticed when slotted in between the work of great western comic artists such as Gil Kane and Alex Toth. Despite having Orlando's early work on the series to live up to, on TALES OF THE BLACK FREIGHTER, Feinberg was finally given a chance to shine. For some reason, there are few incidents on record relating friction between Feinberg and Shea, and indeed the two of them continued to work together on the book until issue thirty-one, at which point Shea quit (perhaps the moody and temperamental writer was making a deliberate effort to control his behavior, having been taught an expensive lesson by Orlando's departure).

In any event the next twenty or so issues of the book became every bit as much instant classics as the Orlando issues had, a fact not hindered by Shea's gradually developing skill as a writer.

The stories that came from his pen in this period are uniformly dark and sinister, balancing metaphysical terrors against an unnerving sense of reality, particularly when applied to matters of mortality or sexuality. Readers who came to the series expecting a good rousing tale of swashbuckling were either repulsed or fascinated by what were often perverse and blackly lingering comments upon the human condition. Tales such as "The Figurehead", which deal unflinchingly with male homosexuality, and the harrowing "Marooned" spring most readily to mind.

In "Marooned", a two-part story occupying issues twenty-three and twenty-four of the book's run, we see Feinberg and Shea at their blood-freezing best. Unusual in that it is a one-character story narrated mostly in captions, "Marooned" tells the story of a young mariner whose vessel is wrecked by the Black Freighter before it can return to its hometown and warn it of the hell-ship's approach. Cast adrift on an uninhabited island with only his dead shipmates for company, we experience the frantic mariner's torment at the knowledge that while he is trapped on his island, the bestial crew of the Freighter are surely bearing down upon his town, his home, his wife and his children. Driven by his burning desire to avert this calamity, we see the mariner finally

escape from the island by what may be one of the most striking and horrific devices thus far in pirate comic books: digging up the recently buried and gas-bloated corpses of his shipmates, the mariner lashes them together and uses them as the floats on an improvised raft on which he hopes to reach the mainland (hence the title of this chapter.) On reaching the mainland safely

upon his horrific craft we see the increasingly distraught and dishevelled mariner trying desperately to reach his home, even resorting to murder to acquire a horse for himself. In the final scenes, thanks to the skillful interplay of text and pictures, we see that the mariner, though he has escaped from his island, is in the end marooned from the rest of humanity in a much more terrible fashion.

Problems set in for the book around issue twenty-five, when Shea began his controversial

TALES OF THE BLACK FREIGHTER

run of issues based around the contents of plundered books in the library of the Freighter's captain, including banned tomes supposedly originally headed for eternal suppression within the vaults of Vatican city when stolen en route by the pirates. Described as 'blatantly pornographic', four of the projected five stories were rejected by DC, which brought about the argument in which Shea quit the book and comics as well, going on to write such classic novels as the twice-filmed FOGDANCING.

At the time of this writing, Shea's whereabouts are unknown. In circumstances as strange as those in any of his stories, the writer apparently vanished from his home one morning and has not been seen since, although police are continuing their inquiries. In his wake he leaves not only a string of excellent novels and screenplays, but also an exemplary run of pirate stories which today fetch mint prices of almost a thousand dollars according to the Overstreet Guide. Stories there to be rediscovered and reexamined, like so many of the fascinating sunken treasures lurking just beneath the surface of this fabulous and compelling genre.

CHAPTER VI

FROM THE NOTES OF DR. MALCOLM LONG, OCTOBER 25TH, 1985.

OKAY, NOW I GUESS YOU KNOW WHAT *THIS* IS...

FIRST INTERVIEW WITH *KOVACS* ...HE'S EVEN MORE DISTURBED THAN I'D HEARD, BUT I'M *OPTIMISTIC*. A SUCCESS HERE COULD MAKE MY *REPUTATION*.

I WANT YOU TO *LOOK* AT IT AND TELL ME WHAT YOU SEE.

HE'S VERY *WITHDRAWN*, WITH NO EXPRESSION IN EITHER FACE OR VOICE. GETTING A RESPONSE IS OFTEN *DIFFICULT*.

WILL YOU *LOOK* AT IT, WALTER?

WILL YOU *DO* THAT FOR ME?

PHYSICALLY, HE'S FASCINATINGLY UGLY. I COULD STARE AT HIM FOR HOURS...EXCEPT THAT HE STARES *BACK*, WHICH I FIND *UNCOMFORTABLE*. HE NEVER SEEMS TO *BLINK*.

NEVERTHELESS, I'M CONVINCED I CAN HELP HIM. *NO* PROBLEM IS BEYOND THE GRASP OF A GOOD *PSYCHOANALYST*, AND THEY TELL ME I'M *VERY* GOOD. GOOD WITH *PEOPLE*.

WELL WALTER? WHAT *IS* IT?

WHAT CAN YOU *SEE*?

A PRETTY BUTTERFLY.

HIS RESPONSES TO THE *RORSCHACH BLOT TESTS* WERE SURPRISINGLY BRIGHT AND POSITIVE AND HEALTHY. I REALLY THINK HE MIGHT BE GETTING *BETTER*.

I JUST WISH HE WASN'T SO *INTENSE*.

1

THE ABYSS GAZES ALSO

HIS FULL NAME IS *WALTER JOSEPH KOVACS*, BORN 1940. MOTHER'S NAME: SYLVIA JOANNA KOVACS, FORMERLY SYLVIA GLICK. HIS FATHER'S NAME IS UNKNOWN.

LET'S TRY *ANOTHER*, SHALL WE?

HE'S 5'6" TALL AND WEIGHS 140 LBS. FOR HIS *AGE*, HE'S IN EXCELLENT PHYSICAL SHAPE DESPITE A LOT OF BRUISES AND LACERATIONS MOSTLY SUSTAINED DURING HIS *ARREST*.

HOW ABOUT *THIS* ONE?

THE POLICE HAVE BEATEN ON HIM PRETTY BADLY. DURING THE POLICE STRIKE OF '77 HE MADE SEVERAL INFLAMMATORY ANTI-COP STATEMENTS, AND THEY'VE NEVER FORGOTTEN.

C'MON, WALTER...DO IT FOR *ME*, HUH?

THE *COPS* DON'T LIKE HIM; THE *UNDERWORLD* DOESN'T LIKE HIM; *NOBODY* LIKES HIM. I'VE NEVER MET ANYONE QUITE SO ALIENATED. HOW ON EARTH DID HE *GET* LIKE THIS?

WALTER?

GOOD. THAT'S VERY *GOOD*.

OKAY, WALTER, NOW I WANT YOU TO TELL ME WHAT'S ON THE CARD...

2

3

I said *FORGET* it. HERE'S FIVE BUCKS. IT'S MORE'N YOU'RE *WORTH.*

FIVE...?

FIVE BUCKS? YOU LOUSY *BASTARD!* DON'T YOU *DARE* WALK OUT ON ME. DON'T YOU *DARE!*

OUTTA MY *WAY*, RETARD.

M-MOM?

MOM, I'M *SORRY.* I, I THOUGHT HE WAS *HURTING* YOU. I THOUGHT ...

YOU LITTLE *SHIT!*

OOAH!

YOU KNOW WHAT YOU JUST *COST* ME, YOU UGLY LITTLE *BASTARD?*

I SHOULDA LISTENED TO EVERYBODY *ELSE!* I SHOULDA HAD THE *ABORTION!*

AAAAAAH! MOMME*EEE...*

AOH

AAAHAH

AAA

WELL, WALTER?

WHAT DO YOU MAKE OF IT?

4

SOME NICE FLOWERS.

WONDERFUL. WALTER, I'M VERY *PLEASED* WITH YOUR *RESPONSES* THIS AFTERNOON, AND I WANT YOU TO *KNOW* THAT.

I REALLY THINK THERE'S *HOPE*, WALTER. DON'T *YOU*?

UHH... WELL, OKAY, WALTER, I THINK THAT'S *ENOUGH* FOR TODAY...

THE *GUARDS* WILL TAKE YOU BACK TO YOUR, UH, YOUR *QUARTERS* NOW.

I'LL SEE YOU *TOMORROW*.

HEY! HEY *RORSCHACH*! YOU *DEAD*, MAN...

YEAH, BUT YOU'RE GONNA BE OUR *WOMAN* FIRST, RORSCHACH. HOWD'YA LIKE *THAT*?

GONNA *CUT* YOU, SISSY. GONNA HOLD YOU DOWN AN' PEEL YOU LIKE A *GRAPE*...

RORSCHACH...

TICK IT IN IL YOU SCREAM CUT YOUR THRO RORSCHACH

YOU'RE GONNA *BEG*. YOU'RE GONNA MAKE IN YOUR *GRAYS*, MAN...

ROR-SCHACH

'RE *DEAD* ORSCHACH...

5

UGLIER WITHOUT THE MASK

RORSCHACH

YOU GOT A *MOTHER*? SHE'S *DEAD*. YOU GOT *KIDS*? THEY'RE DEAD. A SISTER? *DEAD...*

MAKE YOU BLEED AN' BLEED AN' BLEED... ROR-SCHACH

YOU GOT A *DOG*? IT'S...

RORSCHACH

AN' BLEED AN' BLEED AN'BLEED AN' COLD MEAT COLD MEAT COL...

RORSCHACH

HATE YOU, RORSCHACH

UT YOUR TONGUE OUT AND SHOVE IT U...

BONE YOU LIKE A *FISH* AND THEN I'LL

ROR-SCHACH!

IN YOUR MOUTH AND THEN I'LL

DEAD, RORSCHACH

INTO A RAG AND THEN TIE IT ROUND YOUR EYES AND THEN I'LL

RORSCHACH

SOONER OR *LATER*, RORSCHACH

STINK, RORSCHACH

OFF YOUR CLOTHES AND ROLL YOU IN BROKEN PEPSI BOTTLES

AN' BLEED AN' BLEED AN' BLEED AN' BLEED

...TALKING TO *YOU*, RUNT.

YEAH, WHATSA MATTER? YA *DEEF* OR *WHAT*?

I...I HAVE TO *GET* SOMETHING. FROM THE *STORE*. FOR MY MOTHER...

HA HA HA. *I* GOT SOMETHIN' I COULD GIVE YOUR MOMMA.

SURE. WHY NOT? EVERY-BODY *ELSE* DOES, WAY I HEAR IT...

IS THAT *RIGHT*, KID? IS YOUR MOM A *HOO-ER*?

SURE SHE IS. HE'S GONNA FIX US *UP* WITH HER, AIN'T THAT *RIGHT*, WHORESON?

LET ME *BY*! I HAVE TO GO TO...

YOU DON'T HAVE TO GO *NO PLACE*...

...WHORESON.

6

EHHAHAHA! LOOK AT 'IM...

OOK AT 'IM *NUTHIN'*, JU' SMELL HI'

WHORE-SON.

PROBABLY GOT *COOTIES*. PROBABLY GOT *DISEASES*.

EHHAHAHAHA!

YOU GOT ANY *DISEASES*, WHORESON?

WHORESON.

OUGHTTA GIVE THE LITTLE BASTARD AN *EXAMINATION*

EHHAHAHAHA!

IT, HE COULD HAVE ALL KINDA *DISEA*

WHORE-SON.

IKE IN THE ARMY. MY *DAD* SEZ THAT...

OKAY, WHORESON, GET YA *PANTS* DOWN. WE GONNA GIVE YA AN EXAMI-...ATION.

HEY, RICHIE, *WATCH* HIM, HE'S...

HUH? YOU LITTLE SON OF...

EEEEE EEEEYEEE EEEEIGH

EEEEEE! EEEEEE-EEIIIGH!

AAAAA! GET *OFF*! GET *OFFA* ME!

JESUS CHRIST, WILLYA LOOKIT *THAT*...

OH, *GOD*, LOOK, THAT FILTHY LITTLE *ANIMAL*. LOOK HE'S...

OKAY! OKAY! THAT'S *ENOUGH*! THAT'S...

PULL HIM *OFF*! FOR GOD'S SAKE SOMEBODY PULL HIM OFF BEFORE

AAAAAAA! OH, *GOD*! NO NO NO NO NO

HOLD HIS *ARMS*! HOLD HIS *ARMS*!

HTTA BE LOCKED *UP*. SEE HIM BITING THAT

LIKE AN *ANIMAL*. LIKE A *MAD DOG*...

BLAME THE *PARENTS*.

EXACTLY LIKE A MAD *DOG*...

IN 1951, HE ATTACKED AN OLDER CHILD, PARTIALLY BLINDING HIM WITH A LIGHTED CIGARETTE. HE WAS TEN YEARS OLD.

7

ONCE HIS *HOME LIFE* HAD BEEN INVESTIGATED, HE WAS REMOVED FROM HIS MOTHER'S CUSTODY AND PUT INTO *CARE.* AWAY FROM HER, HE SEEMED TO *IMPROVE.*

EXCELLING AT SCHOOLWORK, KOVACS GREW INTO A *BRIGHT* BUT UNUSUALLY *QUIET* CHILD.

EVEN IN 1956, WHEN INFORMED OF HIS MOTHER'S BRUTAL MURDER, HE RESTRICTED HIS COMMENTS TO *ONE WORD:*

MAL?

"GOOD."

MAL, IT'S *LATE.* ARE YOU DONE WITH THIS *RORSCHACH* CASE YET?

NOT RORSCHACH. WALTER *KOVACS.* RORSCHACH'S AN UNHEALTHY *FANTASY* PERSONALITY. Y'KNOW, HE WOULDN'T *ANSWER* TO ANYTHING ELSE DURING HIS *BAIL HEARING?*

ON THE *NEWS* HE SOUNDED *FRIGHTENING.* DON'T GET TOO *WRAPPED UP* IN THIS ONE, MAL. IT MIGHT RUIN YOUR *CHEERFUL DISPOSITION.*

GLORIA, I'M TOO *FAT* AND *CONTENTED* FOR ANYTHING TO RUIN MY *DISPOSITION...*

...ALTHOUGH SOME OF THE STUFF ABOUT HIS *EARLY LIFE,* FANTASIES ABOUT A FATHER HE NEVER *KNEW...*

SHH. LEAVE IT AT THE *OFFICE.* YOU GOT A NICE LIFE, *I* GOT A NICE LIFE. NOBODY ELSE *MATTERS.*

I GUESS *NOT.* IT'S JUST THAT HE'S *WITHDRAWN* AND *DEPRESSED,* AND I REALLY FEEL I CAN GUIDE HIM *OUT* OF IT.

WELL, IF ANYBODY CAN, IT'S *YOU...*

YOU'RE THE *NICEST,* MOST *POSITIVE* PERSON I *KNOW.* THAT'S WHY YOU GOTTA LOOK *AFTER* YOURSELF. I MEAN, ARE YOU *SURE* YOU'RE *SAFE* WITH THIS *KOVACS* GUY?

DON'T WORRY. WHILE HE'S AT *SING-SING* AWAITING *TRIAL* HE'S UNDER *HEAVY GUARD.* HE'S NO *THREAT.*

NOT ANY *MORE.*

WELL, LET'S HOPE NOT. NOW C'MON... FORGET WORK. IT'S A *BEAUTIFUL NIGHT...*

"...LET'S SEE IF WE CAN MAKE IT LAST *FOREVER.*"

8

GOOD *MORNING,* WALTER. TODAY, I'D LIKE...

≷HAAA-HHHORRM≷

SORRY, LATE NIGHT. TODAY, I'D LIKE TO DO SOME-THING *DIFFERENT.* FRANKLY, WALTER, I'D LIKE TO *TALK.*

I'D LIKE TO TALK ABOUT *RORSCHACH.*

WILL YOU *DO THAT FOR ME,* WALTER?

WILL YOU TELL ME ABOUT *RORSCHACH?*

YOU KEEP CALLING ME *WALTER.*

I DON'T LIKE YOU.

UHH...

YOU...YOU DON'T *LIKE* ME. ALRIGHT. ALRIGHT.

WUR, WHY *IS* THAT, EXACTLY?

FAT. WEALTHY. THINK YOU UNDERSTAND *PAIN.*

I'LL TELL YOU SOME-THING, DOCTOR.

I'LL TELL YOU ABOUT *RORSCHACH.*

9

"1956. AGED 16. LEFT CHILDREN'S HOME. BECAME UNSKILLED MANUAL WORKER, GARMENT INDUSTRY.

"JOB BEARABLE BUT UNPLEASANT. HAD TO HANDLE FEMALE CLOTHING.

"1962. SPECIAL ORDER FOR DRESS IN NEW DR. MANHATTAN SPIN-OFF FABRIC. VISCOUS FLUIDS BETWEEN TWO LAYERS LATEX, HEAT AND PRESSURE SENSITIVE.

"CUSTOMER YOUNG GIRL, ITALIAN NAME. NEVER COLLECTED ORDER. SAID DRESS LOOKED UGLY.

"WRONG. NOT UGLY AT ALL.

"BLACK AND WHITE. MOVING. CHANGING SHAPE... BUT NOT MIXING. NO GRAY.

"VERY, VERY BEAUTIFUL.

"NOBODY WANTED IT. MEANT FOR ME. TOOK IT HOME. LEARNED TO CUT IT USING HEATED IMPLEMENTS TO RESEAL LATEX.

"WHEN I HAD CUT IT ENOUGH, IT DIDN'T LOOK LIKE A WOMAN ANYMORE."

SOON, BECAME BORED. FABRIC HAD NO USE. LEFT IT IN TRUNK. FORGOT ABOUT IT.

TWO YEARS PASSED. MARCH, 1964. STOPPED AT NEWSSTAND ON WAY TO WORK, BOUGHT PAPER. THERE SHE WAS. FRONT PAGE.

"WOMAN WHO'D ORDERED SPECIAL DRESS.

"KITTY GENOVESE.

New York Gazet

WOMAN KILLE
WHILE NEIGHE
LOOK ON

"I'M SURE THAT WAS THE WOMAN'S NAME.

"RAPED. TORTURED. KILLED. HERE. IN NEW YORK. OUTSIDE HER OWN APARTMENT BUILDING.

"ALMOST FORTY NEIGHBORS HEARD SCREAMS. NOBODY DID ANYTHING. NOBODY CALLED COPS. SOME OF THEM EVEN WATCHED. DO YOU UNDERSTAND?

"SOME OF THEM EVEN WATCHED.

"I KNEW WHAT PEOPLE WERE, THEN, BEHIND ALL THE EVASIONS, ALL THE SELF-DECEPTION. ASHAMED FOR HUMANITY, I WENT HOME. I TOOK THE REMAINS OF HER UNWANTED DRESS..."

...AND MADE A FACE THAT I COULD BEAR TO LOOK AT IN THE MIRROR.

10

A FACE. I SEE.

WALTER, IS WHAT HAPPENED TO *KITTY GENOVESE* REALLY PROOF THAT THE WHOLE OF *MANKIND* IS *ROTTEN*?

I THINK YOU'VE BEEN *CONDITIONED* WITH A *NEGATIVE* WORLD VIEW. THERE ARE *GOOD* PEOPLE, TOO, LIKE...

LIKE *YOU*?

ME? OH, *WELL*, I WOULDN'T SAY *THAT*. I...

NO. YOU JUST *THINK* IT. THINK YOU'RE 'GOOD PEOPLE.'

WHY ARE YOU SPENDING SO MUCH TIME WITH *ME*, DOCTOR?

UH...WELL, BECAUSE I *CARE* ABOUT YOU, AND BECAUSE I WANT TO MAKE YOU *WELL*...

OTHER PEOPLE, DOWN IN CELLS. BEHAVIOR MORE EXTREME THAN MINE.

YOU DON'T SPEND ANY TIME WITH *THEM*...

...BUT THEN, THEY'RE NOT FAMOUS. WON'T GET YOUR NAME IN THE JOURNALS.

YOU DON'T WANT TO MAKE ME WELL. JUST WANT TO KNOW WHAT MAKES ME SICK.

YOU'LL FIND OUT.

HAVE PATIENCE, DOCTOR.

YOU'LL FIND OUT.

FROM THE NOTES OF DR. MALCOLM LONG, OCTOBER 26TH, 1985.

OF COURSE, WHAT WE HAVE HERE IS A CLASSIC CASE OF MISDIRECTED AGGRESSION.

KOVACS HATED HIS MOTHER. AFTER HER DEATH, HE NEEDED SOMEWHERE TO PUT THE ANGER, AND SO HE CHOSE THE CRIMINAL FRATERNITY.

THE FLIMSY STORY ABOUT KITTY GENOVESE IS OBVIOUSLY THERE TO JUSTIFY HIS BEHAVIOR TO HIMSELF.

IT'S PERFECTLY SIMPLE. CASE SOLVED.

" YOU'LL FIND OUT."

I WONDER WHAT HE MEANT?

11

LATER: THE DEPUTY WARDEN JUST CALLED. APPARENTLY, KOVACS WAS INVOLVED IN AN INCIDENT TODAY, JUST AFTER HE'D SEEN ME. IT HAPPENED DURING LUNCH, IN THE CANTEEN...

RORSCHACH...

HEY, RORSCHACH...YOU'RE PRETTY *FAMOUS*, RIGHT?

BOY, Y'KNOW, I'D SURE LIKE YOUR *AUTO-GRAPH*.

I GOT MY AUTOGRAPH BOOK RIGHT HERE IN MY *POCKET*...

IT'S NOTCHED UP QUITE A FEW *FAMOUS* NAMES OVER THE YEARS...

...AND I'D SURE LIKE TO ADD YOU TO THE *LIST*.

HEY! HEY, DON'T *TOUCH!* WHAT ARE YOU DOI...

12

THE GUARDS INTERVENED, DRAGGING KOVACS AWAY TO SOLITARY AND THE OTHER MAN TO THE PRISON HOSPITAL.

ACCORDING TO THE DEPUTY WARDEN, HIS BURNS WERE HORRIFIC. HOT COOKING FAT... I DON'T LIKE TO THINK ABOUT IT.

AS THEY DRAGGED HIM AWAY, RORSCHACH SPOKE TO THE OTHER INMATES.

HE SAID "NONE OF YOU UNDERSTAND. *I'M* NOT LOCKED UP IN HERE WITH *YOU*. *YOU'RE* LOCKED UP IN HERE WITH *ME*."

MY EARLIER OPTIMISM WAS OBVIOUSLY UNFOUNDED. HE'S GETTING WORSE.

SO AM I. JUST READ BACK WHAT I'VE WRITTEN ABOVE. THE SIXTH LINE DOWN SHOULD READ "KOVACS SPOKE TO THE OTHER INMATES."

KOVACS.

NOT RORSCHACH.

MAL? YOU'RE *NEVER* GONNA SLEEP WITH ALL THAT *COFFEE* INSIDE YOU.

OH. HI, GLORIA. ACTUALLY, I WASN'T PLANNING ON SLEEPING JUST YET.

THIS KOVACS CASE. YOU KNOW ...REQUIRES A LOT OF *ATTENTION*...

REMEMBER LAST *NIGHT*, MAL? WHEN *I* REQUIRED ATTENTION?

GLORIA, *PLEASE!* THEN WAS *THEN*, NOW IS *NOW*...

...AND FRANKLY I THINK IT'S UNFAIR OF YOU TO BRING UP *SEX* WHEN YOU KNOW I NEED TO *WORK*.

OH. WELL, MAYBE I JUST SOMETIMES NOTICE HOW OFTEN YOU BRING UP *WORK* WHEN YOU KNOW I NEED *SEX*.

GOOD NIGHT, MAL.

WAIT! GLORIA, WHAT DO YOU *MEAN?* COME *BACK* HERE. WE CAN *TALK*...

"YOU'RE LOCKED UP IN HERE WITH ME," HE SAID.

HE'S RIGHT.

ABSOLUTELY RIGHT.

13

ALRIGHT, ROR...

ALRIGHT, WALTER...THIS AFTERNOON I WANT TO PICK UP WHERE WE LEFT OFF...

AFTER THE MURDER OF KITTY GENOVESE, YOU DECIDED TO VENT YOUR HOSTILITY UPON THE UNDER-WORLD...

MAKING A MASK FOR YOURSELF, YOU DECIDED TO BECOME RORSCHACH AND...

DON'T BE STUPID.

I WASN'T RORSCHACH THEN.

THEN I WAS JUST KOVACS.

KOVACS PRETENDING TO BE RORSCHACH.

"BEING RORSCHACH TAKES CERTAIN KIND OF INSIGHT. BACK THEN, JUST THOUGHT I WAS RORSCHACH. VERY NAIVE. VERY YOUNG.

"VERY SOFT."

SOFT? HOW DO YOU MEAN?

SOFT ON SCUM. TOO YOUNG TO KNOW ANY BETTER. MOLLY-CODDLED THEM.

"LET THEM LIVE."

AS OPPOSED TO MR. JACOBI AND THE OTHER MURDERS YOU'RE CHARGED WITH, PRESUMABLY.

WELL, LOOKING AT YOUR FILE, THERE'S NO RECORD OF SERIOUS VIOLENCE AGAINST CRIMINALS BEFORE 1975...

LIKE I SAY. SOFT.

KOVACS, W.

"HADN'T REALIZED THE STAKES WE WERE PLAYING FOR BACK THEN.

"ALL OF US...ME, MY FRIENDS: ALL SOFT."

YOU HAVE FRIENDS?

14

KOVACS HAD FRIENDS. OTHER MEN IN COSTUMES. ALL KOVACS EVER WAS: MAN IN A COSTUME.

NOT RORSCHACH.

NOT RORSCHACH AT ALL.

"IN 1965, WORKED WITH NITE OWL BRINGING STREET GANGS UNDER CONTROL. TACKLED THE BIG FIGURE TOGETHER. BROUGHT DOWN UNDERBOSS TOGETHER. GOOD TEAM.

"UNTIL HE GOT SOFT, LIKE REST.

"UNTIL HE QUIT."

NO STAYING POWER. NONE OF THEM.

EXCEPT COMEDIAN. MET HIM IN 1966. FORCEFUL PERSONALITY. DIDN'T CARE IF PEOPLE LIKED HIM. UNCOMPROMISING.

ADMIRED THAT.

"OF US ALL, HE UNDERSTOOD MOST. ABOUT WORLD. ABOUT PEOPLE. ABOUT SOCIETY AND WHAT'S HAPPENING TO IT.

"THINGS EVERYONE KNOWS IN GUT. THINGS EVERYONE TOO SCARED TO FACE, TOO POLITE TO TALK ABOUT.

"HE UNDERSTOOD."

UNDERSTOOD MAN'S CAPACITY FOR HORRORS AND NEVER QUIT. SAW THE WORLD'S BLACK UNDERBELLY AND NEVER SURRENDERED.

ONCE A MAN HAS SEEN, HE CAN NEVER TURN HIS BACK ON IT. NEVER PRETEND IT DOESN'T EXIST.

"NO MATTER WHO ORDERS HIM TO LOOK THE OTHER WAY.

"WE DO NOT DO THIS THING BECAUSE IT IS PERMITTED. WE DO IT BECAUSE WE HAVE TO.

"WE DO IT BECAUSE WE ARE COMPELLED."

KEENE ACT PASSED: VIGILANTES ILLEGAL

15

FROM THE NOTES OF DR. MALCOLM LONG. OCTOBER 27TH, 1985 =

HIS LAST WORDS TODAY WERE "WE DO IT BECAUSE WE ARE COMPELLED."

BUT HE NEVER SAYS WHAT IT *IS* THAT COMPELS HIM. IT'S NOT HIS *CHILDHOOD*, HIS *MOTHER* OR *KITTY GENOVESE*. THOSE THINGS JUST MADE HIM *OVER-REACT* TO THE *INJUSTICE* IN THE WORLD.

THEY'RE NOT WHAT SENT HIM OVER ITS EDGE.

THEY'RE NOT WHAT TURNED HIM INTO RORSCHACH.

IT'S AS IF CONTINUAL CONTACT WITH SOCIETY'S *GRIM* ELEMENTS HAS SHAPED HIM INTO SOMETHING *GRIMMER*, SOMETHING EVEN *WORSE*.

IF ONLY I COULD CONVINCE HIM THAT LIFE ISN'T *LIKE* THAT. THE *WORLD* ISN'T LIKE THAT.

I'M *POSITIVE* IT ISN'T.

BOUGHT A GAZETTE ON WAY HOME, INCLUDING A SMALL PIECE ABOUT KOVACS WHICH THE NEWSVENDOR POINTED OUT EXCITEDLY. I GUESS HE DOES THAT TO EVERYBODY.

APPARENTLY, KOVACS VISITED HIS NEWSSTAND REGULARLY.

THE COINCIDENCE IS TRIVIAL, BUT UNSETTLING.

SO WAS THE FRONT PAGE. RUSSIAN TANKS HAVE ENTERED PAKISTAN.

ON SEVENTH AVENUE, SOMEONE HAD SPRAYED SILHOUETTE FIGURES ONTO THE WALL. IT REMINDED ME OF THE PEOPLE DISINTEGRATED AT *HIROSHIMA*, LEAVING ONLY THEIR INDELIBLE SHADOWS.

AT HOME, GLORIA SEEMED ANXIOUS TO SWEETEN THINGS AFTER YESTERDAY AND TOLD ME SHE'D INVITED RANDY AND DIANA TO DINNER TOMORROW.

WAS TOO EXHAUSTED TO TAKE IN ALL THE DETAILS AND SUGGESTED AN EARLY NIGHT.

16

TODAY HE TOLD ME EVERYTHING.

HELLO, RORSCHACH. HOW ARE YOU TODAY?

IN PRISON. YOURSELF?

UH... FINE. I'M FINE.

I THOUGHT WE'D TRY SOME MORE *BLOT* TESTS.

HOW ABOUT TAKING A LOOK AT *THIS* ONE FOR ME?

SEEN THIS ONE BEFORE.

YES. I KNOW. I ... UH... I THOUGHT YOU MIGHT HAVE BEEN HOLDING *BACK* BEFORE AND I WANTED TO TRY IT *AGAIN*.

GO ON. TELL ME WHAT YOU *REALLY* SEE.

DOG.

DOG WITH HEAD SPLIT IN HALF.

I...I SEE.

AND, UH, WHAT DO YOU THINK SPLIT THE, UH, SPLIT THE DOG'S HEAD.

IN HALF.

I DID.

17

1975. KIDNAP CASE. PERHAPS YOU REMEMBER.

BLAIRE ROCHE. SIX YEARS OLD. KIDNAPPERS BELIEVED SHE WAS CONNECTED TO ROCHE CHEMICAL FORTUNE.

STUPID MISTAKE. FATHER WAS BUS DRIVER. NO MONEY AT ALL.

DAYS DRAGGED BY. NO WORD FROM KIDNAPPERS. THOUGHT OF LITTLE CHILD, ABUSED, FRIGHTENED. DIDN'T LIKE IT. PERSONAL REASONS.

DECIDED TO INTERVENE. PROMISED PARENTS I'D RETURN HER UNHARMED.

VISITED UNDERWORLD BARS AND BEGAN HURTING PEOPLE. PUT FOURTEEN IN HOSPITAL NEEDLESSLY.

"FIFTEENTH GAVE ME AN ADDRESS. DISUSED DRESS-MAKERS IN BROOKLYN.

"BAD NEIGHBORHOOD. SMELLED OF DAMP PLASTER AND STAINED MATTRESSES.

"ARRIVED THERE AT DUSK. NO LIGHTS ON IN BUILDING.

"SOMETHING WAS MAKING NOISE IN WASTELAND AT REAR.

"ATTACK DOGS. TWO GERMAN SHEPHERDS, FIGHTING OVER KNOB OF BONE. DIDN'T SEEM INTERESTED IN ME.

"DECIDED NOT TO USE REAR ENTRANCE ANYWAY.

"WENT IN THROUGH FRONT, LIKE RESPECTABLE VISITOR.'"

18

19

20

SHOCK OF IMPACT RAN ALONG MY ARM. JET OF WARMTH SPATTERED ON CHEST, LIKE HOT FAUCET.

IT WAS KOVACS WHO SAID "MOTHER" THEN, MUFFLED UNDER LATEX. IT WAS KOVACS WHO CLOSED HIS EYES.

IT WAS RORSCHACH WHO OPENED THEM AGAIN.

ACCORDING TO MY INFORMANT, MAN USING PREMISES NAMED GERALD GRICE.

OUT DRINKING WHEN I CALLED. RETURNED TO DRESSMAKERS AT TEN FORTY-FIVE.

DARK BY THEN.

DARK AS IT GETS.

21

HELLO, FRED? BARNEY? I'M HOME.

C'MON... WHO'S GOT A BARK FOR DADDY?

HMP.

22

EEEE - YYUUUGH! GET OFF!

SOMEBODY GET IT OFF ME!

OOUGHH.

OH, NO. OH, PLEASE... I HAVEN'T DONE ANY-THING...

OOUUH. OH, WAIT! WAIT, PLEASE, PLEASE, WHAT ARE YOU GOING TO DO..?

LOOK...LOOK, I KNOW WHAT YOU THINK...

YOU THINK I'M SOMETHING TO DO WITH THAT LITTLE GIRL.

WELL WELL, I'M NOT, OKAY? OKAY?

OH, GOD, PLEASE... WHAT DO YOU WANT?

Y-YOU CAN'T PROVE ANYTHING. I MEAN, WH-WHERE'S THE EVIDENCE? YOU CAN'T DO ANYTHING TO...

...ME...

24

HEY, **WAIT A MINUTE.** THAT'S **MINE!**

WHAT **IS** THIS?

YOU'RE **GIVING** ME THIS? IS **THAT** IT?

LOOK, PLEASE, IF YOU'D JUST **SAY** SOMETHING...

HEY! HEY, ARE YOU **CRAZY?**

THAT'S **KEROSENE!**

YES.

SHOULDN'T BOTHER TRYING TO SAW THROUGH HANDCUFFS.

NEVER MAKE IT IN TIME.

WHAT DO YOU **MEAN?** WHAT AM I SUPPOSED TO...

OH, GOD.

OH, JESUS, **NO.** YOU'RE **KIDDING.** YOU **HAVE** TO BE KIDDING.

EEEEAAAGH   YI¡IAAAGH

"STOOD IN STREET. WATCHED IT BURN."

"IMAGINED LIMBLESS FELT TORSOS INSIDE; BREASTS BLACKENING; BELLIES SMOLDERING; BURSTING INTO FLAME ONE BY ONE."

"WATCHED FOR AN HOUR."

NOBODY GOT OUT.

25

"STOOD IN FIRELIGHT, SWELTERING. BLOOD STAIN ON CHEST LIKE MAP OF VIOLENT NEW CONTINENT.

"FELT CLEANSED. FELT DARK PLANET TURN UNDER MY FEET AND KNEW WHAT CATS KNOW THAT MAKES THEM SCREAM LIKE BABIES IN NIGHT.

"LOOKED AT SKY THROUGH SMOKE HEAVY WITH HUMAN FAT AND GOD WAS NOT THERE. THE COLD, SUFFOCATING DARK GOES ON FOREVER, AND WE ARE ALONE...

"LIVE OUR LIVES, LACKING ANYTHING BETTER TO DO. DEVISE REASON LATER.

"BORN FROM OBLIVION; BEAR CHILDREN, HELL-BOUND AS OURSELVES; GO INTO OBLIVION.

"THERE IS NOTHING ELSE."

EXISTENCE IS RANDOM. HAS NO PATTERN SAVE WHAT WE IMAGINE AFTER STARING AT IT FOR TOO LONG.

NO MEANING SAVE WHAT WE CHOOSE TO IMPOSE.

THIS RUDDERLESS WORLD IS NOT SHAPED BY VAGUE METAPHYSICAL FORCES. IT IS NOT GOD WHO KILLS THE CHILDREN. NOT FATE THAT BUTCHERS THEM OR DESTINY THAT FEEDS THEM TO THE DOGS.

IT'S US.

ONLY US.

STREETS STANK OF FIRE. THE VOID BREATHED HARD ON MY HEART, TURNING ITS ILLUSIONS TO ICE, SHATTERING THEM.

WAS REBORN THEN, FREE TO SCRAWL OWN DESIGN ON THIS MORALLY BLANK WORLD.

WAS RORSCHACH.

DOES THAT ANSWER YOUR QUESTIONS, DOCTOR?

26

WALKED HOME ALONG 40TH STREET. A BLACK MAN TRIED TO SELL ME A ROLEX WATCH. WHEN I KEPT WALKING HE STARTED SHOUTING "NIGGER! HEY, NIGGER!"

IGNORED HIM. BOUGHT PAPER. RUSSIANS CLAIM THAT FIGHTING SPILLING INTO PAKISTAN WAS ACCIDENTAL. NIXON SAYS U.S. WILL MEET CONTINUED SOVIET AGGRESSION WITH "MAXIMUM FORCE."

INSIDE ARTICLE ON NUCLEAR ALERT PROCEDURE.

FINAL New York Gazette
NIXON PROMIS[E]
MAXIMUM FOR[CE]

IT SAYS THAT ANY DEAD FAMILY MEMBERS SHOULD BE WRAPPED IN PLASTIC GARBAGE SACKS AND PLACED OUTSIDE FOR COLLECTION.

ON 7TH AVENUE, THE HIROSHIMA LOVERS WERE STILL TRYING INADEQUATELY TO CONSOLE ONE ANOTHER.

HOME: GLORIA REMINDED ME THAT RANDY AND DIANA WERE COMING TONIGHT. LOOKED CROSS WHEN I CONFESSED I'D FORGOTTEN. WE DRESSED FOR DINNER IN SILENCE.

DINNER DIDN'T GO VERY WELL.

SO, MAL, HOW ARE THINGS GOING WITH THIS FAMOUS *MASKED MANIAC* OF YOURS?

OH, *YES, TELL US.* HAS HE TOLD YOU ANYTHING *WEIRD* OR *KINKY* YET?

YES. YES, HE HAS.

TODAY HE TOLD ME ABOUT A GIRL WHO GOT KIDNAPPED.

LOOK, MAYBE THIS ISN'T SUCH A GOOD IDEA RIGHT NOW...

OH, BOY! WAS SHE TIED UP AND GAGGED AND HELP-LESS?

RAN-DEE!

NO. SHE WAS SIX. HER ABDUCTOR KILLED HER, BUTCHERED HER AND FED HER TO HIS GERMAN SHEPHERDS.

GLORIA?

WHERE ARE YOU GOING?

DIANA REMEMBERED THAT THEIR BABYSITTER HAD TO BE HOME EARLY AND THEY LEFT SOON AFTER DINNER.

GLORIA WENT INTO THE BEDROOM. I FOLLOWED HER. SHE WALKED OUT AGAIN, INTO THE HALL.

I SAT ON THE BED.

SHE CAME IN, WEARING HER COAT, SUBJECTED ME TO A LOT OF CRUDE SEXUAL INSULTS, WENT OUT. THE FRONT DOOR SLAMMED.

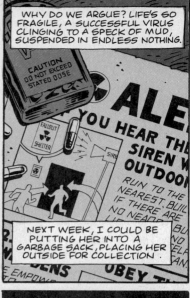

WHY DO WE ARGUE? LIFE'S SO FRAGILE, A SUCCESSFUL VIRUS CLINGING TO A SPECK OF MUD, SUSPENDED IN ENDLESS NOTHING.

NEXT WEEK, I COULD BE PUTTING HER INTO A GARBAGE SACK, PLACING HER OUTSIDE FOR COLLECTION.

I SAT ON THE BED.

I LOOKED AT THE RORSCHACH BLOT.

I TRIED TO PRETEND IT LOOKED LIKE A SPREADING TREE, SHADOWS POOLED BENEATH IT, BUT IT DIDN'T.

IT LOOKED MORE LIKE A DEAD CAT I ONCE FOUND, THE FAT, GLISTENING GRUBS WRITHING BLINDLY, SQUIRMING OVER EACH OTHER, FRANTICALLY TUNNELING AWAY FROM THE LIGHT.

BUT EVEN THAT IS AVOIDING THE REAL HORROR.

THE HORROR IS THIS: IN THE END, IT IS SIMPLY A PICTURE OF EMPTY MEANINGLESS BLACKNESS.

WE ARE ALONE.

THERE IS NOTHING ELSE.

Battle not with monsters, lest ye become a monster,

and if you gaze into the abyss, the abyss gazes also into you.

—Friedrich Wilhelm Nietzsche

New York
Police Department

MANHATTAN

FOR INTER-DEPARTMENTAL USE ONLY

(Please type or print clearly)

Name KOVACS, Walter Joseph

Address TRANSIENT

Born 3/21/40

Mothers name KOVACS, Sylvia Joanna (née GLICK)

Fathers name Unknown

62186   62186

LEFT THUMB PRINT | RIGHT THUMB PRINT

DETAILS OF ARREST   COPIES:

Walter Joseph Kovacs, A.K.A. RORSCHACH, was arrested on the night of Monday, October 21st when a squadron of police officers led by Detectives FINE and BOURQUIN surrounded the house of EDGAR WILLIAM JACOBI, A.K.A. EDGAR WILLIAM VAUGHN, A.K.A. WILLIAM EDGAR BRIGHT, A.K.A. MOLOCH, following an anonymous tip: Kovacs, who was on the premises at the time, injured two police officers while resisting arrest. Officer SHAW was admitted to the hospital with minor burns, while Officer Greaves, who was shot at point blank range with a gas-powered grappling gun, has a shattered sternum and is still on the hospital's critical list as of this writing (10/22/85).

When the house was explored, the body of Edgar Jacobi was discovered in the kitchen, shot through the head. The murder weapon was found less than two feet away, and although there were no fingerprints on the gun it should be remembered that since Kovacs was wearing gloves when arrested, this lack of prints is hardly remarkable. Although Kovacs has denied the murder of Jacobi, given his previous history of violence against other criminals and his location in the murder house at the time, few other conclusions seem possible. Curiously, Kovacs has not denied the two other murders attributed to him, those of GERALD ANTHONY GRICE, unemployed, in the summer of 1975, and of wanted multiple rapist HARVEY CHARLES FURNISS two years later in the summer of 1977, immediately following the passage of the Keene Act into law.

At the time of his arrest, the contents of Kovacs' pockets were as follows: 1 battery powered flashlight; 5 individually wrapped cubes 'Sweet Chariot' chewing sugar; 1 map New York underground and subway system, dated 1968 with recent alterations drawn in with a red ballpoint pen; withered remains one red rose; one dollar fifty-nine cents in assorted loose change; one pencil; one notebook, pages filled with what is either an elaborate cypher or handwriting too cramped and eccentric to be legible; one broken bottle 'Nostalgia' cologne for men, possibly broken during leap from Jacobi's second story window during arrest; a residue of ground black pepper.

(If second sheet is needed refer to Form 6-2)

New York State Psychiatric Hospital
West Branch

EARLY HISTORY: A SUMMARY:

    Sylvia Kovacs came to New York from Ohio in the spring of 1935
with her husband, Peter Joseph Kovacs, whom she divorced in 1937 amidst
mutual accusations of adultery and mental cruelty. After the divorce
she had no further contact with her former husband, and for the next
three years, she lived in a number of low-rent apartments, both alone
and with a number of male acquaintances. Exactly when she drifted
into prostitution as a means of meeting her mounting debts is uncertain,
but it seems likely that her last semi-permanent relationship was with
the true father of Walter Kovacs, who left her two months before the
baby was born. Mrs. Kovacs was either unable or unwilling to provide
any details concerning him other than that his name was 'Charlie'.
Sicne shortly after the birth of her son we see Mrs. Kovacs' first
arrest on charges of prostitution, we can perhaps assume that the addi-
tional cost of keeping an infant child may have been what necessitated
this new occupation, and perhaps also speculate as to whether the above
factors were the cause of the resentment and cruelty which Sylvia Kovacs
showed to her son as he grew older.
    In the July of 1951, the boy was admitted into care after vi-
ciously attacking two older boys in the street, partially blinding
one of them. When questioned, Kovacs refused to talk about what had
caused him to attack the boys, so it must be presumed that it was an
unprovoked assault. Nerertheless, investigation of the circumstances
the boy lived in revealed that he was regularly beaten and exposed
to the worst excesses of a prostitutes lifestyle, and it was decide to
place the child under care. He was admitted to the Lillian Charlton
Home for Problem Children in New Jersey, where he remained until 1956,
when it was decided that he was intelligent and stable enough to func-
tion in normal society. During his time at hte home, removed from
his mother's negative influence, Kovacs did very well at schoolwork,
excelling particularly in the fields of literature and religious ed-
uscation as well as possessing an impressive skill in the areas of
gymnastics and amateur boxing. While quiet and
shy, especially with women, Kovacs was capable
of long and well-reasoned conversations with his
classmates and instructors, and struck most peop
as a serious but likeable child who was merely a
bit withdrawn.

     ~~~~~~~this aside, it is clear that his loathin
of his mother remained undiminished. Shortly
before Kovacs left the Charlton home in 1956,
news was received that his mother, who had never
made any attempt to contact her child and who ha
continued to become further involved in the worl
of small-time vice, had been murdered. Her body
had been found in a back alleyway in the South
Bronx, the cause of death being the forced ing
estion of Drano cleaning fluid. A man named George
Paterson, Mrs. Kovacs' pimp, was later charged

New York State Psychiatric Hospital
West Branch

with her murder. When the news was broken to Walter Kovacs, then aged sixteen, his only comment was 'Good.' Shortly after this, Kovacs left the home to take up residence in the first of a series of small apartments and also take up full employment in a menial capacity within the garment industry, an occupation he apparently remained in up until the mid-seventies, maintaining a dual life between his daytime employment and his nocturnal activities in the guise of 'Rorschach'.

Very little physical evidence existsthat gives a clear insight into the psychology of this troubled man. Some police officers have tentatively identified hima s a prophet-of-doom sandwich-board man seen locally over the last several years, but as Kovacs refuses to divulge his current address, if any, this is not provable at such an early stage in the investigation. Similarly, material relating to his early years is scarce, although I have been able to obtain photocopies of two pieces written by Kovacs during his stay at the Charlton Home, one being an essay written on the set topic of 'My Parents' when Kovacs was eleven, the other being a transcription of Kovacs' verbal recounting of a nightmare he suffered when he was thirteen.

Charlton Home

by Walter Kovacs

My Parents

I have two parents, although actually, I don't have any. I never see my mom, but that's okay, although I would like to see my dad sometimes. I have never met my dad and I would sure like to. He had to leave our house when I wasn't even born, I guess because he couldn't get along with my mother. I would of done the same if I was him.

I used to ask my mom about my dad, but she doesn't talk much about him. His name was charlie, which is short for Charles although it has the same number of letters. She says she doesn't know his second name although how can you live with somebodt if you don't know who they are? It is just stupid.

My mom told me she threw my dad out because he was always getting into political arguments with her because he liked President Truman and she didn't. I think perhaps my dad was some sort of aide to President Truman, because he liked him so much. Most probably he was out of the country during the war when I was growing up on some sort of mission. I think he was the kind of guy who would fight for his country and what was right. Maybe he got killed fighting the Nazis and he's with God now and that's how come he never managed to find me.

I like President Truman, the way Dad would of wanted me to. He dropped the atom bomb on Japan and saved millions of lives because if he hadn't of, then there would of been a lot more war than there was and more people would of been killed. I think it was a good thing to drop the atomic bomb on Japan.

That is all I have to say about my parents.

Charlton Home

CONFIDENTIAL

DREAM, 5/27/63

" A man was in my old house, with my mom. They were eating some stuff like raw dough, and my mom choked on a piece. The guy with her tried to fish it out of her throat. He got his whole hand in her mouth and then it was like he had his whole arm down her throat. He told me to get a doctor, so I ran out of the room but the house was all different and there wasn't any doctor there anyway, so I went back to find mom. I was walking down this sort of hallway, and it was dark and I saw what looked like my mom and this guy dancing, old fashioned dancing at the other end of the room, and they didn't have any clothes on. They were sort of clopping around like a horse in a pantomine with two guys in a suit. When they got nearer, I saw they weren't dancing at all, they were squashed together like siamese twins, joined at the face and chest and stomach. They didn't have any face, you could only see their ears, two on either side of the head facing towards each other. Their hands were growing into each other as well, but they had all four legs free and they were sort of dancing sideways towards me down the dark hall like a crab, and there was something tripping 'em up, wrapped around their feet, and I looked down and I saw it was trousers and underwear and stuff. They were coming towards me, and then I woke up. I had feelings when I woke up. Dirty feelings, thoughts and stuff. The dream it sort of upset me, physically. I couldn't help it. I feel bad just talking about it."

MY dReaM by W.J. KOVACS aGe 13

From the desk of: Dr. Malcolm

10/

Walter Joseph Kovacs promises to a complex case, especially in l of the extreme nature of his vigilante activities. It may be possible to identify a new syndrome that will help us to understand those other people who have in the past shared Kovacs masked vigilante activit In any event, keep notes with an eye to possible future publication.
First interview with Kovacs is Friday afternoon. looking forward to it.

CHAPTER VI

1

A BROTHER TO DRAGONS

LAURIE? DID YOU *SHOUT?*

EVERYTHING *OKAY* DOWN THERE?

MAYBE.

OR MAYBE SOMEONE'S PICKING OFF COSTUMED HEROES.

OH, GOD.

LAURIE?

LAURIE, HANG *ON,* I'M COMING!

THE COMEDIAN MURDERED. DR. MANHATTAN EXILED.

TWO OF US GONE. ALL WITHIN A WEEK.

WHO NEXT? VEIDT? JUSPECZYK? ME?

YOU?

LAURIE?

FIRE EXTINGUISHERS! WHERE THE HELL ARE THE *FIRE EXTINGUISHERS?*

3

OVER HERE.

LAURIE, WHAT HAPPENED? I THOUGHT...

LOOK, I'M REALLY SORRY. I WAS JUST POKING AROUND DOWN HERE. I SAW THE LIGHTS ON IN THE SHIP...

SEE, I WAS LOOKING FOR THE DASH LIGHTER...

I DON'T SMOKE. THAT WAS THE FLAME-THROWER.

YEAH, WELL, I KNOW THAT NOW. LOOK, DAN, I'M REALLY SORRY...

HEY, IT'S OKAY. MY FAULT. I WAS DOWN HERE CHECKING OUT THE SYSTEMS EARLIER. I LEFT EVERYTHING SWITCHED ON WHEN I WENT OUT TO THE STORE.

YOU'RE NOT HURT?

ME? I'M FINE... BUT LOOK AT YOUR BEAUTIFUL SHIP...

AHH, THAT'S MOSTLY JUST SOOT. IT'LL WIPE OFF. I'M JUST GLAD YOU'RE OKAY.

WHEN YOU SCREAMED, I THOUGHT ...WELL, Y'KNOW. EVER SINCE THE COMEDIAN DIED...

OH, COME ON, DAN... YOU'RE NOT STARTING TO TAKE RORSCHACH'S 'MASK KILLER' BULL-SHIT SERIOUSLY?

I MEAN, HE'S PSYCHOTIC. TO HIM, EVERY-THING'S A CONSPIRACY.

I DON'T KNOW ...THE COMEDIAN MURDERED, JON EXILED, SOME-ONE TRIES TO SHOOT ADRIAN, RORSCHACH HIMSELF GETS TAKEN BY THE POLICE...

IT JUST MAKES ME FEEL UN-EASY.

IS THAT WHY YOU WERE TUNING YOUR SHIP?

WHAT? OH, NO, NO, NOTHING LIKE THAT. I WAS JUST TINKERING, YOU KNOW, NOTHING SERIOUS...

YOU'VE GOT SOME WONDERFUL STUFF DOWN HERE. IT'S LIKE A MAGICIAN'S CAVE OR SOME-THING...

WHAT, WITH ALL THESE LEAKS AND PUDDLES?

NO... MAYBE IT USED TO SEEM LIKE THAT TO ME ONCE, BUT THESE DAYS IT'S SORT OF AN EMBARRASSMENT.

LOOKING BACK IT ALL SEEMS SO ...WELL, CHILDISH, I GUESS.

JUST A SCHOOLKID'S FANTASY THAT GOT OUT OF HAND.

THAT'S, Y'KNOW, WITH HINDSIGHT...

...ON REFLECTION.

4

YEAH, WELL, AT LEAST YOU WERE LIVING OUT YOUR *OWN* FANTASIES. I WAS LIVING OUT MY *MOTHER'S.*

Y'KNOW, I'M REALLY *IMPRESSED* BY ALL THIS *EQUIPMENT.* IT MUST HAVE COST YOU A *FORTUNE.*

WHAT'S THIS *CABINET* OVER HERE?

OH, THAT'S JUST *SOUVENIRS* AND JUNK LIKE THAT.

AS FOR THE *MONEY,* MY DAD WAS IN *BANKING.* HE LEFT ME A LOT OF MONEY WHEN HE *DIED.*

I WAS ALWAYS KIND OF *SURPRISED* ABOUT THAT.

I MEAN, HE ALWAYS SEEMED *DISAPPOINTED* IN ME. HE WANTED ME TO FOLLOW HIM INTO *BANKING,* BUT I WAS JUST INTERESTED IN *BIRDS* AND *AIRPLANES* AND *MYTHOLOGY.* YOU KNOW. *KID'S* STUFF.

HMM. WHAT'S *THIS?*

THAT? OH, THAT ISN'T ANYBODY. IT'S JUST THIS *VICE QUEEN* I PUT AWAY BACK IN '68. CALLED HERSELF *DUSK WOMAN* OR SOMETHING.

"*THE TWILIGHT LADY*"

SHE SENT YOU HER *PICTURE?*

From one 'Night Bird' to Another. Love from The Twilight Lady x

YEAH, WELL, I GUESS SHE HAD SORT OF A *FIXATION.* SHE WAS A *VERY* SICK WOMAN.

I KEEP MEANING TO THROW THAT PICTURE *AWAY,* BUT YOU KNOW HOW IT *IS...*

MMM.

I SEE YOU HAVE A LOT OF PICTURES OF *BIRDS* AND STUFF. THAT WAS MY *FANTASY,* WHEN I WAS A *KID:* TO WORK WITH *ANIMALS...*

I JUST LIKED *BIRDS,* MOSTLY. JUST THE IDEA OF *FLYING...*

AS A KID, I READ ABOUT *PEGASUS,* FLYING CARPETS, THEN LATER ABOUT *BIRDS* AND *PLANES.*

FINALLY, I MASTERED IN AERONAUTICS AND ZOOLOGY AT *HARVARD.*

GUESS IT HELPED ME DESIGN THIS *JALOPY* HERE.

JALOPY? THAT'S A WORD I HAVEN'T HEARD IN A LONG TIME.

HEH. I PROBABLY PICKED IT UP FROM *HOLLIS.*

HOLLIS WAS SOMETHING *ELSE* THAT INFLUENCED ME AS A KID. I *IDOLIZED* HIM...

...BUT THEN I GUESS THAT'S PRETTY *OBVIOUS.*

WELCOME *ABOARD.* YOU WANT TO TAKE A LOOK *AROUND* WHILE I FINISH CHECKING THE *SHIP* OUT?

SURE. AND DON'T *WORRY...* I WON'T *TOUCH* ANYTHING.

5

OH, HEY, LISTEN, I'M NOT WORRIED. THAT FLAME THROWER BUTTON CONFUSES EVERYBODY. THE COMEDIAN ALMOST DID THE SAME THING, BACK IN '77.

MM.

DAN, I'M SAFELY ON BOARD. YOU CAN LET GO OF MY HAND NOW.

OH. I'M SORRY. I, UH...

LISTEN, I'D BETTER CHECK OUT THE SHIP'S OTHER SYSTEMS. YOU, UH, YOU JUST TAKE A LOOK AROUND.

I LIKE THE DESIGN. ALL CURVES AND NO CORNERS.

WELL, UH, ACTUALLY, ALONG WITH THE CONCEALED VENTS AND TURBINES, HAVING NO CORNERS HELPS MAKE THE SHIP RADAR INVISIBLE.

HMM. THIS CHAIR CONTROL IS STICKING A LITTLE...

RADAR INVISIBLE? BOY, YOU REALLY HAVE GOT ALL THIS STUFF FIGURED OUT, DON'T YOU?

WHAT'S THIS CLOSET HERE?

SPECIAL AUXILIARY COSTUMES. AH...THAT'S BETTER.

HEY, THESE ARE TERRIFIC. IT'S LIKE WHEN I WAS SMALL, MOM GOT ME THIS G.I. JOE WITH ALL THESE NEAT LITTLE SPARE UNIFORMS.

WHAT'S THIS GREEN ONE?

UNDERWATER WORK. LET'S SEE ...FLAMERS FUNCTIONING, WATER CANNON FUNCTIONING...

PUBLIC ADDRESS SYSTEM AND SCREECHERS FUNCTIONING...

AIR-TO-AIR MISSILES FUNCTIONING...

FOG-SCREENS FUNCT...

AIR-TO-AIR MISSILES?

SURE. BUTTON RIGHT NEXT TO THE FLAME THROWER.

FOGSCREENS FUNCTIONING... RADIATION SHIELDS FUNCTIONING...

THAT'S IT! THAT DOES IT! NO MORE SMOKING. I'M ALL THROUGH. I QUIT!

I MEAN, TALK ABOUT DANGEROUS HABITS...

6

ELECTRO-MAGNETIC SYSTEMS FUNCTIONING ...YUP. EVERYTHING'S OKAY.

I ALREADY STOPPED A COUPLE OF TIMES BEFORE, BUT IT GOT SO *BORING* AROUND THE ROCKEFELLER BASE, MY *WILL* POWER NEVER HELD OUT LONG.

PROBABLY WON'T *THIS* TIME, EITHER.

WELL, Y'KNOW, THAT'S A VERY NEGATIVE *ATTITUDE* ...I MEAN, *I* HAD A DANGEROUS HABIT *MYSELF* ONCE.

YOU DID? WHAT *HAPPENED?*

I QUIT. NO PROBLEM.

OH, I MEAN, SURE, AT FIRST I USED TO GET *CRAVINGS* BUT I HELD ON *IN* THERE.

THESE DAYS IT HARDLY BOTHERS ME AT *ALL.*

YOU'RE TALKING ABOUT, Y'KNOW, WHAT WE *DID.* YOU STILL *MISS* ALL THAT STUFF?

NO. NO, NOT *REALLY.* JUST *SENTIMENT,* I GUESS.

C'MON ... I'M FINISHED HERE. TAKE THE REAR EXIT SO YOU WON'T GET *DIRTY* CRAWLING UNDER *ARCHIE.*

ARCHIE?

OH, UH, WELL, IT'S SHORT FOR *ARCHIMEDES,* MERLIN'S PET *OWL* IN *'THE SWORD IN THE STONE'.* I SAW THE *DISNEY* VERSION ONCE AND... WELL. YOU KNOW. IT'S JUST A STUPID *NICKNAME.*

HERE'S THE *EXIT.* WATCH YOUR *STEP.*

YOU WERE REALLY INTO ALL THAT KNIGHTS-IN-ARMOR FANTASY STUFF AS A KID?

YEAH. I GUESS IT *FIGURES* ...Y'KNOW, BEING A *CRIMEFIGHTER* AND EVERYTHING. IT WAS JUST THIS ADOLESCENT, *ROMANTIC* THING.

NOTHING WRONG WITH ADOLESCENT ROMANCE, ALTHOUGH *MOST* PEOPLE DON'T SPEND SO MUCH MONEY *GETTING* IT.

I MEAN, THIS *BASE-MENT,* IT'S *ENORMOUS.* WHY NOT SELL SOME OF THIS OLD *EQUIPMENT* AND TURN IT INTO, I DUNNO, A *GYM* OR SOMETHING?

ALREADY *GOT* ONE.

NO... I DON'T KNOW *WHY* I HANG *ONTO* THIS STUFF. I MEAN, I *KNOW* THE ROMANCE IS *OVER,* ...

...I GUESS I JUST DON'T HAVE THE HEART TO THROW OUT ALL THE *ENGAGEMENT* PRESENTS.

7

OH, DAN! YOU SOUND LIKE MY MAIDEN AUNT BELLA.

WHAT GOT YOU INTO THIS BUSINESS IN THE FIRST PLACE?

WELL, I WAS RICH, BORED, AND THERE WERE ENOUGH OTHER GUYS DOING IT SO I DIDN'T FEEL RIDICULOUS...

I GUESS HOLLIS WAS MY HERO. HE WAS RETIRING WHEN I WAS STARTING OUT, SO I WROTE AND ASKED IF I COULD CARRY ON HIS NAME.

I REMEMBER VISITING HIS GARAGE, THAT FIRST TIME. I WAS AWESTRUCK.

I MEAN...THERE I WAS, HANGING OUT WITH A REAL HERO, BEING HIS FRIEND AND EVERYTHING.

BEING A CRIME-FIGHTER, Y'KNOW? LIKE PART OF A BROTHERHOOD OR SOMETHING...

THAT'S WHY I SORT OF REGRETTED THE CRIMEBUSTERS FALLING THROUGH BACK IN SIXTY-WHENEVER-IT-WAS.

IT WOULD HAVE BEEN LIKE JOINING THE KNIGHTS OF THE ROUND TABLE; BEING PART OF A FELLOWSHIP OF LEGENDARY BEINGS...

...BUT EVENTUALLY I REALIZED THE COMEDIAN WAS RIGHT: IT'S ALL CRAP DRESSED UP WITH A LOT OF FLASH AND THUNDER.

I MEAN, WHO NEEDS ALL THIS HARDWARE TO CATCH HOOKERS AND PURSE-SNATCHERS? I MEAN REALLY?

HMM. WHAT'S THAT?

PROTOTYPE EXO-SKELETON. FIRST TIME I TRIED MOVING IN IT, IT BROKE MY ARM. NEVER AGAIN.

JESUS. THAT SOUNDS LIKE THE SORT OF COSTUME THAT COULD REALLY MESS YOU UP.

IS THERE ANY OTHER SORT?

8

I MEAN, LOOK AT *RORSCHACH* THE CONDITION HE'S IN. HE WAS *NORMAL* ONCE.

SURE, HE WAS *QUIET*, HE WAS *GRIM*, BUT HE STILL HAD ALL THE *BUTTONS* ON HIS *OVER-COAT*.

SOON AFTER I STARTED OUT, WE BLITZED THE *BIG FIGURE* TOGETHER. TACTICALLY, RORSCHACH WAS *BRILLIANT*. HE WAS SO *UNPREDICTABLE*.

WHAT I'M *SAYING* IS, HE WAS *RATIONAL* THEN.

OVER THE YEARS, THAT *MASK'S* EATEN HIS *BRAINS*.

WASN'T ANYTHING *GOOD* ABOUT THOSE YEARS? I MEAN, ALL THESE *GADGETS* YOU DESIGNED... IF THAT WAS *ME*, I'D FEEL *PROUD*.

YOU'RE *REALLY* INTEREST- ED IN ALL THIS STUFF?

WELL, UH, DID I SHOW YOU MY *GOGGLES*?

I MEAN, IF YOU *LIKE* THIS SORT OF GARBAGE... I GUESS IT'S PRETTY *KITSCH* OR *CAMP* OR WHAT- EVER...

DAN, DON'T BE SO SELF- DEPRECATING. I WAS ADMIRING THE GOGGLES *EARLIER*.

THOSE LENSES ARE PRETTY *DUSTY*...

HMM. THEY WORK BEST IN *DARKNESS*, SO I'LL KILL THE LIGHTS. I'VE GOT THIS LITTLE *CONSOLE* IN MY *BELT* HERE...

WHAT *ELSE* HAVE YOU GOT IN THERE? CHOCOLATE RATIONS? BOY SCOUT KNIFE? ARMY ISSUE CONTRACEP- TIVES?

HA HA HA HA. NO, IT'S MOSTLY PRETTY *BORING*... RESPIRATOR MASKS, SMOKE BOMBS, FINGERPRINT KIT, POCKET LASER, THIS LITTLE *CONSOLE*...

YOU KNOW.

THE *USUAL* STUFF.

OKAY, NOW IF I SNUFF THE LIGHTS IN THE SHIP'S *CABIN* AND IN THE KITCHEN *UPSTAIRS*...

HA! SHOW- OFF.

HEY, WHAT ARE THESE *GOGGLES* SUPPOSED TO DO? I CAN'T *SEE* ANYTHING. ARE THEY *BROKEN*?

NO. YOU JUST PRESS *HERE* TO ROTATE THE LENSES A QUARTER TURN, LIKE THIS.

AS I REMEMBER, THEY WORK PRETTY GOOD. NO MATTER HOW *BLACK* IT GOT, WHEN I LOOKED THROUGH THESE GOGGLES...

...EVERYTHING WAS *CLEAR* AS DAY.

OOOOH!

9

DAN, THIS IS *FABULOUS*. THIS MUST BE WHAT IT'S LIKE HAVING *POWERS*...Y'KNOW, SPECIAL VISION AND LIKE THAT.

HM. WELL, IT'S GETTING *LATE*...

IT MUST BE SO STRANGE BEING *JON*. HE CAN SEE *NEUTRINOS*...

OH, OKAY. I'M ALL THROUGH *PLAYING* WITH THEM, ANYWAY.

...THOUGH MAYBE I'LL BORROW THEM FOR *PALE HORSE'S* MADISON SQUARE GARDEN CONCERTS IN EARLY *NOVEMBER*. THEY'RE KINDA *DEVO*.

DEVO?

JUST A *SECOND*... LET'S PUT THE LIGHTS ON UP-STAIRS.

SURE. DEVO. *"ARE WE NOT MEN?"* BAND FROM *OHIO*. LATE *SEVENTIES*.

OH. WELL, I'M MOSTLY INTO BILLIE HOLIDAY, NELLIE LUTCHER, LOUIS JORDAN... STUFF LIKE THAT.

DO YOU MISS JON?

JON? NO... ALTHOUGH I KEEP THINKING I *SHOULD*.

BUT, YOU SEE, EVEN WHEN I WAS *WITH* HIM, HE WAS NEVER REALLY *THERE*. THERE WAS NO REAL HUMAN *CONTACT*; NO *PHYSICAL* CONTACT...

I WAS SO *LONELY*...

YES. I KNOW. LAURIE SOMETIMES I'VE FELT...

...AND, LIKE, IT WASN'T JUST THE *ISOLATION*. I USED TO WORK OUT IN A *GYM* A LOT AS A KID, ALL BY MYSELF, SO BEING *ALONE'S* NO BIG DEAL.

I MEAN, TAKE *YOU*, FOR EXAMPLE. YOU *LIKE* LIVING HERE ON YOUR *OWN*, SO...

DAN? WHAT ARE YOU *DOING*?

UHH, NOTHING. JUST TRYING TO KEEP THESE LICKS OF HAIR IN *FRONT* TIDY. PLEASE ... CARRY ON.

WELL, WHAT I'M *SAYING* IS THAT AT *ROCKEFELLER* I GOT THE *BAD* SIDE OF ISOLATION WITHOUT THE *COMPENSATIONS*, LIKE *PRIVACY*.

THERE WAS NOBODY TO *TALK* TO, BUT I'D ALWAYS FEEL LIKE I WAS UNDER *OBSERVATION*.

HMM.

IT MUST BE GREAT FOR YOU, HAVING A *SECRET IDENTITY*, A SECRET *PLACE* NOBODY *KNOWS* ABOUT.

YOU CAN JUST COME DOWN HERE TO HANG OUT AND THERE'S NOBODY CHECKING *UP* ON YOU....

NOBODY *WATCHING* YOU.

ISN'T THERE?

THESE DAYS, I FEEL LIKE SOMETHING'S WATCHING MY EVERY MOVE.

10

DAN, YOU SOUND LIKE 'RORSCHACH.' THIS 'MASK KILLER' THING, IT DOESN'T HOLD UP.

WHERE'S THE CONSPIRACY?

I MEAN, JON LEFT EARTH OF HIS OWN FREE WILL; RORSCHACH WAS CAUGHT RED-HANDED COMMITTING MURDER, FOR GOD'S SAKE...

I WASN'T REALLY THINKING ABOUT THE MASK KILLER, BUT...

I DON'T KNOW. THAT RORSCHACH MURDER THING SOUNDED FUNNY. HE WOULDN'T JUST SHOOT SOMEBODY. IT'S TOO ORDINARY.

ANYWAY, IT'S ALMOST SIX O'CLOCK NEWS TIME. WANT COFFEE?

SURE. BLACK AS THE DEVIL AND SWEET AS A STOLEN KISS.

WHAT?

NO MILK; TWO SUGARS. POLISH FOLK SAYING. OH, INCIDENTALLY, DID YOU SEE THAT PACKAGE THAT ARRIVED FOR ME?

UH, NO. I DIDN'T.

JUST MY CLOTHES, FORWARDED FROM ROCKEFELLER. MY OLD COSTUME, STUFF LIKE THAT.

OH, YEAH, AND A LETTER TELLING ME I DON'T HAVE CANCER. HOPE YOU DON'T MIND ME USING YOUR ADDRESS.

LONG AS YOU LIKE.

WELL, I JUST DON'T WANT TO GET IN THE WAY OF YOUR WORK OR ANYTHING.

SEE, I'M NOT REALLY THAT SOLITARY BY INCLINATION.

WHAT IS IT THAT YOU DO, ACTUALLY?

OH, WELL, Y'KNOW. NOT A LOT, I GUESS. I SOMETIMES WRITE PIECES FOR ORNITHOLOGICAL JOURNALS.

REALLY? YOU DO A LOT OF THAT?

...LATEST IN A SERIES OF TENEMENT FIRES ALLEGEDLY DESIGNED TO REMOVE SITTING TENANTS...

NO. NOT MUCH. I HAVEN'T WRITTEN ANYTHING SINCE LAST APRIL. MOST PEOPLE FIND IT ALL PRETTY BORING, I GUESS...

...MEANWHILE, INVESTIGATIONS INTO CAPTURED VIGILANTE RORSCHACH ARE CONTINUING...

USUALLY, AS SOON AS I MENTION ORNITHOLOGY, FOLKS SORT OF SWITCH OFF AND...

SHHHH!

TODAY, POLICE ALLOWED NEWS CAMERAMEN INTO THE APARTMENT USED BY RORSCHACH, REAL NAME WALTER JOSEPH KOVACS.

HIS LANDLADY, MS. DOLORES SHAIRP, DESCRIBED KOVACS AS 'A NAZI PERVERT' AND SAID THAT HE'D FREQUENTLY PROPOSITIONED HER SEXUALLY...

HA! I KNEW IT!

SHE POINTED OUT STACKS OF RIGHT WING LITERATURE INCLUDING BACK ISSUES OF THE NEW FRONTIERSMAN.

11

We asked **Hector Godfrey**, the *Frontiersman's* editor, if he had any comment...

Frankly, isn't it time we **reassessed** Rorschach, as a **patriot** and **American**?

...And did you **see** that **room**? I mean, was that **gross**?

Yeah. He's not gonna be easy for a jury to sympathize with...

Sympathize? After he shoots a **cop** with a **grappling hook gun**?

Following a tense **bail** hearing, Kovacs awaits trial, pending **psychiatric examination**.

Don't **remind** me. It was me who **made** that thing for him.

Dr. **Malcolm Long**, carrying out the examination, has his first interview with Kovacs this afternoon.

He told pressmen he felt 'confident and optimistic'.

I never **dreamed** he'd ever **shoot** anybody with it.

What really worries me is him being in **jail**. The other prisoners'll **kill** him...

Yeah, well things are tough all over.

Meanwhile, in **Afghanistan**, the fighting **spreads**...

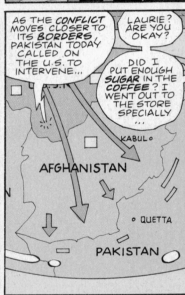

As the **conflict** moves closer to its **borders**, Pakistan today called on the U.S. to intervene...

Laurie? Are you **okay**?

Did I put enough **sugar** in the coffee? I went out to the store specially...

KABUL

AFGHANISTAN

QUETTA

PAKISTAN

No. No, the coffee's fine.

Dan, does this sort of stuff on the news scare the hell out of **you** too, or is it just **me**?

Addressing Congress, President Nixon said that America would 'consider her options'...

Thus, while Russia claims to be merely securing her borders, western experts see only opportunistic hostility in the wake of Dr. Manhattan's departure.

I mean, is this another **false alarm** or has the big **countdown** finally started?

I don't like **thinking** about it. During **Hiroshima Week**, I read an article in **Time** magazine, with **pictures**: kids' bodies, skin burned **black**.

Ough. Dan, **don't**...

Meanwhile, America's European military installations have been placed on **full alert**...

Sorry. It's just **disturbing** that faced with such **heat**, people remain so **cool**, so **apathetic**...

At England's **Greenham Common** base, women **peace** demonstrators were **arrested** during scuffles with **police**...

Me, I wish I could just **split**, like **Jon**.

OH, RIGHT. THE OLD *MANHATTAN TRANSFER*...

WHAT? 'MANHATTAN TRANSFER'?

HA HA HA HA!

...AND THROUGH-OUT THE WORLD THERE IS *TENSION* WITH NO SIGN OF A *BREAK-THROUGH.*

MEANWHILE, AT HOME, POLICE STOPPED SEARCHING FOR MISSING WRITER *MAX SHEA*, HAVING FAILED TO OPEN ANY NEW LINES OF *INVESTIGATION*...

HA HA HA...HAVE YOU *ALWAYS* CALLED JON'S TELEPORTATION *THAT?*

WELL, NOT TO HIS *FACE*...

HA HA HA HA HA.

SHEA, WHO WROTE CHILDREN'S *PIRATE COMICS* BEFORE GRADUATING TO MODERN CLASSICS SUCH AS ' *THE HOODED BASILISK*' AND '*FOGDANCING*', VANISHED FROM HIS BOSTON HOME TWO YEARS AGO...

HMM.

WHY, MR. *DREIBERG* ...YOU'RE *RAVISHING.*

I'M *WHAT?*

OH ... NO, NO, I JUST GOT SOME STEAM, FROM MY *COFFEE*, ON THE *LENSES* ...

WHILE IN NEW YORK, THE *INSTITUTE FOR EXTRASPATIAL STUDIES* REPORTS *EXCITING* AND MAYBE *ALARMING* POSSIBILITIES FOR OPENING *NEW DIMENSIONS* ...

INSTITUTE FOR EXTRASPATIAL STUDIES

165

NO, BUT *SERIOUSLY*, YOU LOOK *TERRIFIC* WITHOUT GLASSES. IF WE COULD JUST DO SOMETHING WITH THIS STUPID *HAIR*...

HEY, *STOP THAT!*

WE SPOKE TO THE INSTITUTE'S CHIEF *PHYSICIST*, DR. ED *COREY.*

AAAGH. LAURIE, *PLEASE.* I LIKE IT HOW IT *IS.* I DON'T *WANT* TO BE *DEVO*...

WE'RE VERY *EXCITED* AND EXPECTING EARLY *SUCCESS* IN OUR SEARCH FOR EXTRA-DIMENSIONAL *ENERGY SOURCES.*

Y'KNOW *YOUR* TROUBLE? YOU'RE *INHIBITED.*

UH ... *INHIBITED?* IN, UH, IN WHAT *WAY*...?

OH, ALL *KINDS* OF WAYS.

OUR *ACTIVITIES* ARE ENTERING *SPACES* WE THOUGHT *IMPOSSIBLE.*

...AND THAT'S THE WORLD TONIGHT. AFTER THE *BREAK*, ADRIAN VEIDT'S NEW YORK ASTRO-DOME *CHARITY PERFORMANCE* ...

UH, *LAURIE?* SHOULD I *MOVE*, OR...

UH...

OH, MY *DARLING*, IT'S *INCREDIBLE*, THAT SOMEONE SO UNFORGET-TABLE ...

...SHOULD THINK *I* AM *UNFORGETTABLE*, TOO.

13

NOSTALGIA ...BY VEIDT.

FOR UNFORGETTABLE YOU.

JESUS, LAURIE, ARE YOU SURE YOU...

SHH.

AND NOW, IN A REPEAT SHOWING OF LAST JULY'S CHARITY SPECTACULAR, WE BRING YOU OZYMANDIAS HIMSELF, ADRIAN VEIDT, AT THE NEW YORK ASTRODOME.

M.

LADIES AND GENTLEMEN, PERFORMING LIVE IN AID OF THE INDIAN FAMINE APPEAL WE PRESENT ADRIAN VEIDT THE ONE, THE ONLY...

...OZYMANDIAS!

HERE ...LET ME MOVE AROUND. MY ELBOW'S PRESSING ON YOUR CHEST...

THANK YOU. I HOPE YOU'LL FORGIVE ME WHILE I WARM UP. I HAVEN'T DONE THIS IN A WHILE.

HA HA HA HA

THAT BETTER?

UH-HUH.

...AND JUST LOOK AT THE CONFIDENCE AS HE LEAPS UP AND GRABS THE BAR, BEGINNING HIS MANEUVER.

OH, I'M SORRY. AM I CRUSHING YOU?

NO. IT'S OKAY. DON'T WORRY. EVERYTHING'S OKAY...

MMM...

MOVING UP INTO THE HANDSTAND NOW... NOTICE THERE'S NOT THE SLIGHTEST TREMOR OF EFFORT. IT'S ALL ONE SMOOTH, SEAMLESS FLOW OF MOTION...

UH, I CAN'T SEEM TO...

WHAT? OH ... HERE, LET ME DO THAT...

...AND AS HE MOVES INTO HIS FIRST SET PIECE, THE AUDIENCE IS ON THE EDGE OF THEIR SEATS.

BELIEVE ME, THIS IS ABSOLUTELY BREATH-TAKING...

OH.

OHH, DAN...

WHAT'S THE MATTER?

THE GRACE OF EACH MOVEMENT IS EXTRAORDINARY. THIS IS A MAN IN HIS FORTIES...

NOTHING. IF YOU COULD JUST LIFT YOURSELF A LITTLE, I COULD ...

THAT'S ENOUGH. THAT'S GREAT...

OOOOOOHH

JUST LISTEN TO THAT CROWD AS HE SWITCHES HIS GRIP THERE...

UM. OOOMMMMM.

14

DAN?

IT'S OKAY. I JUST NEED A COUPLE OF MINUTES TO...

AW, HELL.

...SPINNING THROUGH THE AIR AGAINST THE LIGHTS, JUST *PERFECT* ...

...AND HE'S DOWN! A PERFECT *HECHT DISMOUNT*...

OH, LAURIE, I'M *SORRY*. IT ISN'T *YOU*, IT'S JUST...

HEY, *RELAX*. IT'S *OKAY*. WE DON'T HAVE TO *RUSH* THINGS...

WE'VE GOT AS LONG AS IT *TAKES*. AND DON'T *WORRY*. YOU'RE DOING *FINE*.

THANK YOU. THANK YOU VERY MUCH.

KLAP KLAPKLAP KLAPKLAP KLAP

...AND WITH THE *ELEVEN O'CLOCK NEWS* COMING UP NEXT, THAT'S ALL WE HAVE *TIME* FOR.

SO FROM ME, BENNY ANGER, AND PALE HORSE'S *RED D'EATH*, IT'S THANK YOU AND *GOOD NIGHT!*

STILL NOTHING?

UH-UH.

HM.

MMMMMM- MMELTDOWNS...

NOW LET'S TAKE A BREAK FROM OUR *MIDNIGHT MOVIE* FOR *THIS*...

WITH *FRUITY FALLOUT* AND A *DELICIOUS* MOLTEN CENTER. THEY'LL BLOW YOU ALL THE WAY TO *CHINA*...

AND THAT'S *IT* FROM *ABC* TONIGHT. WE'LL BE BACK TOMORROW MORNING. BUT UNTIL THEN, TAKE A *BREAK*, TAKE A *NAP*, AND MOST OF *ALL*, TAKE *CARE* OF EACH OTHER.

abc

DAN?

MMHUH?

CAN YOU MOVE *OVER* A LITTLE?

UHM SURRY ...

IT DOESN'T MATTER. I KNOW HOW IT IS WHEN SOMETHING'S NOT RIGHT.

WE'LL SLEEP NOW, OKAY?

JUST *SLEEP*.

15

16

UHHMN, JON..?

DID YOU SHUB UBBUH NUHNUHDUH ....

MMM.

17

18

DAN?

DAN? WHERE ARE YOU?

DID YOU GO TO THE **BATHROOM**, OR ...

DOWN HERE.

DOWN...? WHAT ARE YOU DOING DOWN **HERE**? I WOKE UP, AND THE T.V. WAS STILL ON AND EVERY-THING...

I MEAN, IT'S ONLY A QUARTER AFTER **THREE**...

YES.

I KNOW.

DAN?

UH ... HEY, ARE YOU **OKAY**? I MEAN, YOU SOUND **UPSET**...

A **DREAM**. I ... I JUST HAD A DREAM IS ALL.

W-WE WERE **KISSING**, AND THEN THIS NUCLEAR **BOMB**, IT JUST ...

IT'S THIS **WAR**, THE FEELING THAT IT'S UN-**AVOIDABLE**. IT MAKES ME FEEL SO **POWER-LESS**.

WE BURNED **UP**. WE WERE **GONE**. EVERY-THING WAS GONE ...

SO **IMPOTENT**.

19

OH, DAN.

NO, LISTEN, IT'S NOT *JUST* THE WAR OR THE FACT I'M *EMOTIONALLY* CHURNED UP RIGHT NOW...

IT'S THIS *MASK KILLER* THING... I MEAN *SERIOUSLY:* BLAKE DEAD, JON EXILED, ADRIAN SHOT AT, RORSCHACH CAPTURED...

I CAN JUST FEEL THIS *ANXIETY,* THIS *TERROR* BEARING DOWN...

I CAME DOWN HERE, FOR MY *COSTUME*...I DUNNO, I FEEL *WORRIED, CONFUSED.* I JUST NEED TO TAKE THE *AIR,* TO BLOW AWAY THE COBWEBS. I...

AHH, HELL...

HELL, I GUESS I MUST LOOK PRETTY *DEVO,* RIGHT?

HA HA HA HA!

AHH, YOU'RE *RIGHT.* IT'S A STUPID, MID-LIFE CRISIS KIND OF IDEA. I DON'T EVEN KNOW WHAT I WAS PLANNING TO *DO*...

MAYBE TAKE THE *SHIP* OUT OR SOMETHING, GET MYSELF *STRAIGHT*...

SO? WHO'S TO *KNOW*?

WHAT?

WHO'S TO *KNOW*? YOU SAID IT'S *RADAR INVISIBLE.*

YES, BUT...

LISTEN, YOU GET THE REST OF YOUR *SUIT* ON WHILE I GO GET *DRESSED.*

I USED TO BE A MASKED AVENGER *TOO,* REMEMBER...

I MEAN, I'M *USED* TO GOING OUT AT THREE IN THE MORNING AND DOING SOMETHING *STUPID.*

20

UH, DAN'?

I'M READY.

ME TOO.

LET'S GO.

21

UH, WILL THIS THING STILL *FLY* OKAY AND EVERY- THING?

SURE. I RAN A SCAN ON ARCHIE EARLIER : NOT A FEATHER OUT OF PLACE. LET ME JUST PLUG THE STEERING COLUMN IN OVER *HERE*...

HMM. GOT *SOOT* IN HIS EYES...

OH ! WE'RE *MOVING*.

YES. I'M SORRY... HE ALWAYS GIVES THAT LITTLE *LURCH* WHEN HE STARTS UP. CAN'T SEEM TO IRON IT OUT.

BETTER WASH THESE WINDOWS DOWN BEFORE WE HIT THE *EXIT* TUNNEL...

WOW. IT'S LIKE BEING ON A *GHOST TRAIN*: THE DOORS BUMP *OPEN*, YOU ENTER THE *TUNNEL*...

HEH. ACTUALLY IT'S A FORGOTTEN SECTION OF *SUB- WAY* I CONVERTED AFTER BUYING THE BUILDING *ABOVE*.

LET'S PICK UP A LITTLE *SPEED* HERE.

IS IT OKAY TO *GO* THIS FAST? WHERE DOES THE TUNNEL COME *OUT*?

A DERELICT *WARE- HOUSE* TWO BLOCKS *NORTH*. I OWN THAT, TOO.

LET'S JUST HOPE THE STEEL *FLOOD DOORS* OVER THE END OF THE *TUNNEL* HAVEN'T *RUSTED SHUT*.

RUSTED *SHUT*? *DAN*! ARE YOU..?

RELAX. JUST KIDDING.

OKAY, IN A MOMENT I'M GOING TO TAKE HIM *UP* JUST HAVE TO ARRANGE SOME *CLOUD COVER* WITH THE *FOG- SCREENS*...

FOG- SCREENS?

DRY ICE. ARCHIE BREATHES *SMOKE* AS WELL AS *FIRE*.

OKAY NOW, HOLD *TIGHT*. I'M ROLLING BACK THE WAREHOUSE ROOF.

HERE WE *GO*...

THIS IS *GREAT*, REMEMBERING WHICH *SWITCHES*; WHICH *SEQUENCES*. IT'S LIKE THE OLD INSTINCTS ARE *IMPRINTED* ON MY *FINGER-TIPS*...

THERE'S THE *ASTRODOME*, LIKE A *BUMPER* ON A GIANT *PINBALL MACHINE*...

DAN? WHAT'S THAT DOWN ON OUR *RIGHT*?

WAIT A MINUTE. LET'S GET SOME CAMERAS ON THAT SO WE CAN...

HMM. *TENEMENT* BUILDING ON FIRE. LOOKS LIKE PEOPLE TRAPPED THERE ON THE UPPER *STORYS*.

OH, JESUS. I SEE *KIDS*. CAN YOU DO ANYTHING?

"LET'S HOPE SO. TAKING HIM DOWN NOW..."

OUTTA MY *WAY*, BITCH, I CAN'T *BREATHE* ...

OH, *GOD*, PLEASE *SAVE* US! WE AIN'T *DONE* ANYTHING! MY *BABY* HE AIN'T DONE NOTHIN'. OH *JESUS*, LORD, I'M *PRAYING* TO YOU...

MOMEE*EEE*!

PLEASE STAY CALM. YOUR PREDICAMENT HAS BEEN NOTICED AND THE SITUATION IS BEING ATTENDED TO.

23

OKAY, THERE'S *WATER CANNONS* TRAINED ON THE *LOWER STORYS* TO SLOW DOWN THE *FIRE.*

ALL YOU *PEOPLE* IN THERE, PLEASE GET TO THE *TOP FLOOR.* WE'LL JOIN YOU IN A *MOMENT.*

THANK YOU.

I'LL EXTEND A *RAMP* FROM THE *REAR DOOR* TO A *WINDOW,* SO WE CAN SHEPHERD EVERYBODY ONTO THE *SHIP.*

HMM. IF I'M GOING TO BE WORKING CLOSE TO THE *BLAZE,* I WON'T NEED MY *COAT.*

WELL?

UH?

WUH, WELL *WHAT?*

WELL WHAT ABOUT THE *RAMP?* THERE'S A BUNCH OF PEOPLE STILL NEED THEIR *ASSES* HAULED OUT OF THE *FIRE,* REMEMBER?

OH. OH, RIGHT. SURE...

THE RAMP. ABSOLUTELY...

GET BACK! IT'S *POKIN'* SOMETHIN' AT THE *BUILDING!*

MOM? THAT GUY IN THE SPACE ROCKET, IS THAT *JESUS?*

24

OKAY, EVERYBODY. COMING THROUGH...

OH, MAN, I DON'T *BELIEVE* THIS...

SO WHY'S *SHE* DRESSED LIKE THAT? IT'S *US* WHO JUST GOT WOKE UP AT FOUR IN THE A.M.!

HI.

IF YOU COULD ALL FORM A *LINE* BY THE *WINDOW*, WE'LL HAVE YOU OUT OF HERE IN JUST A *MOMENT*.

DA... UH, *NITE OWL*, THERE'S AN AWFUL LOT OF *PEOPLE* IN HERE.

NO PROBLEM. I CAN MAKE MORE SPACE BY TAKING THE *STEERING COLUMN* AND JACKING IT IN UP ON THE *ROOF*...

THESE *FLAMES* ARE CLIMBING PRETTY FAST. HOW'S THE *EVACUATION* COMING?

OH, YOU KNOW. THE *USUAL*. WILL YOU GO *ACROSS*, PLEASE?

ARE YOU WITH THE *FIRE DEPARTMENT*?

LISTEN, I'M SMOKEY THE BEAR'S SECRET MISTRESS. NOW WILL YOU PLEASE JUST *MOVE* OR THROW YOURSELF OVER THE *SIDE* OR SOMETHING?

WELCOME ABOARD. PLEASE MAKE YOURSELVES COMFORTABLE, BUT TRY NOT TO TOUCH ANY *BUTTONS*. WE'LL BE SERVING COFFEE IN A FEW MOMENTS.

IS EVERYBODY *OUT* YET?

HERE'S THE *LAST*. LISTEN, I DON'T *CARE* ABOUT YOUR '*ALLERGIES*' OR YOUR '*MEDICINE*'! JUST GET IN THE *SHIP*, YOU ASSHOLE.

UHH, FINE. OKAY, LET'S *RIDE*.

I'LL PUT SOME *MUSIC* ON THE IN-SHIP *STEREO*...

YOU'RE MY THRILL YOU DO SOMETHING TO ME YOU SEND CHILLS RIGHT THROUGH ME WHEN I LOOK AT YOU, 'COS YOU'RE MY THRILL...

YOU'RE MY THRILL HOW MY PULSE INCREASES I JUST GO TO PIECES WHEN I LOOK AT YOU, 'COS YOU'RE MY THRILL.

25

MMMMMMM-MMMMM NOTHING SEEMS TO MATTER...

THERE'S A **COFFEE MACHINE** BEHIND A PANEL ON THE STAR-BOARD WALL. YOU **GOT** IT?

UH, YEAH. YEAH, I GOT IT. HOW ARE YOU DOING UP THERE? DON'T FALL OFF...

OH, DON'T **WORRY** ABOUT **ME.** I'M FINE.

JUST FINE.

MMMMM-MMMM HERE'S MY HEART ON A SILVER PLATTER.

OKAY, WE'RE OVER THE OPPOSITE **ROOF** NOW. EVERYBODY PLEASE LEAVE THE SHIP THE WAY THEY CAME **IN**...

DON'T **TOUCH** THAT! YOU WANT TO BURN DOWN THE WHOLE **NEIGHBOR-HOOD?**

WHERE'S MY WILL? WHY THIS STRANGE DESIRE...

...THAT KEEPS MOUNTING HIGHER? WHEN I LOOK AT YOU, I CAN'T KEEP STILL 'COS YOU'RE MY **THRILL.**

OKAY, FOLKS, THE FIRE DEPARTMENT WILL HANDLE THE REST. WHEN YOUR COFFEE'S FINISHED, PLEASE HEAD DOWN TO THE STREET.

GOOD-NIGHT, NOW.

YOU KNOW, I CAN'T BELIEVE WE JUST **DID** THAT. YOU REALIZE THEY'LL PROBABLY LOCK US UP WITH **RORSCHACH?**

AHH, WHO **CARES?** WORLD WAR THREE COULD START **TOMORROW,** RIGHT?

WHO WAS THAT **SINGING?**

OH, THAT WAS **BILLIE HOLIDAY,** "YOU'RE MY **THR**..."

UH, LAURIE, WHAT ...?

IT'S OKAY. I THINK I CAUGHT THE TITLE.

26

27

I THOUGHT YOU'D *QUIT*, LAURIE.

DANGEROUS *HABITS*, REMEMBER?

THERE'S NO SUCH THING AS QUITTING. JUST SOMETIMES THERE'S A LONGER PAUSE BETWEEN *RELAPSES*, RIGHT?

DAN, WAS TONIGHT GOOD? DID YOU LIKE IT?

UH-HUH.

DID THE COSTUMES MAKE IT GOOD?

DAN...?

YEAH.

YEAH, I GUESS THE COSTUMES HAD SOMETHING TO DO WITH IT. IT JUST FEELS *STRANGE*, YOU KNOW? TO COME OUT AND *ADMIT* THAT TO SOMEBODY.

TO COME OUT OF THE *CLOSET*.

DOES IT FEEL *GOOD*?

OH, YES. JESUS, YES.

I FEEL SO *CONFIDENT* IT'S LIKE I'M ON *FIRE*. AND ALL THE *MASK KILLERS*, ALL THE *WARS* IN THE *WORLD*, THEY'RE JUST *CASES*--JUST *PROBLEMS* TO SOLVE.

HMMM. Y'KNOW, YOU SOUND REAL *PASSIONATE*. I DIDN'T KNOW YOU COULD *SMOLDER*.

I'D *HOPED* TONIGHT MIGHT WAKE SOMETHING *INSIDE* YOU, BUT IT SOUNDS LIKE IT'S AWOKEN WITH AN *APPETITE*.

YOU'RE RIGHT. IT HAS A *BIG* APPETITE.

MMMMM. *INSATIABLE*, HUH? WELL, I'M OPEN TO *SUGGESTIONS*. WHAT SHALL WE DO *NEXT*?

I'VE BEEN *THINKING* ABOUT THAT, AND I FEEL WE HAVE CERTAIN OBLIGATIONS TO OUR *FRATERNITY*.

I THINK WE SHOULD SPRING RORSCHACH.

WHAT?

I am a brother to dragons, and a companion to owls. My skin is black upon me, and my bones are burned with heat.

JOB chapter 30, verses 29-30

28

The following text is reprinted from the Journal of The American Ornithological Society, Fall 1983.

BLOOD·FROM·THE
SHOULDER·OF·PALLAS
BY DANIEL DREIBERG

Is it possible, I wonder, to study a bird so closely, to observe and catalogue its peculiarities in such minute detail, that it becomes invisible? Is it possible that while fastidiously calibrating the span of its wings or the length of its tarsus, we somehow lose sight of its poetry? That in our pedestrian descriptions of a marbled or vermiculated plumage we forfeit a glimpse of living canvases, cascades of carefully toned browns and golds that would shame Kandinsky, misty explosions of color to rival Monet? I believe that we do. I believe that in approaching our subject with the sensibilities of statisticians and dissectionists, we distance ourselves increasingly from the marvelous and spell-binding planet of imagination whose gravity drew us to our studies in the first place.

This is not to say that we should cease to establish facts and to verify our information, but merely to suggest that unless those facts can be imbued with the flash of poetic insight then they remain dull gems; semi-precious stones scarcely worth the collecting.

When we stare into the catatonic black bead of a Parakeet's eye we must teach ourselves to glimpse the cold, alien madness that Max Ernst perceived when he chose to robe his naked brides in confections of scarlet feather and the transplanted monstrous heads of exotic birds. When some ocean-going Kite or Tern is captured in the sharp blue gaze of our Zeiss lenses, we must be able to see the stop motion flight of sepia gulls through the early kinetic photographs of Muybridge, beating white wings tracing a slow oscilloscope line through space and time.

Looking at a hawk, we see the minute differences in width of the shaft lines on the underfeathers where the Egyptians once saw Horus and the burning eye of holy vengeance incarnate. Until we transform our mere sightings into genuine visions; until our ear is mature enough to order a symphony from the shrill pandemonium of the aviary; until then we may have a hobby, but we shall not have a passion.

When I was a boy, my passion was for owls. During the long summers of the early fifties, while the rest of the country was apparently watching the skies for incoming flying saucers or Soviet missiles, I would hare across the New England fields in the heart of the night, sneakers munching through the dried grass and bracken towards my watch, where I would sit peering upwards in hope of a different sort of spectacle, ears straining for the weird scream that meant an old bird was out combing the dark for sustenance, a mad hermit screech, glaringly distinct from the snoring hiss of a younger owl.

Somewhere over the years; sometime during the yawning expanse between those snug years in the afterglow of a war well won and these current times, huddled in the looming shadow of a war unwinnable; someplace along the line my passion got lost, unwittingly refined from the original gleaming ore down to a banal and lusterless filing system. This gradual tarnishing had gone unnoticed, unchecked, finally calcifying into unthinking habit. It was not until comparatively recently that I managed to catch a dazzling glimpse of the motherlode through the accumulated dust of methodical study and academia: visiting a sick acquaintance at a hospital in Maine on behalf of a mutual friend, walking back across the shadowy parking lot with my mind reduced to blankness by the various concerns of the day, I suddenly and unexpectedly heard the cry of a hunting owl.

It was a bird advanced in years, its shriek that of a deranged old man, wheeling madly through the dark and freezing sky against the ragged night clouds, and the sound halted me in my footsteps. It is a fallacy to suppose that owls screech to startle their prey from hiding, as some have suggested; the cry of the hunting owl is a voice from Hell, and it turns the scrabbling voles to statues, roots the weasel to the soil. In my instant of paralysis there on the glistening macadam, between the sleeping automobiles, I understood the purpose behind the cry with a biting clarity, the way I'd understood it as a boy, belly flat against the warm summer earth. In that extended and timeless moment, I felt the kinship of simple animal fear along with all those other creatures much smaller and more vulnerable than I who had heard the scream as I had heard it, were struck motionless as I was. The owl was not attempting to frighten his food into revealing itself. Perched with disconcerting stillness upon its branch for hours, drinking in the darkness through dilated and thirsty pupils, the owl had already spotted its dinner. The screech served merely to transfix the chosen morsel, pinning it to the ground with a shrill nail of blind, helpless terror. Not knowing which of us had been selected, I stood frozen along with the rodents of the field, my heart hammering as it waited for the sudden clutch of sharpened steel fingers that would provide my first and only indication that I was the predetermined victim. The feathers of owls are soft and downy; they make no sound at all as they drop through the dark stratas of the sky. The silence before an owl swoops is a V-Bomb silence, and you never hear the one that hits you.

Somewhere away in the crepuscular gloom beyond the yellow-lit hospital grounds I thought I heard something small emit its ultimate squeal. The moment had passed. I could move again, along with all the relieved, invisible denizens of the tall grass. We were safe. It wasn't screaming for us, not this time. We could continue with our nocturnal business, with our lives, searching for a meal or a mate. We were not twitching nervelessly in stifling, stinking darkness, head first down the gullet of the swooping horror, our tails dangling pathetically from that vicious scimitar beak for hours before finally our hind legs and pelvic girdle are disgorged, our empty, matted skin curiously inverted by the process.

Although I had recovered my motor abilities in the aftermath of the owl's shriek, I found that my equilibrium was not so easily regained. Some facet of the experience had struck a chord in me, forged a connection between my dulled and jaded adult self and the child who sprawled in faint starlight while the great night hunters staged dramas full of hunger and death in the opaque jet air above me. An urge to experience rather than merely record had been rekindled within me, prompting the thought processes, the self-evaluation that has led to this current article.

As I remarked earlier, this is not to suggest that I immediately foreswore all academic endeavor and research pertaining to the field in order to run away and eke out some naked and primordial existence in the woods. Quite the contrary: I hurled myself into the study of my subject with renewed fervor, able to see the dry facts and arid descriptions in the same transforming magical light that had favored them when I was younger. A scientific understanding of the beautifully synchronized and articulated motion of an owl's individual feathers during flight does not impede a poetic appreciation of the same phenomenon. Rather, the two enhance each other, a more lyrical eye lending the cold data a romance from which it has long been divorced.

Immersing myself avidly in dusty and long untouched reference books I came across forgotten passages that would make me almost breathless, dreary-looking tomes that would reveal themselves to be treasure houses of iridescent wonder. I rediscovered many long-lost gems amongst the cobwebs, antique and functional stretches of descriptive prose which nonetheless conveyed the violent and terrible essence of their subject matter effortlessly.

I stumbled once more across T.A. Coward's engrossing account on an encounter with an Eagle Owl: "In Norway I saw a bird that had been taken when in down from the nest, but it not only assumed the typical terrifying attitude, but made frequent dashes at the wire, striking with its feet. It puffed its feathers out, framed its head in its wings, and fired off a volley of loud cracks from its snapping beak, but what struck me most was the scintillating flash of its great orange eyes."

Then of course there is Hudson's account of the Magellanic Eagle-Owl which he wounded in Patagonia: "The irides were of a bright orange color, but every time I attempted to approach the bird they kindled into great globes of quivering yellow flame, the black pupils being surrounded by a scintillating crimson light which threw out minute yellow sparks into the air." In long-buried words such as the foregoing I caught some of the searing, apocalyptic intensity that I had felt in that wet hospital parking lot in Maine.

Nowadays, when I observe some specimen of *Carine noctua*, I try to look past the fine grey down on the toes, to see beyond the white spots arranged in neat lines, like a firework display across its brow. Instead, I try to see the bird whose image the Greeks carved into their coins, sitting patiently at the ear of the Goddess Pallas Athene, silently sharing her immortal wisdom.

Perhaps, instead of measuring the feathered tufts surmounting its ears, we should speculate on what those ears may have heard. Perhaps when considering the manner in which it grips its branch, with two toes in front and the reversible outer toe clutching from behind, we should allow ourselves to pause for a moment, and acknowledge that these same claws must once have drawn blood from the shoulder of Pallas.

HELLO? HELLO, IS THAT *SALLY*? *SALLY!* HOW ARE YOU? I ...

HOLLIS.

HOLLIS MASON.

HOLLIS? OH *GOD*, I'M *SORRY*. I DIDN'T RECOGNIZE YOUR *VOICE*. IT'S BEEN *AGES*.

SO, HOW'S *THINGS?* ALL THIS TIME YOU HAD MY *NUMBER;* YOU WAIT TILL WE'RE BOTH IN OUR *SUNSET YEARS* TO *USE* IT!

WELL, I RECKONED THIS WAS A *SPECIAL OCCASION,* SAL.

PAPERS REPORT A *TENEMENT FIRE* LAST NIGHT: TRAPPED PEOPLE RESCUED BY AN *AIRSHIP.* THE PILOT WORE *GOGGLES.*

SEEMS HE HAD A *WOMAN* WITH HIM.

YOU'RE TALKING ABOUT THAT KID WHO SUCCEEDED YOU? SO WHO'S THIS *WOMAN?* I ...

LAURIE? MY DAUGHTER LAURIE? BUT SHE *HATED* ADVENTURING! WHY SHOULD SHE...?

LIVING WITH HIM? A WEEK AFTER *JON* SPLITS? JESUS. FAST *WORK.*

HMM. WELL, THE *MEDIA* HAVEN'T *REALIZED* YET, BUT *I* DID, SOON AS I *HEARD.*

DAN *CONFIRMED* IT WHEN HE CALLED CANCELLING TONIGHT'S *BEER SESSION.* DIDN'T *SAY* MUCH, BUT HE'S *PLANNING* SOMETHING...

TAKES YOU *BACK,* HUH?

TO OUR SORDID *PAST?* YEAH, I GUESS IT *DOES.* I'VE BEEN THINKING ABOUT OLD TIMES A *LOT* LATELY, WISHING I'D KEPT IN *TOUCH* WITH PEOPLE...

HOW ARE *YOU,* HOLLIS? BET YOU HAVEN'T CHANGED A *HAIR.*

OH, I'VE CHANGED *SEVERAL* HAIRS. STILL, I TRY TO KEEP IN *TRIM,* WORKING DOWN IN THE *REPAIR SHOP* AND EVERYTHING.

HOW ABOUT *YOU?* FROM YOUR VOICE, YOU'RE SOUNDING *YOUNGER* THAN *EVER.*

WHY, *BLESS YOU,* HOLLIS, BUT THAT'S PROBABLY JUST *SENILITY.*

NO, I'VE GAINED SOME *WEIGHT,* BUT I CAN STILL SQUEEZE INTO THE OLD *COSTUME* IF I DON'T BREATHE IN.

YOU EVER TRY ON *YOUR* OLD *DUDS?*

NAH. IT'S *DIFFERENT* FOR GUYS. I'D FEEL *STUPID...*

...ALTHOUGH ALL THE *KIDS* ROUND HERE ARE PREPARING FOR *HALLOWEEN* NEXT WEEK, SO WHO *KNOWS?* MAYBE I'LL DIG OUT THE OLD THREADS AND GO *TRICK-OR-TREATIN'.*

1

HAHAHA! WELL, IF YOU RUN INTO *LAURIE* AND HER NEW BOYFRIEND WHILE YOU'RE BOBBING FOR APPLES, TELL HER *MOM* SAYS HI.

JEEZ. LAURIE BACK IN *COSTUME.* MAYBE SHE'LL FINALLY THANK ME FOR ALL THAT *TRAINING* I MADE HER DO.

AH, WELL, YOU KNOW *KIDS.* NO *GRATITUDE* TILL IT'S TOO *LATE.* I WAS JUST THE *SAME.*

I OFTEN WISH I COULD THANK *MY* OLD MAN FOR GIVING ME A *CAREER,* A LIVING I *ENJOY...*

OH *SURE.* CHOOSING THE RIGHT *LIFESTYLE'S* JUST *SO* IMPORTANT, AND SOMETIMES YOU NEED *GUIDANCE.*

I NEVER *HAD* GUIDANCE, SO I'M *INDECISIVE.* I MEAN, SHOULD I BOOK EXTRA *ANALYSIS* OR *AEROBICS*? A DECISION *YOU'D* MAKE *INSTANTLY*!

HM. UH, WELL, LISTEN, IT'S BEEN GREAT *TALKING* TO YOU, SALLY, BUT CALLING *CALIFORNIA* IS *EXPENSIVE.*

I BETTER *GO* BEFORE I PUT TOO MUCH STRAIN ON MY *BANK ACCOUNT.* GOD KNOWS IT DOESN'T NEED ANY *MORE.*

YEAH, WELL, THAT'S *NIXONOMICS.* WE'RE ALL FEELING THE *PINCH,* I GUESS.

ANYWAY, THANKS FOR THE NEWS, AND DON'T GET *TOO* MISTY-EYED THINKING ABOUT OLD TIMES. IT AIN'T *HEALTHY.*

YOU TAKE *CARE* NOW, HOLLIS.

'BYE.

OLD GHOSTS

"IT'S LIKE ALL OUR OLD NIGHTMARES COME BACK TO HAUNT US, Y'KNOW?"

ADRIFT AND STARVING, MY DARKEST IMAGININGS WELLED UP UNCHECKED, SPILLING FROM BRAIN TO HEART LIKE BLACK INK, IMPOSSIBLE TO REMOVE.

"RED INVASIONS, MASKED MEN... SEEN THIS WEEK'S NOVA EXPRESS? 'SPIRIT OF '77'. I MEAN, I REMEMBER 1977..."

"GOD SPARE US."

I PICTURED DAVIDSTOWN'S QUIET STREETS OVERRUN BY TATTOOED FIENDS. RECALLING THEIR BRUTALITY, I MOANED.

"EVERYTHING'S GOING TO HELL. I'M JUST GLAD MY ROSA AIN'T ALIVE TO SEE."

THE FREIGHTER HAD SURELY REACHED DAVIDSTOWN ALREADY. MY WIFE WAS ALMOST CERTAINLY DEAD. THESE NOTIONS TRANSFIXED ME, STOPPING TIME IN ITS TRACKS.

"TODAY WOULDA BEEN OUR ANNIVERSARY. SUNDAY, 27TH OCTOBER. FUNNY, THIS TIME O'YEAR SHE'S ALWAYS ON MY MIND."

I REMEMBERED HER WAVING GOODBYE FROM THE VERANDAH SHADOWS, SUNLIGHT ILLUMINATING ONE CHEEK BONE.

DEAD?

"SHE'DA HATED HOW THIS SUPER-HERO THING TURNED OUT: DOC MANHATTAN EXILED, OZYMANDIAS SHOT AT ..."

"... AN' RORSCHACH! SEE INNA GAZETTE HE ATTACKED SOME OTHER PRISONER WITH HOT FAT? JESUS."

"THOSE GLORIOUS DAYS; THAT INNOCENCE..."

DEAD?

"I STILL CAN'T BELIEVE IT... HIM COMIN' HERE EVERY DAY, NOBODY REALIZIN'. STILL, THAT'S LIFE: LOTTA STUFF HAPPENS UNDER THE WATERLINE..."

DEAD: I IMAGINED MY SHIPMATES' BLOATED CORPSES, CARRYING MY RAFT ON FISHEATEN BACKS...

"IN FACT... OH, GAZETTE? SURE. HEY, SEE THIS RORSCHACH ITEM? HE WAS A CUSTOMER HERE. ALWAYS KINDA SUSPECTED, BUT, HEY, PRETTY INCREDIBLE, RIGHT?"

"KOVACS...? UH, YES. INCREDIBLE. THANK YOU."

DEAD: THE PUTREFYING SHARK, ITS SNARL NO LONGER CONVINCING...

"BYE. HAVE A NICE DAY."

DEAD: I HEAR HER PLEADING; SEE THEIR YELLOWED SMILES, THEIR CUTLASSES CARVING RELENTLESSLY UNTIL ALL HER PERSONALITY, ALL HER SUBTLETIES OF POSTURE AND EXPRESSION ARE OBLITERATED, REDUCED TO MEAT...

DEAD.

"HMM. PREOCCUPIED TYPE. PROBABLY A TEACHER, THINKIN' ABOUT ALGEBRA, RELATIVITY, WHATEVER. WHADDA THOSE GUYS KNOW ABOUT LIFE? WORLD'S GOING CRAZY, THEY DON'T EVEN NOTICE!"

FINALLY, FACED WITH HORRORS BOTH INTOLERABLE AND UNAVOIDABLE, I CHOSE MADNESS.

3

THIS IS INSANITY.

WE'RE YOUNG *LOVERS*, THE WORLD COULD END *TOMORROW* AND HOW ARE WE SPENDING SUNDAY *EVENING*? WE'RE PLANNING TO BUST A *HOMICIDAL MANIAC* OUT OF *SING-SING*!

LISTEN, I'LL LOAD THOSE *HOVER BIKES* AFTER THIS *CIGARETTE*, OKAY?

SURE.

AND IT'S NOT INSANITY. *SOMETHING'S* GOING ON: FOUR ADVENTURERS ATTACKED WITHIN *ELEVEN DAYS* ISN'T *COINCIDENCE*.

MAYBE THAT CANCER-SCARE *MEDIA ASSAULT* THAT PROMPTED JON'S *EXILE* WAS PART OF SOMEBODY'S *PLAN*. MAYBE SOMEONE *INTENDED* TO START WORLD WAR *THREE*.

OH DAN, COME ON...

LAURIE, YOU *LIVED* WITH JON. *YOU* DIDN'T CONTRACT *CANCER* FROM HIM. MAYBE *NOBODY* DID.

MY COMPUTER LISTS MOST PEOPLE *NOVA EXPRESS* MENTIONED AS EMPLOYED BY A *RESEARCH COMPANY* CALLED "DIMENSIONAL DEVELOPMENTS" BETWEEN '67 AND '85. WEIRD, HUH?

JANEY *SLATER*, WALLY *WEAVER*... THEY EVEN GAVE *MOLOCH* A TEMPORARY JOB WHEN HE LEFT PRISON.

THEY FUND THE *INSTITUTE FOR EXTRASPATIAL STUDIES*; ANOTHER COMPANY, *PYRAMID DELIVERIES*, FUNDS *THEM*. THIS CORPORATE STRUCTURE STUFF'S A *MAZE*...

YEAH? WELL THAT AND YOUR LOGIC BOTH. I MEAN, WHY RISK SPRINGING A *LIABILITY* LIKE *RORSCHACH*? WE TOOK *ENOUGH* CHANCES WITH THAT *TENEMENT RESCUE*.

RORSCHACH'S BEEN INVESTIGATING THIS THING ALL *ALONG*. WE NEED HIS *INFORMATION*.

... AND WE MAY NOT HAVE LONG TO *GET* IT. TODAY'S *GAZETTE* MENTIONS DEATH THREATS FOLLOWING YESTERDAY'S *HOT FAT INCIDENT*.

IT'S *IMPORTANT*, LAURIE. IF JON'S *EXILE* AND ITS *CONSEQUENCES* WERE *PREMEDITATED*, MAYBE IT'S THE *MOST IMPORTANT THING IN THE WORLD*.

REDS CROSS PAKISTAN BORDER

4

SUPERHERO SAVES WORLD, HUH? THIS IS SOME ELABORATE SCAM TO GET ME BACK INTO MY COSTUME, RIGHT?

HA HA. LAURIE, THE COSTUME WAS *YOUR* IDEA...

WHAAAT? THAT'S RIDICULOUS! I *LOATHE* THAT HALLOWEEN SUIT. OBVIOUSLY, I WORE IT TO HELP *YOU*.

OH, *OBVIOUSLY*.

OWN *UP*, LAURIE: DOESN'T THIS BRING ALL THOSE OLD TIMES FLOODING BACK? *NIGHT* PATROLS; HAVING A *SECRET*...

WELLL... YEAH, *PATROLS* WERE OKAY. I HAD NINE DIFFERENT ROUTES OVER WASHINGTON'S *ROOFTOPS*. ROUTE *FIVE* WAS BEST.

THAT HAD THE *WHITE HOUSE*, THE LINCOLN MEMORIAL AND THEN *HOME* TO ME AND JON'S FABULOUS APARTMENT. WE WERE *HAPPY* THERE. WE...

OH *DAN*, I'M SORRY. I KEEP MENTIONING JON. HE JUST *POPS UP* WHEN I DON'T *EXPECT* IT.

DON'T WORRY. IT'S EARLY DAYS. A FEW *SKELETONS* ARE BOUND TO KEEP JUMPING OUT OF THE CLOSET.

I WAS JUST THINKING ABOUT *ADRIAN*. WE OUGHT TO *CONTACT* HIM, BUT MAYBE NOT TILL *AFTER* THE JAILBREAK.

I MEAN, IN *HIS* POSITION, KNOWING *BEFORE-HAND* WOULD BE *COMPROMISING*. HE MIGHT FEEL OBLIGED TO *STOP US*.

DAN, SOME-TIMES, I FEEL OBLIGED TO STOP US. I MEAN, A *JAILBREAK*. I CAN'T BELIEVE WE'RE TAKING THIS *SERIOUSLY*.

ASSUMING SOMEBODY'S USING *JON* TO TRIGGER *ARMAGEDDON*, THEN HOW *SHOULD* WE TAKE IT? IT'S *SERIOUS*...

...AND FOR *RORSCHACH*, IF THE MOOD AROUND THAT PRISON GETS ANY *UGLIER*, IT'S A MATTER OF LIFE OR *DEATH*.

5

UHH.... WHAT DO **YOU** GUYS WANT?

HEY, LOOK, THIS IS THE **SOLITARY** WING. YOU'RE NOT SUPPOSED TO **BE** HERE. IF ANYBODY **SEES**, WE COULD **ALL** GET INTO TROUBLE.

HEY, C'MON, GIMME A **BREAK**, HUH?

HOW'S THE WIFE, MULHEARNEY?

WHAT? HEY, LISTEN, SHE'S NOTHING TO **DO** WITH THIS, OKAY? YOU BETTER LEAVE...

...AND THE **KID?** YOU STILL HAVE A **KID.** THAT'S **RIGHT**, ISN'T IT?

Y-YEAH. BUT I ...

AW CHRIST. LOOK, WHAT DO YOU **WANT?**

FIVE MINUTES ALONE WITH THE BABY YOU'RE MINDING. DON'T WORRY. WE WON'T HURT HIM.

WE JUST WANT TO SAY HELLO.

WELL...WELL, ALRIGHT. FIVE MINUTES. BUT THAT'S ALL, OKAY?

OKAY, FELLAS?

OKAY. OKAY, FINE...

RORSCHACH.

IT'S BEEN A LONG TIME.

BIG FIGURE.

SMALL WORLD.

6

HA HA. "*SMALL WORLD*". I *LIKE* THAT. THAT'S VERY *GOOD*.

BUT Y'KNOW, YOU'RE *RIGHT*. THIS *IS* A SMALL WORLD. I'VE BEEN IN IT NOW FOR HOW LONG IS IT, MICHAEL?

TWENTY YEARS, MR. FIGURE.

TWENTY YEARS...

IT'S A LONG *TIME*. YOU MUST HAVE THOUGHT YOU COULD *FORGET* WHAT YOU DID TO ME, YOU AND THAT *OWL* GUY. FUNNY, AIN'T IT, HOW...

⌐ *FFP* ⌐ THANK YOU, LAWRENCE...

...HOW THESE THINGS COME BACK TO *HAUNT* US?

INCIDENTALLY, THAT *GUY* YOU *BURNED* IS *DYING*: MAYBE TOMORROW, MAYBE THURSDAY, FRIDAY. BUT DON'T *WORRY* ...IT'LL NEVER REACH *COURT*.

YOU NEITHER.

SEE, WHEN HE *CROAKS*, THIS PLACE *BLOWS*...

...AND THEN YOU DIE BY *INCHES*.

TALL ORDER.

LEMME GET *MULHEARNEY* TO UNLOCK THIS *CAGE*! I WANNA TEAR THIS GUY A NEW *HOLE*...

NO. NOT *YET*, MICHAEL. I'VE WAITED *TWENTY YEARS*. THERE'S NO *HURRY*.

HE'LL GET HIS SOON *ENOUGH*...

...AND NOBODY IS GOING TO *CARE*. I HEAR EVEN HIS *SHRINK* RESIGNED TODAY.

YOU'RE ALONE IN THE *VALLEY* OF THE *SHADOW*, RORSCHACH, WHERE YOUR PAST HAS A LONG *REACH* AND BETWEEN *YOU* AND *IT* THERE'S ONE CRUMMY *LOCK*.

THINK ABOUT IT.

7

EXCUSE ME? MY NAME'S DETECTIVE STEVEN *FINE*, I'M LOOKING FOR A DANIEL *DREIBERG*.

I'M DAN DREIBERG.

UH, YOU BETTER COME *IN*...

ALMOST *THROUGH* HERE, MR. DREIBERG. THIS BABY'LL HOLD OFF AN *ARMY*. SORRY WE KEPT YOU *WAITING* FOR THE *INSTALLATION*.

THAT'S OKAY. WELL, DETECTIVE, HOW CAN I *HELP* YOU?

EDWARD BLAKE. HOMICIDE VICTIM. YOU *KNEW* HIM.

UH, YES. VAGUELY.

YOU KNEW HIM WELL ENOUGH TO ATTEND HIS *FUNERAL.* I SAW THE *PHOTOGRAPHS:* YOU, ADRIAN *VEIDT*, DOC *MANHATTAN.*

YOU KEEP *HEAVY* COMPANY, MR. DREIBERG.

I MET BLAKE THROUGH *VEIDT.* I, UH, ONCE DONATED SOME *MONEY* TO ONE OF VEIDT'S *CHARITIES.*

UH-HUH.

BIG *GUY*, THAT BLAKE. FOR A *DIPLOMAT.* QUITE A *HEROIC FIGURE.* MAYBE HE WORKED *OUT*, HUH?

FUNNY... THERE'S BEEN A *LOT* OF "HEROIC FIGURES" IN THE NEWS LATELY: *RORSCHACH* CAPTURED, *VEIDT* SHOT AT, *DOC MANHATTAN* LEAVES *EARTH*, DAMN NEAR KICKING OFF WORLD WAR *THREE*...

CIGARETTE, MR. DREIBERG?

NO. THANKS. I DON'T.

New York Ga—

TANKS MASS I EASTERN EUROPE

'PURELY DEFENSIVE' SAY REDS.

CALIFORNIA: GOVE. REAGAN URGES HARD LINE

VERY WISE.

...AND THEN THERE WAS THAT THING LAST *WEEKEND.* YOU *READ* ABOUT THAT? THAT *TENEMENT FIRE?*

ALL FINISHED, MR. DREIBERG. YOU GOT *MAXIMUM SECURITY.*

GORDIAN KNOT

UH, *RIGHT.* RIGHT, *THANKS!* I'LL SETTLE BY *CHECK...*

CRAZIEST STORY... THIS *AIRSHIP* RESCUES ALL THESE *PEOPLE*, HOVERING DOWN BETWEEN THE *BUILDINGS.* AIN'T MANY AIRSHIPS CAN DO *THAT.*

NO?

NO. INTERVIEWED SOME *WITNESSES*, BUT THE DETAILS WERE *GARBLED:* PILOT WORE *GOGGLES;* HAD A FEMALE *ACCOMPLICE;* PLAYED *MUSIC;* SERVED *COFFEE...*

HEY..."*SWEET CHARIOT*"SUGAR *CUBES!* ONLY COME IN *CATERING PACKS*, RIGHT?

UH, YES. I BELIEVE SO. WHY?

EET CHAR SUGAR ATERING PACK

NO REASON.

Y'KNOW, THE ONLY SHIP I EVER HEARD OF COULD MANEUVER BETWEEN *BUILDINGS* BELONGED TO ONE OF THOSE MASKED *ADVENTURERS* THEY OUTLAWED IN '77.

COULDN'T HAVE *BEEN* HIM, NATURALLY... HE'D BE IN HIS *FORTIES* NOW.

SUGAR

8

I MEAN, GUYS THAT AGE LIKE US, WE'RE UNHEALTHY. WE GET UP IN THE MORNING AND COUGH OUR LUNGS UP, WE...

...OH, BUT THEN I FORGOT. YOU DON'T SMOKE, DO YOU?

NO. LISTEN, WHAT'S THIS ABOUT?

AIN'T ABOUT NOTHING. I'M NOT EVEN ON DUTY. JUST CALLED TO SEE IF YOU KNEW ANYTHING ABOUT BLAKE.

I'M AFRAID NOT. WE WEREN'T CLOSE.

UH, THAT LEADS TO THE LUMBER ROOM. KEY'S LOST, I'M AFRAID.

NO SWEAT. I GOTTA GO, ANYWAY. SAY, I NOTICED THIS CALENDAR EARLIER. NICE OWL.

Y'KNOW, TWO KINDS OF PEOPLE HAVE CALENDARS: PEOPLE WHO PEEK AT NEXT MONTH'S PICTURE IN ADVANCE AND PEOPLE WHO DON'T. WHICH ARE YOU?

I DON'T.

YOU OUGHTTA. IT PAYS TO LOOK AHEAD.

HMM. NOVEMBER'S A HAWK TAKING A SPARROW IN FLIGHT. OMINOUS KINDA PICTURE, HUH?

AW HELL... I HOPE I DIDN'T SPOIL THE SURPRISE FOR YOU?

OH, DON'T WORRY. LIFE HAS ENOUGH SURPRISES.

I'LL BET. INCIDENTALLY, I'M SORRY FOR BORING YOU WITH THAT TALK ABOUT ADVENTURERS. IT'S A KINDA HOBBY HORSE OF MINE.

SINCE I ARRESTED RORSCHACH, THEY'VE BEEN PREYING ON MY MIND.

I MEAN, RESCUING FIRE VICTIMS, NOBODY CONDEMNS THAT, BUT IF IT WENT ANY FURTHER,...IT'S LIKE NOVA EXPRESS SAYS: "SPIRIT OF '77". BRRR.

THOSE CHARACTERS: THAT DAME, THE SILK SPECTRE; WHERE'S SHE NOW, I WONDER?

...AND RORSCHACH, HEH! KNOW WHAT HE HAD IN HIS POCKETS WHEN WE COLLARED HIM?

SUGAR CUBES. WEIRD SHIT, HUH?

I'LL BE SEEING YOU, MR. DREIBERG. YOU TAKE CARE, NOW.

I WILL. GOOD EVENING, DETECTIVE.

DAN? WHO WAS THAT? I WAS JUST IN THE BATH BUT I HEARD THE LAST OF IT.

WHAT HE SAID ABOUT 1977... WHAT DID IT MEAN?

IT MEANS TIME'S RUNNING OUT. MAYBE HE'S ALREADY CALLED ROCKEFELLER BASE. MAYBE HE ALREADY KNOWS YOU'RE HERE. SPRINGING RORSCHACH ANY LATER THAN TOMORROW ISN'T SAFE.

SUDDENLY, WE HAVE A DEADLINE.

9

"OCTOBER... THIRTY-FIRST... NINETEEN...EIGHTY-FIVE." THAT'S ALL STRAIGHT.

UH, RIGHT HERE, MR. GODFREY...

SEYMOUR, COME ON, THIS HAS TO BE PASTED UP, PRINTED AND OUT BY THIS AFTERNOON. GIMME THE HEADLINE. WHERE'S THE PICTURES?

WELL, DON'T JUST STAND THERE LIKE AN ASSHOLE, WE STILL NEED THAT FILLER IN BACK. SOMETHING OUTTA THE CRANK FILE.

Y'KNOW, THIS IS MY GREATEST HEADLINE YET. SO MUCH FOR NOVA EXPRESS: "SPIRIT OF '77". SHIT.

UH, IS THIS OKAY? IT'S ADDRESSED "TO THE PEOPLE OF THE JEWNITED STATES OF AMERICA"...

SURE, FINE, WHATEVER. WHERE THE HELL IS THAT OTHER PICTURE? THERE'S ONLY TWO HERE.

FIND IT. PLUS THE PICTURES FOR OUR 'MISSING WRITER' FOLLOW-UP...

MY GOD, THIS PIECE IS HOT! IT CATCHES THE MOOD ON THE STREET; THE WAR PARANOIA AND NOW ALL THIS MASKED MAN STUFF...

Y'KNOW, IT'S RUMORED A MASKED MAN PULLED THAT TENEMENT RESCUE...

I GOT 'EM.

WILL THIS PICTURE DO, OF THE WRITER? I KNOW WE USED IT BEFORE...

SEYMOUR, JUST GET OUT OF MY GODDAMNED FACE! I CAN'T SEE WHAT I'M DOING!

HUH. APPROPRIATE MATERIAL FOR THE HALLOWEEN EDITION.

OKAY. THAT'S IT... LISTEN, YOU GO OUT AND GRAB LUNCH... AND NO GUNGA DINER SHIT, NO HANKY-HEAD GARBAGE! GET ME A HAMBURGER. AN AMERICAN HAMBURGER!

MEANWHILE, I'LL GET THIS WHOLE PANTOMIME READY TO HIT THE STREETS.

10

STILL *SKETCHING,* MS. *MANISH?* I THOUGHT YOU'D BE GLAD TO SEE THE *BACK* OF THE DAMNED THING.

I AM. I JUST NEEDED SOME FINAL STUDIES OF THE *FACIAL ASSEMBLY.*

YOU'RE BLOCKING MY *LIGHT.*

OH, *I'M* SORRY. PLEASE EXCUSE AN OLD DRUNK WHO'S JUST OUT ADMIRING THE COAST OF MOSQUITOES AND DAYDREAMING ABOUT GETTING BACK TO THE *MAINLAND.* THREE MORE *DAYS...*

HOW CAN YOU DRAW IT UNDER THAT *TAR-PAULIN?*

THEY LIFTED IT FOR ME TO SEE THE *BEAK* STRUCTURE.

IT'S BEAUTIFUL *WORK.* I HOPE THEY KEEP IT PROPERLY *RE-FRIGERATED* ON ITS *VOYAGE.* IF IT *DECAYS...*

FPP? OH, IT'S PLENTY COLD ENOUGH WHERE *THAT'S* HEADED.

A LOT COLDER THAN WHERE *I'M* HEADED WHEN I LEAVE HERE.

I TELLYA, THIS PLACE... GODDAMNED PARANOID *MOVIE COMPANIES!* IT'S BEEN LIKE BEING *SHIP-WRECKED.* I REMEMBER, I WROTE THIS *STORY* ONCE...

MORE PLEASANT THAN YOUR *CURRENT* ONE, I HOPE. ILLUSTRATING THAT SEQUENCE WHERE THE YOUNG CHEW THEIR WAY *OUT* OF THEIR MOTHER'S WOMB WAS QUITE AN *EXPERIENCE.*

THERE. FINISHED. SHALL WE GO AND WAVE OUR BABY *GOODBYE,* MR. SHEA?

BABY? HA! IF THAT'S ANY BABY OF *MINE* THERE'S JUST *GOTTA* BE A MORE EN-JOYABLE WAY OF *MAKING* 'EM!

OKAY, C'MON... WE'LL GO CHECK FOR A *FAMILY RESEMBLANCE.* LET'S GIVE THE TYKE A FINAL *ONCE-OVER.*

MANISH 10/31/85

11

...MY OPINION, NUCLEAR WAR IS QUITE POSSIBLE WITHIN THE NEXT *TEN DAYS*, INCONCEIVABLE AS THAT MIGHT SEEM. GOD KNOWS WHAT THESE PEOPLE HAVE INSTEAD OF *BRAINS*...

THANK YOU, PROFESSOR. MOVING *ON* NOW...

TODAY'S *NEW FRONTIERSMAN* MAKES AN APPEAL FOR CLEMENCY ON BEHALF OF *COSTUMED ADVENTURERS.*

IT'S BEEN DESCRIBED BY *NOVA EXPRESS* WRITER-EDITOR *DOUG ROTH* AS "ATTEMPTING TO GRAFT AN ACCEPTABLE FACE ONTO GLORIFIED KLAN-STYLE BRUTALITY."

THE FRONTIERS-MAN PIECE WAS, UH, AN *ATTACK* UPON *MYSELF* AND MY *MAGAZINE.*

IT CLAIMED WE WERE, HA, FUNDED BY COMMUNISTS, IN OUR *DR. MANHATTAN EXPOSE* AND OUR CURRENT "*SPIRIT OF '77*" FEATURE...

THERE. LIKE RODIN, HUH?

IT'S PURE *COMEDY. NOVA EXPRESS* IS FINANCED BY, OF ALL THINGS, A VERY *ORDINARY,* VERY *ALL-AMERICAN* DELIVERY COMPANY. CERTAINLY NOT BY *MOSCOW.*

AS FOR THEIR *EDITORIAL,* I'D CALL IT "SPIRIT OF *NUREMBERG.*"

WAIT A MINUTE...

DOUG ROTH. MEANWHILE, AS PUBLIC RESENTMENT GROWS TOWARDS MASKED HEROES FOLLOWING DR. MANHATTAN'S ABANDONMENT OF EARTH, POLICE ADMIT HAVING NO EVIDENCE TO SUPPORT RUMORS OF VIGILANTE INVOLVEMENT IN SATURDAY'S *TENEMENT RESCUE*...

LEMME JUST PUT THIS IN HERE...

JUST COMING IN; THE PRISONER SCALDED BY CAPTURED VIGILANTE *RORSCHACH* DIED THIS AFTERNOON.

FEARING A *RIOT,* PRISON SPOKESMEN SAY THEY'RE "LOOKING INTO THE JAWS OF HELL".

PRETTY *GOOD.* CAN HARDLY WAIT TILL IT'S *DARK.*

12

GAZETTE? SORRY, PAL...SHOULD BE HERE ANY MINUTE, YOU WANNA WAIT.

BEEN TO THE *UTOPIA*? THOSE OLD *MOVIES*... *RAVES* OUTTA THE *GRAVE*, RIGHT?

In my ravings, desperate for company it seemed I conversed with my perished shipmates.

YEAH, THIS *SPACE GUY* COMES TO WARN EVERYBODY ABOUT *NUCULER WAR*...

TEN DAYS. ON T.V. THEY SAID TEN *DAYS*! JESUS, DERF, GIMME SOME *KATIES*! I WANNA GET *CRAZY*.

Their voices spoke from beneath the raft; thick; bubbling...

HI. GIMME A *GAZETTE*. I WANNA LOOK IN *APARTMENTS* TO *RENT*. I BUSTED UP WITH *ALINE*.

UH, HI, JOEY. JOEY, THE GAZETTE AIN'T *ARRIVED*...

THESE *SUPERFAGS*...THEY'RE THE GUYS I HATE.

DERF...

The conversation of the dead: dreary, bitter, endlessly sad...

HEY!

THAT *MANHATTAN* GUY...IT'S *HIM* WHO BROUGHT ALL THIS DOWN. AND THAT *TENEMENT RESCUE*. I HEARD...

DERF, I KNOW YOU GOT SOME, YOU BASTARD...

Interminable bad news from mouths wherein the little fishes dart.

HI. HERE THEY ARE...

HEY, GIMME ONE OF THOSE!

...I HEARD *THAT* WAS SUPERHEROES TOO. IT'S LIKE THE SPIRIT OF SEVENTY-SIX!

SEVENTY-*SEVEN*. GIMME THOSE *KATIES*...

We talked together my rotted fellows and I...

...OF LIFE, AND ITS ENDINGS. OF THE TERRIBLE SENTENCE UPON US ALL.

OH JESUS. SEE *THIS*? "SING-SING ERUPTS: CAPTURED VIGILANTE SPARKS RIOT: FIVE DEAD."

WELL, I GUESS THAT'S *IT*. I GUESS THE *BALLOON'S* GONE UP.

13

RORSCHACH...

FIGURE, YOU BETTER LET US *AT* HIM! AFTER *OTIS* CROAKED, THAT *LOONEY TUNE'S* GOT HIS COMING!

OFF HIS EYELIDS AND THEN I'LL FIGURE.

YEAH! WE *WANNA* PIECE, FIGURE!

SURE. THANKS-GIVING'S *EARLY* THIS YEAR, BUT EVERYBODY GETS A PIECE OF *TURKEY*.

IT'S JUST I GET TO *CARVE*. NOW *BEAT* IT.

LAWRENCE, HURRY THE GOD-DAMNED *ARC WELDER* UP. WE *ALREADY* GOT DELAYED BUSTING IT OUT OF THE *MACHINE SHOP*...

...AND I WANT TO TAKE MY *TIME* OVER THIS.

WELL, RORSCHACH? HERE IT *IS*! HALLOWEEN, WHEN THE DEAD THINGS RETURN AND DEVILS ARE FREE TO ROAM THE *NIGHT*!

WHATSA-MATTER? TOO *WARM* IN THERE? GONNA GET PLENTY *WARMER*.

RII-I-IGHT! HEY *BOSS*, YOU *NOTICE*? SUDDENLY HE AIN'T GIVING YOU NO "TALL ORDER, SMALL WORLD" SHIT.

MAYBE HE FIGURED OUT THAT ONCE WE SLICE THESE BARS WE'RE GONNA MAKE *HIM* A LITTLE SHORTER.

FAT CHANCE.

FAT...? YOU LOUSY LITTLE *BASTARD*! I'LL TEAR YOUR GODDAMNED *HEART* OUT! YOU'RE *DEAD*, YOU UNNER-STAND? *DEAD*!

WE GOT A JAIL FULL OF GUYS OUT HERE HATE YOUR *GUTS*. WHAT IN HELL DO *YOU* GOT?

YOUR HANDS.

MY PERSPECTIVE.

14

YOU STUPID, FAT SON OF A **BITCH!** NOW WE CAN'T GET AT THE **LOCK!**

MICHAEL, REACH **THROUGH** THERE! CUT WHAT'S **TYIN'** HIM!

AWW SHIT. MY **FINGERS.** HE BROKE MY **FINGERS** ...

CAN'T **REACH.** CAN WE CUT THE **BARS** INSTEAD OF THE **LOCK?**

TOO **SLOW.** THIS RIOT WON'T **LAST,** AND I MUSTN'T BE **INTERRUPTED** BEFORE I'M THROUGH. UNFORTUNATELY, LAWRENCE IS IN THE WAY OF MY **REVENGE.**

KILL HIM.

BOSS, **JESUS,** YOU'RE **KIDDING!** YOU DON'T WANT HIM **THAT** BAD. MIKE, FOR CHRIST'S **SAKE** ...

NOTHING PERSONAL, LARRY.

KKUHH ...

SHIT, THIS IS A MESS. WHAT DO WE DO NOW?

WE **GET** HIM IS WHAT WE DO! WE'RE GONNA CUT THROUGH THERE AND THEN THAT BASTARD'S GONNA FIND OUT WHAT THE **SCORE** IS!

...HHUH-GHLUH-HHH...

ONE-NOTHING.

YOUR MOVE.

COME AND GET ME.

LOOK... *CONVICTS.* WE'RE IN THE *OCCUPIED* SECTION.

HOW DID YOU TALK ME *INTO* THIS? THIS IS GETTING *SCARY...*

DON'T WORRY. PUT IN YOUR EARPLUGS SO WE CAN HIT THE GROUND RUNNING. I'M TURNING ON THE SCREECHERS *NOW...*

16

ALMOST *IN*...

JEEZ, THIS *SMELL*, IT'S PRETTY *OBNOXIOUS*... AND DO YOU HEAR THAT SORTA *SCREAMING*, LIKE A *SIREN* ?

IGNORE IT! JUST OPEN THE DOOR SO I CAN SMELL *THIS* SON OF A *BITCH* COOKING!

OH *YEAH*. OH, FOR *SURE*. ANY *SECOND*.

AW, LOOK, HE'S CLIMBIN' UP ON HIS *BUNK*, LIKE A LITTLE *KID*. ANY TIME NOW HE'S GONNA *CRY*. SHIT, I LOVE IT WHEN THEY DO THAT...

JUST *HURRY*.

HA! THERE IT *IS*! THERE SHE *GOES*!

I *GOT* YOU, YOU RUNTY LITTLE *BASTARD*!

YOU'RE GONNA BE *HAMBURGER*! YOU'RE GONNA BE *SMOKED* MEAT, YOU STINKING, *LOUSY*...

...*LITTLE*...

HURRM. NEVER DISPOSED OF SEWAGE WITH TOILET BEFORE. OBVIOUS, REALLY.

TWO— NOTHING.

YOUR *MOVE*.

...EXTINGUISHED! ALL THE LIGHTS, THEY JUST WENT OUT...

SPEAK UP, I CAN HARDLY HEAR YOU.

IT'S SOME SORT OF POWER FAILURE, OBVIOUSLY. EMERGENCY LIGHTS SHOULD KICK IN SOON, PROVIDING NOBODY'S BEEN TOO ROUGH WITH THE ELECTRICALS.

DAN, THIS IS HORRIBLE. WHEN WE HEARD ABOUT THE RIOT, I THOUGHT IT WOULD JUST PROVIDE COVER FOR THE ESCAPE. I HADN'T IMAGINED THIS...

OLD GRUDGES GET WORKED OUT IN THESE THINGS.

OLD GRUDGES AND BAD BLOOD.

BUT THIS IS PANDEMONIUM! EVEN ASSUMING THAT NOBODY KILLED HIM ALREADY, THAT HE'S STILL ALIVE; HOW ARE WE SUPPOSED TO FIND HIM?

HE'S SUPPOSEDLY IN THE SOLITARY SECTION. HE SHOULDN'T BE TOO DIFFICULT TO TRACK DOWN...

I STILL DON'T SEE YOU NEED HIM. WHAT DID HE DO FOR YOU LATELY?

NOTHING. BUT MEETING HIM RECENTLY, IT'S LIKE HE WANTS TO MAKE FRIENDS WITHOUT KNOWING HOW.

AS IF THE GAP BETWEEN US WERE NARROWING.

IT'S JUST SO HARD, REACHING HIM. I MEAN, ALL THIS STUFF, THIS HORROR AND MADNESS, HE ATTRACTS IT. IT'S HIS WORLD. THIS IS WHERE HE LIVES...

...IN THIS SORDID, VIOLENT TWILIGHT ZONE...

...UNDER THIS SHADOW.

18

WELL? DID WE FIND THE RIGHT CELL? IS HE THERE?

FROM THE SMELL THIS WHOLE PLACE HAS HIS STAMP ON IT.

NO. NO, HE ISN'T HERE...

...BUT I THINK HE'S BEEN HERE.

COME ON. IF WE DON'T FIND HIM SOON, OUR WHOLE PLAN IS IN THE TOILET.

B WING

MEN'S ROOM

ALONG HERE, MAYBE?

I DON'T KNOW. IF ONLY THERE WAS SOME SIGN...

MEN'S ROOM

HEY! IS THAT HIM ALONG THERE? THERE WAS THAT PICTURE IN THE PAPERS, HIM WITHOUT HIS MASK...

I--I'M NOT SURE. IT LOOKS LIKE HIS POSTURE...

HEY, RORSCHACH?

RORSCHACH? IS THAT...? YES. YES, IT'S YOU.

COME ON, MAN. WE CAME TO BUST YOU OUT AND WE BETTER HURRY BEFORE, UH...

UH, WE'RE NOT INTERRUPTING ANYTHING?

19

NO.

EXCUSE ME. HAVE TO VISIT MEN'S ROOM.

OH, FOR CHRIST'S SAKE...

UH, LOOK, IT'S OKAY. I MEAN, IT HAPPENS TO EVERYBODY, RIGHT? I REMEMBER ONCE I LOST A BIG ARREST LIKE THAT...

I WAS CLOSING ON THIS DOPE DEALER AND I NEEDED TO TAKE A LEAK. BY THE TIME I'D GOT IN AND OUT OF MY COSTUME, HE'D VANISHED.

I RE-DESIGNED IT SINCE THEN.

OH, SURE. EVERY-BODY'S DONE THAT...

WHAT PISSES ME OFF, WE CAME TO RESCUE HIM, HE DOESN'T EVEN THANK US! DOESN'T EVEN SAY HELLO!

HELL, WHAT'S HE DOING IN THERE? THAT BUMPING...

IT'S OKAY... I THINK I JUST HEARD HIM FLUSH...

AT LAST!

SHHH.

THERE. DID WHAT HAD TO BE DONE. CAN LEAVE NOW.

REALLY? I MEAN, ARE YOU SURE? WE DON'T WANT TO GET TOO RECKLESS AND GO DIVING HEAD-FIRST INTO THINGS!

HURM.

GOOD ADVICE.

SURE THERE ARE MANY WHO'D AGREE WITH YOU.

20

INCIDENTALLY, GOOD SEEING YOU IN UNIFORM, DANIEL. LIKE OLD TIMES.

AND MISS JUSPECZYK. ALTHOUGH NEVER LIKED YOUR UNIFORM. NOTHING PERSONAL.

UH, MAYBE I BETTER KILL THE *SCREECHERS* SO ARCHIE DOESN'T *DEAFEN* YOU WHEN I BRING HIM *UP*.

HURRM. OWLSHIP. SCREECHERS. BELT CONSOLE. ALL THE OLD TOYS. I REMEMBER.

WHAT BROUGHT YOU OUT OF RETIREMENT? TAKING MASK KILLER SERIOUSLY AT LAST?

WELL...

NO. LEASTWAYS, I'M NOT.

NO? BUT THEN YOU HAVEN'T BEEN ATTACKED YET. FUNNY. MOST EVERYONE ELSE HAS.

RORSCHACH, FOR GOD'S *SAKE*, MAN, DON'T YOU *EVER* LET UP? SHE JUST *RESCUED* YOU...

WHAT'S HE *IMPLYING*? I JUST DON'T BUY THIS *CONSPIRACY* IS ALL!

I MEAN, TO ME, THIS WHOLE *SITUATION'S* GROTESQUE. DAN THOUGHT SPRINGING YOU MIGHT HELP; I PLAYED ALONG.

FRANKLY, I WISH I *HADN'T*. I WISH JON WAS HERE TO *STRAIGHTEN* EVERYTHING AND...

OH, *DAN*, I'M *SORRY*.

FORGET IT. HERE'S *ARCHIE*...

HURRY. WITHOUT THE *SCREECHERS* KEEPING FOLK *AWAY* WE'LL SOON START DRAWING *FIRE*.

ALSO, I WANT TO VISIT MY PLACE ONE LAST TIME BEFORE *THIS* CAPER BRINGS THE *POLICE* DOWN ON IT. THERE'S *EQUIPMENT* TO COLLECT.

Y'KNOW, THIS IS GETTING *HEAVY*. AS DAN DREIBERG, YOU'LL BE *WANTED*.

THE WORLD SHOULD *LAST* SO LONG. NO, IT'S OKAY. I SET UP *EMERGENCY* IDENTITIES YEARS AGO. *THEY'LL* CONCEAL US.

HOLD *TIGHT*. WE'RE GOING HOME TO *ROOST*...

NOVEMBER

M	T	W	T	F	S	S
				1	2	3
4	5	6	7	8	9	10
11	12	13	14	15	16	17
18	19	20	21	22	23	24
25	26	27	28	29	30	

OKAY, THAT'S EVERYTHING FROM UP *HERE*, BUT I HAVE SOME STUFF TO LOAD DOWN IN THE *BASEMENT*, SO...

UH, *LAURIE*? WHAT ARE YOU *DOING*?

CHANGING YOUR *CALENDAR*. ANOTHER *HOUR*, IT'LL BE *NOVEMBER*.

YOU SOUND *UPSET*. IS EVERYTHING *OKAY*?

YEAH. IT'S JUST STUFF CATCHING *UP* WITH ME ...THE *JAILBREAK*, THIS *WAR* THING ...EVERYTHING'S JUST SO SHITTY.

GUESS I WANT SOMEBODY TO WAVE A *WAND* AND MAKE IT ALL *BETTER*, Y'KNOW?

...BUT THERE'S NOBODY WHO CAN DO THAT, IS THERE?

LISTEN, I HAVE TO COLLECT SOME JUNK FROM THE *LIVING ROOM*... STUFF MY *MOTHER* INSISTED I HAVE, PERSONAL EFFECTS AND LIKE THAT...

BE RIGHT WITH YOU.

HELLO.

22

JON? OH JESUS, I...

I, I MEAN THEY SAID YOU'D *GONE*. THEY SAID YOU WERE ON *MARS*...

I *AM* ON MARS.

NOW, I BELIEVE WE HAVE A *CONVERSATION* SCHEDULED. YOU WANT TO *TALK* TO ME.

GOD, *YES*. YES, I WAS JUST THINKING ...BUT JON, HOW DID YOU *KNOW*? I NEED TO *SEE* YOU, YOU *APPEAR*...I MEAN, IT'S ALL SO *DEUS EX MACHINA* ...

"THE GOD OUT OF THE MACHINE". YES. YES, I SUPPOSE IT IS ...

...BUT THE RULES ARE *DIFFERENT* FOR ME. PLEASE TRY TO UNDER-STAND.

AN HOUR INTO MY *FUTURE* WE'RE ON *MARS*, TALKING. I THOUGHT I'D *COLLECT* YOU IN *READINESS*.

MARS? OH NO! YOU'RE KIDDING! WHY MARS?

LAURIE? WHO ...?

BECAUSE THAT'S WHERE I *AM*. BECAUSE THAT'S WHERE OUR *CONVERSATION* IS GOING TO TAKE PLACE. YOU'RE GOING TO TRY TO CONVINCE ME TO SAVE THE *WORLD*.

TO *SAVE* ...? I HAVE TO *CONVINCE* YOU? JON, THIS IS *INSANE* ...

JON? LAURIE? WHAT'S *HAPPENING*? I ...

DAN? HE JUST *APPEARED*. HE WANTS ME TO *GO* WITH HIM. I--I THINK I BETTER DO AS HE *SAYS*. I *KNOW* HIM! HE DOESN'T CHANGE HIS *MIND*.

DANIEL? DOORBELL RINGING ...

LAURIE, *WAIT!* WHAT *IS* THIS? WHAT ARE YOU GOING TO *DO*?

W--WE'RE GOING TO *TALK*. MAYBE WE'LL FIND SOME WAY *OUT* OF THIS MESS.

IT'LL BE OKAY, DAN. REALLY. YOU TAKE *CARE*.

PEOPLE OUTSIDE, DANIEL. POLICE.

HAMMERING NOW. BEST HURRY. WE ...

LAURIE! DON'T....

DANIEL, DOOR WON'T HOLD LONG. MUST GO NOW BEFORE... WHERE IS MISS JUSPECZYK?

SHE... SHE WON'T BE TRAV-ELLING WITH US.

LET'S GO.

23

COME ON, THE PLACE IS LIT UP, THEY COULD STILL BE HERE...

THEY BETTER BE! STEVE, YOU'RE TELLING ME YOU KNEW DREIBERG WAS THIS OWL-MAN AND YOU NEVER...

I MADE A MISTAKE, THOUGHT A WARNING WOULD BE ENOUGH. HELL, I DIDN'T KNOW HE WAS PLANNING HIS PAL'S ESCAPE...

DOWN THOSE STAIRS! I KNEW HE HAD SOMETHING HIDDEN BACK THERE FROM HIS ATTITUDE ...

STEVE, IF THOSE GUYS AREN'T DOWN THERE, YOU BETTER START THINKING ABOUT THE CAPTAIN'S ATTITUDE.

IT AIN'T GONNA BE SWEETNESS AND LIGHT.

I'LL BE DAMNED.

OH SURE.

AT THE VERY LEAST.

24

OUR DAMNATION: IT OBSESSED THE SODDEN DEAD, DOMINATING THEIR BUBBLING DIALOGUES.

FUH- FIRST, THERE'LL BE THIS BIG FLASH...

AY! DERF!

YEAH! AN' IT'S HIS FAULT, DR. BLUE ASS MANHATTAN!

THEY SPOKE OF A HEAVEN, WHERE ONCE WE ALL LIVED AND DIED, SENTENCED FOR OUR SINS TO THIS PANDEMONIUM WE CALL THE WORLD.

...AND THEN THERE'S THIS TERRIBLE NOISE...

AY, DERF, ON THE RADIO, YOU HEAR WHAT WENT DOWN?

I HEARD ABOUT THE RIOT...

OLD NEWS. SOME SUPER DUPERS SPRUNG THAT BLOT-FACE GUY.

...AND, OH THE FASTEST WIND...

TRULY, LIFE IS HELL AND DEATH'S ROUGH HAND OUR ONLY DELIVERANCE.

SPRUNG HIM? THOSE BASTARDS, THEY DO WHAT- EVER THEY LIKE!

YEAH, SOME OWL CHAR- ACTER DID IT...

NITE OWL? MY DAD KNOWS HIM... LIVES OVER SOME GARAGE NEAR HERE. WE OUGHTTA GO KICK HIS ASS!

...AND THEN THE SHOCK- WAVE...

YEAH! KICK ASS! GREAT CONCEPT. I SAY RUN WITH IT, GIVE HIM HELL...

I COULD ENDURE NO MORE. THOUGH DREADING SUCH A BLACK, BREATH- LESS END, I LEAPT, FEET FIRST INTO HORROR...

...THE SKY, BURNING...

FEET FIRST INTO COLD AND DANK MORTALITY.

YEAH, THAT'S RIGHT, TAKE IT SOME PLACE ELSE, YOU GODDAMN KATIE HEADS. WHO NEEDS IT? MOBS IN THE STREET, GUYS RUNNIN' AN' YELLIN'...

JUST LIKE OLD TIMES.

Oh how the ghost of you clings...

Nostalgia by VEIDT

W! 86 BUICKS! NOW!

25

...BUT THE WATER'S SURFACE SEEMED AS **STONE** BENEATH MY TIMBER-BLISTERED SOLES, AND THE OCEAN'S DEPTHS REFUSED TO SWALLOW ME.

WHAT NEW TORTURE WAS THIS? I STOOD UPON THE CALM SEA, A CHARNEL MESSIAH, UNABLE TO SINK BENEATH IT TO THE OBLIVION I CRAVED.

WHEN WOULD MY SUFFERING CEASE? WHEN WOULD DEATH DEIGN TO CALL UPON ME? HAD HIS TERRIBLE SHADOW PASSED ME BY?

I LIFTED MY UNCOMPREHENDING EYES TO THE HEAVENS...

...AND SAW INSTEAD THE EARTH.

ACCUSTOMED TO A MISERABLE, SHIFTING LANDSCAPE OF IRON GREEN, MY MIND COULD NOT AT FIRST GRASP THE **MEANING** OF THIS SANDBAR, BLOND AND SOLID.

IT MEANT THAT MY LURCHING JOURNEY THROUGH DARKNESS WAS ENDED.

IT MEANT THAT I HAD REACHED MY DESTINATION.

THEY'D LEFT ME FOR DEAD, THE FIENDS WHO'D DOUBTLESS BUTCHERED MY KIN, BUT NOW I WAS **RETURNED**, UPON MY **CORPSE BOAT**...

A TERROR THEY'D IMAGINED THEMSELVES **SAFE** FROM...

A SPECTRE OF **REVENGE**, RIDING THE FLOW TIDE **HOME**.

MASON'S AUTO REPAIRS

WHO WATCHES

26

HEH. OKAY, OKAY, I *HEAR* YA... YOU CAN QUIT *BANGING*.

JUST GIVE ME A *MOMENT* HERE. LEMME SEE... APPLES, CANDY...THAT'S IT, I GUESS.

ALRIGHT, ALRIGHT, I HEAR YA. I'M COMING.

THERE. HAPPY *HALLOWEEN*, KIDS. I...

"*AAK!* YOU OLD SON OF A *BITCH*, YOU *HIT* ME! YOU..."

"*GET THE DOG!* SOMEBODY GET THE *DOG!*"

"WATCH *OUT*, HE'S TRYING TO GET *UP*..."

"*DERF*, JESUS, LOOK, THIS IS AN *OLD GUY*. WE OUGHTTA *SPLIT* BEFORE..."

"*SPLIT?* WHATSA-MATTER, CAN'T YOU JERKS DO ANYTHIN' WITH-OUT I SHOW YOU HOW? GIMME SOME-THIN' *HEAVY*..."

"*HEY!* HEY, *GRANPA!* HEADS *UP!*"

"TRY AN' PUT A *BRAVE FACE* ON *THIS*..."

27

HHUUGGHH

DERF? DERF, WHAT DID YOU DO? THESE *KATIES,* I CAN'T...

SHUT UP. WE'RE FINISHED HERE.

BUT *DERF,* I MEAN, SHIT, MAN, *LOOK* AT THE GUY! YOU...

I SAID WE'RE *FINISHED* HERE. LET'S GO.

MR. MASON? IT'S US, SAME AS *LAST YEAR.* WERE THOSE GUYS WHO JUST LEFT *FRIENDS* OF YOURS?

MR. MASON? HEY, C'MON, TRICK OR *TREAT?*

MR. MASON?

On Hallowe'en the old ghosts come about us, and they speak to some; to others they are dumb.

—*Hallowe'en*
Eleanor Farjeon

28

Thursday, October 31st, 1985

50 cents

NEW FRONTIERSMAN

Issue IVII
No. 21

★★★★ ▬▬▬▬▬▬▬▬▬▬

HONOR IS LIKE THE HAWK: SOMETIMES IT MUST GO HOODED

Hector Godfrey, Editor

RED ARMAGEDDON!

In this, the eleventh hour, with the world poised on the brink of Red Armageddon, it is vital that we, as a nation, should rally around those symbols that are closest to the great, warm, red-white-and-blue beating heart of this beleaguered country. They are our hope and our inspiration, the legends that urge our people onward even in times of deepest crisis.

Would our sense of national identity, our pride, our sense of honor; would these things be so enduring were it not for such great symbols of freedom as Paul Revere's midnight ride, or the Alamo, or the Gettysburg address? I think not. And yet, it seems there are those who, even in the dire adversity that besets us, see fit to ridicule and deride the very notions that have made America what she is today!

←cont. on pg. 2

Honor is like . . . (cont.)

WHO THE HELL DO THEY THINK THEY ARE?

For any citizen who has been watching the newsstands over this last, unbearable month, there can be little doubt who I am referring to. In the current edition of pseudo-intellectual Marxist-brat rock-star monthly *Nova Express*, cocaine-advocating editor DOUGLAS ROTH makes a vitriolic and unfounded attack upon the tradition of the masked lawman in our culture and attempts to stir up old prejudices and hatreds into a bloody wave of civil disorder.

It is hardly necessary for me to remind readers that in a previous edition of his inflammatory publication, Roth had spearheaded the cancer-smear character assassination of Dr. Manhattan. This wild and hysterical attack led to our country's greatest tactical asset leaving this world for self-imposed exile upon another. Ultimately, it may lead to searing nuclear apocalypse or our subjugation as a nation beneath the cossack boot of the U.S.S.R.

Nova Express, heaping libel upon libel, has followed up this potentially catastrophic feature with an article in its current edition that attempts to draw tenuous links between recent news items involving former masked adventurers and work them into some wild-eyed conspiracy theory, apparently forgetting that most of the "news items" involved were generated as a direct result of *Nova Express* and its irresponsible scaremongering! Roth refers gloatingly in his article to the fact that back copies of the *New Frontiersman* were found in the rented apartment of captured vigilante Rorschach after his arrest, citing this as "proof" of the aforementioned hero's poor character. He seems to suggest, with typical pothead disregard for logic, that Rorschach must be bad if he reads the *New Frontiersman*, while simultaneously implying that the *New Frontiersman* must be slightly disreputable if someone like Rorschach reads it! The overall effect of the piece is that of a snotty-nosed and unsubstantiated attack not only upon this paper and upon the individual costumed adventurers themselves, but also upon a whole American institution! Who the hell do Roth and his cringing staff of pinko sycophants think they are???

RIPPED OUT GUTS

The institution that Roth and his cronies are so casually ripping the guts out of is that of hooded justice, of a force for righteousness that dares to tread where the wimpy and useless laws laid down by the spineless dupes and fellow travellers in our judiciary forbid it to.

What about the Boston Tea Party? What about the spirit of the Lone Ranger? What about all those occasions when men have found it necessary to go masked in order to preserve justice above the letter of the law? *Nova Express* makes many sneering references to costumed heroes as direct descendants of the Ku Klux Klan, but might I point out that despite what some might view as their later excesses, the Klan originally came into being because decent people had perfectly reasonable fears for the safety of their persons and belongings when forced into proximity with people from a culture far less morally advanced.

No, the Klan were not strictly legal, but they did work voluntarily to preserve American culture in areas where there were very real dangers of that culture being overrun and mongrelized. Similarly, during our perfectly justified retaliatory bombing of Beirut in 1979, there were many of our so-called fair-weather-friend European allies who were bleating about supposed infringements of international law. Yet what are laws made for, if not to serve mankind? And if those laws through unforeseen circumstance become no longer applicable, is it not more noble to follow the course of right and justice; to serve the spirit of the law rather than its every dot and comma? In my book, anyone answering that question in the negative is someone without the moral backbone necessary to call himself an American. In the case of the *Nova Express* articles and their perpetrators, I would go so far as to call such a denial of time-tested patriotic virtues as being most definitely ANTI-American.

COKED-OUT COMMIE COWARDS

I've had it up to here with those coked-out commie cowards, and I think it's time we started to ask ourselves just who stands to benefit most from *Nova Express*' ridiculing of American legends and the subsequent subversion and undermining of our national morale? Can there be any doubt that the only beneficiary is the cause of international communism? Should we not perhaps call upon our authorities to take a closer look at exactly who is funding this pernicious piece of propaganda in pop star's

cont. on pg. 3

(open up para. #

As we see it . . .

Honor is like . . . (cont.)

clothing that finds its way onto our newsstands each week? Regular readers will know that I have already voiced my suspicions concerning a red hand in the denunciation and subsequent exile of Dr. Manhattan (see *N.F.*, Sunday 20th October: "Our country's protector smeared by the Kremlin") and will no doubt join me in perceiving this renewed assault by *Nova Express* upon our traditions and values as further proof of where that magazine's interests lie: Due East, and don't you forget it.

Hector Godfrey, Editor

MISSING WRITER
VANISHED PERSONS LIST
GROWS AS HUNT CALLED OFF

Earlier this week, police called off their inquiry into the mysterious disappearance of author Max Shea, citing lack of evidence as a principal contributing factor in their decision. *New Frontiersman* would like to remind both the authorities concerned and our readers of the overwhelming evidence already tabulated by this paper to suggest that Shea's disappearance was part of a carefully orchestrated conspiracy, the roots of which may yet be traced back to sinister Cuban interests.

Although it is true to say that Shea did indeed vanish without trace, leaving no clue whatsoever as to his destination, by considering the extraordinary amount of similar disappearances reported at approximately the same time, it is possible to glimpse a larger and more frightening picture as it emerges. In the two months leading up to Shea's disappearance, no less than four prominent creative figures also seemingly dropped from the face of the earth. These included radical architect Norman Leith, surrealist painter Hira Manish, and respected "hard" science fiction author James Trafford March. Admittedly, the circumstances in each case are wildly different and seem to allow for a simple, meaningless coincidence of human destinies . . . Manish was apparently suffering profound difficulties with her marriage, making her apparent abandonment of her husband and two sons somewhat less than surprising. March owed massive debts to the IRS, who had frozen his earnings. Leith was reportedly depressed and even suicidal during the run-up to his disappearance, as was fellow missing person, avant-garde composer Linette Paley. As reasons for disappearance, these each seem individually credible enough to make any notion of conspiracy unnecessary, and yet a doubt still remains: Can *four* such prominent people simply dematerialize in the space of half as many months, leaving such bright and promising

careers and reputations behind them?

Added to this, we must consider those prominent people in other fields, who, although less prominent and thus less easy to gauge numerically, have also apparently melted into thin air during this period. I have on record an unusually high number of disappearances from amongst the scientific community, which, although consisting largely of semi-skilled menial workers, does include such notable names as that of Dr. Whittaker Furnesse, the brilliant eugenics specialist who according to his wife left the family home one evening to walk the family dog and quite simply never returned.

Odder still, and quite probably entirely unconnected, there is the disappearance of *part* of a person after his death, recorded on the same week Shea's vanishing act reached the public awareness. Parents and relatives of so-called psychic and clairvoyant Robert Deschaines, attending his funeral following the young medium's fatal stroke, were horrified to learn that ghoulish vandals or practical jokers had stolen the corpse's head from its body while it lay unattended upon a mortuary slab. Police voiced a few tenuous opinions concerning possible involvement by black magic cultists, but since then no further evidence has come to light.

Even discounting this last curiosity, is there nobody who is prepared to look into this bizarre glut of disappearances and see what emerges? Can it be that our increasingly shrill and nervous judiciary are actually afraid to look too far under this particular rug for fear of what they might find hidden there? The *New Frontiersman* repeats it warning: Talented and prominent Americans are being spirited away from under our noses.

Isn't it time somebody found out just where they are going?

Photo to Come

"LAURIE?"

WHAT'S HAPPENING? I...

DAN? HE JUST APPEARED. HE WANTS ME TO GO WITH HIM. I...I THINK I BETTER DO AS HE SAYS. I KNOW HIM. HE DOESN'T CHANGE HIS MIND.

DANIEL? DOORBELL RINGING...

LAURIE, WAIT! WHAT IS THIS? WHAT ARE YOU GOING TO DO?

W-WE'RE GOING TO TALK. MAYBE WE'LL FIND SOME WAY OUT OF THIS MESS.

IT'LL BE OKAY, DAN. REALLY. YOU TAKE CARE.

PEOPLE OUTSIDE, DANIEL. POLICE.

HAMMERING NOW. BEST HURRY. WE...

LAURIE!

"DON'T..."

1

THE DARKNESS OF MERE BEING

OF COURSE. IT IS HERE ON MARS THAT WE DEBATE EARTH'S DESTINY.

JON, PLEASE, I MEAN, *THIS,* JUST *BEING* HERE, IT'S GIVING ME *PROBLEMS,* OKAY?

I CAN'T TAKE YOUR PREDESTIN-ATION TRIP RIGHT NOW.

WHY DOES MY PERCEPTION OF TIME DISTRESS YOU?

WHY *ASK?* YOU ALREADY *KNOW* MY ANSWER: IT'S *STUPID.* WHEN I LEFT YOU, WHEN *NOVA EXPRESS* ATTACKED YOU, YOU WERE *SURPRISED.*

WHY, IF YOU *KNEW* IT WOULD HAPPEN?

EVERY-THING IS PREORDAINED. EVEN MY *RESPONSES.*

AND YOU JUST GO THROUGH THE *MOTIONS,* ACTING THEM *OUT?*

IS THAT WHAT YOU *ARE?* THE MOST POWERFUL THING IN THE *UNIVERSE* AND YOU'RE JUST A *PUPPET* FOLLOWING A *SCRIPT?*

WE'RE ALL PUPPETS, LAURIE. I'M JUST A PUPPET WHO CAN SEE THE *STRINGS.*

WE SHALL GO UP TO THE BALCONY. YOU CAN SEE THE NODUS GORDII MOUNTAINS FROM THERE.

WELL, WHAT IF I *DON'T?*

HUH?

WHAT HAPPENS IF I JUST STAY DOWN HERE AND SCREW ALL YOUR *PREDICTIONS,* HUH?

WHAT HAPPENS *THEN?*

JON?

I SAID "WHAT HAPPENS *THEN?*"

5

THIS IS WHERE WE HOLD OUR CONVERSATION.

IT COMMENCES WHEN YOU SURPRISE ME WITH THE INFORMATION THAT YOU AND DREIBERG HAVE BEEN SLEEPING TOGETHER.

Y--YOU *KNOW* ABOUT ME AND DAN?

NO. NOT YET. BUT IN A FEW MOMENTS YOU'RE GOING TO *TELL* ME.

AAAAAGH!

JON, WHAT ARE YOU TRYING TO *DO* TO ME? WHEN YOU'RE LIKE *THIS* I CAN'T EVEN *TALK* TO YOU, LET ALONE DEBATE THE WHAT WAS IT...

DESTINY OF THE WORLD.

DESTINY OF THE WORLD.

I MEAN, THIS IS *RIDICULOUS*. WHY HOLD A *DEBATE* WHEN YOU ALREADY KNOW THE GODDAMNED *OUTCOME*?

BECAUSE...

"BECAUSE THAT'S HOW IT *HAPPENS*!" I KNOW, I KNOW...

OH *GOD*...

LISTEN, JON, OKAY, I'LL PLAY IT *YOUR* WAY... BUT YOU HAVE TO HELP ME *UNDERSTAND*. I MEAN, I CAN'T TELL THE *FUTURE*...

THERE *IS* NO FUTURE. THERE *IS* NO PAST. DO YOU *SEE*?

TIME IS *SIMULTANEOUS*, AN INTRICATELY STRUCTURED *JEWEL* THAT HUMANS INSIST ON VIEWING ONE EDGE AT A *TIME*, WHEN THE WHOLE *DESIGN* IS VISIBLE IN EVERY *FACET*.

WHAT IS YOUR EARLIEST *MEMORY*?

HUH? MY EARLIEST *MEMORY*?

I ...I DUNNO. AROUND WHEN MY *FOLKS* SPLIT UP, I GUESS...

I CAN REMEMBER A *TOY*, ONE OF THOSE *SNOWSTORM* BALLS, BUT...

NO. NO, IT'S GONE.

IT *ISN'T* GONE. IT'S STILL HERE. LET YOURSELF *SEE* IT.

"WELL, I ...I WAS FIVE, SOMETHING LIKE THAT. I MUST HAVE GOT WOKEN UP ...THERE WAS SHOUTING DOWNSTAIRS...

"MY MOM AND DAD. GOD, I CAN HEAR THEM NOW."

6

...SHOUTED AT HIM, HE LOOKED **SURPRISED**, COULDN'T IMAGINE WHY I'D BEAR A GRUDGE. SEE, IT'S **DIFFERENT** FOR HIM, AND I JUST COULDN'T **SUSTAIN** IT, THE **ANGER**...

GOD, YOU KNOW, REALLY, YOU NEED ANALYSIS, I'M SERIOUS...

HOW WOULD **YOU** KNOW HOW A WOMAN FEELS? SHIT, HOW A **MAN** FEELS, FOR THAT MATTER?

OH, THAT'S **CHEAP**. EVEN FOR **YOU**, THAT IS **CHEAP**!

WELL, C'MON, LET'S HEAR THE **REST**...

WHY? SO YOU CAN PUT IT IN A LETTER TO ONE OF THOSE **MAGAZINES** YOU READ? "MY WIFE DESCRIBED HOW HIS ROUGH HANDS SLOWLY SQUEEZED..."

STOP THAT!

YOU WANTED TO **HEAR**, SO OKAY, YOU LISTEN:

FIRST OFF, HE WAS **THERE**, RIGHT?

PLUS, HE WAS **GENTLE**. YOU KNOW WHAT GENTLENESS **MEANS** IN A GUY LIKE THAT? EVEN A GLIMMER OF IT?

OH **SPARE** ME.

IT MEANS YOU **REACHED** SOMETHING. IT MEANS YOU REACHED SOME OF THAT MAGICAL ROMANCE AND BULLSHIT THAT THEY PROMISE YOU WHEN YOU'RE A KID...

IT **ALSO** MEANS A BROKEN **MARRIAGE**; AN UNCERTAIN **FUTURE** FOR OUR CHILD...

MY CHILD. THAT'S WHAT ALL THIS IS **ABOUT**, REMEMBER?

ANYWAY, DON'T YOU WORRY ABOUT **HER** FUTURE. THAT'S TAKEN **CARE** OF.

"I TIPTOED DOWNSTAIRS TO THE T.V. ROOM. IT WAS DARK AND NEXT DOOR THEY WERE SHOUTING...

"NOBODY KNEW I WAS THERE. THESE MOMENTS WERE JUST MINE. EVERYTHING FELT **SECRET** AND **ENCHANTED**...

"...AND THERE WAS THIS **TOY**, THIS SNOWSTORM BALL, WITH A TINY **CASTLE** INSIDE, EXCEPT IT WAS LIKE A WHOLE **WORLD**; A WORLD INSIDE THE **BALL**...

"IT WAS LIKE A LITTLE GLASS BUBBLE OF SOMEWHERE **ELSE**.

"I LIFTED IT, STARTING A BLIZZARD. I KNEW IT WASN'T **REAL** SNOW, BUT I COULDN'T UNDERSTAND HOW IT FELL SO **SLOWLY**.

"I FIGURED INSIDE THE BALL WAS SOME DIFFERENT SORT OF **TIME**.

"**SLOW** TIME.

7

"AND THEN..." LAUREL JANE?

AAA!

WHAT ARE YOU DOING DOWN HERE? WHAT...

LARRY, DON'T YOU *DARE* TAKE THIS OUT ON HER! SHE'S ONLY A *KID!* SHE'S VULNERABLE...

"...FRAGILE..."

"...AND INSIDE THERE WAS ONLY WATER.

"MY DAD YELLED AND SENT ME TO BED. HE WAS ALWAYS YELLING, PROBABLY BECAUSE HE KNEW I WASN'T *HIS.*

"MY REAL DAD, I'M PRETTY SURE, WAS MOM'S OLD BOY-FRIEND, HOODED JUSTICE."

I SEE. THEN YOUR MOTHER'S HUSBAND WASN'T ...AHH. LOOK OVER THERE: A DUST STORM RISING.

YEAH. VERY NICE.

NO, SCHEXNAYDER WASN'T ANYTHING EXCEPT A DOMINEERING *BULLY.* HE REALLY USED TO *PICK* ON ME.

THAT'S PROBABLY WHY I'M *EDGY* IN RELATIONSHIPS WITH STRONG, *FORCE-FUL* GUYS...

I MEAN, WITH *DAN,* IT ISN'T *LIKE* THAT. AS A *LOVER* HE'S MORE SORT OF *RECEPTIVE;* THE TYPE YOU CAN POUR YOUR *TROUBLES* OUT TO...

YOU MEAN THAT YOU'RE SLEEPING WITH DREIBERG?

B-BUT ...YOU ALREADY *KNOW.* I MEAN, YOU SAID...

I *SAID,* OFTEN, THAT YOU WERE MY ONLY *LINK,* MY ONLY CONCERN WITH THE WORLD.

WHEN YOU LEFT ME, I LEFT EARTH. DOES *THAT* NOT SAY SOMETHING?

NOW YOU HAVE REPLACED ME, AND THAT LINK IS SHATTERED. DON'T YOU SEE WHAT THAT MEANS?

DON'T YOU SEE THE FUTILITY OF ASKING ME TO SAVE A WORLD THAT I NO LONGER HAVE ANY STAKE IN?

8

JON, DON'T BE *RIDICULOUS*! EARTH'S TOO *IMPORTANT* TO HINGE ON ONE *RELATION-SHIP*!

NOT TO ME. MY RED WORLD HERE MEANS MORE TO ME THAN YOUR BLUE ONE. I WILL SHOW YOU AROUND IT IF YOU WISH...

OH NO! I'VE HAD ENOUGH OF *THAT*, THROWING *UP* AND YOU FORGETTING I NEED TO *BREATHE*. I'M NOT DOING ANY MORE HOPPING AROUND.

AS YOU PLEASE. THERE ARE OTHER METHODS.

HUH? WHAT DO YOU...?

HEY! HEY, EVERYTHING'S *SHAKING!* JON, ARE *YOU* DOING THIS? I'M NOT IN ANY MOOD FOR *CLOWNING AROUND*...

NOR I. BELIEVE ME, I FULLY UNDERSTAND THE SERIOUSNESS OF OUR CIRCUMSTANCES...

...THE *GRAVITY* OF THE SITUATION.

9

A— AND THIS IS SO I DON'T GET *TRAVEL SICK?*

I NEED A DRINK. WHAT'S IN THE *BOTTLE?*

WHAT DO YOU *WANT* TO BE IN THE BOTTLE?

WHAT DO...?

UH, WATER. JUST WATER.

AS YOU WISH.

JON, I...I JUST CAN'T *TAKE* THIS, SIGHTSEEING ON *MARS,* DRINKING INSTANT *WATER* WHEN DOWN *THERE* THE MISSILES COULD BE FLYING RIGHT *NOW.*

HUMANITY IS ABOUT TO BECOME *EXTINCT.* DOESN'T THAT *BOTHER* YOU? ALL THOSE PEOPLE *DEAD*...

ALL THAT PAIN AND CONFLICT *DONE* WITH? ALL THAT NEED- LESS *SUFFERING* OVER AT *LAST?* NO...

NO, THAT DOESN'T BOTHER ME.

ALL THOSE GENERATIONS OF *STRUGGLE,* WHAT *PURPOSE* DID THEY EVER ACHIEVE?

"ALL THAT *EFFORT,* AND WHAT DID IT *EVER* LEAD TO?"

10

HAAHHH

...AGREE. IT'S FUN SEEING ALL YOU GUYS AND... ONCE IN A WHILE, BUT... POINT, REALLY? I MEAN ...THOSE YEARS WE WORKED OUR ASSES ...DID WE ACHIEVE?

SHOULDN'T HAVE TO **ASK**, HOL... WE'RE AN INSPIRATION... THAT NEW BOY ...PAPERS...FEEL PROUD?

...ELL, AS FOR ME...WHAT I ACHIEVED... *SITTING* IN IT ...AND AS ...WHAT I ACHIEVED IT *WITH*...

...I'M SITTING **ON IT!** HA HA HA HA!

AHEH. SALLY. REALLY ...

UH-OH. BETTER CLEAN UP YOUR **ACT,** SAL. WE GOT **COMPANY.**

AAH, SHE'S HEARD IT ALL BEFORE.

HI THERE, SUGAR TUSH. HOW'D THE WORKOUT GO? YOU GONNA BE A BIG TOUGH SUPER- LADY, LIKE MOM?

YEAH. I GUESS.

ATTA GIRL. NOW LEMME **SEE**... UNCLE HOLLIS YOU **KNOW,** BUT THIS BIG HUNK OVER **HERE,** THIS IS YOUR UNCLE **NELSON.** YOU'VE SEEN THE **PICTURE**...

OH, YEAH. CAPTAIN METROPOLIS. YOU WERE SKINNIER BACK THEN.

UH.... RIGHT.

UH, WELL, LISTEN, SALLY, I'D BETTER GO CHECK **OUTSIDE.** HE SHOULD **ARRIVE** SOON, AND I PROMISED I'D **MEET** HIM...

HI THERE, PUMPKIN. SO, DID YOU READ MY **BOOK** YET?

SURE.

BOOK?

SURE. **"UNDER THE HOOD."** I GAVE SALLY ONE TO PASS **ON**...

I, UH, I DIDN'T GIVE IT TO HER YET. I FIGURED "SHE'S YOUNG, DON'T WANNA READ THAT OLD STUFF."

MAYBE WHEN YOU'RE OLDER...

11

MOM, I'M **THIRTEEN**! **WHY** CAN'T I READ UNCLE HOLLIS'S BOOK? I DO ALL THIS **TRAINING** TO BE A COSTUME HERO, I CAN'T EVEN **READ** ABOUT THEM?

UH, NOW, HONEY, MAYBE MOM KNOWS **BEST**. I GUESS I WASN'T **THINKING**...

WELL, I JUST GUESS YOU **WEREN'T**! ALL THOSE **STORIES** YOU TOLD OUT OF **SCHOOL**...

SALLY, REALLY, I'M SORRY, I FORGOT... **HEY, EVERYBODY**! LOOK WHO MADE THE REUNION **AFTER** ALL!

BYRON! OH **BYRON**, IT'S SO GOOD TO **SEE** YOU! CAN WE FIX YOU, UH...

JUST A CLUB SODA FOR MR. LEWIS.

MY FRIENDS. ALL MY FRIENDS. WHAT TIME IS IT?

UH...IT'S, UH, **HIGH TIME WE ALL GOT TOGETHER** IS WHAT IT IS! HERE...HERE'S YOUR SODA, BYRON...

MOM? WHO...?

SHHH. AN OLD FRIEND. I'LL EXPLAIN **LATER**.

HE'S ONE OF **YOU**, RIGHT? JESUS, IS **THAT** WHAT I'M TRAINING FOR? WHAT I GOT TO LOOK **FORWARD** TO?

LAURIE, SHUT **UP**! BYRON'S **FINE**. HE JUST...

ARE...ARE MY RELATIVES HERE?

UH...MR. LEWIS...

I--I'M JUST SORRY. I'M SORRY FOR US **ALL**...

BYRON, CAREFUL! YOUR **GLASS**, YOU'RE...

"...SPILLING EVERYTHING..."

"LAURIE? ARE YOU LISTENING TO ME?"

I WAS ASKING THE **POINT** OF ALL THAT **STRUGGLING**; THE PURPOSE OF THIS ENDLESS LABOR; ACCOMPLISHING NOTHING, LEAVING PEOPLE EMPTY AND DIS-ILLUSIONED...

LEAVING PEOPLE BROKEN.

12

OKAY. OKAY, I'LL ADMIT LOTS OF PEOPLE HAVE MESSED-UP LIVES THAT DON'T ACCOMPLISH ANYTHING *VISIBLE*, BUT...

BUT DON'T WE HAVE SOME *IMPORTANCE* TO THE UNIVERSE *BEYOND* THAT? I MEAN, JUST THE *EXISTENCE* OF LIFE, ISN'T *THAT* SIGNIFICANT?

IN MY OPINION, IT'S A HIGHLY *OVERRATED* PHENOMENON. MARS GETS ALONG PERFECTLY WITHOUT SO MUCH AS A *MICRO-ORGANISM*.

SEE: THERE'S THE *SOUTH POLE* BENEATH US NOW...

NO LIFE. NO LIFE AT ALL, BUT GIANT STEPS, NINETY FEET HIGH, SCOURED BY DUST AND WIND INTO A TOPO-GRAPHICAL MAP, FLOWING AND SHIFTING AROUND THE POLE IN RIPPLES TEN THOUSAND YEARS WIDE.

TELL ME...

WOULD IT BE GREATLY IMPROVED BY AN OIL PIPE-LINE?

JON, IN *THOSE* TERMS, SURE, MANKIND HASN'T *HELPED* THE ENVIRONMENT, BUT *AGAINST* THAT, YOU HAVE TO MEASURE THE LIVES OF *ARTISTS*, *SCIENTISTS*, *POETS*...

HELL, EVEN *MY* LIFE. THAT HAS TO BE WORTH *SOMETHING*...

GOD DAMN, WHY WON'T THIS THING *LIGHT*?

NOT ENOUGH *OXYGEN*. I COULD EXTEND YOUR *AURA*...

SO I CAN FILL IT WITH *SMOKE*? *FORGET* IT. I'LL HAVE SOME...UH...MILK, INSTEAD...

LOOK, ABOUT THE *ENVIRONMENT*: WITHOUT *LIFE*, THERE WOULDN'T EVEN BE AN ENVIRONMENT!

YOUR DEFINITION IS *NARROW*; LIFE INSISTING ON LIFE'S *VIEWPOINT*, WHEN *ALTERNATIVES* EXIST.

THOSE JUMBLED *BOX CANYONS* BELOW, WHERE VOLCANOES BOILED THE *PERMAFROST* INTO SCALDING *GEYSERS*: ONCE THEY COULD HAVE BEEN *FOUNTAINS OF LIFE*.

13

THE GROUND CRUMBLED WHEN THE SUBTERRANEAN ICE MELTED, RELEASING TORRENTS OF WATER TO FORM VAST RIVERS, NOW LONG DRY.

LIFE COULD HAVE FLOURISHED HERE THEN, BUT MARS DID NOT CHOOSE LIFE. IT CHOSE *THIS*.

IT'S CALLED *CHAOTIC TERRAIN*.

YEAH? WELL, ORDINARY LIFE; *MY* LIFE; *THAT'S* GOT "CHAOTIC TERRAIN" *TOO*... OR IS THAT TOO *ABSTRACT*, TOO *UNQUANTIFIABLE*?

I MEAN, YOU'RE SO FASCINATED BY *ROCKS* GETTING TWISTED INTO *WEIRD SHAPES*, JESUS *CHRIST*, YOU SHOULD HAVE SEEN ME BEFORE I MET *YOU*!

MY *MOTHER*, SHE ERODED MY *ADOLESCENCE*, CHIPPING ME INTO THE SHAPE *SHE'D* HAVE BEEN IF SHE HADN'T HAD *ME*.

SHE PUSHED ME INTO *ADVENTURING*, FUSSING OVER "MY *CAREER*," TRYING TO LIVE *HER* LIFE THROUGH *ME*...

"REMEMBER THAT *CRIME-BUSTERS* THING IN THE *SIXTIES*? DID I TELL YOU SHE *DROVE* ME THERE IN A *LIMO*, AND WAITED *OUTSIDE* LIKE IT WAS MY FIRST *SCREEN TEST* OR SOMETHING?

BLACK UNREST

"I WAS *SIXTEEN*. I FELT LIKE A JERK.

14

"I REMEMBER STARING AT *YOU*. I JUST COULDN'T GET USED TO YOU. I MEAN, YOU HAD A GREAT BODY, BUT, Y'KNOW, IT WAS *BLUE*."

"YOUR *GIRLFRIEND*, JANEY, SHE GLARED AT ME ALL THE WAY THROUGH."

"THEN IT *COLLAPSED*: EVERYBODY *LEAVING* EXCEPT NELSON AND ADRIAN. BIG DISAPPOINTMENT..."

"I GUESS I SORTA WONDERED WHAT IT WOULD BE LIKE, SLEEPING WITH YOU, BUT YOU SEEMED KINDA SPOKEN FOR. NOBODY ELSE THERE INTERESTED ME."

"OUTSIDE, I WATCHED THEM GO: DAN IN HIS SHIP, RORSCHACH SNEAKING AWAY INTO THE BUSHES. HE GAVE ME THE CREEPS."

"I FELT LET DOWN, RESTLESS, HORNY AND I NEEDED A CIGARETTE. I WAS LEAVING NELSON'S MANSION..."

"...WHEN SOMEBODY CALLED MY NAME."

LAUREL? LAUREL JANE, IS THAT RIGHT?

SO YOU'RE SALLY'S KID?

UH, YEAH. YEAH. YOU'RE THE *COMEDIAN.* I CAUGHT YOUR ACT IN THERE. YOU WERE PRETTY COOL.

WELL YOU DON'T LOOK LIKE YOU GREW UP TOO BAD *YOURSELF.* HERE... LEMME TAKE A *LOOK*...

HEH. YEAH, THERE'S HER EYES...EVEN GOT THAT FUNNY LITTLE MOLE...

YOU AIN'T GOT HER HAIR, BUT OTHER- WISE, YOU'RE LIKE HER. YOU'RE A LOOKER.

WELL, UH, THANK YOU.

UH, SAY, I NEED A *CIGARETTE,* BUT I DON'T HAVE A *LIGHT.* DO YOU...?

SURE. HEY, LISTEN, YOUR MOM—SHE TALK ABOUT ME MUCH?

NO. NOT MUCH.

HEH. IT FIGURES. HERE'S YOUR LIGHT. I...

HELL. GONE OUT. HERE, LEMME...

IT'S OKAY. I'LL STEADY IT.

THERE. THAT'S BETTER.

YOU TAKE YOUR HANDS *OFF* HER!

15

HI, SAL. LONG TIME NO SEE.

NOT LONG ENOUGH IN MY BOOK, EDDIE.

LAUREL JANE, YOU PUT THAT THING OUT AND COME HERE IMMEDIATELY. WE'RE GOING HOME.

...AND AS FOR *YOU*, ARE THERE NO DEPTHS YOU WON'T SINK TO?

CHRIST, WE WERE JUST *TALKING*! CAN'T A GUY TALK TO HIS, Y'KNOW, HIS OLD FRIEND'S DAUGHTER? I MEAN, WHAT DO YOU THINK I *AM*?

I *KNOW* WHAT YOU ARE, EDWARD BLAKE. I'VE KNOWN WHAT YOU WERE FOR TWENTY-FIVE YEARS, AND DON'T YOU EVER FORGET THAT.

GET IN THE CAR, LAURIE.

SALLY, LISTEN, I THOUGHT WE'D SETTLED ALL THAT A *LONG* TIME AGO.

NO. THINGS LIKE THAT DON'T EVER GET SETTLED. NOT COMPLETELY...

I SAID GET IN THE *CAR*, GIRL!

...AND THEY'RE NOT GOING TO HAPPEN TO MY *DAUGHTER*.

GOODBYE, EDDIE.

"WE DROVE AWAY IN SILENCE. I LOOKED BACK AND HE JUST STOOD THERE, WATCHING US GO. HE LOOKED SAD. I FELT SORRY FOR HIM.

"OF COURSE, *THEN* I DIDN'T KNOW WHAT THE BASTARD HAD *DONE*!

"THAT'S WHY MOM WAS SO PROTECTIVE. IT HAD BROUGHT BACK ALL THOSE TERRIBLE *MEMORIES*.

"WE DROVE THREE BLOCKS AND THEN SHE PULLED THE CAR OVER AND JUST SAT THERE...

"...AND IT ALL CAME POURING OUT."

HER *PAIN*, HER *FEARS*, HER WHOLE *LIFE*, Y'KNOW?

I MEAN, *ORDINARY PEOPLE*, RIGHT? ALL THE THINGS THAT *HAPPEN* TO THEM...

DOESN'T *THAT* MOVE YOU MORE THAN A BUNCH OF *RUBBLE*?

16

IT STRETCHES MORE THAN THREE THOUSAND MILES, SO THAT ONE END KNOWS DAY WHILE THE OTHER ENDURES NIGHT.

TEMPERATURE DIFFERENCES BREED SHRIEKING WINDS THAT HERD OCEANS OF FOG ALONG A CANYON FOUR MILES DEEP.

DOES THE HUMAN HEART KNOW CHASMS SO ABYSMAL?

YES! YES, MINE, RIGHT NOW! JON, YOU'VE SEEN PEOPLE *DEPRESSED*. ME, WHEN I'M MISERABLE, WHEN I'VE HAD TOO MUCH TO *DRINK*...

YES. I REMEMBER A BANQUET IN 1973...

OH, DON'T *REMIND* ME. I ACTED LIKE AN *IDIOT*...

...BUT I GUESS THAT'S IN KEEPING WITH THE REST OF MY LIFE, HUH? I MEAN, YOU SAY IT'S ALL *WORTHLESS*, RIGHT? THAT WE'RE ALL BLIND, STUPID THINGS, STUMBLING THROUGH OUR LIVES...

"...HOPELESSLY LOST IN THE FOG."

19

"THE FOG I WAS LOST IN THAT NIGHT WAS SCOTCH MIST. I MUST HAVE DRUNK HALF A BOTTLE.

"IT WAS A DINNER IN HONOR OF *BLAKE*. I REMEMBER THINKING '*WHY?*' Y'KNOW? JUST '*WHY?*'"

" WHY ALL THIS SUDDEN *POPULARITY? NIXON* WASN'T THERE, BUT EVERYBODY ELSE WAS: FORD, LIDDY, AL HAIG... NO,... WAIT, HAIG QUIT BEFORE THEN', DIDN'T HE?

"THERE WERE CAMERAS. FORD SHOOK BLAKE'S HAND. EVERY-BODY SEEMED REAL PLEASED WITH HIM ...

" ... BUT NOT ME.

"SEE, BY THEN I'D READ '*UNDER THE HOOD*,' ABOUT HIM ASSAULT-ING MY MOM. THAT BANQUET, IT WAS THE FIRST TIME I'D SEEN HIM SINCE I FOUND OUT ...

"...AND I WAS MEAN DRUNK.

"EVERYBODY WAS *TALKING*,..."

SEE THOSE *POST REPORTERS* THEY FOUND IN THAT *GARAGE*? WOODWARD AND WHAT'S HIS NAME? JEWISH NAME...

BERNSTEIN. YEAH, I UNDERSTAND THE UNDERGROUND PAPERS ARE ALREADY YELLING *CONSPIRACY*.

WELL, EDDIE? ANY OPINIONS?

THAT PIECE IN THE *BERKELEY BARB*? WELL, I GUESS YOU SMOKE ENOUGH *WEED* YOU CAN IMAGINE ALMOST *ANY-THING*.

NAH... I'M CLEAN, GUYS. JUST DON'T ASK WHERE I WAS WHEN I HEARD ABOUT J.F.K.

HA HA HA HA!

HA HA HA! THAT'S *GOOD*! DICK'LL LOVE THAT.

Y'KNOW, ED, YOU'RE OKAY. SOMEBODY A GUY CAN *RELAX* WITH... NOT GIVING EVERYBODY THE CREEPS LIKE GODDAMN *MR. SPOCK* OVER THERE...

SHH.

MISS *JUSPECZYK*. GOOD TO SEE YOU.

"JUSPECZYK," WHAT'S THAT? GRANDMOTHER'S NAME? DIDN'T LIKE *JUPITER*, HUH?

DIDN'T TAKE YOUR OLD MAN'S NAME EITHER...

WHAT'S MY NAME TO YOU?

NOTHING.

Y'KNOW, YOU'RE A PRETTY GIRL. I JUST GOTTA LOOK AT YOU, I SEE YOUR MOM. HEH ...

Y'KNOW, YOUR MOTHER, SHE WAS A *PEACH*...

IS THAT WHAT YOU TOLD HER BEFORE YOU TRIED TO RAPE HER?

20

BEFORE YOU **HIT** HER? BEFORE YOU **KICKED** HER? THAT ISN'T THE WAY YOU TREAT **PEACHES**?

UH, MISS JUSPECZYK...

SOMEBODY GET HER **BOY-FRIEND**.

KID, ARE YOU SURE YOU WANNA TAKE THIS ALL THE WAY?

DAMN **STRAIGHT**; DAMN **STRAIGHT** I DO! I MEAN, WHAT KIND OF MAN **ARE** YOU, YOU HAVE TO TAKE SOME WOMAN, YOU HAVE TO FORCE HER INTO HAVING SEX AGAINST HER **WILL**...

ONLY ONCE.

"ONLY **ONCE**, AS IF, Y'KNOW, IT WAS BETTER THAN DOING IT TWICE OR FIFTY TIMES! AND HIS **SCAR**...IT ALWAYS LOOKED LIKE HE WAS **SNEERING**...

"HAD SEVEN SCOTCHES INSIDE ME, ONE IN MY HAND...

"I LET HIM HAVE IT."

...AND THEN YOU CAME, AND YOU WERE ANGRY, AND YOU TOOK ME HOME.

IT WAS THE FIRST TIME YOU EVER TELEPORTED ME ANYWHERE...

FIRST TIME I THREW UP.

...BUT, I MEAN, WHY BOTHER TELLING YOU ALL THIS? IT JUST **CONFIRMS** THINGS, RIGHT? ALL THESE WRETCHED, GRUBBY LITTLE HUMAN ENCOUNTERS: BETTER OFF WITHOUT 'EM!

NONE OF IT EVER MEANT A DAMN THING, ANYWAY.

I MEAN, THESE, MY MOTHER'S CLIPPINGS; HER WHOLE **LIFE**, RIGHT **THERE**! WHAT'S IT **MEAN**?

IN **YOUR** TERMS, NEXT TO A ...A **NEUTRINO**, NEXT TO SOMETHING YOU CAN'T EVEN **SEE**, FOR CHRIST'S SAKE! IT MEANS **NOTHING**!

LAURIE...

DON'T "**LAURIE**"ME! IT'S POINTLESS DEBATING WHEN YOU OBVIOUSLY DON'T SEE ANY-THING TERRIBLY **MIRACULOUS** IN LIFE. MAYBE QUANTUM PHYSICS DOESN'T **ALLOW** MIRACLES ...

NO. "THERMO-DYNAMIC MIRACLES" ARE...

OH, FOR GOD'S **SAKE**, JON, JUST **LAND** THIS THING.

NOW.

21

ON THE ARGYRE PLANITIA?

AS YOU WISH.

THERE. OKAY. THAT'S IT.

YOU CAN TAKE ME BACK TO EARTH TO *FRY* WITH *DAN* AND MY *MOM* AND ALL US OTHER WORTHLESS HUMANS. THE CONVERSATION'S *OVER*...

...AND *LISTEN*, YOU WERE *WRONG*, SEE? YOU SAID IT ENDED WITH ME IN *TEARS*, AND *LOOK* AT ME: NOT A MOIST EYE IN *SIGHT*!

YOU WERE WRONG ABOUT THAT. MAYBE ABOUT A *LOT* OF THINGS...

I MEAN, MAYBE YOU WERE WRONG ABOUT THE STREETS FULL OF *CORPSES* TOO!

JON? CAN YOU *HEAR* ME?

PERFECTLY.

22

AA! JESUS, JON...

"LAURIE, YOU COMPLAIN, PERHAPS *RIGHTLY*, THAT I WON'T SEE EXISTENCE IN HUMAN TERMS...

...BUT YOU YOURSELF REFUSE TO CONSIDER *MY* VIEWPOINT, LETTING YOUR EMOTIONS *BLIND* YOU. *LOOK* AT YOURSELF: ANGRY, SHOUTING..."

"...SHOUTED AT HIM, HE LOOKED *SURPRISED*, COULDN'T IMAGINE WHY I'D *BEAR* A GRUDGE. SEE, IT'S *DIFFERENT* FOR HIM, AND I JUST COULDN'T *SUSTAIN* IT, THE *ANGER*..."

"IF YOU'D ONLY *RELAX* ENOUGH TO SEE THE WHOLE *CONTINUUM*, LIFE'S *PATTERN* OR *LACK* OF ONE, THEN YOU'D UNDER-STAND MY *PERSPECTIVE*.

YOU'RE *DELIBERATELY* SHUTTING OUT UNDERSTANDING, AS IF YOU'RE *AFRAID*; AS IF YOU'RE TOO *DELICATE*..."

"MOM, I'M *THIRTEEN*! WHY CAN'T I READ UNCLE HOLLIS'S BOOK? I DO ALL THIS *TRAINING* TO BE A COSTUME HERO, I CAN'T EVEN *READ* ABOUT THEM?"

"UH, NOW, HONEY, MAYBE MOM KNOWS *BEST*. I GUESS I WASN'T *THINKING*..."

I'M *THROUGH* THINKING ABOUT MY LIFE, LOOKING BACK ON ALL MY *STUPID* MEMORIES.

I DON'T WANT TO SEE IT. I DON'T WANT TO TALK ABOUT IT.

IT'S BEEN A *DUMB* LIFE, AND IF THERE'S ANY *DESIGN*, IT'S A *DUMB* DESIGN.

"CHRIST, WE WERE JUST *TALKING*. CAN'T A GUY TALK TO HIS, Y'KNOW, HIS OLD FRIEND'S DAUGHTER? WHAT DO YOU THINK I AM?"

"...HIS, Y'KNOW, HIS OLD FRIEND'S DAUGHTER?"

"WHAT DO YOU THINK I *AM*?"

I THINK YOU'RE *AVOIDING* SOME-THING.

DON'T BE *STUPID*. THERE'S N-NOTHING TO *AVOID*...

"...HIS, Y'KNOW, HIS OLD FRIEND'S DAUGHTER? WHAT DO YOU THINK I *AM*?"

I-I'VE *NEVER* HAD ANY OCCASION TO AVOID THE TRUTH...

"ONLY ONCE."

"WHAT DO YOU THINK I *AM*?"

"...OLD FRIEND'S DAUGHTER?"

"WHAT DO YOU THINK..."

"...HIS, Y'KNOW, HIS..."

"WHAT DO YOU THINK I AM?"

"...FRIEND'S DAUGHTER?"

I-I MEAN *LOOK*, HERE, MY *LIFE*, MY MOM'S LIFE, THERE'S NOTHING THERE *WORTH* AVOIDING, IT'S ALL JUST MEANING-LESS...

"...HIS, Y'KNOW, HIS'..."

"...ONLY ONCE."

"...Y'KNOW, HIS OLD FRIEND'S DAU..."

NO.

23

NO.

NO NOT HIM NOT...

NO.

NO. NO, SHE **WOULDN'T.** SHE **COULDN'T** HAVE NOT AFTER HE...

"...JUST COULDN'T SUSTAIN THE **ANGER.**"

"WHAT DO YOU THINK I **AM?**"

LAURIE?

NO! NO, YOU'RE **NOT.** YOU'RE **NOT!**

YOU'RE NOT MY FUH, MY FUH, FUH...

"CHRIST, WE WERE JUST **TALKING.** CAN'T A GUY TALK TO HIS, Y'KNOW, HIS..."

NO!

"...DAUGHTER?"

NNNAAAAOOOHH!

"...AND THERE WAS THIS **TOY,** THIS SNOWSTORM BALL, WITH A TINY **CASTLE** INSIDE, EXCEPT IT WAS LIKE A WHOLE **WORLD,** A WORLD INSIDE THE **BALL...**

"IT WAS LIKE A LITTLE GLASS BUBBLE OF SOMEWHERE **ELSE.**

"I LIFTED IT, STARTING A BLIZZARD. I KNEW IT WASN'T **REAL** SNOW, BUT I COULDN'T UNDERSTAND HOW IT FELL SO **SLOWLY.**

"I FIGURED INSIDE THE BALL WAS SOME DIFFERENT SORT OF **TIME.**

"**SLOW** TIME.

"...AND INSIDE THERE WAS ONLY WATER."

24

LAURIE?

ARE YOU ALRIGHT?

OF *COURSE* NOT! *BLAKE,* THAT *BASTARD,* AND MY M-*MOTHER,* THEY ...THEY PULLED A *GAG* ON ME IS WHAT THEY DID!

MY WHOLE *LIFE'S* A JOKE. ONE BIG, STUPID, MEANINGLESS ...AW *SHIT...*

I DON'T THINK YOUR LIFE'S MEANINGLESS.

OH NO, WELL, *OBVIOUSLY* THAT'S WHAT *YOU'RE* GOING TO SAY BECAUSE ANYTHING *I'M* STUPID ENOUGH TO BELIEVE IS TRUE, YOU JUST *DISAGREE* WITH IT AND...

...UH...

YOU *DON'T?*

NO.

BUT... LISTEN, YOU'VE JUST BEEN *SAYING* LIFE *IS* MEANINGLESS, SO HOW CAN...?

I CHANGED MY MIND.

BUT... *WHY?*

THERMO- DYNAMIC MIRACLES ...EVENTS WITH ODDS AGAINST SO ASTRONOMICAL THEY'RE EFFECTIVELY *IMPOSSIBLE,* LIKE *OXYGEN* SPONTANEOUSLY BECOMING *GOLD.* I LONG TO OBSERVE SUCH A THING.

AND YET, IN EACH HUMAN COUPLING, A THOUSAND MILLION SPERM VIE FOR A SINGLE EGG. MULTIPLY *THOSE* ODDS BY COUNTLESS *GENERATIONS,* AGAINST THE ODDS OF YOUR ANCES- TORS BEING *ALIVE; MEETING; SIRING THIS* PRECISE SON; *THAT* EXACT DAUGHTER...

26

... UNTIL YOUR MOTHER LOVES A MAN SHE HAS EVERY REASON TO *HATE*, AND OF THAT *UNION*, OF THE THOUSAND MILLION CHILDREN COMPETING FOR FERTILIZATION, IT WAS *YOU*, ONLY *YOU*, THAT EMERGED.

TO DISTILL SO *SPECIFIC* A FORM FROM THAT CHAOS OF *IMPROBABILITY*, LIKE TURNING *AIR* TO *GOLD*...

THAT IS THE CROWNING *UNLIKELIHOOD.*

THE THERMO-DYNAMIC *MIRACLE.*

"BUT... IF ME, MY BIRTH, IF *THAT'S* A THERMODYNAMIC MIRACLE... I MEAN, YOU COULD SAY THAT ABOUT ANYBODY IN THE *WORLD!*"

"YES.

"ANYBODY IN THE WORLD.

"... BUT THE WORLD IS SO *FULL* OF PEOPLE, SO *CROWDED* WITH THESE MIRACLES THAT THEY BECOME *COMMONPLACE* AND WE *FORGET*...

"*I* FORGET.

" WE GAZE CONTINUALLY AT THE WORLD AND IT GROWS DULL IN OUR PERCEPTIONS. YET SEEN FROM ANOTHER'S VANTAGE POINT, AS IF NEW, IT MAY STILL TAKE THE BREATH AWAY."

27

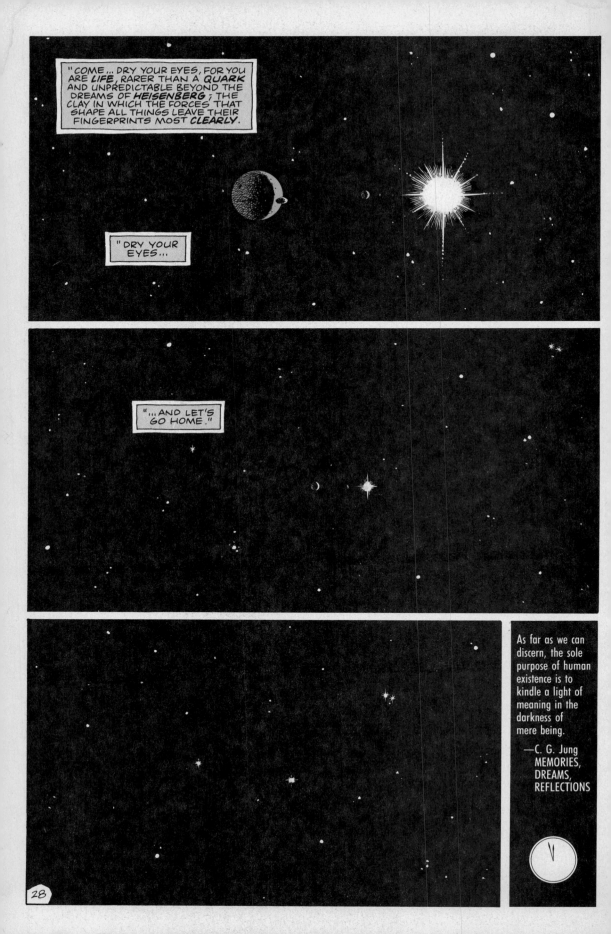

"COME... DRY YOUR EYES, FOR YOU ARE *LIFE*, RARER THAN A *QUARK* AND UNPREDICTABLE BEYOND THE DREAMS OF *HEISENBERG*; THE CLAY IN WHICH THE FORCES THAT SHAPE ALL THINGS LEAVE THEIR FINGERPRINTS MOST *CLEARLY*.

"DRY YOUR EYES...

"...AND LET'S GO HOME."

As far as we can discern, the sole purpose of human existence is to kindle a light of meaning in the darkness of mere being.

—C. G. Jung
MEMORIES, DREAMS, REFLECTIONS

28

VILLAINS VIE FOR VOLUPTUOUS VIGILANTE

Goons are going ga-ga over the test do-gooder to pull on a tight ostume and jump aboard the asked vigilante bandwagon. Why? ell, maybe it's because *this* cosumed cutie is a *girl*! Shapely 18-ear-old redhead Sally Jupiter 36-24-36) has taken the alluring nd mysterious monicker of "Silk pectre" as she dons the shortest ng underwear yet and becomes e first feisty female to join the ght against felony.

Miss Jupiter's agent, Mr. Larry hexnayder, says that former aitress and burlesque dancer ally is such a hit with the hoods at they're practically tripping ver each other in the rush to get abbed by her! In testimony, he prouced Mr. Claude Boke of no fixed ddress, currently out on parole fter Sally, who happened to be on and, arrested him during an atempted liquor store robbery.

"She beat me fair and square, but don't hold no grudges. She's a retty-looking young woman and I'd ather have her take me in than two at old cops anytime," says Claude, ho received a light fine and has ince quit drinking and taken a job umping gasoline.

Sally, who eventually hopes to nove on to modeling work or novies, tells us that there is already movie about her life in the works.

"It's called 'Silk Spectre: The ally Jupiter Story,'" enthuses Sally, and it's already in the planning tages. Larry and I have met with Mr. King Taylor of Hollywood, and verybody's very excited about it ll."

I'm sure we all wish spunky Sal uck in her future endeavors, and if he above movie gets made, who nows? Maybe Sally will have to rganize a special premiere . . . just or the criminal fraternity!

reports are true, she certainly has some explaining to do to her hubby and two kids back home on the ranch.

Meanwhile, over with the cape-and-mask crowd, lips are buzzing and tongues are wagging about cheesecake crime-crusher **Sally Jupiter**, alias the **SILK SPEC-TRE**. It seems that she and veteran vigilante **HOODED JUSTICE** are something of an item, and seldom out of each other's company. Can wedding bells be too far away? If you want evidence, just look whose arm our Sal is hanging onto in the recently released publicity photographs of that tights-and-trunk-clad team, **The Minutemen.** Between you and me, your Zelda wonders: Does he keep that hood and noose on *all* the time?

• • •

Spotted dancing cheek to cheek

King Taylor Productions

8-22-45

Sal and Larry

Hi, kids! I know, I know, it's been ages, but I think things are finally moving with "She Devils In Silk." (That's the latest title, by the way. Maurie dreamed it up. Hope you like it. We decided that "Sally Jupiter: Law In Its Lingerie" was too long, after all.)

The latest version is looking good — we've retained a lot of the plot elements from the saturday morning Matinee approach we adopted after junking the documentary idea, and we've kept a lot of the footage we shot with you way back then. This new version has some added material to make it accessible to a more adult market, and I think you'll find it kinda fun. We have a young discovery named Cherry Dean that I'm very excited about, and she stands in for you in the new scenes. From the back, she's a dead ringer! It's phenomenal!

Anyway, I'll keep touching base with you as things progress.

Hugs and kisses,
King

Sal — thought you'd like this for your scrapbook

MARINE LIEUTENANT USMC
NELSON GARDNER

FREE–LANCE CONSULTANT

KL5–22

Dear Miss Jupiter,

Having seen you in the news lately, I wished to introduce myself. My name is Captain Metropolis, and I too am a costumed adventurer,
with a keen interest in stamping out crime and injustice wheresoever
it should rear its ugly head. I am delighted to find that you share
these inclinations.

I note also from my perusal of the press that there are several
other people of our persuasion stepping forward to join the struggle
across America, and, being a military man by nature and career it
struck me that it might be a distinct strategic advantage if we were
to organize ourselves into some sort of battalion, ready to do our
country's bidding at a moment's notice.

I suggest that such a group might be called 'The New Minute Men
of America', and I have already devised such things as codes and pass-
words and strategic exercises that would serve us well in our war on
infamy.

If you are interested in this proposal, please contact me through
my representative, former Marine Lieutenant Nelson Gardner, whose card
is enclosed.

I look forward very much to hearing from you.

Your costumed Comrade in the campaign against crime,

Captain Metropolis

Sally – thought there might be mileage in this – P. Revise I.S.

*Larry –
Jesus Christ! Are
you kidding –!*

February 3rd, 1948

Dear Sally,

        Haven't been in touch lately because I thought you should
have time to get over poor Bill's funeral. However, there's things
that need talking over.

        Nelly called last night, upset over yet another tiff with
H.J. Those two are getting worse. The more they row and act like an
old married couple in public, the harder they are to cover for. I
know that you've provided a pretty steady alibi for H.J. up to now,
and that the publicity we got from that hasn't exactly hurt you either,
but it can't last much longer. Nelly says he's always out when Nelly
calls, out with boys, and apparently there's a lot of rough stuff going
on. One of these punks only has to go to the cops with a convincing
story and some convincing bruises to back it up and it would be the
Silhouette fiasco all over again.

        I honestly wonder how long it can last. Lewis is drinking
harder all the time, and has been very low since the thing with Bill.
Mason is a big bouncy boy scout, same as ever, but with Nelly and H.J.
acting up it's a pretty sorry spectacle at the meetings these days.
Maybe now is the time to pull out and cut our losses. We've made
quite a sum, you know, and I've often talked about a place out west
somewhere; maybe now's the time we could take it on as a viable partner-
ship proposition together? Anyways, at least think it over.

                                With fond regards,

                                        Larry

*nearest thing I ever
got to a proposal*

SCREEN REVIEWS
■■■■■■■■■■■■■■■■■■■■■■■■■■■■

SILK SWINGERS OF SUBURBIA
DIR: Edmund "King" Taylor
STARRING: Cherry Dean, Rod Don-
ovan, Dana Young, Lola Booker, Harry
J. Peters, Sally Juniper.

If you like tasteful and sensually artistic modern cin-
ema, then I recommend that this film be avoided at all
costs. Cheaply made even by "B"-movie standards,
this appears to have started life as a children's adventure serial, complete with unconvincing and dated
footage of a stuntwoman in an antique chorus girl
costume engaging in poorly staged fights with stock
heavies. Edited into this unpromising and juvenile
scenario with astonishing clumsiness, we have scenes
of Miss Dean—similarly attired and being tied up,
whipped and fondled by "Rod Donovan," who must
surely be a relative of well-known hack director "King"
Taylor, so close is the resemblance between the two
men. Too awful even to be dignified with the term
"pornography," the only real act of sadism in this film
lies in releasing it; the only masochism in watching it.

PROBE PROFILE: SALLY JUPITER

an interview with a forties glamour girl and the seamier side of her crimefighting career.

PROBE: Sally, how much would you say that it's a sex thing, putting on a costume?

SALLY: No. I don't . . . Well, let me say this, for me, it was never a sex thing. It was a money thing. And I think for some people it was a fame thing, and for a tiny few, God bless 'em, I think it was a goodness thing. I mean, I'm not saying it wasn't a sex thing for some people, but, no, no, I wouldn't say that's what motivated the majority . . .

PROBE: There was Ursula Zandt, the Silhouette . . .

SALLY: Uh-huh. Well, sooner or later, okay, that's going to come up, so let me deal with that . . . First off, I didn't like her as a person. I mean, she was not an easy person to get along with. But, when the papers got hold of it, her being a—what is it—a gay woman they say nowadays, when that happened, I thought it was wrong. I mean, Laurence, who was my first husband, he got everybody to throw her out of the group to minimize the P.R. damage, but . . . I mean, I voted along with everybody else, but . . . well, it wasn't fair. It wasn't honest. I mean, she wasn't the only gay person in the Minutemen. Some professions, I don't know, they attract a certain type . . .

PROBE: Who else was gay?

SALLY: I'm not naming anybody. It was a couple of the guys, and they're both dead now. One died recently. I'm not saying who

it was, I'm just saying that we all knew, and we knew she wasn't the only one, and we slung her out just the same. When she got murdered like that . . . I mean, I never really liked her. Ursula. Was that her real name? I didn't know that. I didn't like her, but . . . throwing her out. We shouldn't have done that. I feel bad about that.

PROBE: On the subject of the Minutemen, in Hollis Mason's autobiography . . .

SALLY: Uh-oh! Here it comes.

PROBE: . . . he alleges that you were sexually assaulted by the Comedian, who, as you know, is still active. You've never said too much about this incident yourself . . .

SALLY: Well, why break a lifetime's habit?

PROBE: You won't comment upon that?

SALLY: I . . . Look, I don't bear any grudges. That's all. I know I should, everybody tells me I should but . . . look, I don't have to justify this, okay? It's just that nothing's that simple, not even things that are simply awful. You know, rape is rape and there's no excuses for it, absolutely none, but for me, I felt . . . I felt like I'd contributed in some way. Is that misplaced guilt, whatever my analyst said? I really felt that, that I was somehow as much to blame for . . . for letting myself be his victim not in a physical sense, but . . . but,

it's like what if, y'know? What if, just for a moment, maybe I really did want . . . I mean, that doesn't excuse him, doesn't excuse either of us, but with all that doubt, what it is to come to terms with it, I can't stay angry when I'm so uncertain about my own feelings . . .

PROBE: You're retired now, and it seems your daughter has been groomed to follow in your footsteps. Having seen the lifestyle for yourself, how do you feel about that?

SALLY: Mm. That's tough. I guess, in a lot of ways, it was me who pushed Laurie, that's my daughter, pushed her into this line of work . . . I know that when she's upset about something she always blames me for shoving her into such a weird career, but underneath somewhere, I think she secretly kinda likes it. She likes to bitch about it, but what else would she have done? Been a housewife? Got a job in a bank? So she didn't have a normal life! What's so great about normal life? Normal life stinks! You can ask anybody! No, no, of course, I'm her mother, I get worried about her. But in the end, I think she'll see what it was I gave her. I think she'll start to see her life next to the lives of other kids and she'll start thinking in terms of what I saved her from instead of what I condemned her to.

PROBE: You think so?

SALLY: I hope so.

"You know, rape is rape and there's no excuse for it, absolutely none, but for me, I felt . . . I felt like I'd contributed in some way."

TWO RIDERS WERE APPROACHING...

THEY'RE IN THE 'COPTERS.

'COPTERS PROCEED TO ENTRANCE ALPHA. ENTRANCE ALPHA, STAND BY...

CARS ONE AND TWO NOW APPROACHING MAIN CONCOURSE...

THE PRESIDENTIAL PARTY IS NOW INSIDE THE COMPLEX. ENTRANCE ALPHA REMAIN OPEN UNTIL DEFCON ONE IS ACHIEVED. MAIN CONCOURSE, ALL UNITS PREPARE TO RECEIVE VISITORS...

2

MR. PRESIDENT. YOU WERE ABLE TO SEE MRS. NIXON TO SAFETY, I TAKE IT?

UH, YES, YES, PAT, SHE, UH, THAT IS, MRS. NIXON, SHE WASN'T TOO HAPPY ABOUT, WELL, YOU KNOW, BUT SHE'S OKAY NOW, I GUESS.

HOW ARE THINGS HANGING HERE?

WELL, AS YOU KNOW, I SEE NO PROFIT IN EMPLOYING MAD BOMBER TACTICS.

DON'T...DON'T YOU START THAT 'MAD BOMBER' SHIT. THAT WHOLE IMAGE, IT WAS *YOUR* SUGGESTION. I...

MR. PRESIDENT, OUR ANALYSIS SHOWS GOOD PERCENTAGES ON A FIRST STRIKE...

DON'T *PRESSURE* ME. LIDDY, YOU'RE EX-C.I.A., I KNOW YOUR LOYALTIES IN THIS, BUT I WILL NOT BE PRESSURIZED! I'M TENSE *ENOUGH*. NOW, WHAT'S THE *LATEST*?

EAST GERMANY: TANKS MASSING, ALLEGEDLY IN RESPONSE TO 'WESTERN ALARMISM'.

DEFCON 2

UH, THAT MIGHT POSSIBLY BE GENUINE. THIS LAST WEEK WE'VE *BOTH* BEEN ON FULL ALERT...

THE QUESTION *IS*, WHAT DO WE DO *NEXT*?

WE DO WHAT WE CAME *DOWN* HERE FOR: WE STAY AT DEFCON TWO...

AND WE SIT...

AND WE *WAIT*.

3

HOW MUCH LONGER? TIRED OF SKULKING DOWN HERE. IMPATIENT. WORK TO BE DONE.

RORSCHACH, WE JUST GOT YOU **OUT** OF PRISON. EVERY-BODY'S LOOKING FOR US, AND UNLESS WE **BOTH** WANT TO GO **BACK** THERE WE'D BETTER BE **CAREFUL**.

DOWN HERE HOURS ALREADY. NEED TO COLLECT SPARE UNIFORM AND PERSONAL EFFECTS, SO THAT WE CAN PROCEED.

ALL RIGHT, ALL RIGHT. THAT'S WHAT I'M **DOING**. WE'RE NEAR THE WHARVES BACKING ONTO YOUR NEIGHBOR-HOOD RIGHT NOW.

I'M TAKING HER UP.

AT LAST.

IT FEELS GOOD TO BE WORKING WITH YOU AGAIN, DANIEL. PITY MISS JUSPECZYK COULDN'T STAY WITH US.

YES.

YES, IT'S A PITY.

HUNH. STILL HERE. GOOD. POLICE DIDN'T FIND IT.

: MPH :

EXACTLY WHAT, UH, PERSONAL EFFECTS WERE YOU LOOKING FOR?

SPARE CLOTHES. SPARE FACE. FINAL DRAFT OF JOURNAL. POLICE ONLY FOUND ROUGH NOTES.

GLOVES. HAT. SHOES. THERE. THINK THAT'S EVERY-THING. WE...

OH GOD!

I--IT'S...OH GOD, WHAT ARE YOU DOING HERE? I... LOOK, PLEASE, I DON'T WANT ANY TROUBLE, OKAY? I...

MRS. SHAIRP.

LONG TIME NO SEE.

TOLD PRESS I'D MADE SEXUAL ADVANCES TO YOU. NOT TRUE.

VERY BAD.

NO! I NEVER SAID THAT! I GOT MISQUOTED! OH GOD, PLEASE, DON'T...

RORSCHACH? COME ON, MAN. LEAVE IT...

CAN'T. SERIOUS BUSINESS. SLUR ON REPUTATION.

HOW MUCH DID THEY PAY YOU TO LIE ABOUT ME, WHORE?

OH PLEASE, DON'T SAY THAT. NOT IN FRONT OF MY KIDS...

PLEASE. THEY...

THEY DON'T KNOW.

GOT WHAT WE CAME FOR. FINISHED HERE NOW.

LET'S GO.

6

WELCOME BACK, SIR. IT IS GOOD TO HAVE YOU SAFE WITH US. WE RECEIVED BULLETINS FROM NEW YORK...

THE ATTEMPTED SHOOTING? AH YES. YES, THESE ARE DANGEROUS TIMES...

HELLO, BUBASTIS. HELLO, OLD GIRL.

DO YOU STILL WISH TO STUDY THE **MONITORS** AND RECORD YOUR **OB-SERVATIONS** BEFORE DINNER? IF YOU ARE **HUNGRY**...

NO. LET DINNER WAIT. THE WORK COMES FIRST, AS EVER. THERE ARE THINGS TO DO, PROBLEMS TO SOLVE...

IT'S THE SAME OLD STORY.

INCIDENTALLY, DID THE DELIVERY RUN SMOOTHLY IN MY ABSENCE?

OH YES. WE THREE SUPERVISED THE RECEPTION UN-AIDED, AS INSTRUCTED.

THE MONITORS HAVE BEEN PREPARED, SIR. HOW MANY SCREENS DID YOU WISH TO VIEW?

ALL OF THEM. RANDOM CHANNEL CHANGE EVERY HUNDRED SECONDS.

THE PLANET IS CURRENTLY SWARMING WITH EVENTS. IN SUCH TIMES, **NONE** OF THEM ARE INSIGNIFICANT.

I NEED INFORMATION. INFORMATION IN ITS MOST CONCENTRATED FORM.

HA HA! SIR, DO YOU NOT FEAR THAT YOU MIGHT BECOME **DRUNK** UPON SO CONCENTRATED A DRAFT OF KNOWLEDGE?

HA HA HA. NO, I DON'T THINK SO.

INDEED, IT IS THE MOST SOBERING POTION THAT I KNOW.

7

HM. LET ME *SEE*...

FIRST IMPRESSIONS: OILED MUSCLEMAN WITH MACHINE-GUN... CUT TO PASTEL BEARS, VALENTINE HEARTS. JUXTA-POSITION OF WISH FULFILMENT VIOLENCE AND INFANTILE IMAGERY, DESIRE TO REGRESS BE FREE OF RESPONSIBILITY...

THIS ALL SAYS "WAR". WE SHOULD BUY ACCORDINGLY.

BUT... SIR, WE HAVE *NEVER* BOUGHT INTO *MUNITIONS*...

OF COURSE NOT. YOU'RE IGNORING THE *SUBTEXT*: INCREASED SEXUAL IMAGERY, EVEN IN THE CANDY ADS.

IT IMPLIES AN EROTIC UNDER-CURRENT NOT UNCOMMON IN TIMES OF WAR. REMEMBER THE *BABY BOOM*...

SO, SHOULD WE BUY INTO ... UH...?

INTO THE MAJOR EROTIC VIDEO COMPANIES. THAT'S *SHORT* TERM. ALSO, WE SHOULD NEGOTIATE CONTROLLING SHARES IN SELECTED *BABY FOOD* AND *MATERNITY GOODS* MANUFACTURERS.

I THINK I'M READY TO BEGIN *RECORDING* NOW.

VERY GOOD. THE EQUIPMENT IS READY, SIR. WE SHALL RETIRE AND LEAVE YOU TO YOUR WORK. WE KNOW THAT YOU PREFER TO BE *ALONE* DOWN HERE.

YES, THAT'S RIGHT. ALL ALONE...

JUST ME AND THE WORLD.

8

HATE THIS. ALL DAY ON RIVER BED. DROWNED CORPSES MORE USEFUL. YOU SAID WE COULD PROCEED.

THESE **COMPUTER SEARCHES** I'VE BEEN RUNNING **ARE** PROCEDURE. WHEN IT'S **DARK** AGAIN, WE'LL GO **UP**.

THIS IS NO **PICNIC** FOR ME, EITHER.

IMPLYING SOMETHING?

ABOUT COAT PERHAPS? OLD. SLIGHTLY MUSTY. APOLOGIES. CAN'T ALL BE **FASTIDIOUS**. CAN'T ALL KEEP HANDS CLEAN.

I WASN'T... LOOK, I JUST MEANT WE TOOK **ENOUGH** UNNECESSARY RISKS RETRIEVING YOUR **OUTFIT** THIS MORNING...

UNNECESSARY? COWERING DOWN HERE IN SLUDGE AND POLLUTION, CONJURING NAMES ON SCREENS, LEARNING NOTHING = THAT IS UNNECESSARY.

GIVE ME SMALLEST FINGER ON MAN'S HAND. I'LL PRODUCE INFORMATION. COMPUTER UNNECESSARY.

THIS FACE ALL THAT'S NECESSARY ...

ALL I NEED.

THAT'S BULLSHIT. YOU NEED **DARKNESS** TO WORK WITH, JUST LIKE **I** DO. AND WE **BOTH** NEEDED THE **SLEEP** WE GRABBED.

RIGHT **NOW**, I NEED SOME **PATTERN** THAT MAKES SENSE OF THE **DATA** WE HAVE...

THE **COMEDIAN** MENTIONED AN **ISLAND** AND SOME PLOT AGAINST **JON**. MY **COMPUTERS** SUGGEST JON COULD HAVE BEEN **SET UP**, POSSIBLY BY THE COMPANY ALL HIS SUPPOSED 'VICTIMS' **WORKED** FOR...

"POSSIBLY."

WE SHOULD ASK QUESTIONS IN THE UNDERWORLD.

ISN'T THAT WHAT I'M **DOING**?

9

DON'T PLAY GAMES WITH ME.

YOU WASTE TIME LOOKING FOR PATTERN WHEN PATTERN IS OBVIOUS. THE MASK KILLER...

IF YOU'D *LISTEN* THAT'S WHAT I'M TRYING TO *SAY!* WHAT IF THERE *IS* NO MASK KILLER?

LOOK, THE COMEDIAN LEARNED, *ACCIDENTALLY,* ABOUT SOME *ISLAND,* SOME SCHEME AGAINST *JON.*

THE PLOT AGAINST JON COMES *FIRST. BLAKE'S* KILLED WHEN HE *DISCOVERS* IT.

WHO KNEW BLAKE SUSPECTED ANYTHING?

THIS *DIMENSIONAL DEVELOPMENTS* COMPANY EMPLOYED *MOLOCH.* MAYBE HIS PLACE WAS *BUGGED* WHEN BLAKE *VISITED?*

THAT'D ALSO EXPLAIN HOW THEY KNEW ABOUT *YOUR* INVESTIGATIONS AND WERE ABLE TO *FRAME* YOU...WITHOUT *REQUIRING* ANY 'MASK KILLER'.

AND VEIDT?

MM. ADRIAN'S A *PROBLEM.* THAT *WAS* A CLEAR-CUT ASSASSINATION ATTEMPT, USING A HIRED *KILLER...*

EXACTLY. SO TRACE KILLER. VISIT BARS. SQUEEZE PEOPLE.

BEEN LAZING AROUND A LONG TIME. MAYBE YOU'VE FORGOTTEN HOW WE DO THINGS.

JOURNAL 1985 1985

LAZING...?

LISTEN, I'VE *HAD* IT! WHO THE HELL DO YOU THINK YOU *ARE?* YOU *LIVE* OFF PEOPLE WHILE *INSULTING* THEM, NOBODY COMPLAINS BECAUSE THEY THINK YOU'RE A GODDAMNED *LUNATIC*...

YOU KNOW HOW *HARD* IT IS, BEING YOUR *FRIEND?*

I...LOOK, RORSCHACH, I'M *SORRY.* I SHOULDN'T HAVE SAID ALL THAT...

LISTEN, YOU'RE *RIGHT.* WE'VE BOTH BEEN DOWN HERE TOO LONG. IT MUST BE DARK ENOUGH TO SURFACE BY NOW. I'LL TAKE HIM UP.

DANIEL...

YOU ARE...A GOOD FRIEND.

I KNOW THAT.

I AM SORRY...THAT IT IS SOMETIMES DIFFICULT.

UH...HEY...

HEY, FORGET IT. IT'S OKAY, MAN!

IT'S OKAY.

10

UHH...

WELL, ANYWAY, THERE'S...

∴NG∴

...THERE'S NO SENSE WAITING DOWN HERE ANY LONGER.

I MEAN, DOWN HERE IN THIS *JUNK GARDEN,* IS THIS ANY PLACE TO HOLD THE REUNION OF THE *NITE OWL-RORSCHACH* TEAM?

LET'S GO UP TO VISIT THE *CRIMINAL FRATERNITY,*...AND *REALLY* START PLUMBING THE DEPTHS.

Y'KNOW, SOME NICE STRAIGHTFORWARD BRUTALITY, AFTER WADING KNEE-DEEP IN THIS *CONSPIRACY* WEIRDNESS FOR SO LONG...

HELL, IT'LL BE LIKE COMING *HOME.*

11

I WAS RETURNED, SPLASHING NOISILY THROUGH THE EN-CUMBERING SHALLOWS, SUN MULLING THE HORIZON BEHIND ME, A POKER IN A GLASS OF SACK.

I COULD BE NO MORE THAN TWENTY MILES FROM DAVIDSTOWN.

I WAS HOME.

IN BROAD CHARCOAL STROKES, NIGHT SHADED THE SKY.

I SAT AMONGST SKULL-COLORED DUNES, SHARP GRASS CLINGING LIKE HAIR IN BLACK, OBSTINATE TUFTS. BY NOW, DAVIDSTOWN WAS OVER-RUN, MY FAMILY SLAUGHTERED. ONLY REVENGE REMAINED.

DELIBERATING UPON THIS, I STARTLED AT THE SOUND OF HORSES APPROACHING, PICKING DAINTILY ACROSS THE SHINGLE; VOICES, MALE AND FEMALE...

HUDDLED IN THE DUNE'S LAP, I WATCHED THROUGH A CURTAIN OF WHISPERING MARAM GRASS.

DISMOUNTING, THEY TETHERED THEIR STEEDS TO DARK WOODEN GROINS, JUTTING OUT LIKE CHARRED RIBS FROM THE BEACH.

I RECOGNIZED THE MAN: A MONEYLENDER FROM DAVIDS-TOWN. LAUGHING, HE WALKED HIS WOMAN OVER PEBBLES, DOWN TOWARDS THE SURF.

WITH DAVIDSTOWN CAPTURED, WHY WOULD BRIGANDS ALLOW THIS SCOUNDREL FREE PASSAGE FOR HIS MIDNIGHT TRYSTS? HAD HE COLLABORATED?

THE RIBALD CHUCKLING REACHED THE WATER'S EDGE; CEASED; BECAME A SCREAM.

MY RAFT WAS DISCOVERED.

HE COMFORTED THE WEEPING, HYSTERICAL WOMAN, AND MY HEART GREW COLD. WAS MY WIFE COMFORTED BEFORE HER EXECUTION, WHILE THIS COLLABORATOR AND HIS PIRATE MASTERS SNEERED?

NOW THEY WOULD REPORT MY RAFT.

MY DECISION WAS HURRIED, BUT NOT DIFFICULT.

SCREAMING MY HATRED, I RUSHED DOWN THE NIGHT SLOPE TOWARDS THEM, BUT ALL THAT ESCAPED MY LIPS WAS THE BLACK LANGUAGE OF GULLS.

CLUTCHING THE ROCK, MY HAND FELT HUGE, DEFORMED. STARTLED, THEY TURNED.

OVER-RIPE, THE MONEYLENDER'S HEAD BURST WITH A SINGLE BLOW, EXPLODING AS IF PRESSURIZED BY THE GUILT WITHIN.

SUDDENLY SLICK, THE ROCK SHOT FROM BETWEEN MY RED FINGERS AND WAS LOST.

THE WOMAN I STRANGLED.

THIS TOOK CONSIDERABLY LONGER THAN I HAD ANTICIPATED.

12

Y'KNOW, I DIDN'T EXPECT ALL THIS TO TAKE SO *LONG*. DIDN'T EXPECT THIS *WAITING*...

LOOK: EVERYBODY'S SCARED THEY'LL DROP IT TONIGHT, GATHERIN' ON CORNERS, LOOKING FOR *TROUBLE*...

AT DEATH'S APPROACH, ALL CREATURES DISCOVER AN APTITUDE FOR VIOLENCE.

FLAILING, SCRATCHING, SHE WAS A BRIAR ROSE IN THE WIND. THE WIND DROPPED. HER THRASHINGS BECAME WEAKER...

THE HORSES WATCHED, UNDERSTANDING ONLY A LITTLE.

LIKE, IT'S TOO BIG TO TAKE *IN*, BUT PEOPLE KNOW SOMETHING *BAD'S* HAPPENING...

PEOPLE KNOW SOMETHING'S *COMING.*

ASK ME, IT'S *DOOMSDAY,* LIKE IN THE BOOK O' REVOLUTIONS. I MEAN, TANKS IN EAST GERMANY, THERE'S NO MISTAKIN' IT...

WHEN DEATH WAS ASSURED, RESIGNATION LENT HER EYES A CERTAIN MATURITY.

THUMBS CROSSED, I CLOSED HER WINDPIPE. A BUCCANEER'S WHORE DESERVED NO PITY.

EVENTUALLY I STOOD, LEGS TREMBLING, BARELY SUPPORTING ME. IN THE FOAM ABOUT MY ANKLES, TWO WORLDS LAY ENDED.

MAYBE TODAY, MAYBE TOMORROW, BUT *SOON* FOR SURE.

GOOD DAY, SIR. I'D LIKE TO PURCHASE A GAZETTE, IF I MAY.

UH, SURE. THAT'S WHAT I'M *HERE* FOR...

MY PURPOSE ALMOST FORGOTTEN IN THE GIDDY WHIRL OF MURDER ITSELF, I GAZED STUPIDLY AT THE HORSES.

RECOVERING, I BECAME MORE RATIONAL. SEEKING VENGEANCE, MIGHT I TURN THIS UNFORESEEN CIRCUMSTANCE TO MY ADVANTAGE? AN IDEA BLOSSOMED, PLAUSIBLE, TEMPTING...

THERE. NOW, WE'VE BOUGHT ONE OF *YOUR* PAPERS. PERHAPS YOU'D LIKE TO TRY *OURS*?

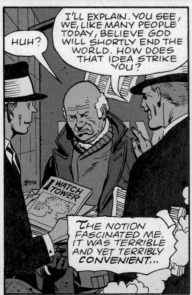

HUH?

I'LL EXPLAIN. YOU SEE, WE, LIKE MANY PEOPLE TODAY, BELIEVE GOD WILL SHORTLY END THE WORLD. HOW DOES THAT IDEA STRIKE YOU?

THE NOTION FASCINATED ME. IT WAS TERRIBLE AND YET TERRIBLY CONVENIENT...

BALONEY! END THE *WORLD*? NO WAY, JOSÉ!

OH, I SEE. WELL, WE'RE JUST *LEAVING*...

THIS COUPLE LEFT DAVIDSTOWN UNHINDERED, DESPITE THE PIRATE SENTRIES THERE MUST BE THEY'D BE ALLOWED BACK, ALSO...

TIED TO HER SADDLE, SHE LOOKED QUITE NATURAL.

GODDAMN *FANATICS.* ITCHIN' TO SAY "I TOLD YA SO!"

WOULDN'T GIVE 'EM THE *SATISFACTION*!

TWO FIGURES HAD RIDDEN HERE, NOW TWO RODE BACK. SOON. SOON I WOULD VENTURE AMONGST EVIL MEN, AND MAKE THEM FEAR ME...

New York Gazette

ASTERN EUROPE: TANKS MASS AS ONFLICT ESCALATES

13

OH NO.

OH YES.

MISSED YOU WHILE IN PRISON, BOYS. FEELS GOOD TO BE BACK.

VISITED TWO BARS BEFORE THIS. YOU MAY HAVE HEARD AMBULANCES. HOPEFULLY, LUCKIER HERE.

NEED INFORMATION: ADRIAN VEIDT SHOT AT. PRESS GAVE KILLER'S NAME AS ROY VICTOR CHESS.

DEAD NOW.

SOMEBODY KNEW ROY CHESS. SOMEBODY HIRED HIM.

DON'T WORRY...

WON'T INSULT LEGENDARY UNDERWORLD SOLIDARITY BY SUGGESTING YOU SURRENDER NAME WITHOUT TORTURE.

YOU BASTARDS! I BUY YA DRINKS, YOU SELL ME OUT! WHAT KINDA TOWN IS THIS?

YOU KEEP AWAY FROM ME! YOU COME ANY CLOSER, YOU'RE GONNA GET THIS IN YOUR GODDAMN SQUIDGY FACE!

YOU'RE GONNA...

AAAAOOOGODDD!

STUPID.

ALL RIGHT ...EVERYBODY STAY CALM, WE'LL TRY TO KEEP THIS BRIEF.

NO! NO, DON'T SQUEEZE IT...

ROY CHESS.

HOW'S YOUR GAME?

14

LISTEN, PLEASE, I JUST HANDED OVER THESE **ENVELOPES** TO THE GUY. I DON'T KNOW ANYTHING ABOUT **AAAA**!

WHAT **ENVELOPES**?

SEALED ENVELOPES, ONE WITH **CASH**, ONE WITH **INSTRUCTIONS**. I HAD TO FIND A RELIABLE CONTRACT **HIT**, GIVE HIM **BOTH**. NOBODY MENTIONED **VEIDT**!

GOT OFFERED THE ERRAND BY MY **BOSS**, FREIGHT CO-ORDINATOR AT PYRAMID DELIVERIES...

AH.

POISON CAPSULES=IN ENVELOPES?

M-MAYBE. HELL, I DUNNO. I TOOK THE JOB, LOT OF OTHER GUYS WERE GETTIN' SOME ACTION, I FIGURE WHY **NOT**? NOW EVERYBODY'S GETTIN' **KILLED**, MY LIFE'S A **NIGHTMARE**...

KILLED?

ALL THE OTHER **FREIGHT HANDLERS** WHO WERE **IN** ON THINGS. SUPPOSED TO BE **ACCIDENTS**; OVERDOSES... **BULL**SHIT!

MY BOSS, GUY GAVE ME THE ENVELOPES, HE FELL UNDER A **SUBWAY** TRAIN.

I'M NEXT. I NEED **PROTECTION.**

SEE, I **UNDERSTAND**, YOU GUYS ARE PISSED, YOUR OWN PEOPLE ARE THREATENED, THAT'S **UNDERSTANDABLE**, BUT I **SWEAR**, NOT 'TIL I SAW CHESS ON THE **NEWS**, I DIDN'T KNOW **VEIDT** WAS THE **CONTRACT**.

SOMETHING **BOTHERING** YOU, SON?

I'D NEVER **CROSS** ONE O' YOU PEOPLE. NOT **KNOWINGLY**...

I **KNEW** IT! I **KNEW** YOU'D **VICTIMIZE** ME! GET OFF MY **CASE**! WEARING A **KNOT** DOESN'T MEAN I'M CONNECTED WITH THAT STUFF LAST **NIGHT**. LOTTA PEOPLE DRESS LIKE THIS, MAN.

I **HEARD** THE **NEWS**, BLAMING THAT **MASON** GUY'S MURDER ON KNOT TOPS, I THOUGHT "SHIT! LIKE THEY **NEEDED** EXCUSES TO **HASSLE** US!"

SO YOU GOTTA **PROTECT** ME. SOMEBODY'S **AFTER** ME, AND THESE DAYS **NOBODY'S** SAFE!

PROTECT YOU? BECAUSE YOU WERE **UNAWARE** WHOSE **EXECUTION** YOU WERE **ARRANGING**?

MAYBE PERSON ARRANGING YOURS DOESN'T KNOW **EITHER**. NOTHING PERSONAL, HEHN?

HOPE THAT THOUGHT COMFORTS YOU WHILE WAITING FOR AX TO FALL.

YI¡AAAAAGH!

15

WHO **DID** IT? TELL ME WHO **DID** IT, YOU **SLIME!** WHO MURDERED **HOLLIS?**

KCUH...NO. DON'T KNOW... GHUCH...GANG... KIDS SAW GANG ...RUNNING AWAY...

YOU **TELL** THEM! TELL THEM THEY'RE **DEAD!** YOU KNOW HOW MUCH **FIRE POWER** I HAVE FLOATING OUT THERE?

I OUGHTTA TAKE OUT THIS ENTIRE RAT-HOLE **NEIGHBORHOOD!** I OUGHTTA... OUGHTTA BREAK YOUR NECK, YOU...YOU...

OH GOD **DAMN.**

GOD DAMN GOD DAMN GOD **DAMN!**

NOT IN FRONT OF CIVILIANS. WE HAVE THE KNOWLEDGE THAT WE WANTED...

YEAH.

YEAH, AND THEN SOME. HELL, LET'S GET **OUT** OF HERE.

HOLLIS. OH **CHRIST,** MAN, **WHY?**

W-WE MUST HAVE **MISSED** IT ON THE NEWS. PROBABLY NOT **IMPORTANT** ENOUGH FOR REPEAT BULLETINS. JUST SOME...SOME USELESS OLD **GUY...**

OH SHIT. TAKE THIS AND BRING ARCHIE DOWN. I CAN'T SEE.

HAPPY HARRY'S

BAR GRILL

BRONX

UNIDENTIFIED GANG MURDERS MASON. SUPPORTS MASK-KILLER THEORY...

LOOK, I DON'T **CARE!** RIGHT NOW I DON'T **CARE** ABOUT WHOSE THEORY IS BEST! JUST **SHUT UP** AND BRING THE **SHIP** DOWN.

MERELY **SUGGESTING** THAT BY FINDING MASK KILLER, CAN HAVE REVENGE FOR MASON'S DEATH. MEANT TO **COMFORT** YOU.

COMFORT ME? WHO IN THEIR RIGHT MIND COULD TAKE COMFORT FROM ...UH ...

YEAH, OKAY. THANKS, RORSCHACH. REALLY. THANK YOU.

YOU'RE WELCOME.

NOW KNOW WHO PAID TO KILL VEIDT. INFORMATION SHOULD CONVINCE HIM TO HELP US.

SURE.

I CAN'T BELIEVE HE'S DEAD. I REMEMBER **ADRIAN** ONCE TELLING ME THAT THE **EGYPTIANS** REGARDED DEATH AS A **VOYAGE...**

HURN. NICE IDEA IF YOU CAN AFFORD TO GO FIRST CLASS, WITH PHARAOHS...

...BUT JUDGING BY OUR DEPARTURES, MOST OF US TRAVEL STEERAGE.

16

"OOPS. MR. SHEA, IT'S VERY *DARK* DOWN HERE. WHAT IF SOMEONE SHOULD *DISCOVER* US?"

"RELAX. EVERYBODY'S UP ON DECK FOR THE *EVACUATION* PARTY. ONCE THE LAST OF THE EQUIPMENT'S ABOARD, THE SHIP'S READY TO PUT OUT."

"HOW ABOUT YOU?"

"WHAT...? MR. *SHEA,* *REALLY*! HA HA HA HA!"

"HIRA, COME *ON,* WE'RE CELE-BRATING. TONIGHT WE *LEAVE* THIS PLACE AFTER ALL THESE *MONTHS.* HELL, I SAW NORM LEITH AND LIN PALEY UP ON DECK. EVEN *THEY* WERE SMILING..."

"WELL, THEY'RE BEING PAID ENOUGH TO *VANISH* AND FORGET THEIR *CARES.* YOU KNOW, THIS *MOVIE* HAS INVOLVED EXTRA-ORDINARY *SECRECY*..."

"YEAH... AND I KNOW *WHY.* THAT *GENETICIST* GUY, *FURNESSE,* TOLD ME THEY'D USED A HUMAN *BRAIN* MAKING THAT GOD-DAMNED *SPECIAL EFFECT.*"

"PROBABLY ILLEGAL, BUT WHO CARES? *I'M* CONTENT TO BE A RICH MISSING PERSON AND FINALLY OFF THAT *ISLAND.*"

"LIKE YOUR SHIPWRECKED *VOYAGER*? DID HE ESCAPE *HIS* ISLAND?"

"WELL, YES, BUT... HEY! FEEL *THAT*? WE'RE *MOVING.*"

"THAT ISN'T *ALL* I CAN FEEL. MAX, PLEASE, AT LEAST LET ME PUT DOWN MY *DRAWING* EQUIPMENT... THERE. HOW'S *THAT*?"

"MMM. HIRA, MEETING YOU MAKES UP FOR *EVERYTHING.* WE'LL FIND SOME PLACE TOGETHER AND ..."

"HELL, WHAT'S *DIGGING* INTO MY *ARM*?"

17

FORGET IT, WHATEVER IT IS. I CAN'T WAIT UNTIL A HOTEL ON THE *MAINLAND*. AFTER YEARS WITH THAT *SEXLESS* OAF AND HIS SPOILED SONS, I'M *IMPATIENT*.

SOME KINDA BOX UNDER THE *TARPAULIN*. LEMME SWITCH THIS *LIGHT* ON ...

MAX, *PLEASE*...

WHAT'S THAT *COUNTER*? LET ME *SEE* THAT. IT'S...

MAX, FOR GOD'S SAKE, CONCENTRATE ON *ME*. THE CREW MUST *VISIT* THIS PART OF THE SHIP, AND I THINK WE MIGHT NOT HAVE VERY LONG.

MAX? YOU'RE SO *PALE*. WHAT'S *WRONG*?

NOTHING, LOVE.

NOTHING'S WRONG.

HOLD ME.

18

19

DANIEL? FOUND SOMETHING?

OH GOD, YES. YES, I'VE FOUND SOMETHING...

RORSCHACH, I THINK WE'RE IN *BAD* TROUBLE. THE PERSON *BEHIND* THIS, THE PERSON WE'RE *UP* AGAINST...

PYRAMID DELIVERIES FINANCIAL ANALYSIS YEAR ENDING 3:31:85

NET INCOME [$M] 115.49

BREAKDOWN FOLLOWS ▮

I THINK IT'S ADRIAN.

ALL THIS *EGYPTIAN* STUFF... I THOUGHT I'D CHECK OUT PYRAMID DELIVERIES ON HIS COMPUTER. AS PASSWORD I TRIED RAMESES II, THE EGYPTIAN NAME FOR *OZYMANDIAS.*

HE *RUNS* IT, RORSCHACH! *RUNS* PYRAMID DELIVERIES, DIMENSIONAL DEVELOPMENTS, THE WHOLE SHOW!

BUT VEIDT WAS TARGET.

OZYMANDI SOUTHERN I FAMINE RELIEF

I KNOW IT'S CRAZY, AND I DON'T WANT TO *BELIEVE* IT, BUT PERHAPS WE SHOULD FIND ADRIAN *FAST.*

"KARNAK"... RAMESES BUILT A GIGANTIC *HALL* THERE; A *MONUMENT.* KARNAK MUST BE VEIDT'S ANTARCTIC *RETREAT.*

BETTER GRAB THOSE PAPERS FROM HIS *DESK...*

IT'S A LONG *JOURNEY,* AND THEY'LL MAKE BETTER READING THAN THE *LIFEJACKET* INSTRUCTIONS.

21

RORSCHACH'S JOURNAL. NOVEMBER 1ST, 1985. =

Final entry? Left Veidt's office just before midnight.

Dreiberg, convinced Veidt's behind everything, is serious about visiting Antarctica. Owlship capable, apparently, but are we?

Veidt. Cannot imagine more dangerous opponent.

Assuming journey possible, tracking him to his lair only option. Still feel uneasy. Unfamiliar territory...

He could kill us both, there in snow. Nobody would ever know...

First night in november.

I am cold tonight.

Veidt is faster than Dreiberg. Perhaps faster than me. Return from mission seems unlikely.

This last entry. Will shortly mail journal to only people can trust.

Tell Dreiberg I need to check my maildrop. He believes me.

Appreciate your recent support and hope world survives long enough for this to reach you, but tanks are in east Berlin, and writing is on wall.

For my own part, regret nothing. Have lived life free from compromise...

Offices below, headstones marking daily graves of thousands. Inside, across clock faces, as observed as those of celebrities, hands commence final laps.

Oblivion gallops closer, favoring the spur, sparing the rein.

I think we will be gone soon.

NOVEMBER 2ND PALE HO IN CONCERT, WITH KRYSTALNACH MADISON SQUARE

If reading this now, whether I am alive or dead, you will know truth: whatever precise nature of this conspiracy, Adrian Veidt responsible.

Have done best to make this legible. Believe it paints disturbing picture.

...and step into the shadow now without complaint.

RORSCHACH, NOVEMBER 1ST, 1985.

22

IT AIN'T *FAIR.* WE DIDN'T ASK FOR NO *WAR.* THERE'S NO GODDAMN *JUSTICE* IN THIS WORLD!

Unrecognizable in corpse's clothing, I was the concealed implement of God's retribution.

ALL THIS *CRAZINESS* GOIN' DOWN, THE ORDINARY GUY GOT NO *PROTECTION.* LIKE A *TURTLE* WITH NO *SHELL.* HE'S ALL WASHED UP!

Abandoning the naked moneylender to the cold surf, I led the horses from the beach.

Ahead, Davidstown lay sleeping, little dreaming what approached.

I MEAN, AT LEAST THOSE *SUPER* GUYS *TRIED* TO PROTECT FOLK. MAYBE WE SHOULDA *LISTENED.* MAYBE THEY HAD A *MESSAGE,* Y'KNOW?

I MEAN, THERE'S GOTTA BE *SOMEBODY* LOOKIN' OUT FOR US, RIGHT?

Cantering down moonlit lanes, I spied the dark, unmoving form of a pirate sentry, watching sullenly from atop an embankment. I held my breath...

...dreading lest he should attempt conversation.

HI THERE! BOY, THIS *WAR* BUSINESS, HUH? *CRAZY!* ME, I ALWAYS BIN AGAINST THAT *ATOMIC WEAPONS* STUFF.

UH, JUST 'A GAZETTE, PLEASE. NO OFFENSE, MAN...

...BUT I'M IN KIND OF A *RUSH.*

Trotting unhurriedly to avoid suspicion, I rode past. If he noted the lovers' unusually early return from their assignation, the sentinel said nothing, perhaps assuming we'd ARGUED.

The woman's head lolled stupidly. No LIVING companion was ever so agreeable.

HI, JOEY. HOW'S *THINGS*?

DUNNO. *ALINE'S* MEETING ME FROM *WORK* TONIGHT, TO *DISCUSS* THINGS. *NOW* SHE'S PISSED 'CAUSE THAT CLASHES WITH *PALE HORSE'S* MADISON SQUARE *GIG!*

I spurred the horses on, whinnying, unnerved by death's scent, towards that inevitable confrontation.

HEY, LIGHTEN UP. IT AIN'T THE END O' THE *WORLD*...

"Dear God, let me have vengeance, then die swiftly..."

...UH...

...I MEAN, AT LEAST, Y'KNOW, FIGURATIVELY *SPEAKIN'.*

...delivered at last into the hands of a higher JUDGMENT.

23

US MAIL SORTING DEPOT

URGENT

...S NOW NOR...
...LOOM OF NIGHT...
...AY THESE COURI...
...HE SWIFT COMPLE...
...R APPOINTED TA...

US MAIL

PIONEER PUBLISHING INC.

MAIL FOR YA.

UH, THANKS...

SEYMOUR, BRING THAT IN HERE AND *OPEN* IT! MAYBE THAT LAZY JERK *FEINBERG* MANAGED TO GET HIS *EDITORIAL CARTOON* IN ON TIME!

NEW FRONTIERSMAN

URGENT

I MEAN, RED HOLOCAUST ABOUT TO *BREAK*, EVERYTHING HAPPENING AT *ONCE*, AM I SUPPOSED TO HANDLE THINGS BY *MYSELF*?

UH, THIS *FIRST* ONE'S SOME *JOURNAL*...

"DEAD DOG IN ALLEY THIS MORNING, TIRE TREAD ON BURST STOMACH..."

JESUS, WHO'S IT *FROM*? SON OF *SAM*? SLING IT ON THE *CRANK FILE*. NEW YEAR, WE'LL BURN THAT GARBAGE HEAP AND START *OVER*!

HERE'S ONE ABOUT FLUORIDE TURNING PEOPLE INTO *HOMOS*...

CRANK FILE! THROW 'EM ALL ON THE CRANK FILE AND GET SOME *WORK* DONE!

WAR'S COMING, AND THIS PAPER HAS A *MISSION*, GODDAMNIT. I WON'T SEE *TRUTH* AND *INTEGRITY* BURIED BENEATH AN *AVALANCHE* OF *DRIVEL*!

WHILE WE STAND AROUND SORTING *JUNK MAIL*, WE COULD MISS SOMETHING *IMPORTANT!* HELL, *FACE* IT, THE REDS COULD HAVE EMPTIED THEIR SILOS FIVE MINUTES AGO...

THE BIRDS COULD BE IN THE AIR RIGHT *NOW!*

24

HOW MUCH FURTHER? SAID WE WERE OVER ANTARCTICA HOURS AGO.

VEIDT'S FORTRESS IS NEARBY, ALONG THE COASTLINE. THAT'S WHAT I'M FOLLOWING.

LISTEN, I DON'T LIKE THE WAY ARCHIE'S HANDLING. I'M GOING TO TAKE HIM DOWN.

SENSIBLE MOVE. MAKE FINAL APPROACH LOW, BENEATH RADAR.

I DON'T THINK WE'VE GOT MUCH CHOICE. YOU FEEL THAT SORT OF KICKING IN THE ENGINE, LIKE IT'S ABOUT TO SEIZE?

ICE. SHIT, I BET IT'S ICE...

I HAD HIM SOAKING ON A RIVER BED ALL YESTER- DAY, THEN BRING HIM STRAIGHT INTO SUB-ZERO TEMPERATURES! WHY DIDN'T I THINK?

DANIEL... COMING IN TOO LOW TOWARDS CLIFFS...

DON'T WISH TO INTERFERE WITH RUNNING OF SHIP, BUT SHOULD PERHAPS PULL UP SHARPLY BEFORE...

I'M TRYING! I'M TRYING TO PULL HIM UP, GODDAMN IT!

WAIT! WAIT, I THINK IT'S COMING. I THINK WE'VE...

...MADE IT!

DANIEL...

IT'S *OKAY*, WE DID IT! WE CLEARED THE...

DANIEL, ENGINE JUST STOPPED.

WHAT?

SAID ENGINE JUST...

ALRIGHT ALRIGHT, I *KNOW*! JESUS CHRIST...

LEMME TRY TO... WHOO-OOAH...

ENNK...

HOLD *ON* TO SOMETHING! I'M *LOSING* IT! HE'S *ROLLING*. I THINK WE'RE GOING TO...

OW.

YOU OKAY?

TWISTED ANKLE, NOTHING SERIOUS. LANDED ON IT BADLY NIGHT POLICE TOOK ME.

HOW BAD IS DAMAGE TO SHIP?

DIFFICULT TO SAY. PROBABLY NOTHING I COULDN'T FIX GIVEN A FEW HOURS...

IT'D BE QUICKER TO COVER THE REMAINING DISTANCE ON THE HOVERBIKES. THE INSTRUMENTS PUT US WITHIN TWENTY MILES OF VEIDT'S FORTRESS.

YOU BREAK OUT THE BIKES WHILE I GET INTO MY SNOW SUIT.

UH...YOU'RE SURE I CAN'T FIT YOU OUT IN SOMETHING A LITTLE WARMER?

FINE LIKE THIS.

WELL, WHATEVER YOU WANT. GIVE ME A SECOND AND I'LL OPEN THE REAR DOOR SO YOU CAN UNLOAD THOSE...

USED THESE WHEN WE TOOK UNDERBOSS. REMEMBER RIDING ALONG SEWER.

GOD, YES! THEY KNEW WE COULDN'T GET ARCHIE DOWN THERE AND FIGURED THEY WERE SAFE...

THEN YOU SHOOT OUT OF THAT TUNNEL, WITH THE GAS CLOUD, ALL THE RATS RUNNING AHEAD OF YOU...

MAN, THEIR FACES!

YES. GOOD NIGHT. THINK OF IT OFTEN.

AS I RECALL, CONTROLS SIMPLE; JUST TWO PEDALS AND STEERING COLUMN.

YOU GOT IT.

TCH. LOOK AT THAT ICE. BETTER FIX IT SOON AS WE GET BACK...

IF WE GET BACK.

YEAH.

YEAH. IF WE GET BACK. I'M GOING TO SECURE THE SHIP ANYWAY.

THERE. OKAY, I GUESS THAT'S IT...

WHAT ARE WE WAITING FOR?

27

Outside in the distance a wild cat did growl, two riders were approaching, the wind began to howl.

— Bob Dylan

Leo Winston
President
Marketing and Development

Dear Adrian,

Even though you vetoed an expanded range of dolls based upon former advesaries, I still feel that the Ozymandias action figure line needs to attain a higher profile on the marketplace, and that to me indicates an extended range of product. Several possibilities have ocurred to me, outlined below.

Firstly, figurines based upon Rorschach and Nite Owl seem to be viable. From a legal viewpoint, we're currently investigating the situation regarding the trademark and copyright laws. Our lawyers seem to think that since the costumed identities themselves are outlawed and illegal, there can be no legal claim to copyright upon their costumed images, leaving us free to register a copyright ourselves. This seems okay to me, but I'm advised that since you may have some personal connection with these individuals, there's a possibility that you'll feel differently.

Secondly, the Moloch figurine. Since Edgar Jacobi died recently, there may be a question of taste, but from what our lawyers can determine, Jacobi left no estate likely to oppose such a marketing move. Also, once again there can be no legal claim on Jacobi's part concerning infringement of an identitiy which is illegal in the first place.

Thirdly, and on a somewhat lighter note, I hope you will approve the inclusion of Bubastis. I know that she really didn't play any part in your exploits while you were an adventurer, but I understand that the people doing the Saturday morning Ozymandias cartoon show, scheduled for next fall, are keen that Bubastis should play a major role as a feline sidekick, making it therefore appropriate to play her up in our other merchandising.

Anyway, in anticipation of your approval concerning this expansion of the line and in the absence of any immediate legal difficulties, I had some of the boys in production put together this dummy promotional leaflet. Hope you get a kick out of it, and I'll be calling next week to discuss the "Ziggurat of Death" role playing game, so we can discuss all this then.

Best, as always,

Leo Winston

Leo Winston
Marketing and Development

26

(OZ0001): Ozymandias:
This fully posable action doll, with removable cloak, tunic, and headband, is authentically molded to duplicate accurately the world-famous physique of athlete and former adventurer Adrian Veidt.

(OZ0002): Rorschach:
New Figure! Fully jointed and posable, this scale facsimile of the feared vigilante has a removable trenchcoat and hat.

(OZB001): Rorschach's Grappling Gun:
New Accessory! This scale model of the famous gas-powered grappling gun is spring loaded, and will fire a miniature hook, along with a length of line. Safe for children over five.

(OZ0003): Nite Owl:
New Figure! With removable cowl and belt, this fully posable model of the former nocturnal adventurer offers hours of exciting fun.

(OZB002): The Owlship:
New Accessory! Painstakingly assembled from existing photographs of this famous craft, our Owlship has an accessible and fully detailed cabin area, built to scale with **OZ0003**. Fully lighted cabin! Batteries not included.

(OZ0004): Moloch:
New Figure! With detachable handgun and stage magician's jacket, now you can thrill to the misdeeds of the infamous crown prince of the underworld in the safety of your own home.

(OZB003): Bubastis:
New Accessory! Fully posable, see the giant mutant Lynx of Ozymandias. Now she can help Adrian Veidt fight evil and help the innocent in *your* adventures, just like she does on TV.

Jeb—

Agree with you re: expansion of line. My study of recorded sales figures in a historical context suggests an increase in the sale of soldiers and action figures in times immediately prior to a period of anticipated war or bloodshed, and we should take advantage of this syndrome for as long as it lasts.

However, ethically very uncertain about Rorschach, Nite Owl and Moloch, plus accessories. Suggest instead we create costumed army of terrorists, introduce as main villains in Saturday cartoon, then duplicate here along with weapons, accessories and vehicles. More militaristic flavor will sell better. The American public has never really gone in for super-heroes in a big way. We'll discuss this next week.

Best,
Adrian Veidt

P.S.— loved Bubastis. As soon as they're made, I must have one to give to her. Regards to Josephine and your children.

VEIDT Adrian Veidt
President and C.E.O.

Angela Neuberg
Director
Veidt Cosmetics & Toiletries

Dear Angela,

Enclosed you'll find a representative sample of our current magazine and bill-board advertising, promoting Nostalgia.

The sexual imagery is obvious, the woman adjusting her stocking being overtly erotic, yet layered with enough romantic ambiance to avoid offense. In our choice of models for the Nostalgia ads I note that we have consistently chosen models with a slightly androgynous quality to their beauty, which I presume is to afford us a window into the gay marketplace, a tendency more pronounced in the ads for Nostalgia aftershave. This is all well and good, but it avoids the most significant element of the Nostalgia campaign:

In the soft focus imagery and romantic atmosphere, the advertisements conjure an idyllic picture of times past. It seems to me that the success of the campaign is directly linked to the state of global uncertainty that has endured for the past forty years or more. In an era of stress and anxiety, when the present seems unstable and the future unlikely, the natural response is to retreat and withdraw from reality, taking recourse either in fantasies of the future or in modified visions of a half-imagined past.

While this marketing strategy is certainly relevant and indeed successful in a context of social upheaval, I feel we must begin to take into account the fact that one way or another, such conditions cannot endure indefinitely. Simply put, the current circumstances out civilization finds itself immersed in will either lead to war, or they won't. If they lead to war, our best plans become irrelevant. If peace endures, I contend that a new surge of social optimism is likely, necessitating a new image for Veidt cosmetics, geared to a new consumer.

To this end, starting next year we will begin to phase out the Nostalgia line of ladies' and men's cosmetics, successful though they be, and replace them with a new line that better exemplifies the spirit of our anticipated target group. This new line is to be called the "Millenium" line. The imagery associated with it will be controversial and modern, projecting a vision of a technological Utopia, a whole new universe of sensations and pleasures that is just within reach.

I would like the new line to be ready for launch in the summer, and would appreciate it if some dummy ad copy and artwork could be assembled for my perusal and comment sometime before Christmas.

Anticipating your cooperation, and looking forward to working with you on this one. My fondest regards to Frank. We must have lunch soon.

Love,

Adrian Veidt

VEIDT
Adrian Veidt
President and C.E.O.

Attached, manuscript for revised Introduction, updated "Veidt Method" self-improvement booklet. Please forward to relevant department.

—V.

THE VEIDT METHOD : AN INTRODUCTION

Hello. If you're reading this, it's because you sent away for my course, and if you did THAT, it's because you think you need a change in your life. A better body? Increased confidence and magnetism? Advanced mental techniques that will help you at home or in business? Well, yes, we can offer you all these things... but in order to have and enjoy them, there's got to be a new YOU! More than just a bodybuilding course, the Veidt Method is designed to produce bright and capable young men and women who will be fit to inherit the challenging, promising, and often difficult world that awaits in our future. The course is designed to be easy to read and to understand, and if you follow it through, I can assure you that you and your friends will quickly notice the results as a whole new realm of ability and experience is opened up to you. Below is a brief summary of what you can expect to find in the later chapters of this volume.

UNDERSTANDING THE SELF

Both the body and the mind are parts of a biological robot that our immaterial souls inhabit. Like any machines, they can be tuned, improved and made to run more efficiently, as long as one understands the process for doing so. Through meditation and intellectual exercise, we may come to use our minds in ways that we never thought possible. In this first chapter of our manual we will discuss lateral thinking, Zen meditation, and the power of dreaming and the subconscious, along with other useful techniques for the advancement of the mind and intellect. Though not a religion, there are powerful spiritual disciplines behind the Veidt Method that must be understood if the student is to proceed.

HEALTH AND THE BODY

In our second chapter, we explore the connection between body and mind, and learn how this helps us to conquer pain and illness without recourse to drugs and medicines. We will show you, step by step, a number of techniques for focusing the mind's healing power upon any ailing part of the body. In relation to this, we also examine how the actions of the body can be used to aid and focus the mind, taking into account Yogic doctrines and martial training.

CREATING A NEW YOU

Our third and longest chapter presents a carefully coordinated series of physical and

intellectual exercise systems which, if followed correctly, can turn YOU into a superhuman, fully in charge of your own destiny. All that is required is the desire for perfection and the will to achieve it. No special equipment or other hidden cash extras are necessary. The Veidt Method paves the way for a bright and hopeful future in which anyone can be a hero.

YOU AND THE WORLD

Just as you are a whole organic being, complete unto yourself, so are you also part of a larger social organism consisting of the people around you, the people you work with, and ultimately the whole world. When you yourself are strong and healthy in mind and body, you will want to react in a healthy and positive way to the world around you, changing it for the better if you are able, and improving the lot of both yourself and your fellow man. Our final chapter will help you to understand the organism that is the world, and your part in it. You will learn that one can either surrender responsibility for one's actions to the rest of the social organism, to be pulled this way and that by society's predominating tensions, or that one can take control by flexing the muscles of the will common to us all, affecting our environment positively and responsibly.

So, in conclusion, welcome to the Veidt Method for physical fitness and self-improvement, a step by step guide to realizing exciting potentials latent within every one of us. I hope that you'll be intrigued by what you find within, and I know that if you persevere you'll walk away from this book a different person.

There's a bright new world just around the corner. It's going to need heroes just as badly as this one does, and one of them could be YOU!

All best wishes and encouragement,

Adrian Veidt

Adrian Veidt

CHAPTER XI

OBSERVATION=

MULTI-SCREEN VIEWING IS SEEMINGLY ANTICIPATED BY BURROUGHS' *CUT-UP* TECHNIQUE. HE SUGGESTED RE-ARRANGING WORDS AND IMAGES TO EVADE RATIONAL ANALYSIS, ALLOWING SUBLIMINAL HINTS OF THE *FUTURE* TO LEAK THROUGH...

AN IMPENDING WORLD OF EXOTICA, GLIMPSED ONLY PERIPHERALLY.

PERCEPTUALLY, THIS SIMULTANEOUS INPUT ENGAGES ME LIKE THE KINETIC EQUIVALENT OF AN ABSTRACT OR IMPRESSIONIST PAINTING...

PHOSPHOR-DOT SWIRLS JUXTAPOSE; MEANINGS COALESCE FROM SEMIOTIC CHAOS BEFORE REVERTING TO INCOHERENCE.

TRANSIENT AND ELUSIVE, THESE MUST BE GRASPED *QUICKLY:*

COMPUTER ANIMATIONS IMBUE EVEN *BREAKFAST CEREALS* WITH AN HALLUCIN-OGENIC FUTURITY; MUSIC CHANNELS PROCESS *INFOR-MATION-BLIPS*, AVOIDING LINEAR PRESENTATION, IMPLYING LIMITLESS PERSONAL CHOICE...

THESE REFERENCE POINTS ESTABLISHED, AN EMERGENT *WORLDVIEW* BECOMES GRADUALLY *DISCERNIBLE* AMIDST THE MEDIA'S *WHITE NOISE*.

THIS JIGSAW-FRAGMENT MODEL OF TOMORROW ALIGNS ITSELF PIECE BY PIECE, SPECIFIC AREAS NECESSARILY OBSCURED BY INDETERMINACY.

HOWEVER, BROAD ASSUMPTIONS REGARDING THIS POSTULATED FUTURE MAY BE DRAWN. WE CAN IMAGINE ITS *AMBIENCE*. WE CAN HYPOTHESIZE ITS *PSYCHOLOGY*.

IN CONJUNCTION WITH MASSIVE FORECASTED TECHNOLOGICAL ACCELERATION APPROACHING THE MILLENNIUM, THIS OBLIQUE AND SHIFTING CATHODE MOSAIC UNCOVERS THE BLUEPRINT FOR AN ERA OF NEW SENSATIONS AND POSSIBILITIES.

AN ERA OF THE CONCEIVABLE MADE *CONCRETE*...

...AND OF THE CASUALLY *MIRACULOUS*.

1

LOOK ON MY WORKS, YE MIGHTY...

AS AN *AFTERTHOUGHT*, THE METHOD HAS AN *EARLIER* PRECURSOR THAN BURROUGHS IN THE *SHAMANISTIC* TRADITION OF DIVINING RANDOMLY SCATTERED *GOAT INNARDS...* THE SUBJECT FOR A SUBSEQUENT DISCOURSE, PERHAPS.

OBSERVATION ENDS.

VEIDT. NEW YORK TIME, ELEVEN EIGHTEEN P.M. LOG AND FILE.

HOUF

IT'S ALL RIGHT, GIRL. NO NEED FOR RESTLESS-NESS. THE INSIGHT WASN'T MAJOR, BUT DESERVED RECORDING. BESIDES, WE'RE IN NO HURRY.

IN *THESE* CONDITIONS, OUR VISITORS WON'T YET BE WITHIN TEN *MILES* OF KARNAK.

LET'S TAKE A *LOOK* ...

NEW YORK

AA. YOU *SEE?*

REALLY, GETTING EVEN *THIS* FAR IS A *BREATH-TAKING* EFFORT, GIVEN THEIR *LIMIT-ATIONS.*

IT MUST BE SO *DISORIENTATING.* THEIR PURSUIT LEADS THEM DEEPER INTO MORAL AND INTEL-LECTUAL REGIONS AS UNCHARTED AND DEVOID OF LANDMARK AS THE TERRITORIES CURRENTLY *SURROUND-ING* THEM.

OF COURSE, THE ICE THEY'RE *SKATING* ON IS *SLIPPERY*, AND THINNER THAN IT *LOOKS.*

LET'S HOPE THEY DON'T BECOME TOO *RECKLESS* AND OVERSTEP THEM-SELVES.

LET'S HOPE THEY KNOW WHERE TO *STOP.*

2

OKAY... THERE IT *IS*, UP AHEAD.

LOOKS LIKE THERE'S NO OPTION OTHER THAN A DIRECT APPROACH. WE CAN'T CREEP *UP* WITHOUT *COVER*, AND IT'S POINTLESS WAITING FOR *DARKNESS* UP HERE...

THERE *ISN'T* ANY.

UNTRUE. JUST ISN'T ANY OF KIND WE CAN USE.

IF VEIDT TRULY ENGINEERING THIRD WORLD WAR, WE ARE APPROACHING HEART OF DARKNESS.

HMM. I'VE BEEN *WONDERING* ABOUT THAT...

THOSE *BROCHURES*, ALL THAT CRAP WE TOOK FROM HIS *DESK*...THE *TONE* WAS WRONG, SOMEHOW.

NOT *OPTIMISTIC* EXACTLY, BUT...WELL, 'PLANNING' FOR A *FUTURE*.

IT DIDN'T READ LIKE SOMEONE OUT TO CARVE A *HEADSTONE* FOR HUMANITY.

...AND *ANYWAY*, THIS IS *ADRIAN*, FOR GOD'S *SAKE*! WE *KNOW* HIM. HE NEVER *KILLED* ANYBODY, EVER. WHY WOULD HE WANT TO DESTROY THE *WORLD*?

RONCH

RONCH

RONCH

INSANITY PERHAPS?

HA. WELL, THAT'S A *TRICKY* ONE...

I MEAN, WHO'S QUALIFIED TO *JUDGE* SOMETHING LIKE *THAT*? THIS IS THE WORLD'S SMARTEST *MAN* WE'RE TALKING ABOUT HERE, SO HOW CAN YOU *TELL*?

HOW CAN ANYONE TELL IF HE'S GONE *CRAZY*?

3

98

22

⁚HHAHHH⁚ AH WELL.

COME ON, OLD GIRL. WE HAVE A FEW MATTERS TO ATTEND TO BEFORE THEY GET HERE.

I SUPPOSE I'VE BEEN WAITING FOR AN OPPORTUNE MOMENT, BUT THERE'S NO POINT PUTTING THINGS OFF ANY *LONGER*...

TOKYO

LONDON

NEW YORK

... AND NO TIME LIKE THE *PRESENT*.

4

NOT COMING ANY FURTHER? NO?

FAIR ENOUGH. YOU WAIT THERE. THIS WON'T TAKE A MOMENT.

HELLO, MY FRIENDS. I'VE FINISHED MY WORK NOW, AND I'D BE HONORED IF THE THREE OF YOU WOULD JOIN ME FOR A SMALL DRINK IN THE VIVARIUM, BEFORE DINNER.

I HAVE SOMETHING TO CELEBRATE.

THANK YOU.

VEIDT OUT.

5

PARTYIN'! HOLOCAUST COMIN', GODDAMN **KNOT-HEADS** GOTTA **PARTY**! I CAN HEAR THAT GOD-FORBID-I-CALL-IT-MUSIC CLEAR FROM **MADISON SQUARE!**

YANG YANG YANG! MUSIC TO DROP **BOMBS** BY IS WHAT IT IS...

DAVIDSTOWN SLEPT, DESERTED SAVE FOR SILENCE.

TETHERING BOTH HORSES TO THE VERANDAH, I ENTERED MY FORMER RESIDENCE NOISELESSLY, CAREFUL NOT TO ROUSE THE BUTCHERS OCCUPYING IT FROM THEIR DEBAUCHED SLUMBER.

THEY'LL ALL COME OUT FIGHTIN' **DRUNK**, COVERED IN **TATTOOS** AND **EAR-RINGS**...

AN' IT'S RIGHT DOWN THE **AVENUE**! I **TELLYA**, THIS IS A **BAD** INTERSECTION. YOU NEVER KNOW WHAT'S GONNA TURN UP **NEXT**.

UNAWARE THAT DEATH WAS AMONGST THEM, THEY'D KNOW ITS DARK EMBRACE WITHOUT EVER UNDERSTANDING WHY.

ONE, HOWEVER, WAS AWAKE.

FRANTIC LEST HE SHOULD RAISE ALARUMS, I SET UPON HIM AS HE ENTERED THE NIGHT-WRAPPED CHAMBER.

IN FACT, I SEE ONE MORE STUPID **HAIRCUT**, I'M GONNA ...

OH. HI. GETCHA SOMETHING?

NAH. GUESS **JOSEPHINE** POSTED THIS, LIKE SHE SAID. Y'KNOW, SOMETIMES SHE REALLY **TRIES**. SHE FINISHED **WORK** YET?

JOSEPHI...? OHH...**JOEY**! YOU MUST BE HER... UH...

GIRL-FRIEND. EX. WE'VE BEEN **FIGHTING**.

IN CATARACT DARKNESS, I BLUDGEONED HIM, HIS SCREAMS UNNERVINGLY SHRILL.

OH. WELL, I AIN'T SEEN HER LATELY...

NO SWEAT. I'LL WAIT OUTSIDE THE **PROMETHEAN**. I'M NOT **RELISHING** THE ENCOUNTER.

NO PIRATES CAME, BUT SOMETHING WORSE. I LOOKED UP INTO FACES FAMILIAR SAVE FOR THEIR TERROR.

LISTEN, TELL HER **HUSTLER'S** DUE IN TOMORROW!

HUSTLER? GOD, IF IT'S OKAY, I'LL LET HER FIND OUT **HERSELF**.

THE CHILDREN WAILED. I LOOKED DOWN AT THE FIGURE BENEATH ME. THROUGH PUFFED AND BLOODIED LIPS SHE MOUTHED MY NAME.

HUH? WHADDI **SAY**? DON'T GO AWAY MAD...

THERE CAME AN UNDERSTANDING SO LARGE, IT LEFT NO ROOM FOR SANITY. AS I FLED PAST THE MOUNTED CADAVER OUTSIDE, LANTERNS FLARED IN NEARBY WINDOWS.

HUH! TIMES LIKE **THESE**, PEOPLE GOTTA BE **HOSTILE**? ME AN' **ROSA** SHOULDA QUIT THIS TOWN LIKE SHE **WANNED**, AN' ESCAPED FROM **EVERYTHING**.

I RAN, BUT THE KNOWLEDGE OF MY DAMNATION PACED ME, GLOATING, CELEBRATING ITS AWFUL VICTORY.

6

MR. VEIDT. THIS IS INDEED AN HONOR. MIGHT WE ENQUIRE WHAT IT IS THAT PROVIDES *OCCASION* FOR SUCH GENEROSITY?

A LIFE SUCH AS *MINE* OFFERS *MANY* THINGS WORTHY OF CELEBRATION, MY FRIEND. YOU NEED ONLY LOOK *ABOUT* YOU.

MIGHT I NOT CELEBRATE THE FORTUNES THAT HAVE MADE THIS *VIVARIUM* POSSIBLE? A MIRACULOUS BUBBLE OF *TROPICANA* SET INTO ENDLESS SUB-ZERO *WASTES*...

TWO ALIEN *UNIVERSES*, SEPARATED BY A MEMBRANE OF FRAGILE *GLASS*.

WHAT, IN MY LIFE, DOES NOT DESERVE CELEBRATING?

...BUT YOU ARE *RIGHT*, OF COURSE. TODAY MARKS AN EVENT *ESPECIALLY* WORTHY OF SUCH ATTENTIONS.

IN MANY WAYS, IT REPRESENTS THE CULMINATION OF A DREAM MORE THAN TWO THOUSAND YEARS OLD.

7

... ALTHOUGH TO UNCOVER THE REASONS FOR MY CURRENT ELATION, ONE NEED NOT DELVE QUITE SO DEEPLY INTO ANTIQUITY.

A MERE FORTY YEARS WILL SUFFICE, BACK TO MY CHILDHOOD.

"MY PARENTS REACHED AMERICA THE YEAR I WAS BORN, 1939."

"ENTERING SCHOOL, I WAS ALREADY EXCEPTIONALLY BRIGHT, MY PERFECT SCORES ON EARLY TEST PAPERS AROUSING SUCH SUSPICION THAT I CAREFULLY ACHIEVED ONLY AVERAGE GRADES THEREAFTER."

WHAT CAUSED SUCH PRECOCIOUSNESS? MY PARENTS WERE INTELLECTUALLY UNREMARKABLE, POSSESSING NO OBVIOUS GENETIC ADVANTAGES.

PERHAPS I DECIDED TO BE INTELLIGENT, RATHER THAN OTHERWISE? PERHAPS WE ALL MAKE SUCH DECISIONS, THOUGH THAT SEEMS A CALLOUS DOCTRINE.

"BY SEVENTEEN, MY PARENTS WERE BOTH DEAD AND I FACED A DIFFERENT DECISION.

"MY INHERITANCE OFFERED LIFELONG IDLE LUXURY, AND YET, NEEDING NOTHING, I BURNED WITH THE PARADOXICAL URGE TO DO EVERYTHING.

"DO YOU UNDERSTAND?"

MY INTELLECT SET ME APART. FACED WITH DIFFICULT CHOICES, I KNEW NOBODY WHOSE ADVICE MIGHT PROVE USEFUL. NOBODY LIVING.

THE ONLY HUMAN BEING WITH WHOM I FELT ANY KINSHIP DIED THREE HUNDRED YEARS BEFORE THE BIRTH OF CHRIST.

"ALEXANDER OF MACEDONIA. I IDOLIZED HIM. A YOUNG ARMY COMMANDER, HE'D SWEPT ALONG THE COASTS OF TURKEY AND PHOENICIA, SUBDUING EGYPT BEFORE TURNING HIS ARMIES TOWARDS PERSIA...

"HE DIED, AGED THIRTY-THREE, RULING MOST OF THE CIVILIZED WORLD."

RULING WITHOUT BARBARISM! AT ALEXANDRIA, HE INSTITUTED THE ANCIENT WORLD'S GREATEST SEAT OF LEARNING.

TRUE, PEOPLE DIED... PERHAPS UNNECESSARILY, THOUGH WHO CAN JUDGE SUCH THINGS? YET HOW NEARLY HE APPROACHED HIS VISION OF A UNITED WORLD!

"I WAS DETERMINED TO MEASURE MY SUCCESS AGAINST HIS. FIRSTLY, I GAVE AWAY MY INHERITANCE TO DEMONSTRATE THE POSSIBILITY OF ACHIEVING ANYTHING, STARTING FROM NOTHING.

"NEXT I DEPARTED FOR NORTHERN TURKEY, TO RETRACE MY HERO'S STEPS."

I WANTED TO MATCH HIS ACCOMPLISHMENT, BRINGING AN AGE OF ILLUMINATION TO A BENIGHTED WORLD.

HEH.

I WANTED TO HAVE SOMETHING TO SAY TO HIM, SHOULD WE MEET IN THE HALL OF LEGENDS.

8

HI.

BOY, THIS IS SOME KINDA DUMP, RIGHT?

IT'S WHERE I WORK, OKAY? NOT IN SOME DINKY LITTLE MAGAZINE OFFICE WITH A BUNCH OF GUPPIES!

YOU KNOW I DON'T LIKE THAT TERM. WE SHOULD RESPECT GAY PROFESSIONALS WORKING OPENLY...

HEY. HEY, FELLA, EXCUSE ME...

I'M MEETING MY BROTHER, HE'S THE MANAGER HERE. KNOW WHERE HE'S AT?

MILO'S IN THE FRONT OFFICE. GETS OFF AROUND ELEVEN-THIRTY.

JOSEPHINE, CAN WE WALK FOR A WHILE? I DON'T LIKE THIS KIND OF NEIGHBORHOOD.

SURE. YOU'D RATHER BE AT MADISON SQUARE WITH A BUNCH'A DOPED-UP KNOT-TOPS. LIKE THAT'S MORE IMPORTANT THAN US, RIGHT?

OH SHIT, LOOK, THIS ISN'T WORKING OUT. I DON'T THINK THERE'S ANY WAY WE CAN SALVAGE THIS RELATIONSHIP.

UH-HUH. SO THAT'S IT, JUST LIKE THAT? I TRIED MY GODDAMNED BEST, ACTIN' LIKE YOU WANTED ME TO...

SEE? OVER THERE? I PUT YOUR STUPID DYKE DISCO POSTER UP...

SURE. SAME PLACE YOU BUY HUSTLER.

I...LISTEN, I DON'T HAVE TO JUSTIFY ANYTHING TO YOU. I LIKE NICE CHICKS, YOU GIVE ME THIS POLITICAL SHIT...

AW, PLEASE. DON'T CRY.

I'M NOT CRYING! WHO THE HELL SAYS I'M CRYING?

OKAY. I'M SORRY, I...

LOOK, THIS BOOK'S ABOUT RELATIONSHIPS. I THINK IF YOU READ IT, IT'LL HELP YOU UNDERSTAND WHAT'S HAPPENED TO US...

I DON'T WANNA UNDERSTAND SHIT! I JUST WANNA GO TO BED WITH YOU ONE TIME!

I, I WANNA GO TO BED WITH YOU, AND...

JOEY, PLEASE, I CAN'T HANDLE THIS...

...AND I WUH-WANNA BE STRAIGHT...

OH JOEY, DON'T...

...AND, AND I WANNA BE DEAD...!

EVENTUALLY I CAME TO AN ASH-COLORED SHORE, A DISMAL BLACK OCEAN STRETCHING ENDLESS BEFORE ME.

HOW HAD I REACHED THIS APPALLING POSITION, WITH LOVE, ONLY LOVE, AS MY GUIDE?

9

"I FOLLOWED THE PATH OF ALEXANDER'S WAR MACHINE ALONG THE BLACK SEA COAST, IMAGINING HIS ARMIES TAKING PORT AFTER PORT; ANCIENT BLOOD ON ANCIENT BRONZE.

"STRANGELY, BEFORE SUBDUING *PHOENICIA*, HE STRUCK NORTH TOWARDS *GORDIUM*..."

"...PERHAPS BECAUSE OF THE *CHALLENGE* IT PRESENTED: THE ANCIENT WORLD'S GREATEST *PUZZLE* WAS THERE, A *KNOT* THAT COULDN'T BE *UNTIED*.

ALEXANDER CUT IT IN TWO WITH HIS SWORD.

LATERAL THINKING, YOU SEE. CENTURIES AHEAD OF HIS TIME.

" HEADING SOUTH, HE ENTERED EGYPT THROUGH *MEMPHIS*, WHERE THEY PROCLAIMED HIM SON OF *AMON*, JUDGE OF THE DEAD, WHOSE NAME MEANS *'THE HIDDEN ONE'*.

"UNDER RULE FROM ALEXANDRIA, THE CLASSIC CULTURE OF THE GREAT PHARAOHS WAS RESTORED."

I FOLLOWED HIM THROUGH *BABYLON*, UP THROUGH *KABUL* TO *SAMARKHAND*, THEN DOWN THE *INDUS*, WHERE HE FIRST MET ELEPHANTS-OF-WAR.

WHERE HE'D TURNED *BACK* TO QUELL DISSENT AT *HOME*, I TRAVELLED *ON*, THROUGH *CHINA* AND *TIBET*, GATHERING MARTIAL WISDOM AS I WENT.

"ALEXANDER RETURNED TO BABYLON TO DIE OF AN *INFECTION*, AGED *THIRTY-THREE*. AMONGST ITS RUINED ZIGGURATS, I SAW AT LAST HIS *FAILINGS*...

"HE'D NOT UNITED *ALL* THE WORLD, NOR BUILT A UNITY THAT WOULD *SURVIVE* HIM."

DISILLUSIONED BUT DETERMINED TO COMPLETE MY ODYSSEY, I FOLLOWED HIS CORPSE TO ITS RESTING PLACE IN ALEXANDRIA.

THE NIGHT BEFORE RETURNING TO AMERICA, I WANDERED INTO THE *DESERT* AND ATE A BALL OF *HASHISH* I'D BEEN GIVEN IN *TIBET*.

"THE ENSUING VISION *TRANSFORMED* ME. WADING THROUGH POWDERED *HISTORY*, I HEARD DEAD KINGS WALKING UNDERGROUND; HEARD FANFARES SOUND THROUGH HUMAN SKULLS.

"ALEXANDER HAD MERELY RESURRECTED AN AGE OF *PHARAOHS*. THEIR WISDOM, *TRULY* IMMORTAL, NOW INSPIRED *ME*!"

10

WHAT INTELLECTUAL *MAGNIFICENCE* THEIR SYSTEM ENCOURAGED ...*PTOLEMY*, SEEKING THE UNIVERSE'S *PIVOT* FROM HIS LIGHT-HOUSE AT *PHAROS*; *ERATOS-THENES*, MEASURING THE WORLD USING ONLY *SHADOWS*...

THEIR *GREATEST* SECRETS, HOW-EVER, WERE ENTRUSTED TO THEIR *SERVANTS*, BURIED *ALIVE* WITH THEM IN SAND-FLOODED *CHAMBERS*.

"ADOPTING RAMESES THE SECOND'S GREEK *NAME* AND ALEXANDER'S FREE-BOOTING *STYLE*, I RESOLVED TO APPLY ANTIQUITY'S *TEACHINGS* TO TODAY'S *WORLD*.

"THUS BEGAN *MY* PATH TO CONQUEST...CONQUEST NOT OF *MEN*, BUT OF THE EVILS THAT *BESET* THEM."

TODAY, THAT CONQUEST BECOMES *ASSURED*, IN WHICH YOUR UNQUESTIONING *ASSISTANCE* HAS PROVEN *INVALUABLE*.

DO YOU COMPREHEND THE *TRIUMPH* TO WHICH YOU HAVE *CONTRIBUTED*, THE *SECRET GLORY* THAT IT AFFORDS?

DO YOU UNDER-STAND MY *SHAME* AT SO INADEQUATE A *REWARD*?

11

12

BEHIND ME, DISTANTLY, A LYNCH-MOB HOWLED. THE MONEYLENDER FLOATED AT MY FEET. NOBLE INTENTIONS HAD LED ME TO ATROCITY. THE RIGHTEOUS ANGER FUELING MY INGENIOUS, AWFUL SCHEME WAS BUT DELUSION.

MORALLY, WE OUGHTTA STRIKE **FIRST**.

WE GOTTA PROTECT **OUR** WOMEN AND KIDS, EVEN IF **THEIRS** DIE. THAT'S MORALLY **LOGICAL**.

WHERE WAS MY **ERROR**? THE FREIGHTER WAS HEADING FOR **DAVIDS-TOWN**. IT SHOULD HAVE ALREADY **ARRIVED**. MY DEDUCTION WAS FLAW-**LESS**, STEP BY STEP...

PAUSING, I STOOD PANTING, SOBBING, LISTENING TO THE WINDBORNE SOUND OF MY PURSUERS, CLOSER NOW AS BREATH RETURNED. PLANNING TO RESUME MY FLIGHT, I RAISED MY HEAD...

EXCUSE ME?

OH. HI.

...AND SAW HER.

MY HUSBAND'S A GENTLEMAN OF **COLOR**, BUYS HIS **PAPER** HERE NIGHTS? HAS HE BEEN **BY**?

HM. DUNNO. MAYBE THE BLACK GUY SELLS WATCHES UP THE **STREET** KNOWS HIM...

*SHE SEEMED TO BE **WAITING**, NOT HOVERING TO **STRIKE**...*

WHAT? YOU THINK WE'RE ALL IN SOME **NEGRO** CLUB; THAT WE ALL **KNOW** EACH OTHER?

HUH? SAY, I DIDN'T MEAN NO **HARM**...

GRADUALLY, I UNDERSTOOD WHAT INNOCENT INTENT HAD BROUGHT ME TO, AND, UNDERSTANDING, WADED OUT BEYOND MY DEPTH.

LOOK, FORGET IT. I SEE MY HUSBAND NOW. THANKS FOR YOUR **TIME**.

SURE. DON'T MENTION IT.

THE UNSPEAKABLE TRUTH LOOMED UNAVOIDABLY BEFORE ME AS I SWAM TOWARDS THE ANCHORED FREIGHTER, WAITING TO TAKE EXTRA HANDS ABOARD.

THERE'D BEEN NO PLAN TO CAPTURE DAVIDS-TOWN. WHAT COULD A MORTAL TOWNSHIP OFFER THOSE WHO'D REAPED THE WEALTH OF THE SARGASSO?

SEE? BRINK O' **WAR**, EVERY-BODY GOTTA **FIGHT**!

THE SHIP WAS LARGER, NEARER. I KEPT SWIMMING.

THAT'S WHAT'S **WRONG** WITH THIS WORLD: NO INCENTIVE TO BE **NICE**: YOU TRY TO **HELP**, YOU WIND UP IN **TROUBLE**...

ALL MY WELL-MEANING PLANS HAD COME TO THIS. I CHOKED, SPAT OUT BRINE AND STRUCK GRIMLY ON.

...SO WHERE'S THE **PERCENT-AGE**?

THEY'D COME TO DAVIDSTOWN TO WAIT UNTIL THEY COULD COLLECT THE ONLY PRIZE THEY'D EVER VALUED, CLAIM THE ONLY SOUL THEY'D EVER TRULY WANTED.

MY SHOULDERS ACHED. THE SHIP WAS MASSIVE NOW.

13

ON THE ...THINK... SEE AN ENTRANCE ...

GOING TO ...HER UP...

WHAT?

HURM.

YEAH... IT'S SOME SORT OF *DOOR*. I THINK I CAN BURN OUT THE *LOCK* MECHANISM.

PALM TREES, BURIED IN SNOW. DOESN'T MAKE SENSE.

PLEASE, LET'S JUST GET *INSIDE* AND WORRY ABOUT ONE MYSTERY AT A *TIME*. ALL THIS *WHITENESS*, I'M FEELING SORT OF *EXPOSED*.

UP *HERE*, WE DON'T HAVE ANY *CAMOUFLAGE*. WE'RE OUT OF OUR NATURAL *ENVIRONMENT*.

THERE. OPEN SESAME.

NERVOUS?

WELL, MY *STOMACH* FEELS WEIRD AND MY *BALLS* ARE ALL SHRIVELLED UP, SO, YEAH, I GUESS "NERVOUS" WILL DO.

Y'KNOW, THIS MUST BE HOW *ORDINARY* PEOPLE FEEL.

THIS MUST BE HOW ORDINARY PEOPLE FEEL AROUND *US*.

14

JESUS, *LOOK* AT THIS PLACE. I THOUGHT *I* HAD SOME *STUFF* IN THE *OWL'S NEST*...

I MEAN, WHAT THE HELL IS *THAT* THING? HALF THIS EQUIPMENT I DON'T EVEN *RECOGNIZE*...

CAN ASK VEIDT WHEN WE FIND HIM.

NOTHING.

HM. ACTUALLY, THAT'S A *POINT*. HOW *DO* WE APPROACH HIM? WHAT DO WE *SAY*?

SUBDUE HIM FIRST, IF POSSIBLE. MAY NOT GET SECOND CHANCE. ASK QUESTIONS LATER.

YEAH. I SUPPOSE YOU'RE RIGHT, BUT IT'S GOING TO FEEL AWFULLY *STRANGE*. HE'S SUCH A CARING, CONSCIENTIOUS *GUY*. HE'S A *PACIFIST*, A *VEGETARIAN* ...

HITLER WAS VEGETARIAN. IF BOTHERS YOU, LEAVE VEIDT TO ME.

SUGGEST WE PROCEED QUIETLY FROM HERE.

15

MANNERS.

ADRIAN...

...DON'T...

...MAKE...

...ME...

KGGUH

NOW...

WHAT CAN I DO FOR YOU?

DAMMIT, YOU *KNOW* WHAT THIS IS ABOUT! *PYRAMID DELIVERIES* ARE BEHIND THIS WHOLE *MESS*, AND *YOU'RE* BEHIND *PYRAMID*.

YOU *KNOW*!

CHRIST, *ADRIAN*. WHAT ARE YOU TRYING TO *DO*?

WHAT WE *ALL* TRIED TO DO, AFTER OUR INITIAL STRUGGLE TO FIND OUR FEET. I'M TRYING TO *IMPROVE* THE WORLD.

LIKE WHEN I STARTED OUT.

"MY FIRST *CASE* MADE IT SEEM POSSIBLE TO END INJUSTICE BY DEMOLISHING *CRIME SYNDICATES*.

"THIS NOTION, THAT CRIMINALS MONOPOLIZED EVIL WAS *ITSELF* DEMOLISHED BY MY *SECOND* CASE."

RESEARCHING MY MASKED *PREDECESSORS* I INVESTIGATED THE MID-FIFTIES DISAPPEARANCE OF *HOODED JUSTICE*.

AN *OPERATIVE*, GOVERNMENT SOURCES REVEALED, HAD TRIED *UN-EARTHING* HIM BACK THEN, REPORTING *FAILURE*...

"UNEARTHING THE OPERATIVE, TRACKING HIM TO *DOCKLAND*, PROVED *EASIER*.

"*EDWARD BLAKE*.

"AS INTELLIGENT MEN FACING LUNATIC TIMES, WE WERE VERY *ALIKE*, DESPISING EACH OTHER *INSTANTLY*."

RECOGNIZING ME, HE ATTACKED *ANYWAY*, "MISTAKING ME FOR A *CRIMINAL*!"

I STUDIED HIS *LIMITATIONS*: SKILLFUL *FEINT*; DEVASTATING *UPPERCUT*; LITTLE *ELSE*...

HE *WON*. IN THE *SHORT* TERM.

"HAD BLAKE *FOUND* HOODED JUSTICE, *KILLED* HIM, REPORTING *FAILURE*? I CAN PROVE NOTHING.

"WE NEXT MET IN 1960. I *AVOIDED* HIM, MORE FASCINATED BY *JON*."

STILL, I *OBSERVED* BLAKE OVER THE *YEARS*...

KNOW WHAT? HE WAS IN *DALLAS*, MINDING *NIXON*, THE DAY *KENNEDY* DIED.

NOBODY'S SURE WHY NIXON WAS THERE.

"EVER READ *J.F.K.'S* INTENDED SPEECH?

"'WE IN THIS COUNTRY, IN THIS GENERATION, ARE BY DESTINY, RATHER THAN CHOICE, THE WATCHMEN ON THE WALLS OF WORLD FREEDOM.'"

18

WAS he *REHEARSING* it, perhaps, as the motorcade reached the *PLAZA*...

...NEVER SUSPECTING THAT ON THE WALLS OF WORLD *TYRANNY*, CROSS-HAIRS WATCHED *HIM*.

"WE ALL REALIZED THEN HOW *BAD* THINGS WERE. I CONTINUED *ADVENTURING*, BUT IT SEEMED *HOLLOW*."

"I FOUGHT ONLY THE *SYMPTOMS*, LEAVING THE DISEASE ITSELF *UNCHECKED*."

I DESPISED MYSELF; MY SHAM *CRUSADE*. KNOWING MANKIND'S PROBLEMS, I'D *BLINDED* MYSELF TO THEM.

I FELT *HELPLESS* AGAINST FORCES GREATER THAN ANY I'D *ANTICIPATED*.

"TOO *COWARDLY* TO *CONFRONT* MY *ANXIETIES*, I HAD LIFE'S BLACK COMEDY EXPLAINED TO ME BY THE COMEDIAN HIMSELF AT THE *CRIMEBUSTERS* FIASCO IN '66.

"I'M SURE YOU *REMEMBER*."

HE DISCUSSED NUCLEAR WAR'S *INEVITABILITY*; DESCRIBED MY FUTURE ROLE AS "SMARTEST GUY ON THE CINDER"...

... AND OPENED MY *EYES*. ONLY THE *BEST* COMEDIANS ACCOMPLISH *THAT*.

"I REMEMBER THE CHARRED *MAP* BETWEEN MY *FINGERS*; NELSON SAYING 'SOMEONE'S GOT TO SAVE THE WORLD', HIS TREMULOUS, COMPLAINING VOICE...

"THAT'S WHEN I UNDERSTOOD."

THAT'S WHEN IT HIT ME.

"CONSOLING NELSON, I *LEFT*. OUTSIDE, BLAKE ARGUED WITH *LAURIE* AND HER MOTHER.

"I SWORE TO DENY HIS KIND THEIR LAST BLACK LAUGH AT EARTH'S EXPENSE."

I *ALSO* SWORE THAT WHEN NEXT I MET *BLAKE* OR ANY *OTHER* FOE, THOUGH PERHAPS NOT ON MY *TERRITORY*...

...IT WOULD CERTAINLY BE ON MY *TERMS*.

19

HI. FANCY MEETING YOU HERE.

GLORIA?

I KNEW YOU CAME THIS WAY *HOME*, SO I FIGURED I'D MEET YOU FROM *WORK*. I'M NOT READY TO VISIT BACK AT THE *APARTMENT* JUST YET.

"JUST *YET*"?

WELL, I *WANT* TO COME BACK. I *MISS* YOU, MALCOLM. I MISS THE PERSON YOU *WERE*...

...BUT I *CAN'T* LIVE WITH SOMEONE WHO FEELS DRIVEN TO HELP *HOPELESS* CASES, THEN LETS *THEIR* MISERY AFFECT *OUR* LIVES.

IF YOU CAN PROMISE ME YOU'LL ASK FOR A TRANSFER TO DIFFERENT WORK WITH DIFFERENT *PATIENTS*, I CAN COME HOME... IF THAT'S WHAT YOU *WANT*.

GLORIA, OF *COURSE* THAT'S WHAT I *WANT*, BUT, UH...

WELL, *DO* IT! I'M NOT GOING TO SHARE YOU WITH A WORLD FULL OF *SCREW-UPS* AND *MANIC DEPRESSIVES*. I'M NOT GOING TO SHARE *MY* LIFE WITH THEM.

MALCOLM?

MALCOLM, ARE YOU *LISTENING* TO ME?

GLORIA, I'M SORRY... THOSE *PEOPLE*... THEY'RE *HURTING* EACH OTHER...

MALCOLM? DON'T YOU *DARE*! DON'T YOU *DARE* GET INVOLVED!

DIDN'T YOU LISTEN TO A WORD I JUST *SAID*?

GLORIA, PLEASE. I *HAVE* TO. IN A WORLD LIKE *THIS*...

I MEAN, IT'S ALL WE *CAN* DO, TRY TO *HELP* EACH OTHER. IT'S ALL THAT *MEANS* ANY-THING...

PLEASE. PLEASE UNDER-STAND.

MALCOLM, I'M *WARNING* YOU! YOU LET YOUR-SELF GET DRAWN TOWARDS ANOTHER HEAP OF SOME-BODY ELSE'S *GRIEF*, I DON'T WANT TO *SEE* YOU AGAIN!

GLORIA ...I'M *SORRY*. IT'S THE *WORLD*...

I CAN'T *RUN* FROM IT.

ITS DARK AND LURCHING MASS FILLED ALL MY VISION. I SAW THE HEADS NAILED TO ITS PROW, HEARD DRUNKEN LAUGHTER; ENCOURAGEMENTS BARKED FROM THE DECKS ABOVE...

CLOSER, IT CAME.

CLOSER.

20

BRUTALLY, I'D BEEN BROUGHT NOSE TO NOSE WITH MANKIND'S **MORTALITY**; THE DREADFUL, IRREFUTABLE **FACT** OF IT.

FOR THE FIRST TIME, I GENUINELY UNDER-STOOD THAT EARTH MIGHT **DIE**. I RECOGNIZED THE **FRAGILITY** OF OUR WORLD IN INCREASINGLY HAZARDOUS TIMES...

...AND YET WHAT COULD I **DO**?

MY **FIRST** STEP WAS TO STAND BACK AS FAR AS I COULD, TO VIEW THE PROBLEM FROM A FRESH **PERSPECTIVE**, MY **VISTA** WIDENING WITH MY **COMPREHENSION**.

I SAW **EAST** AND **WEST**, LOCKED INTO AN ESCALATING **ARMS SPIRAL**, THEIR MUTUAL TERROR AND SUSPICION MOUNTING WITH THE **MISSILES**, MAKING THE POSSIBILITY OF DISARMAMENT PROGRESSIVELY MORE **REMOTE**.

GRADUALLY, I CLOSED UPON THE **HEART** OF THE DILEMMA.

HERE WAS A **KNOT** TO TRY EVEN **ALEXANDER'S** INGENUITY.

BOTH SIDES **REALIZED** THE SUICIDAL **IMPLICATIONS** OF NUCLEAR CONFLICT, YET COULDN'T STOP RACING **TOWARDS** IT LEST THEIR **OPPONENTS** SHOULD **OVERTAKE** THEM.

AFRAID OF THEIR **WEAPONS**, AFRAID OF **LOSING** THEM, AFRAID TO **BLINK** OR TURN THEIR **BACKS**...

MEANWHILE, EXPENSIVE ARSENALS MEANT LESS CASH TO SPEND UPON THEIR **OLD**; THEIR **SICK** AND **HOME-LESS**; ON THEIR CHILDREN'S EDUCATIONS.

AS STOCKPILES **GREW**, AS COMPUTERS REDUCED HUMAN INVOLVEMENT, THE SPECTRE OF ACCIDENTAL APOCALYPSE STALKED EVER **CLOSER**.

SIMPLY GIVEN THE **MATHEMATICS** OF THE SITUATION, SOONER OR LATER CONFLICT WOULD BE INEVITABLE!

HOWEVER, WITHOUT A PRACTICAL **SOLUTION** AT HAND, WHAT USE WAS IT TO SUDDENLY NOTICE THE **PERILS** OF THE SITUATION?

SIMILARLY A **SOLUTION** WOULD BE **EQUALLY** USELESS...

...UNLESS ONE POSSESSED THE **MUSCLE** TO BACK IT UP; THE BRUTE **POWER** TO SEE ONE'S WILL **IMPLEMENTED**.

I TOOK ANOTHER STEP BACK, AND THOUGHT AGAIN.

21

OTHER factors emerged: ARMS EXPENDITURES boosted international LENDING rates. To repay soaring DEBT INTEREST, nations like BRAZIL levelled their FORESTS.

NUCLEAR POWER, providing vital WEAPONS-GRADE WASTE, became MANDATORY.

WAR ASIDE, ATOMIC DEADLOCK guided us downhill towards environmental RUIN.

JON'S PRESENCE ACCELERATED THIS, though less than you'd IMAGINE. Any SIGNIFICANT POWER IMBALANCE would yield SIMILAR results.

NEVERTHELESS, he somehow SYMBOLIZED MANKIND'S PROBLEMS. As tensions ROSE, the ELEVATION of costumed heroes became a DESCENT...

I FORESAW that by the late SEVENTIES, it would reach BOTTOM.

THIS LEFT TEN YEARS to build a FORTUNE and REPUTATION to sustain me BEYOND that point, allowing me the POWER and LEVERAGE I'd surely NEED.

DEVELOPING the basic PATENT for public SPARK HYDRANTS, I financed DIMENSIONAL DEVELOPMENTS with the PROCEEDS.

MY PLAN required PREPARATION for the day when I'd assume the ASPECT of kingly RAMESES, leaving ALEXANDER the ADVENTURER and his TRAPPINGS to gather DUST.

EACH STEP had to be taken CAREFULLY, constantly striving to keep in mind the enormous SCALE of what was at STAKE!

THE EARTH. HUMANITY. All we've ever KNOWN...

"END OF THE WORLD" does the concept no JUSTICE.

THE WORLD'S PRESENT would END. Its FUTURE, immeasurably VASTER, would ALSO vanish.

EVEN OUR PAST would be CANCELLED. Our struggle from the primal OOZE, every CHILDBIRTH, every PERSONAL SACRIFICE rendered MEANINGLESS, leading only to DUST, tossed on the VOID-WINDS.

SAVE FOR RICHARD NIXON, whose name adorns a plaque upon the MOON, no human VESTIGE would remain.

RUINS become SAND, sand blows AWAY... all our RICHNESS and COLOR and BEAUTY would be LOST...

...AS IF IT HAD NEVER BEEN.

22

THE WORLD I'D TRIED TO SAVE WAS LOST BEYOND RECALL. I WAS AMONGST HORRORS MUST I *DWELL*.

A ROPE SNAKED DOWN. SPLUTTERING, I GRABBED IT...

SEE, PEOPLE DON'T REACH *OUT* AND MAKE *CONTACT*.

...AND FROM THE DECKS ABOVE A CHEER WENT UP, BOTH GROSS AND BLACK, ITS STENCH AFFRONTING HEAVEN.

THE END.

THAT'S WHY THERE'S THIS COMMOTION ALL THE TIME, THIS CONFLICT. PEOPLE DON'T CONNECT WITH EACH OTHER.

IT'S LIKE, YOU BEEN COMING HERE WEEKS, READIN' THAT JUNK OVER AN' OVER, AN' YET WE AIN'T EXACTLY CLOSE...

'CAUSE THEY DON'T MAKE SENSE, MAN! THAT'S WHY I GOTTA READ 'EM OVER.

THAT AIN'T THE POINT.

LISTEN, WHEN MY ROSA DIED, MOST OF OUR FRIENDS WERE HER FRIENDS: THEY STOPPED CALLING. I TOOK THIS JOB TO MEET PEOPLE, Y'KNOW?

SO... WHAT'S YOUR NAME? WHADDAYA DOIN' HERE?

MY NAME'S BERNIE. I'M HERE BECAUSE MY MOM'S WORKING, AN' MY SISTER, SHE'S OUT TOO, AND THESE HYDRANTS ARE WARM, Y'KNOW?

BERNIE? SHORT FOR BERNARD? WELL I'LL BE HORSEWHIPPED! THAT'S MY NAME!

SO? AIN'T NO BIG DEAL. LOTTA PEOPLE CALLED BERNARD, MAN. DON'T SIGNIFY FOR NOTHIN'.

WELL, SURE, BUT... WAIT A MINUTE. WHAT THE HELL'S GOING ON...?

FIGHT. PULL OVER.

STEVE, YOU JUST GOT SUSPENDED. THIS AIN'T YOUR PROBLEM. SOME OTHER UNIT CAN HANDLE IT.

I'M STILL ME, JOE. PULL HER OVER.

LISTEN, MILO, YOU LEAVE WORK EARLY FOR A BEER WITH YOUR BROTHER, BUSINESS AIN'T GONNA COLLAPSE.

AW SHIT...

NO, BUT... HEY... POLICE. WHAT'S HAPPENING?

THAT'S JOEY! THAT'S ONE OF MY DRIVERS, IN A FIGHT...

HELL! ANOTHER MINUTE, WE'D HAVE BEEN GONE.

TALK ABOUT LOUSY TIMING!

23

EACH STEP WAS *SYNCHRONIZED.*

JON, BEING TOO *POWERFUL* AND *UNPREDICTABLE* TO FIT MY *PLANS,* NEEDED *REMOVING.* THUS, DIMENSIONAL DEVELOPMENTS HIRED HIS PAST *ASSOCIATES...*

...AND GAVE THEM *CANCER?*

YES. WEAVER FIRST, SLATER AND MOLOCH *LATER.* UNWITTINGLY EXPOSED TO *RADIATION,* THEY WERE CLOSELY *OBSERVED,* CULTIVATED AS WEAPONS AGAINST *JON.*

MEANWHILE, TAKING ADVANTAGE OF NEW *TECHNOLOGY,* I RESEARCHED *GENETICS...* BUBASTIS WAS AN EARLY *SUCCESS...* AND *TELEPORTATION.*

SINCE JON PROVED TELEPORTATION *POSSIBLE,* WHY DEVELOP ELECTRIC *CARS?* MY RESEARCHES WERE *VITAL...* LIKE MY *ISLAND,* SECRETLY PURCHASED IN 1970.

THE ONLY HERO RETAINING PUBLIC *SYMPATHY,* I QUIT TWO YEARS BEFORE THE *KEENE ACT,* CONCENTRATING ON MY *PLAN.*

"UNABLE TO UNITE THE WORLD BY *CONQUEST...* ALEXANDER'S METHOD ...I WOULD *TRICK* IT; FRIGHTEN IT TOWARDS SALVATION WITH HISTORY'S GREATEST *PRACTICAL JOKE.*

"THAT'S WHAT UPSET THE *COMEDIAN,* WHEN AWARENESS OF MY SCHEME CRASHED *IN* UPON HIM:

"PROFESSIONAL *JEALOUSY.*"

BLAKE'S *MURDER.* YOU *CONFESS?*

CONFESSION IMPLIES *PENITENCE.* I MERELY REGRET HIS *ACCIDENTAL INVOLVEMENT.*

RETURNING FROM *NICARAGUA* BY *AIR,* HE SPOTTED A *SHIP* DOCKING AT AN UNCHARTED *ISLAND.* SUSPECTING SANDINISTA BASES, HE RESOLVED TO *INVESTIGATE.*

"I *PICTURE* HIM, SWIMMING TO THE *ISLAND,* DAGGER IN *TEETH,* PENETRATING ITS *INSTALLATIONS.* WHAT HE *FOUND* MUST HAVE COME AS A TERRIBLE *BLOW.*

"IMAGINE...THE PERFECT *FIGHTING MAN* DISCOVERING A PLOT TO PUT AN END TO *WAR...*

"...AN END TO *FIGHTING.*"

24

HOW COULD GENETICS AND TELE-PORTATION END WAR?

WELL, WITHOUT JON'S GUIDING MIND, TELE-PORTATION PROVED LIMITED. ANYTHING LIVING DIED OF SHOCK UPON TRANSFER, OR MATERIALIZED IN AN OCCUPIED SPACE AND EXPLODED...

"...BUT THAT WASN'T WHAT BLAKE FOUND ON THE ISLAND. HE FOUND A COLLECTION OF MISSING ARTISTS AND SCIENTISTS, WORKING UPON A MONSTROUS NEW LIFE FORM.

"UPON LEARNING THE CREATURE'S INTENDED PURPOSE, BLAKE'S PRACTICED CYNICISM CRACKED."

THOUGH APPALLED, EXPOSING MY PLAN WOULD PRECIPITATE GREATER HORRORS PREVENTING HUMANITY'S SALVATION.

EVEN BLAKE BALKED AT THAT RESPONSIBILITY, TELLING ONLY MOLOCH, WHO HE KNEW WOULDN'T UNDERSTAND...

...BUT I HAD MOLOCH'S PLACE BUGGED, AND I UNDERSTOOD PERFECTLY.

"THE PLAN BLAKE HAD UNCOVERED WAS THIS: TO FRIGHTEN GOVERN-MENTS INTO CO-OPERATION, I WOULD CONVINCE THEM THAT EARTH FACED IMMINENT ATTACK BY BEINGS FROM ANOTHER WORLD.

"I'M AFRAID THE DISCOVERY RATHER DROVE THE WIND FROM HIS SAILS."

AHHA...

HA HA HA! ADRIAN, COME ON,... WHAT... YOU'RE SERIOUS?

PERFECTLY. AN INTRACTABLE PROBLEM CAN ONLY BE RESOLVED BY STEPPING BEYOND CONVENTIONAL SOLUTIONS. ALEXANDER UNDERSTOOD THAT, TWO THOUSAND YEARS AGO, IN GORDIUM.

"BLAKE UNDERSTOOD, TOO. HE KNEW MY PLAN WOULD SUCCEED, THOUGH ITS SCALE TERRIFIED HIM. THAT'S WHY HE TOLD NOBODY. IT WAS TOO BIG TO DISCUSS...

"...BUT HE UNDERSTOOD.

"AT THE END, HE UNDERSTOOD.

"HE UNDERSTOOD THE PORTENTS, KNEW A DAZZLING TRANS-FORMATION WAS AT HAND FOR MANKIND.

"THE BRUTAL WORLD HE'D RELISHED WOULD SIMPLY CEASE TO BE, ITS FIERCE AND BRAWLING DENIZENS RUSHING TO JOIN THE MASTODON IN OBSOLESCENCE...

"IN EXTINCTION."

AFTER *BLAKE*, I NEUTRALIZED *JON*. STOLEN *PSYCHIATRIC* REPORTS INDICATED HIS MENTAL *WITHDRAWAL*. THE *CANCER* ALLEGATIONS MADE IT *PHYSICAL*.

BY THEN, RORSCHACH'S *MASK KILLER* HUNT NEEDED STOPPING. MY *OWN* "ASSASSINATION" CONFIRMING HIS ERRONEOUS THEORY, PLACED ME BEYOND SUSPICION.

"I'D HIRED MY OWN KILLER THROUGH A THIRD *PARTY*. WHEN I FED HIM THE *CYANIDE CAPSULE*, PERHAPS HE *REALIZED* THIS.

"I KNEW ONLY *TRIUMPH*... *NOTHING* NOW STOOD BETWEEN *ME* AND MY *GOAL*. HUMANITY'S *FATE* RESTED SAFELY IN MY *HANDS*."

ADRIAN, THIS IS *CRAZY*. WHO'D *BELIEVE* AN ALIEN *INVASION*?

HITLER SAID PEOPLE SWALLOW LIES *EASILY*, PROVIDED THEY'RE *BIG* ENOUGH. I PLANNED TO BUILD MY *MONSTER*, TELEPORT IT TO A CERTAIN *DESTINATION*...

SAID TELEPORTATION UNWORKABLE.

"IT WORKS *FINE*, ASSUMING YOU *WANT* THINGS TO EXPLODE ON *ARRIVAL*.

"TELEPORTED TO *NEW YORK*, MY CREATURE'S *DEATH* WOULD TRIGGER MECHANISMS WITHIN ITS MASSIVE *BRAIN*, CLONED FROM A HUMAN *SENSITIVE*...

"...THE RESULTANT PSYCHIC *SHOCKWAVE* KILLING HALF THE *CITY*."

ADRIAN, I'M *SORRY*...YOU NEED *HELP*. I KNOW THIS "*HALF NEW YORK*" STUFF IS BULLSHIT, BUT I'M *STILL* GLAD WE GOT HERE BEFORE YOU GOT DEEPER *INTO* THIS MESS.

CHRIST, YOU SERIOUSLY *PLANNED* ALL THIS MAD SCIENTIST STUFF?

"I MEAN, WHEN WAS THIS HOPELESS BLACK FANTASY SUPPOSED TO *HAPPEN*?

"WHEN WERE YOU PLANNING TO *DO* IT?"

Gunga Diner

POLICE   POL

26

"DO IT?"

DAN, I'M NOT A REPUBLIC *SERIAL* VILLAIN. DO YOU SERIOUSLY THINK I'D EXPLAIN MY *MASTER-STROKE* IF THERE REMAINED THE SLIGHTEST CHANCE OF YOU AFFECTING ITS *OUTCOME*?

I DID IT THIRTY-FIVE MINUTES AGO.

NEW YORK

27

My name is
Ozymandias,
king of kings:
Look on my works,
ye mighty,
and despair!

—*Ozymandias*
Percy
Bysshe
Shelley

AFTER THE MASQUERADE:

Superstyle and the art of humanoid watching.

DOUG ROTH VISITS ANTARCTICA TO INTERVIEW ADRIAN VEIDT

VEIDT: "The frightening thing about the campaign to re-elect the president is that in the wake of the victory in Vietnam, I don't see how they can fail. C.R.E.E.P.! What a terrible acronym. I wonder who coined that one? Somebody who watched too many 'Man From U.N.C.L.E.' episodes in the sixties . . . Liddy, or one of those other Washington humanoids."

"Humanoids." I'm sitting talking with a retired superhero in a glass dome filled with tropical flowers and hummingbirds, while outside the antarctic wind builds snowdrifts against the glass. I would imagine myself beyond surprise by this point, yet the sudden use of such an odd term is startling. Have I detected a hitherto unnoticed contempt for mere humans behind that eminently likable golden facade? Why "humanoids"? I put this to him, and he chuckles.

VEIDT: "I'm sorry, it's a sort of one-man private joke. I've been referring to Nixon's close subordinates as humanoids since I heard about the banquet . . . and this is true, I promise . . . where one of the presidential aides spilled a glass of water over Vice-President Ford. The aide was incredibly apologetic, obviously, but Ford just smiled and said 'Oh, that's okay. Nobody's human.' (*Laughter*) I've called 'em humanoids ever since."

Continued

The laughter of Adrian Veidt is deep and rich, filled with a warmth I hadn't anticipated as the jet he'd arranged lowered me gently from the blank white antarctic sky towards the dangerously small-looking black hyphen of the landing strip, set into the endless pack ice far below. The landscape was hard and cold, too big to get to grips with, and I expected much the same of any man who'd choose to live in it.

The plane was met at the landing strip by three enthusiastically friendly Vietnamese men who led me between obelisks of dark marble with rolling purple highlights towards the fortress dominating the nude white reaches beyond.

Servants? My liberal sensibilities recoiled at the concept with a predictable knee-jerk. Later, however, on learning that the men had been Vietcong refugees in danger of losing their lives in the purges following America's victory without Veidt's intervention, I wasn't so sure. Since Antarctica is owned by no nation, the men are theoretically safe from extradition, and their nominal boss seems to treat them more as respected friends than as lackeys. Certainly, they themselves seem deliriously happy with both their lot and their landlord.

"Mr. Veidt has made the effort to understand our culture. He talks to us often concerning our religious beliefs, asking many questions." The man who tells me this is sincere and heartfelt in his testimonial, showing an almost fatherly protective anxiety that this magazine should not misrepresent his employer:

"He is not one of your pop music stars. He does not inject drugs, or treat young women badly. Make sure that you say that."

When we reach the fortress, Veidt is still completing his daily workout in a gymnasium of vast, almost dreamlike proportions, where parallel bars meet at infinity. I'm cordially invited to watch while he finishes up, and as I observe that perfect swiss-watch of a body twirling and circling above me in easy defiance of gravity, all my earlier doubts concerning Veidt's accessibility return.

There he is, right up there above me: the man. Adrian Veidt. Ozyman . . . whoops. Uh-uh. We don't call him that anymore, do we? The mask is gone, but as he loops the high bar in slow, graceful centrifuge he still wears the golden leotard, and the headband. Every girlfriend I've had in the past four years has wanted to lay this guy, more than Jagger, more than Springsteen or D'Eath or any of those also-rans, and now here I am, squinting up at him, and yes, goddamn it, I have to goddamned admit that he looks like a goddamned god! I can't quite believe he'll submit to being interviewed by someone so obviously mired in the dregs of the gene pool as myself . . .

. . . but here he comes, dropping to the floor, picking up the purple towel that I realize later is actually the tunic of his costume, and wiping himself beneath the arms with it in a distinctly Homo sapiens fashion. He's walking towards me, his smile somewhere between Jackie Coogan and J.F.K., sticking out a hand that grips mine strongly enough to make me glad it's friendly. He glances towards the gymnasium windows, outside which a blizzard seems to be commencing and smiles again.

"Not the sort of snow you're used to in California, Mr. Roth."

A coke joke! Adrian Veidt, Ozy-freakin'-mandias himself has just told me a _coke joke!_ Whoooo-ee! We fall easily into conversation from that point on, and after he's dressed he takes me for a tour of his fortress, opulent beyond the wildest dreams of Versailles. We end up in a large section of the main hall where one wall appears to be entirely covered with TV screens, all tuned to different channels. It is here that we hold our interview, and I notice his eyes often drifting across the riot of clashing images as we speak. It's only after I express worries concerning background noise and my recording equipment that he thinks to turn the sound of the multiple televisions down. They don't seem to affect _his_ concentration at all.

Before launching into my interview spiel, I take a breath and remember why I'm here. Almost lost in the cacophony surrounding the old Trickster's Constitutional amendment scam, one of America's best-respected and most consistently left-leaning superheroes quietly retired from crimefighting to pursue a career in business. When this magazine phoned him to ask why, he kindly offered to fly me up to his antarctic retreat where we could conduct the interview in comfort. Exhaling, I press the record button and begin.

NOVA: So, how do you get to be a superhero? Were your parents rich? I mean, did that give you advantages?

VEIDT: No more than I could help. My mother left me a lot of money when she died, but I gave it to charity when I was seventeen. I wanted to prove that I could accomplish anything I wanted starting from absolutely nothing. Also, I wanted to free myself of concern for money. Consequently, it's never been a problem for me. To answer your question, you get to be a superhero by believing in the hero within you and summoning him or her forth by an act of will. Believing in yourself and your own potential is the first step to realizing that potential. Alternatively, you could do as Jon did: Fall into a nuclear reactor and hope for the best. On the whole, I think I prefer to stick to my own methods. (_Laughter_)

NOVA: You'll forgive me for saying so, but isn't that philosophy a little Norman Vincent Peale? That self-realization stuff? How exactly do you exploit that potential to the degree that you obviously have?

VEIDT: The disciplines of physical exercise, meditation and study aren't terribly esoteric. The means to attain a capability far beyond that of the so-called ordinary person are within reach of everyone, if their desire and their will are strong enough. I have studied science, art, religion and a hundred different philosophies. Anyone could do as much. By applying what you learn and ordering your thoughts in an intelligent manner it is possible to accomplish almost anything. Possible for the "ordinary person." There's a notion I'd like to see buried: the ordinary person. Ridiculous. There is no ordinary person.

NOVA: Returning to your costumed career, why did you quit?

VEIDT: There were a number of reasons, but I suppose basically it boiled down to my increasing uncertainty about the role of the costumed hero in the seventies. What does fighting crime mean, exactly? Does it mean upholding the law when a woman shoplifts to feed her children, or does it mean struggling to uncover the ones who, quite legally, have brought about her poverty? Yes, I've busted drug rings and been accused of being an establishment pawn for doing so . . . that happened a lot in the sixties. I've also uncovered plots by breakaway extremist factions within the Pentagon, for example the plot to release some unpleasantly specific diseases upon the population of Africa, the exposure of which led to the *New Frontiersman* denouncing me as a "Puppet of Peking" on the strength of my youthful travels through the East. I guess I've just reached a point where I've started to wonder whether all the grandstanding and fighting individual evils does

much good for the world as a whole. Those evils are just symptoms of an overall sickness of the human spirit, and I don't believe you can cure a disease by suppressing its symptoms. That whole *Contac-400* approach to our society's problems, I despair of it. It doesn't work. Maybe as a businessman I can do more good, on a more meaningful scale.

NOVA: What sort of world do you see it being, in the future?

VEIDT: That depends upon us . . . each and every one of us. Futurology interests me perhaps more than any other single subject, and as such I devote a great deal of time to its study. Even so, technology is progressing at an ever-accelerating pace, and by early next century I would hesitate to predict *any* limitations upon what we might be capable of. I would say without hesitation that a new world is within our grasp, filled with unimaginable experiences and possibilities, if only we want it badly enough. Not a utopia . . . I don't believe that any species could continue to grow and keep from stagnation without *some* adversity . . . but a society with a more human basis, where the problems that beset us are at least *new* problems.

NOVA: You don't think there's a possibility we may have damaged the environment beyond repair, or that we might someday have a fatal nuclear showdown with the Soviets?

Continued

Veidt cont.

VEIDT: Of course. Of course I do. I'd be ignoring the facts if I didn't accept those things as strong possibilities. As I said, it all depends on us, on whether we, individually, want Armageddon or a new world of fabulous, limitless potential. That's not such an obvious question as it seems. I believe there are some people who really do want, if only subconsciously, an end to the world. They want to be spared the responsibilities of maintaining that world, to be spared the effort of imagination needed to realize such a future. And of course, there are other people who want very much to live. I see twentieth century society as a sort of race between enlightenment and extinction. In one lane you have the four horsemen of the apocalypse . . .

NOVA: . . . and in the other?

VEIDT: The seventh cavalry. (*Laughter*)

NOVA: Changing the subject entirely, do you listen to much music? I wondered what your tastes might be, as a superhero . . .

VEIDT: I like electronic music. That's a very superhero-ey thing to like, I suppose, isn't it? I like avant-garde music in general. Cage, Stockhausen, Penderecki, Andrew Lang, Pierre Henry. Terry Riley is very good. Oh, and I've heard some interesting new music from Jamaica . . . a sort of hybrid between electronic music and reggae. It's a fascinating study in the new musical forms generated when a largely pre-technological culture is given access to modern recording techniques without the technological preconceptions that we've allowed to accumulate, limiting our vision. It's called dub music. You'd like it, I'm sure.

NOVA: How do you get on with the rest of the superhero fraternity? Some of them seem very right-wing in contrast with your own stance. I'm thinking of Rorschach, the Comedian, Dr. Manhattan . . .

VEIDT: *Jon*? Right-wing? (*Laughs*) If there's one thing in this cosmos that that man *isn't* capable of doing it's having a political bias. Believe me . . . you have to meet him to understand. I mean, which do you prefer, red ants or black ants?

NOVA: Uh . . .? Well, I don't have any particular preference . . .

VEIDT: Exactly. Well, imagine how Jon feels. Rorschach, I don't know very well. I believe he's a man of great integrity, but he seems to see the world in very black and white, Manichean terms. I personally believe that to be an intellectual limitation.

NOVA: And the Comedian? I understand there's no love lost between you. I heard that he beat you in combat, back when you were just starting out . . .

VEIDT: Yes, well, that was a case of mistaken identity and general misunderstanding. For some reason it happens a lot when costumed crimefighters meet for the first time. (*Laughter*)

NOVA: But you and the Comedian don't like each other?

VEIDT: My, but you're determined, aren't you? (*Laughs*) No, we're not great friends. It's largely a political difference. He sees me as an intellectual dilettante dabbling in national affairs that don't concern me. I see him as an amoral mercenary allying himself to whichever political faction seems likely to grant him the greatest license. The difference is as simple and as profound as that.

NOVA: There's no general sense of disillusionment with your fellow crimefighters, then?

VEIDT: Not at all. Some of my dearest friends are numbered amongst them. I wish them all nothing but luck in the years that lie ahead.

NOVA: In closing, you've often been referred to in the press as the world's smartest man. Is that true, and does it bother you?

VEIDT: No, that isn't true, but it's very flattering and I don't mind a bit. If somebody wants to call me the world's best-groomed man, then hey, that's okay too. (*Laughs*) No, no, I don't mind being the smartest man in the world. I just wish it wasn't this one. ✦

THE TIMES THEY ARE A 'CHANGING

NOSTALGIA BY VEIDT

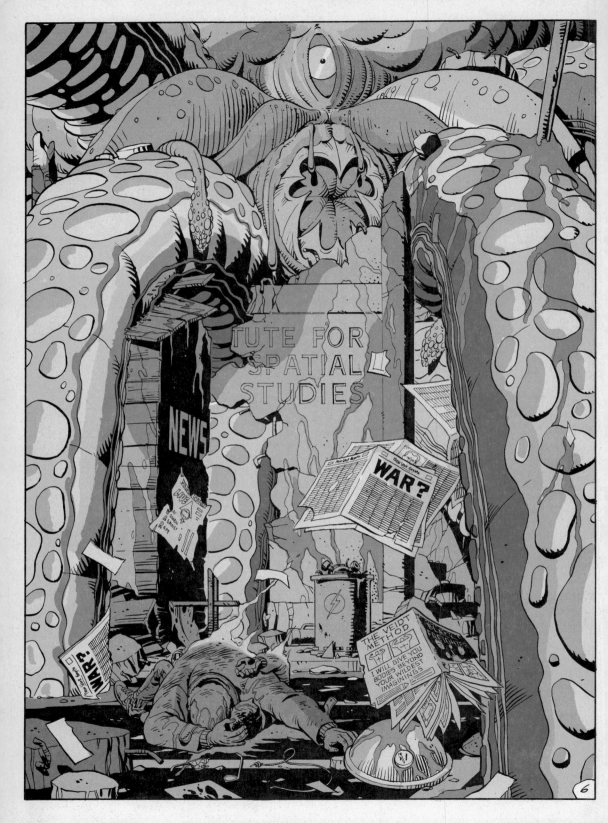

A STRONGER LOVING WORLD

MIDNIGHT.

MIDNIGHT, NOVEMBER SECOND.

THAT'S UNUSUAL. I'D EXPECTED US TO REAPPEAR ON EARTH MUCH *EARLIER*. THE *STATIC INTERFERENCE* I NOTICED *EARLIER* MAKES EVERYTHING SO *UNPREDICTABLE*. OBVIOUSLY, IT WASN'T CAUSED BY A *WAR-HEAD* DETONATION.

WHAT, THEN?

NOT *TACHYONS*, SURELY... YES! *DEFINITELY!* A SQUALL OF *TACHYONS*. WHERE CAN THEY BE *COMING* FROM?

I'D ALMOST *FORGOTTEN* THE *EXCITEMENT* OF NOT *KNOWING*, THE DELIGHTS OF *UNCERTAINTY*...

TANDOORI TO GO. THAT'S ALL THEY WENT OUT FOR, THESE PEOPLE...

TANDOORI TO GO.

7

...AND *INSTEAD*, THEY... THEY GOT...

I MEAN, WH-WHO'S *SAFE*? HOW CAN *ANYONE* PROTECT THEMSELVES AGAINST A WORLD WHERE *THIS* HAPPENS? I...

UHH...

NOW, LET ME *SEE*...

TACHYON PARTICLES, TRAVELLING BACKWARDS IN *TIME*, OCCUR *RARELY*. SOMEONE MUST BE *GENERATING* THEM.

IF I PROBE *FAR* ENOUGH, I SHOULD STUMBLE UPON THE *SOURCE* OF THE DISTURBANCE...

...THOUGH THIS *STATIC* MAKES SCANNING *DIFFICULT*. ALSO, THERE'S APPARENTLY *MORE THAN ONE* GENERATOR.

MOST ARE *FAINT*, BUT A PULSE FROM THE SOUTHERN *POLAR* REGION IS *STRONG*...

REASSURINGLY *POWERFUL*.

LOGICALLY, WE SHOULD INVESTIGATE THE ANTARCTIC SIGNAL *IMMEDIATELY*, ASSESS ITS CONNECTION WITH THIS *CATASTROPHE*...

WORKING *BLIND*, WE CAN'T USEFULLY *PREPARE* OURSELVES...

GET ME OUT OF HERE.

OUT? CERTAINLY. WE CAN TRACE THE TACHYONS TO THEIR *SOURCE*, AND...

JON, I JUST WANNA BE AWAY FROM THESE *PEOPLE*, AND THAT *THING*, AND, AND...

...HHRREUGHH...

I'M SORRY. HOW *THOUGHTLESS* OF ME. THIS MUST BE A *DISTRESSING* TIME FOR YOU...

JON, FOR CHRIST'S *SAKE*! I WANT TO BE *OUT* OF HERE, OKAY?

JUST TAKE IT *AWAY* IS ALL...

TAKE IT AWAY.

8

TAKE CAT AWAY, VEIDT. TAKE CAT AWAY AND FACE ME...

WHOA.

ADRIAN, I'M SORRY, I DON'T BUY THIS *HOAX INVASION* STORY.

COME ON, WHAT ARE YOU *REALLY* UP TO?

≥HHAHHH≤

VERY WELL. ONCE MORE: I ENGINEERED A *MONSTER*, CLONED ITS *BRAIN* FROM A HUMAN *PSYCHIC*, SENT IT TO *NEW YORK* AND *KILLED HALF OF THE CITY*.

ADRIAN, THAT'S *BULL-SHIT*...

NO. TELLING TRUTH. LISTEN TO VOICE.

HE DID IT.

LOOK, *NOBODY* COULD DO THAT. YOU'RE BEING...

HE DID IT.

HALF NEW YORK.

VEIDT, GET RID OF CAT.

NO, I DON'T *THINK* SO. AFTER *ALL*, HER PRESENCE SAVES YOU THE HUMILIATION OF ANOTHER *BEATING*.

HURRR...

RORSCHACH, HE'S KIDDING YOU. HIS *STORY*, IT'S FULL OF *HOLES*...

ADRIAN, YOUR *ASSASSINATION* ATTEMPT: YOU *COULDN'T* HAVE PLANNED IT! WHAT IF HE'D SHOT *YOU* FIRST INSTEAD OF YOUR *SECRETARY*?

I SUPPOSE I'D HAVE HAD TO CATCH THE *BULLET*, WOULDN'T I?

YOU...?

NAHH COME ON. THAT'S *COMPLETELY*...

YOU COULDN'T *REALLY* DO THAT?

9

NO. I JUST DON'T *BUY* IT. *ANY* OF IT. YOU *WOULDN'T* KILL HALF NEW YORK. YOU *COULDN'T*...

I COULD. I DID.

IF YOU LIKE, I'LL TELL YOU *HOW*:

THE *PSYCHIC* WAS THE KEY, POOR YOUNG *ROBERT DESCHAINES.* I ACQUIRED HIS BRAIN AFTER DEATH AND MY GENETICISTS CLONED SOMETHING MUCH *BIGGER* AND MORE *POWERFUL* FROM IT, INCORPORATING IT INTO MY *CREATURE.*

THE BRAIN WAS A PSYCHIC *RESONATOR.* IT WOULD AMPLIFY A *SIGNAL PULSE* AND *BROADCAST* IT, THE SIGNAL TRIGGERED BY THE ONSET OF DEATH.

WE CODED A LOT OF INFORMATION INTO THAT SIGNAL.

TERRIBLE INFORMATION.

MAX *SHEA'S* DESCRIPTIONS OF AN ALIEN *WORLD,* HIRA *MANISH'S* IMAGES AND LINETTE PALEY'S *SOUNDS*...

OTHER THAN THOSE KILLED OUTRIGHT BY THE SHOCK, MANY WILL BE DRIVEN MAD BY THE SUDDEN FLOOD OF GROTESQUE SENSATION...

... AND *SENSITIVES* WORLD-WIDE WILL HAVE BAD DREAMS FOR YEARS TO COME.

NO ONE WILL DOUBT THIS EARTH HAS MET A FORCE SO *DREADFUL* IT MUST BE *REPELLED,* ALL FORMER *ENMITIES* ASIDE.

NO ONE WILL KNOW. THOSE INVOLVED ARE ALL DEAD, KILLED BY KILLERS WHO KILLED EACH *OTHER,* A LETHAL *PYRAMID*...

MY *SERVANTS'* DEATHS FROM EXPOSURE, AFTER DRUNK-ENLY OPENING MY *VIVARIUM,* PROVIDES ITS SILENT *CAP-STONE.*

WHAT ABOUT *US?*

YES. YES, I'D BEEN RATHER *WONDERING* ABOUT THAT, MYSELF...

ORRR?

BUBASTIS? WHAT IS IT, GIRL? IS SOME-BODY OUT THERE?

JUST A MOMENT. I'LL CHECK THE *SCREENS*...

AH.

I SEE.

10

VEIDT. OF COURSE. WHO **ELSE** HAS THE INTELLIGENCE OR RESOURCES FOR **TACHYON** INTERFERENCE?

HMM. EIGHT GENERATORS THROUGHOUT ANTARCTICA, EIGHT IN ORBITING SATELLITES. IT DISPLAYS REMARKABLE FORESIGHT, DON'T YOU THINK?

UCCUK

HUT

AFTER ALL, SINCE TACHYONS ONLY AFFECT **ME**, HE'S OBVIOUSLY ANTICIPATED MY POSSIBLE **DISCOVERY** OF HIS PLOT FOR SOME CONSIDERABLE TIME...

PLOT?

WAIT A MINUTE. I'VE **BEEN** HERE. THIS IS **ANTARCTICA.** THAT'S...

THAT'S ADRIAN'S **FORTRESS.**

A-ARE YOU SAYING SOMEONE **PLANNED** THAT...THAT STUFF IN **NEW YORK?** THAT HE...THAT VEIDT...

YES. YES, HE KILLED BLAKE AND HALF NEW YORK.

EXCUSE ME, RORSCHACH. I'M INFORMING LAURIE NINETY SECONDS AGO.

RORSCHACH? JON, **DON'T!** DON'T START ALL YOUR CRAP **NOW!**

DID HE **KILL** THEM? DID VUH-VEIDT KILL ALL THOSE PUH-PEOPLE?

JON, **ANSWER** ME!

I-I'M SORRY. IT'S THESE **TACHYONS.** THEY'RE MUDDLING THINGS **UP...**

I'D BETTER FOLLOW HIM INSIDE.

NO! DON'T YOU **DARE** LEAVE ME OUT HERE!

JON, **WAIT!**

OH....

26

...DEAR.

11

BUBASTIS. QUICKLY...

NO. DON'T LET HIM ESCAPE.

MUST STOP HIM. KILLED BLAKE. KILLED HALF NEW YORK.

YES. YES, HE KILLED BLAKE AND HALF NEW YORK.

EXCUSE ME, RORSCHACH. I'M INFORMING LAURIE NINETY SECONDS AGO.

WHAT? WHERE'S LAURIE?

JON? ARE... ARE YOU OKAY? YOU SEEM SORT OF... I DUNNO... DRUGGED OR SOMETHING...

I - I'M SORRY. IT'S THESE TACHYONS. THEY'RE MUDDLING THINGS UP...

I'D BETTER FOLLOW HIM INSIDE.

12

VEIDT?

VEIDT, EVEN IF I CAN'T PREDICT WHERE I'M GOING TO *FIND* YOU, I CAN TURN THIS PLACE TO *GLASS*. YOU CAN'T HIDE. YOU'RE BEING *STUPID*.

THE *TACHYONS* WERE CLEVER, BUT THIS IS *STUPID*.

IT ISN'T *LIKE* YOU TO...

AH.

VERY WELL. IF I *MUST*...

IF I *MUST* FOLLOW THIS THROUGH TO THE BITTER *END*...

STAND BEHIND SCREEN WHEN I.F. SUBTRACTOR IS ACTIVATED

BUBASTIS...

FORGIVE ME.

INTRINSIC FIELD SUBTRACTOR

CAUTION

ACTIVATE

AAAA-AAAA-WRRR!

OOWAA-AAAAA-RROWR!

VEIDT? DON'T...

HM.

DO YOU KNOW, I REALLY WASN'T SURE THAT WOULD WORK.

O BEHIND EN WHEN BTRACTOR CTIVATED

OF COURSE, IT WAS THE *TACHYONS* THAT MADE IT POSSIBLE TO GIVE HIM SOMETHING HE WASN'T *EXPECTING*...

14

VEIDT...

YOU'RE AN ASSHOLE.

HHHHIIIIIIII...

YAAA--

15

OH SH...

⸰UUUUUHHH⸰

STAND BEHIN
SCREEN WH
1.F. SUBTRA
IS ACTIVA

THERE.

SOMETHING *ELSE* I WASN'T SURE WOULD WORK.

VEIDT!

OOOO-UUWW...

VEIDT, YOU *BASTARD*. IF YOU'VE *HURT* HER, I'LL...

OH *DANIEL*. DANIEL, DANIEL, DANIEL...

PLEASE...

DO GROW UP.

MY NEW WORLD DEMANDS LESS *OBVIOUS* HEROISM, MAKING YOUR SCHOOLBOY HEROICS *REDUNDANT.*

WHAT HAVE THEY *ACHIEVED?* FAILING TO PREVENT EARTH'S *SALVATION* IS YOUR ONLY *TRIUMPH...*

...AND YET THAT *FAILURE* OVERSHADOWS EVERY PAST *SUCCESS!* BY DEFAULT, YOU USHER IN AN AGE OF *ILLUMINATION* SO *DAZZLING* THAT HUMANITY WILL REJECT THE *DARKNESS* IN ITS HEART...

...AND TURN INSTEAD TOWARDS THE...

UH...

AAAAA!

17

I AM DISAPPOINTED, VEIDT.

VERY DISAPPOINTED.

RESTRUCTURING MYSELF AFTER THE SUBTRACTION OF MY *INTRINSIC FIELD* WAS THE FIRST TRICK I *LEARNED.* IT DIDN'T KILL *OSTERMAN...*

DID YOU THINK IT WOULD KILL ME?

I'VE WALKED ACROSS THE SUN. I'VE SEEN EVENTS SO TINY AND SO FAST THEY HARDLY CAN BE SAID TO HAVE OCCURRED AT *ALL,* BUT YOU...

YOU ARE A MAN.

...AND THIS WORLD'S *SMARTEST* MAN MEANS NO MORE TO ME THAN DOES ITS SMARTEST *TERMITE.*

WHAT'S THAT IN YOUR HAND, VEIDT? ANOTHER ULTIMATE WEAPON?

YES.

YES, YOU COULD SAY THAT.

...FROM NEW YORK. PICTURES COMING UP...

NEWS FLASH

18

I SAVED EARTH FROM **HELL**. NEXT, I'LL HELP HER TOWARDS **UTOPIA**. IT IS AS RAMESES SAID:

"CANAAN IS DEVASTATED, ASHKELON IS FALLEN, GEZER IS RUINED, YENOAM IS REDUCED TO NOTHING..."

"...ISRAEL IS DESOLATE AND HER SEED IS NO MORE, AND PALESTINE HAS BECOME A WIDOW FOR EGYPT..."

WAIT A MINUTE... "**NEXT**"? AFTER WHAT **YOU** DID? YOU CAN'T GET AWAY WITH **THAT**...

"ALL THE COUNTRIES ARE **UNIFIED** AND **PACIFIED**."

CAN'T GET AWAY WITH IT?

WILL YOU **EXPOSE** ME, UNDOING THE PEACE MILLIONS **DIED** FOR? **KILL** ME, RISKING SUBSEQUENT **INVESTIGATION**? MORALLY, YOU'RE IN **CHECKMATE**, LIKE BLAKE.

LET'S COMPROMISE.

WHAAT?

LOGICALLY, I'M AFRAID HE'S **RIGHT**. **EXPOSING** THIS PLOT, WE DESTROY ANY CHANCE OF PEACE, DOOMING EARTH TO **WORSE** DESTRUCTION.

ON MARS, YOU DEMONSTRATED LIFE'S **VALUE**. IF WE WOULD PRESERVE LIFE **HERE**, WE MUST REMAIN **SILENT**.

NEVER **TELL** ANYONE? W-WE REALLY HAVE TO **BUY** THIS?

JESUS, HE WAS **RIGHT**. ALL WE DID WAS FAIL TO STOP HIM SAVING **EARTH**.

JESUS.

HOW...HOW CAN **HUMANS** MAKE DECISIONS LIKE **THIS**? **WE'RE** DAMNED IF WE STAY **QUIET**, EARTH'S DAMNED IF WE **DON'T**. WE...

OKAY.

OKAY, COUNT ME IN. WE SAY NOTHING.

JOKING, OF COURSE.

RORSCHACH...?

RORSCHACH, **WAIT**! WHERE ARE YOU **GOING**? THIS IS TOO **BIG** TO BE **HARD-ASSED** ABOUT! WE HAVE TO COMPROMISE...

NO.

NOT EVEN IN THE FACE OF ARMA-GEDDON.

NEVER COMPROMISE.

20

HMM.

NOW WHAT WOULD YOU CALL *THAT*, I WONDER?

"BLOTTING OUT REALITY" PERHAPS?

AH WELL... IN ALL LIKELIHOOD IT'S OF NO CONSEQUENCE. AS A *RELIABLE WITNESS,* RORSCHACH IS HARDLY... HOW SHALL WE PUT IT..."*WITHOUT STAIN*"? STILL...

STILL.

I THINK I SHALL *MEDITATE* NOW, IN MY *ORRERY.*

OBVIOUSLY, YOU MUST BOTH MAKE YOURSELVES AT *HOME.* THERE ARE SEVERAL *RESTROOMS,* SHOULD YOU WISH TO *FRESHEN UP.*

"*BOTH*"?

I JUST WANT TO GO SOMEPLACE *ELSE.* CAN YOU GET US *OUT* OF HERE, JON?

JON?

WHERE'D HE *GO?* WHERE'D *EVERY-BODY* GO?

I MEAN... IN NEW *YORK,* ALL THOSE *BODIES...* HOW CAN EVERY-BODY JUST WALK *AWAY* FROM THAT?

I *KNOW.* LISTEN, LET'S FIND SOMEPLACE QUIET, AWAY FROM THESE *LIGHTS.* WE NEED TO *THINK,* TO *TALK...*

BUT WHERE'S *JON?* HE'S BEEN ACTING SO *STRANGE:* HE PREDICTED I'D TELL HIM ABOUT *YOU* AND ME, THEN SEEMED *ANGRY* WHEN I *DID!*

UH ...HOW *ANGRY?*

OH, I *DUNNO.* HE *CONFUSES* ME, AND I DON'T *NEED* CONFUSING.

I'M *SCREWED* UP *ALREADY.* I LEARNED STUFF ON *MARS* AND THEN NEW *YORK...*

DEAD. EVERYBODY WAS JUST ...*DEAD.*

I ...I STILL CAN'T *IMAGINE.* THIS WHOLE *THING,* WE'RE JUST, I DUNNO...

OUT OF OUR *DEPTH.*

21

BUT...THERE WERE **PEOPLE**, JUST STEPPED OUT THE GUNGA **DINER**. THAT PINK AND YELLOW **RICE**, IT WAS ALL **SPILLED**, AND...

DAN? CAN WE SIT **DOWN**?

SURE.

LAURIE, LISTEN, ABOUT **US**...DO YOU THINK JON MINDS?

IT DOESN'T **MATTER**. AFTER NEW YORK, **NOTHING** MATTERS. THAT'S WHAT I'M TRYING TO **SAY**.

DAN, PLEASE... SIT WITH ME. I NEED YOU.

I NEED YOU TOO.

NO. I MEAN I **NEED** YOU. NEED YOU **NOW**. DAN, ALL THOSE **PEOPLE**, THEY'RE **DEAD**. THEY CAN'T **DISAGREE** OR EAT INDIAN **FOOD**, OR **LOVE** EACH OTHER...

OH, IT'S **SWEET**. BEING ALIVE IS SO DAMN **SWEET**.

LAURIE? WH-WHAT DO YOU WANT ME TO **DO**?

I WANT YOU TO LOVE ME.

I WANT YOU TO LOVE ME BECAUSE WE'RE NOT DEAD.

HERE... TAKE THESE OFF. I WANT TO **SEE** YOU.

I WANT TO SEE YOU AND **TASTE** YOU AND **SMELL** YOU, JUST BECAUSE I **CAN**.

WHAT **IS** THAT, DAN? WHAT'S THAT YOU SMELL OF?

NOSTALGIA.

22

WHERE ARE YOU GOING?

BACK TO OWLSHIP. BACK TO AMERICA.

EVIL MUST BE PUNISHED.

PEOPLE MUST BE TOLD.

RORSCHACH....

YOU KNOW I CAN'T LET YOU DO THAT.

23

HUHHH.

OF COURSE. MUST PROTECT VEIDT'S NEW UTOPIA. ONE MORE BODY AMONGST FOUNDATIONS MAKES LITTLE DIFFERENCE.

WELL? WHAT ARE YOU WAITING FOR?

DO IT.

RORSCHACH....

DO IT!

24

MOSPHERE HERE'S DIFFICULT TO DESCRIBE: **ELATION** THAT AN ALMOST CERTAIN WAR HAS BEEN **AVERTED,** MINGLED WITH HORROR AND...

...RUSSIA, OFFERING HELP

...ARENTLY, THE CREATURE DIED UPON ACCIDENTALLY BREACHING OUR DIMENSION, BUT, IN ITS DEATH-THROES IT

...HAVE DESCRIBED THE SCENE AS *"LIKE HIROSHIMA BUT WITH BUILDINGS."* WE ASKED

...FROM ANOTHER DIMENSION

...COULD FURTHER ATTACKS BE IMMINENT?

AND LITERALLY MILLIONS ARE

WE THINK NOT. IMAGINE AN ALIEN BEE, NOT VERY INTELLIGENT, THAT STINGS REFLEX-IVELY UPON DEATH. IF

25

HELLO, JON.

I WAS HOPING WE'D HAVE THE CHANCE TO TALK.

JON... I *KNOW* PEOPLE THINK ME CALLOUS, BUT I'VE MADE MYSELF *FEEL* EVERY *DEATH*. BY DAY I IMAGINE ENDLESS *FACES*. BY NIGHT...

WELL, I *DREAM*, ABOUT SWIMMING TOWARDS A HIDEOUS...NO. NEVER MIND. IT ISN'T *SIGNIFICANT*...

WHAT'S SIGNIFICANT IS THAT I *KNOW*. I *KNOW* I'VE STRUGGLED ACROSS THE BACKS OF MURDERED INNOCENTS TO SAVE HUMANITY... BUT *SOMEONE* HAD TO TAKE THE WEIGHT OF THAT AWFUL, NECESSARY CRIME.

I'D HOPED *YOU'D* UNDERSTAND, UNLIKE *RORSCHACH*...

YOU NEEDN'T CONSIDER RORSCHACH. I STRONGLY DOUBT HE'LL REACH CIVILIZATION.

...BUT YES, I UNDERSTAND, WITHOUT CONDONING OR CONDEMNING. HUMAN AFFAIRS CANNOT BE MY CONCERN. I'M *LEAVING* THIS GALAXY FOR ONE LESS *COMPLICATED*.

BUT YOU'D REGAINED INTEREST IN *HUMAN* LIFE...

YES, I HAVE. I THINK PERHAPS I'LL *CREATE* SOME.

GOODBYE, ADRIAN.

JON, WAIT, BEFORE YOU *LEAVE*...

I DID THE RIGHT THING, DIDN'T I? IT ALL WORKED OUT IN THE END.

"IN THE END"?

NOTHING ENDS, ADRIAN. NOTHING *EVER* ENDS.

JON? *WAIT*! WHAT DO YOU MEAN BY...

27

ALL **RIGHT**, I'M **COMING**!

ALREADY I HAD THE **CLEANING PEOPLE** CALLING FOR TIPS! ON CHRISTMAS DAY, PEOPLE GOTTA COME **BEGGING**? JESUS CHRIST, ISN'T ANYTHING **SACRED**? IT NEVER ENDS. NEVER.

AND NOW MORE CHRISTMAS EXCITE- MENT WITH TONIGHT'S RETURN VISIT...

I'M **SORRY**, MS. JUPITER, WE **TRIED** CALLING FROM **RECEP- TION**, BUT YOUR **PHONE** WAS OFF. YOUR FRIENDS MR. AND MRS. **HOLLIS** ARE HERE TO SEE YOU.

WHAT? BUT I DON'T **KNOW** ANY...

...TO THE OUTER LIMITS...

...UH...

...IN WHICH ROBERT CULP IS PHYSICALLY TRANSFORMED BY ...**THE ARCHITECTS OF FEAR**!

...I DON'T KNOW **ANYONE** I'D RATHER **SEE**! COME **INSIDE**! HOW **WONDER- FUL**, MY DEAR FRIENDS, MR. AND MRS. ...

HOLLIS.

HA HA HA! OF **COURSE**! THANK YOU **SO** MUCH FOR BRINGING THEM OVER.

YOU'RE WELCOME. HAVE A NICE DAY.

MOTHER, WE...

WHAT THE **HELL** ARE YOU TRYING TO **DO**? YOU'RE TRYING TO **KILL** YOUR MOTHER WITH A **HEART ATTACK**? I THOUGHT YOU WERE **DEAD**! WHO DID THAT TO YOUR **HAIR**? YOU SHOULD **SUE**, YOU LOOK LIKE A **WAITRESS**...

THERE IS NOTHING WRONG WITH YOUR TELEVISION SE-¾:¾

MOTHER, SHUT **UP**! WE CAN'T STAY **LONG**, BUT WE HAD TO LET YOU KNOW WE'RE **OKAY**.

WE BROUGHT. **FLOWERS**. MERRY CHRISTMAS, MOM.

OH **LAURIE**. OH SWEETHEART, I'M SO GLAD TO **SEE** YOU.

¾ GNFF ¾

SO, WHO'S THE **STUD**?

HE **WAS** DAN **DREIBERG**. WE'RE SAM AND SANDRA **HOLLIS** NOW.

NOT LEGALLY MARRIED, HUH? WELL, LET'S HOPE HE'S **RICH**. DELIGHTED TO **MEET** YOU, DAN.

EQUALLY DELIGHTED, MS. JUPITER. I'M A FAN FROM WAY BACK.

OH, I **LIKE** THIS ONE.

28

NOW, LEMME **SEE**, I MUST HAVE SOME GIFTS FOR **YOU**...

I **KNOW**! THERE'S A NEW **MILLENNIUM** STUFF...

MOM, WE DON'T HAVE **LONG**, AND THERE'S IMPORTANT **THINGS** TO DISCUSS.

AT **CHRISTMAS**, WHAT'S MORE IMPORTANT THAN **GIFTS**? I REMEMBER WHEN YOU WERE A LITTLE **GIRL**, YOU ALWAYS USED TO...

MOM, I FOUND OUT WHO MY REAL DAD WAS.

MOM, I FOUND OUT WHO MY REAL DAD WAS.

YOU...?

OH **JESUS**...

OH **LAUREL**, I'M SO **SORRY**. WH-WHAT MUST YOU **THINK**? IT...IT WAS JUST AN AFTERNOON, IN SUMMER. HE STOPPED BY...

MOM...

I **TRIED** TO BE ANGRY, BUT...I MEAN, I NEVER WANTED YOU TO KNOW. I SHOULD HAVE **TOLD** YOU BUT...I DON'T KNOW, I JUST FELT **ASHAMED**, I FELT **STUPID**, AND...

MOM... IT DOESN'T MATTER.

PEOPLE'S **LIVES** TAKE THEM STRANGE **PLACES**. THEY DO STRANGE **THINGS**, AND...

...WELL, SOMETIMES THEY CAN'T **TALK** ABOUT THEM. I KNOW HOW THAT IS.

I **LOVE** YOU, MOM. YOU NEVER DID ANYTHING WRONG BY ME.

THAT'S ALL I CAME TO **TELL** YOU, I GUESS. WE HAVE TO **GO**, BUT WE'LL VISIT **SOON**.

SURE. LISTEN, TAKE THIS. IT'LL HELP YOU HOLD ONTO **BLONDIE**. GUESS I BETTER FIND **HIM** SOMETHING, TOO...

WELL, YEAH, BUT **HURRY**. I GET **NERVOUS**, WAITING AROUND...

WHAT'S THAT YOU'RE ...**OHH**. **THAT** OLD THING. HOPE IT HASN'T **EMBARRASSED** YOU.

OH **NO**. NOT AT **ALL**. TO TELL THE **TRUTH**, I...

WELL, IN 1952, I **OWNED** A COPY.

YOU **DID**? WHY, **BLESS** YOU, YOU **KEEP** IT.

BUT...THESE ARE **VALUABLE** REALLY, MS. **JUPITER**, I COULDN'T...

SALLY. TAKE IT. JUST DON'T TELL THE WIFE.

DAN...UH, SAM, HONEY? COME ON... WE HAVE TO **GO**.

29

YEAH, WELL, YOU KIDS TAKE *CARE* OF EACH OTHER.

AND DON'T WAIT TOO LONG TO HAVE *CHILDREN!* I'M AN *OLD WOMAN!*

GOOD*BYE,* MOM.

WELL, THAT WAS PRETTY *PAINLESS,* HUH?

Y'KNOW, MAYBE THAT WASN'T SUCH A BAD *IDEA* OF YOUR MOTHER'S...

CHILDREN? FORGET IT. NOT *YET.* YOU WERE TALKING ABOUT *ADVENTURING,* AND *I'M* NOT STAYING HOME CHANGING *DIAPERS.*

"*NITE OWL* AND *SILK SPECTRE*" SOUNDS *NEAT.*

"*SILK SPECTRE'S*" TOO *GIRLY,* Y'KNOW? PLUS, I WANT A BETTER *COSTUME,* THAT *PROTECTS* ME: MAYBE SOMETHING *LEATHER,* WITH A *MASK* OVER MY FACE...

ALSO, MAYBE I OUGHTTA CARRY A *GUN.*

30

THIS IS THE TIME. THESE ARE THE FEELINGS.

MILLENNIUM by V

OOOHH, SO YOU FINALLY CAME **BACK**? WHAT, DID YOU GO TO **DIMENSION X** FOR 'EM? HM?

SEYMOUR, CHRIST, I DON'T KNOW...

THREE MILLION NEW YORKERS DIED AND YOU WEREN'T ONE OF THEM.

I HADDA GO TO THE **BURGERS 'N' BOR** ...

DON'T **SAY** IT. DON'T SAY THAT **WORD**. I'LL EAT **FOOD** FROM THE PLACE IF I **MUST**, BUT I WON'T HAVE **RUSSIAN** SPOKEN IN THIS OFFICE.

SEYMOUR, DON'T YOU HAVE ANY-THING TO DO?

WELL I WAS GONNA **EAT**.

OH NO. YOU GOT TWO MORE **PAGES** TO FILL BEFORE YOU EAT, THANKS TO THIS GODDAMNED, ASS-KISSING **ACCORD**!

I THOUGHT YOUR COLUMN ...

YEAH, WELL, YOU THOUGHT **WRONG**! NOBODY'S **ALLOWED** TO SAY BAD THINGS ABOUT OUR GOOD OL' BUDDIES THE **RUSSIANS** ANYMORE, SO BANG GOES A TWO-PAGE **COLUMN**!

GET SOME **FILLER** FROM SOME-WHERE.

ROBERT REDFORD SAYS HE'LL BE RUNNING FOR PRESIDENT IN '88. WE COULD RUN A PIECE ON ...

SEYMOUR, WE DO **NOT** DIGNIFY **ABSURDITIES** WITH **COVERAGE**. THIS IS STILL **AMERICA**, GOD DAMNIT! WHO WANTS A **COWBOY ACTOR** IN THE WHITE HOUSE?

HM. WELL, THEN I GUESS IT'S SOMETHIN' FROM THE **CRANK FILE**.

YES, YES. WHATEVER'S WITHIN YOUR LIMITED **ABILITIES**. JUST PLEASE LET ME EAT MY LUNCH IN **PEACE**.

WELL, WHICH PIECE SHOULD I **RUN**? I ...

SEYMOUR, FOR GOD'S **SAKE**! I'M **ASKING** YOU TO TAKE **RESPONS-IBILITY** FOR ONCE IN YOUR MISERABLE LIFE, WHILE **I** EAT LUNCH! IS THAT TOO **MUCH**?

GO **ON**. JUST RUN WHICHEVER YOU **WANT** ...

I LEAVE IT ENTIRELY IN YOUR HANDS.

It would be a stronger world, a stronger loving world, to die in.

—John Cale

32

**Quis custodiet
ipsos custodes.**

Who watches the watchmen?

—Juvenal, *Satires,* VI, 347
Quoted as the epigraph of the Tower
Commission Report, 1987